Jules Hardy was born in Bristol and grew up in and around London. She is a trained carpenter and now lives in Bristol, where she teaches creative writing at Bath Spa University College and is studying for a PhD. Her debut novel, *Altered Land*, won the WHSmith Fresh Talent Award. *Mister Candid* is her second novel.

Acclaim for *Altered Land*

'A compelling story about a mother's love for her son, the different ways people survive physical and mental damage, and the persistence of a dream . . . Hardy keeps you hooked from the start. A well crafted, consistent debut' *Arena* magazine

'Her extraordinary deep understanding of heartbreak and the intricacie   human relationships conveys itself via a deft handling   her characters, never judgmental and always compassio   e . . . This is a truly wonderful book; a heart-rending,   lifting tribute to many kinds of love' *Time Out*

'[A] stun   lebut . . . shifting timeframes and shocking revelatio   e this an engrossing read' *Good Housekeeping*

'Her wri   s beautiful – Anita Shreve comes to mind as a comparis   *he Times*

'Heartbr   ig, heart warming and exquisitely written. Sets the scene fc   extremely promising writing career' *Irish News*

'Assure   nd uplifting . . . spare and poetic. A love story in the broades   d best sense of the word. This haunting and tear-jerking ı   l will stay with you long after you've read the last page' *Gl   ır* magazine

'A powerful, heartwarming story about how mother and son try to piece together their lives . . . and overcome devastating psychological damage' *Daily Mail*

Also by Jules Hardy

Altered Land

MISTER CANDID

JULES HARDY

withdrawn from stock

SIMON & SCHUSTER

London · New York · Sydney · Tokyo · Singapore · Toronto · Dublin

A VIACOM COMPANY

First published in Great Britain by Simon & Schuster UK Ltd, 2003
A Viacom company

1 3 5 7 9 10 8 6 4 2

Simon & Schuster UK Ltd
Africa House
64–78 Kingsway
London WC2B 6AH

www.simonsays.co.uk

Simon & Schuster Australia
Sydney

A CIP catalogue record for this book
is available from the British Library

ISBN 0-7432-0746-7

Typeset in Palatino by M Rules
Printed and bound in Great Britain by
The Bath Press, Bath

For my beloved Grandfather, Tom Prout,
who hated this when he read it.

Flanagan would be at a football match, wolfing down a dog with an eye on the game, or perhaps playing with his kids in the yard, when one or other memory (of so many) from those months would swim lazily into his mind. This happened often yet randomly. Sometimes when the images appeared he shifted uneasily, moved awkwardly; other times he walked away from the picture dancing before him. But most often he'd smile, take his eye off the ball or grab and hug his kids, while he relived moments branded so harshly on his mind they were beyond erasure. His thoughts could be kick-started by a smidgen of recollection: the shift of a velvet bustle; a More cigarette burning down (with a sound like a leaf growing); voodoo drums beating on East 82nd Street; the polished chrome of an exotic fender; the ruin of a salt-damaged mansion overlooking The Atlantic Ocean; a Polaroid; a pair of pale blue eyes. A man in a lurid orange jumpsuit, tethered hand and foot, falling. A flock of birds wheeling in a square of wide, blue-blue sky.

Flanagan would lie on his bed, in his bath, his hammock, his porch-swing and relive days or hours of that time, rubbing his capacious mound of a belly as he ruminated. He knew when the memories ended – at what point in time his odyssey came to an end – but he could never be sure when, *exactly* when, his journey started. When he held his gun to the base of a rapist's skull and chose not to fire? Perhaps when he stared into a shallow sandy grave? Was it when he read the articles in the *LA Times* and saw a fine-boned face staring back? Or did his journey begin, when all was said and done, that night at the Police Benefit Ball in Naples, Florida, when the fuse of his curiosity was lit by a woman in a burgundy dress? A fuse which took six months to burn down before blowing.

1997

Twyla Thackeray is an attractive woman in her late forties; slim, tanned and carefully coiffed. Anyone glimpsing her crossing the street or slipping into her low-slung car would admire her for a moment, take subliminal note of her poise, her air of confidence, and possibly feel a pang of envy. If they did feel this last, they would be mistaken to do so – for, despite appearances, Twyla Thackeray is a desperate woman. She is a *divorced* woman, a state in which she never expected to find herself. Eleven years it has been since she saw her now-despised husband; eleven years of supporting herself, fending for herself, feeding herself and drinking herself to death. A packed agenda, which has left her exhausted but still able to maintain appearances. She is the director of the Emerald Rest Home – where she is known, to her annoyance, as the matron. The Emerald Rest Home is the last staging post for the dying and near-dead whose families have sufficient funds to ease their consciences by placing their incurable elderly and infirm in (unappreciated) luxury. The staff there cheerfully ease the passage to the unknown, overseen by the matron.

Tonight, preparing herself for the Police Benefit Ball in downtown Naples, Florida, sipping pepper-flavoured

Absolut as she moisturizes, Twyla Thackeray is particularly
thoughtful. The rest home, despite its appearance of opulence
and languid (yet efficient) Southern solicitousness, is on the
rocks, much like her vodka. She has been covertly downsizing
the workforce – letting casual cleaners go, giving part-time
janitors notice, ending the gardening contracts. The pool has
been emptied, on the grounds that the patients – *customers* –
can hardly avail themselves of its benefits. The windows have
not been cleaned for months, the shutters left untreated,
despite cracks appearing in the wood. She has terminated
contracts with medical supply firms, shaving hundreds of
dollars off the monthly invoices by switching to less reputable
firms. Telephone lines have been cut off and problems with
the software system left unresolved. None of these changes is
easily noticed – the grime on the windows only apparent if a
finger sweeps the glass. But, thinks Twyla Thackeray as she
swills vodka, all she is doing is fiddling while Rome burns.
She walks, naked, to her kitchen and refreshes her glass with
three inches of icy spirits, stands by the sink, looking out over
the parking lot behind her condo and drinks as she calculates.

There is no way of salvaging the Emerald Rest Home – the
funds are simply not there. She has made miscalculations,
overestimated occupancy rates, underestimated the astounding
will to live exhibited by some of the old bastards. Then there
is her own pilfering of the far from petty cash. Her salary,
while generous, is not enough to keep her in the style to
which she has become accustomed – the style to which she
has come to imagine she is entitled. What to do, hmmm?
What to do? She is fortunate that the home is geographically
isolated, down a three-mile, heavily wooded track off

Highway 41 on the perimeter of the Big Cypress National Reserve, where the occupants endure a form of emotional quarantine. These facts may buy her time, but, as the Home deteriorates, even the most guilt-free, amoral, bounty-hunting relative will feel compelled to remove ageing Grandma and place her elsewhere. What to do? Another three inches slosh into the crystal tumbler.

As she slips into a burgundy evening dress, its swooping lines revealing smooth, blemish-free shoulders and a tantalizing glimpse of her bronzed coccyx, Twyla Thackeray reaches the same conclusion that she always reaches at this point down the bottle: what to do? Why – find a man, a man big enough, *worthy* enough, to take her on, and then get the fuck out of Florida.

Malibu, CA – January

M –

I've been sitting on the gallery of this house looking out over the ocean for a few days now. And all the time I've been sitting here I've had a notion I should be doing something, and I know what it is. I should be writing to you. I know, after all this time, I should be writing to you.

The ocean looks diseased today, frothy and speckled, the way the Pacific can be sometimes. Makes me want to pick it up and shake it. My fingers are hurting already, it's been so long since I wrote anything. And I sit here and wonder – did you ever get to the West Coast? I remember sitting in the back of the car, our legs dangling over the seats in front, watching the sun set at Plymouth Bay, the lighthouse turning. We were naked. I'd forgotten that until now. Shit. We were naked just sitting in the car at the end of that track. I also remember you saying then that you wanted to see California. (You looked so beautiful when you said it.) Well, I'm here now and I can tell you it's a pile of crap. But if you ever made it here I guess you'll know that already.

Do you know how many years have passed since we sat there, watching the light turn? Seventeen. Seventeen years.

Yours,

C

Lieutenant Flanagan always enjoys being invited to functions in Naples – Collier County is nothing if not generous and the night of the Police Benefit Ball is no exception. The town hall is draped, inside and out, in blue, gold and silver, balloons bounce lazily against the ceiling and a light jazz quartet is tinkling quietly as he ambles into the reception. He spies the open bar, loaded with Four Roses, Jim Beam, Black Label, Glenmorangie and twenty-five-year-old J&B, and soon he is holding a tumbler of whisky in one huge hand as he selects a meaty chicken thigh with the other.

'Hey, Flanagan!'

He swivels slowly, chewing tender chicken flesh, and sees Captain Brannigan heading towards him across the room, pushing through the crowds. Flanagan swallows, wipes his fingers on his trousers and smiles hugely. 'Hey, Ted. How you doing?'

'Fine, just fine. How're you, Lieutenant?'

'Just fine, too.'

'How's things in big bad Miami?'

Flanagan eyes the spread of food dolefully but swiftly.

'Good as ever. Keeps me busy, that's for sure. Grand turnout tonight.' He motions at the packed floor. 'Who's it in aid of?'

Captain Brannigan sighs. 'Dave Sullivan, shot six months ago on a ten thirteen. Ed Braxton and Louis Grammandi – Louis left three kids under five.'

Flanagan frowns as his throat closes. He remembers Dave Sullivan, he'd worked with him as a rookie. 'How's Jane holding up?'

'Huh?'

'How's Jane Sullivan doing?'

The captain's eyes flicker. 'Uh . . . Jane overdosed about eight weeks ago.' He sketches a faint cross on his chest.

'Jesus.' Flanagan lowers his head and stares at the amber liquid in his glass, drinks it. 'Did you arrest anyone?'

'Wasn't hard to figure. It was a guy Sullivan put away for life twelve years ago. Got paroled early and musta kept the grudge boiling because when he got out he hacked into the police band and sent Sullivan to the address where he was waiting for him. Seems the guy had studied telecommunications while he was inside.' The captain sighs again, gently takes Flanagan's glass from him.

Flanagan is staring furiously at the scuffed pine floor of the town hall. He is thinking of Jane Sullivan and how it must have been for her – how bereft she must have been to take her own life. The Jane Sullivan he remembers was a good, God-fearing Catholic. Flanagan's heart is hammering as Brannigan returns with two more whiskies and the jazz band begins to swing.

'Must congratulate you on the Addis Barbar case, Flanagan. That was some sharp footwork.'

'Huh?'

'The Addis Barbar case, congratulations are in order.'

Flanagan feels his chest is going to burst the constraints of his crumpled jacket. 'Thanks.'

'Couldn't have handled it myself. No way. I know my limitations. What we get around here – drunks, bit of grass, meter violations, maybe the occasional motor death, fraud, robbery – I can deal with that. Kiddie killers, no way.'

Flanagan is aware of someone hovering nearby, nearly at his elbow, but he ignores them, turns his startling lime eyes on Brannigan. 'Ted, you read anything or heard anything about Mr Candid?'

'Mr Candid? Well, sure I have. Everyone has. Load of bullshit, that's all it is – load of bullshit. Can't believe they waste their time on that crap.' Brannigan laughs.

'I dunno, Ted,' Flanagan mumbles. 'Too many coincidences. Too many sightings.'

'There are *no* sightings, Flanagan. None. No two descriptions are the same. It's all bullshit. What kinda name is that anyway? "Mr Candid" – sounds like a frigging shirt-lifter. Oh, shoot – I'm sorry, Mrs Thackeray. I do apologize.'

'Captain Brannigan, I heard nothing,' drawls Twyla Thackeray.

Twyla Thackeray had arrived at the benefit ball an hour before, shrugging off her shawl in the vestibule (delighting the doorman) before stepping daintily into the reception, which was where she first laid eyes on a bear of a man, causing her vodka-scented breath to falter. The man was tall and beefy, his clothes crumpled, his fair hair ruffled. The man wore creased clothes untidily and looked puzzled. The man was Flanagan. For an hour she watched him, mesmerized, all the time drifting towards him, coming to rest at his elbow. She had, in the nick of time, found a man big enough and, she suspected, *worthy* enough, to save her.

'Uh – Mrs Thackeray, may I introduce Flanagan, *Lieutenant* Flanagan, I should say? He works for the Florida Department of Law Enforcement out of Miami, but he was here in Collier County for ten years before he was transferred. Flanagan, Mrs Twyla Thackeray, matron at the Emerald Rest Home.'

Twyla Thackeray lowered her eyes momentarily, then turned the full blaze of her gaze on the lieutenant, who, sadly, missed this as he was glancing at the trays of uneaten food. 'Mrs Thackerby, nice to meet you.' Flanagan takes her bony hand in his paw and shakes it. Unfortunately for Twyla Thackeray, Flanagan is distracted that evening, by hunger and by sadness at the thought of Jane Sullivan's lonely death. He leaves the ball early, but not before writing a cheque for three hundred dollars, a sum which will no longer benefit Jane Sullivan but which might ease the damage done to Louis Grammandi's children. He returns to his hotel and lies on the bed, cogitating as he eats his way though a family bucket of KFC chicken pieces.

'Charlie Kane – he didn't step into the world, he *slithered* into it.' Iris Chandler laughs, an improbable sound.

The nurse glances down at her, adjusts Iris's pillow. 'It'll soon be time for your lunch, Iris,' she bawls into Iris's creased earflap.

Iris's eyes narrow as a shard of clarity pierces her, and she looks up, beyond the vast breasts swaying above her, snug in starched cotton. 'You're new,' she remarks.

'Yes.' Bronwen heaves the frail body higher on the mound of pillows.

Face like a muffin, thinks Iris. 'There are a few things you should know. First, I am *not* deaf. There is no need to shout at me. Jesus, my head's still ringing. Second, I don't like pillows pushed up behind me. And third – and make sure you remember this – I do *not* like having my arm touched.'

Bronwen pulls the pillows away, watches Iris slump down. She stares at the stump that is Iris's right arm. 'And would there be anything else I should know?'

'Why certainly!' Iris's mouth opens wide – a real cakehole, thinks Bronwen – and Iris shouts, 'I am the mother of Charlie Kane!'

And who the fuck is Charlie Kane? Bronwen wonders, as she moves on to the next derelict body.

Malibu, CA – January

M –

I've not had a good day. I had this ache all over me when I woke up and I went and lay in the sun thinking that would make a difference but it didn't. I think the ache is loneliness, which is crazy. I've been on my own for years and I never felt like this before. Or maybe I have. Some days, years ago, I used to wake up and feel like I was lying next to something cold and blue. A large cube. When things were bad, when I was doing too many lines, I called the cube Mrs Blue. How crazy is that? Naming your loneliness and making it a friend?

I'm lying in a hammock. I'm thirty-eight years old and I feel like crying. I wish you were here. I want to tell you what it's like to be here. I'm looking at my hands writing this and even that makes me want to cry. I always wanted to have elegant hands – remember that? I remember lying

in a motel bed and holding my hands up in front of your
face and you laughed. Which made me sad because I
thought they were elegant then. They looked pale and
surprised. You laughed and I wonder what you would do
if you could see them now – given the things they've
done. Sorry about this – I've been drinking.

It's late now. I'll write again.

Yours,

C

The same morning that three more patients – customers – are
removed from the rest home by worried relatives, Bronwen
throws herself, unbidden, on to a chair in the matron's room
and pushes off her shoes. A cheesy odour wafts over to the
desk and Twyla Thackeray looks up, grimacing, from an
invoice for $30,984 for annual employee insurance. Bronwen
sips her tea, producing a sound not unlike the death rattle. The
matron sighs and looks away. 'What can I do for you,
Bronwen?'

'Hmm? Oh, nothing, Matron.'

'I'm very busy.'

Bronwen rubs her plump toes through the damp nylon
mesh of her tights. 'I never expected it to be so hot here. In
Wales it's freezing in January. Cold enough to shatter coal.
Mam and I would have to sit in the same room every evening
to stay warm, Matron, can you believe it? I mean, we only
heated the one room so we'd both go in there. That was after
my father died . . .'

As Bronwen talks of the finer points of heating a small
Victorian house, Twyla Thackeray wonders if all Welsh people
are as boring as this. She has no way of knowing, since

Bronwen is the first (and last) Welsh nurse she has employed. 'Bronwen, I'm real pleased that you want to come in and talk with me, that you feel relaxed enough to do that, but I have a lot of administrative—'

'We always used to visit the matron in Swansea General. Her door was always open and we'd all pop in for a cup of tea and a chat. She was a lovely woman, from Llanerchymydd in Ynys Môn. She was like a mother to us, you know, not strict or anything, so I think I just got in the habit—'

'Bronwen,' Twyla Thackeray cuts in sharply, trying to dam the flood of words. 'Bronwen, we do things differently here at the Emerald Rest Home. You must make an appointment to see me, if you feel you need to discuss anything. Any problems you may have.' She looks at Bronwen's blank, pasty face. It reminds her of someone, or something. '*Do* you have any problems?'

'Oh, no, Matron. I love it here. Only it's too hot. Mam said, when I told her I was moving to Florida, Mam said to make friends with the matron and—'

'Bronwen, as much as I have enjoyed talking with you, I must ask you to leave now, so that I can continue my morning's work. And for the record, my title is director, not matron.'

Bronwen pushes her feet back into her shoes and stands, puffing and wiping sweat from her temples. "Bye, then.' She pauses at the door and turns back. 'There are a couple of things actually, Matron. You know Iris?'

'Yes.'

'Well, I was looking at her notes and it says she's fifty-seven.'

'Yes.' Twyla Thackeray fiddles with her pen, imagines

opening the virgin bottle of Absolut hidden in the locked drawer of her desk.

'Well, she looks about eighty. Is it a mistake?'

'No, Bronwen. We don't make mistakes here at the Emerald Rest Home. Iris is fifty-seven. She's had a hard life; she suffered a massive trauma at some time and she also has a mild form of dementia. What was the other question? I really do have to get on here.'

'Who's Charlie Kane?'

The matron tilts her chin, stretching the skin of her throat. 'Why do you ask that?'

'It's only Iris going on. She's always shouting that she's the mother of Charlie Kane, or Chum Kane, as if it's important. Is he a film star or something?'

'No. No, he's not. Goodbye, Bronwen.' Twyla Thackeray watches Bronwen's swaying rump as she leaves the room, then she realizes: a muffin. Bronwen reminds her of a muffin. She crosses the office, locks the door, unlocks the desk drawer and pours herself two fingers of raw vodka. Before drinking she glances at the clock (8.47 a.m. – the earliest yet at work), pulls a newspaper from her purse and spreads it open on the desk, poring over an artist's impression, a charcoal sketch of a fine-boned face.

Malibu, CA – January

M –

I'm depressed. I write these letters and then I think – where are you? You may be dead. You may be screwing. You may be a corporate executive. I can't help these things. Sorry – I'm feeling loose today. It's this waiting. I have to stay here for a while, but I don't know how long, maybe a few days, maybe a week. Just sitting here, staring at my navel, waiting for a call.

Yours,

C

'Matron,' Twyla Thackeray mutters, as she closes her office door and slips the key into an artful, beautiful pocket adorning an artful, beautiful suit. '*Matron* indeed. "Director of healthcare", rather.' She taps the nameplate on her door with a manicured burgundy fingernail and swivels on her heels, which squeal on the linoleum of the corridor.

As she passes the rooms lining the corridor, rooms tastefully decorated in apricot and sky blue, she nods gravely at the occupants. Some drool in response, some shriek. Some raise the wreck of a hand and wave. Some – they are few – croak a greeting through ravaged larynxes: 'Morning, Matron.' Matron, indeed.

She turns into the farthest room and looks at Iris, asleep in her chair, her mouth agape. The stump that is her arm is raised jauntily, jutting boldly into the air, as if she intends soon and suddenly to hang a right. Matron sits on the edge of the bed, examines a minutely chipped nail and looks up to find Iris's pale blue eyes on her. Matron smiles brightly. 'Good afternoon, Iris! Did you enjoy your lunch?'

'Can't remember.' The stump-arm waggles a little and lowers itself.

'What a delightful room this is.'

'Same as all the others if I rec'llect c'rrectly.' All her life Iris has cracked her vowels in the vice of her mouth when nervous or suspicious. At this moment she is both.

Twyla Thackeray gets up from the bed and smoothes the

tight skirt over her toned, tanned legs. She moves to the dresser in the corner and picks up a photograph, framed in silver. 'Oh, isn't this lovely? Was this your home?' She holds out the picture of a pastel confection of a house, complete with turrets, galleries and balconies, ornate portico leading to vast double doors. Behind the house a pale, wide beach melts into the sea.

'Sure was.'

'You must miss it.'

'Maybe.' Iris begins to suck her lower lip, flubbering a little as her eyes follow the photograph.

Matron turns her back on Iris and frowns. This is not going well. The bitch is sharp today, very sharp. She scans the dresser, finds the picture she knows is there. Wheeling round she sits on the edge of the bed once more, holding the picture in Iris's face. 'And who's this handsome man? You told me once and now I've gone and forgotten.'

A film covers the pale blue eyes and Iris becomes childlike, almost coquettish. 'Why, how can you f'rget that?' She snatches the photograph and puts it in her lap, begins gently to rub the face of the man with her single forefinger, stroking it as she would the neck of a cat. The man's lips look as if they are about to laugh, as if he is hearing a roaring sound. He is handsome – slim and fearless, long of limb and chiselled of face. His pale blue eyes stare back into Iris's own. His foot rests on the gleaming, elegant chrome fender of a car, his hands hanging limp. 'How could you forget? That's Charlie Kane. Charlie Kane – he didn't step into the world, he slithered into it.'

The matron crosses her legs and lights a cigarette, knowing that she has Iris hooked. Be a problem shutting her up now.

'Charlie Kane came into this world blue and cold, like a fish covered in slime. He wasn't even interested in breathing until the nurse whacked his behind. Then he just spit gently and coughed. I remember him looking around as if deciding whether to take another breath or not. Well, he must've seen something he liked the look of because the next thing he was screaming and hanging off my tit like a stripper's tassel.'

Matron rolls her eyes and taps a neat cylinder of warm ash into her soft white palm.

Iris stops rubbing the photograph and looks at it. 'He was something, Charlie Kane. I had another one a couple of years later – Lydia. But then, that's a different . . . I can't talk . . . Anyway, Charlie was a wonder. Made me think of sherbet and leaves and velvet. I could never get enough of him – why, I'd hug him tight every day.' Iris stares out of the window at the diseased trees. 'I'd hold him for ever if I could.'

Matron watches Iris as she plays and replays her pictures on the walls of the empty rooms in her mind. Iris sighs and the photograph slips from her lap. Matron scoops it up and looks at Charlie Kane, licks her lips.

'The time we moved to that house by the sea, the one you looked at – my, they were happy times. Charlie running all over and then Lydia just a baby. But the troubles had already started and things weren't ever really the same again.'

Twyla Thackeray looks up sharply. 'What troubles, Iris? What troubles did you have in that lovely house?'

Iris sucks her lower lip and stares right back, as if making a judgement, as if weighing something in her ransacked mind. She rocks forward and nods, the decision made. 'Well, some might say it couldn't be a trouble, a burden, a tribulation, but I tell you, looking back, it was like a disease.'

Matron is puzzled, her brow furrowed. 'Iris, what can it be?'

'Genius. That was the trouble. Pure genius. Just before we moved to that house, when we were in Manhattan, I came back to the apartment one day from a stint of shopping and all I wanted to do was sit down and have a cup of coffee – you know how it is.'

Matron nods, imagining the lead crystal glass awash with the near-frozen vodka that she sips at breakfast, so cold it moves like the jelly seas around the Antarctic.

'I came home that day to find Charlie Kane sitting in the apartment reading the *New York Times*. Well, we always took the *Post* so I knew something was wrong. Charlie Kane stood in the kitchen, on his tiny little legs, and told me that he thought the *Post* was very "limited" and "parochial" and he hoped I wouldn't get mad but he wanted the *Times* delivered instead.' Iris sucks in her cheeks and sits back. 'Well, I can tell you, I had my coffee but in that cup was a wedge of bourbon.'

Twyla Thackeray waves the burnt butt of the cigarette and asks, 'What did you do with him?'

'I wouldn't have done anything with him. Seemed to me he was happy as he was. I didn't care if he read the *New York Times*, though I never liked it myself – too wordy. Anyway, I said nothing to anyone, just made sure Charlie Kane was happy as he could be. Couldn't last, of course. The day he went to school all hell caught fire. Next thing I know there are psycho-this and psycho-that all over the house and they're running tests on Charlie Kane like he was a car or something. I had calls from people asking for him to go on television, radio and all. I got offers for him to go to college. Go to college.' Iris snorts and rubs her stump. 'The boy was only three years old! Why would he want to be doing with college?'

'What did Charlie think about it? I mean, did he want to go?'

Iris smiles alarmingly. 'No. He wanted to stay right at home with his mother and sister. He said he enjoyed school and he could read what he wanted in the evenings. He used to sit in his room all night, just reading. Course, I couldn't understand half of what he told me, but I could listen and that's surely nearly as good as understanding. As for Lydia, well, shoot, she was simply unfortunate. Couldn't be helped. Couldn't even say "Charlie". Used to call him Chum, and before I knew it everyone was calling him Chum Kane. If I'd wanted people to call him Chum I would have named him so.' Iris draws a breath which stutters in her throat. 'Poor little Lydia.'

Twyla Thackeray sits, cupping ash in one hand, holding the photograph of Charlie in the other, sits and waits for Iris to speak. But the thought of Lydia has dammed Iris's throat. She whimpers and holds out her hand for the image of Chum. The matron asks, 'Where's Chum Kane now?'

Iris throws back her head and shouts. 'I don't know! *I don't know!*'

'And what about Chum's father? Your husband? Where's he, Iris? You've never talked about him.' Iris has never talked about anyone except Charlie Kane, she thinks.

Iris's mouth snaps shut and she shakes her head.

'Oh, Iris, you can tell me.'

Again Iris shakes her head.

Twyla Thackeray lights another cigarette. She goes to the window, opens it and dusts off her palms. She stares at the mouldering sky for a moment and turns back. 'I've always wondered, Iris, I always wondered who pays your fees. Where does the money come from? I mean, you've been here for years now and, Lord knows, I realize it hardly comes cheap. Yet every month there's the banker's draft. Did you sell that lovely house? Is that where the money came from?'

Iris's chin sets like concrete. 'No. I'd never sell that house. What if Charlie Kane came home and found home didn't exist any more? That would be terrible. No, it's sitting there just the same as when he left it all those years ago. They can't sell it without my say-so. He'll come back one day. I know it. He'll come back to say goodbye to his mother.'

'So who pays your fees, Iris?'

Iris shrugs and begins to flubber. Twyla Thackeray looks down at her coolly. Both she and Iris know that this regression is a sham, a play, for Iris's eyes are focused on the matron's face. Twyla Thackeray picks up the photograph and says, 'Can I borrow this for a while? Just a couple of hours? Is that all right, Iris?'

Iris heaves herself out of the chair with a squawk, grabs at the frame with her hand, her stump waving wildly, trying to beat the matron away, but the matron pushes the frail body back into the chair. Iris begins to scream, begins to rock back and forth with her mouth wide open as Twyla Thackeray turns to see Bronwen in the doorway.

'Ah, Bronwen. It's a good thing you arrived. Iris is having a bad day today and I came in to try to calm her. Perhaps you can take over?'

Bronwen nods and waddles into the room.

'Give me back Charlie Kane! *Give me back Charlie Kane!*' The strings holding Iris's neck together are pulled tight, her skin red.

'Why,' says Bronwen, 'she just wants her photo back, that's

all.' She takes it gently from the matron and gives it to Iris. 'There, love, there's your picture.'

Twyla Thackeray glares at Bronwen's back bent over the chair and walks out of the room. Bronwen does not notice Matron leaving. Bronwen does not notice anything; is unaware of her own breathing, unaware even of the odour of Iris's flesh. All Bronwen can see – all she wants to look at ever again – is the vision of Charlie 'Chum' Kane resting his foot on the chrome fender of an unseen car.

Malibu, CA – January

M –

It's maybe four in the morning. I don't know. I can't sleep. I went fishing today for my supper. Didn't amount to much more than three swallows. The electricity went out while I was eating and I lit some candles. I felt crazy sitting there picking at a backbone, all alone by candlelight. I felt deserted. Like the last diner at the Last Supper. *L'Ultima Cena*.

I can't sleep because I've got one of those feelings for which I am – justly – famous. I have the feeling of something slipping, of jaws closing. Someone somewhere has made a decision which narrows the pincers. Could be paranoia. Don't think so. Not sure. Some men are born with endless mountains at the edge of their minds. A sense of space. I was born with the posse at the edge of mine; and I can hear it now.

Yours,

C

'Lieutenant Flanagan, please.' Matron stands in front of the mirror in her bedroom, drink in one hand, cordless telephone in the other. She slips the strap of her dress from her tanned, velvet-smooth shoulder, licks her vermilion lips. As the call is put through, she remembers the thrill of meeting the lieutenant, how she was overwhelmed, almost, by his bulk, his presence, the sharp scent of his testosterone. She near swooned as they were introduced, and every night since then she has caressed herself, imagining the lieutenant's hands mirroring the same moves.

'Flanagan speaking.'

'Why, Lieutenant, you sound so gruff on the phone!' Matron turns and looks at the swooping lines of the burgundy dress as it dips down her back.

'Who is this, please?'

'It's Twyla Thackeray. I don't know if you remember but we met a couple of weeks ago at the benefit ball in Naples?' Matron bites her lip. 'I'm the director of health care over at the Emerald Rest Home.'

'Sure, sure I remember. You were wearing a red dress.'

Matron smiles and fingers the fabric. 'That's the one. You have a good memory.'

'How can I help you?'

Matron walks briskly into her lounge and sits, knees clamped together, back ramrod straight, on the edge of her sofa. 'It's difficult to explain.'

'Try me.'

'Well, I don't know if you remember but when we met you were with Captain Brannigan, talking about those stories about a guy who's some kind of a vigilante, a wanted man. Am I right?'

'Sure, sure. Papers call him Mr Candid.'

'That's the one.'

Lieutenant Flanagan sighs, sending a rush of air into Matron's vodka-sodden mind. 'So, what d'you have to tell me? Sorry, but I'm real busy.'

'Well, I've read that the psychological profiles of the man have pointed to someone in his thirties. And that some psychs have said that he's exceptionally gifted.'

'That's right.' Lieutenant Flanagan smothers a yawn, which reaches into Matron's ear as a numbing sound.

'Thing is, to get to the point, and I guess this is synchronicity or serendipity or something, but the next morning, it was a Sunday – I only have the papers delivered on Sunday, so I know it was – and there was an article about Mr Candid. There was this artist's impression with the piece, one of those pencil drawings. Know what I mean?'

Lieutenant Flanagan grunts.

'Thing is, this drawing looked exactly like the photograph one of our patients – sorry, customers – has in her room. But *exactly*. Almost as if it could have been drawn from that photograph. Am I making any sense here?'

'Some.'

'Anyway, I was kind of interested, because of listening to you and all, and reading this article, so I went to see her today, and guess what?'

'What?'

'She does have a son.' Matron smiles a cat smile.

'Jesus – sorry, I'm sorry, Ms Thackerby. It's just that a lot of people have sons.'

'I know that; of course I know that. But there's something unusual about her circumstances, the customer's, I mean. For example, how many people have their care fees paid by an unknown source?'

'Maybe she has her own money.'

'Ah, no. She don't have two dimes to shove where the . . .' Matron slips from the sofa to the floor, spilling vodka on the red bullet tips of her toes. She realizes she has been slurring. Sitting bolt upright she places the glass on the table and lights a cigarette. 'No, she has no private source of income. And yet she still has her house and I can tell you it's quite a place. I just feel there's some ambiguity here. She never has visitors. Not in all the time she's been here.'

'Uh huh.'

'It seems strange, y'know, what with the photograph and all.' Matron frowns, knows she is not dealing with this well. This conversation is supposed to attract the lieutenant back to her side.

'Well, maybe we'll come and see her when we have time. Thanks for your concern, Ms Thackerby. Very civic-minded of you.'

She has to hook him soon. Now. 'Look, Iris don't make much sense much of the time. I mean, it's very difficult to get her to talk – she had some trauma years ago that seems to have unhinged her or something. No one knows where she comes from. She arrived here with a name tag, a letter detailing bank drafts, two photographs and no memory.'

'How long ago was that?' The lieutenant's interest is being slowly stirred.

Matron smiles, swigs a mouthful and swallows. 'Before I was appointed here. I think she was admitted maybe sixteen, seventeen years ago? I could certainly find out for you. Thing is, I thought maybe I could help you, so I tried to talk to her today. So first of all there's the drawing and the photograph. And also there was one other thing she told me. Her son was conshidered a genius. He was offered a place at college when he was three yearsh old.'

'What's his name? Ms Thackerby, what's his name?'

'Charlie Kane. Also known as Chum Kane.'

Malibu – January

M –

Things haven't been so good the past couple of days. I'm not sleeping. The feeling of an end, of a bolt-hole slamming shut, a caesura closing, persists. Maybe I should move on. I'm waiting for a call from someone in LA. It's difficult to explain, but I need to find a name and number and I've put the word out and all I can do now is wait.

I forgot to tell you – when I was out fishing I sat there in the silence and for the first time in years, I swear I don't know how many, I tested myself. Square root of 68,000. If you took the second prime number in a series predicated on the denary scale and multiplied it by the number of prime numbers in a closed set defined by pi and then shoved it all up your ass, what would happen? Which number would you have if you multiplied it by eight, found the square root of that number, added the digits and subtracted ten? Seventeen. Same number as the years since I've seen you. Keeps bothering me.

Yours,

C

The Emerald Rest Home squats in the swamps where colours are blown in from the Gulf of Mexico to be bleached by a sun peering over the Tropic of Cancer. The winds race over the Keys, bringing with them memories of sweat and snakes, malaria, cayman and mangroves. Around the rest home the gardeners have fought back the marshes and planted palms, which have sucked up the saline water and grown diseased and contorted. Lieutenant Flanagan watches these stunted trees wave listlessly in the breeze as he waits for Matron in her office and tries to imagine a less healthy environment in which to die. As he fails to conjure one single place, the door whispers open and Matron steps into the room.

'Why, Lieutenant Flanagan, how long have you been waiting? No one told me you were here,' she lies, having spent the past ten minutes straightening the seams of her clothes and face.

'No problem.' Lieutenant Flanagan heaves his large frame from the chair and shakes her proffered hand.

Matron simpers and slips into her chair. 'What can we do for you?' She pats her expensively styled, highlighted hair.

'I was wondering if I might meet with this patient—'

'Customer.'

'Sorry, customer, that you called me about.'

'Of course you may. I have to warn you that she can get pretty crazy sometimes. Although' – here the matron dimples deliciously – 'sometimes I reckon she's just going through the motions. Attention-seeking. Here at the Emerald we don't believe in administering drugs on demand so we have to allow them a little latitude.'

'Admirable.' The lieutenant glances at his watch, at the twisted palms.

'Well, I'm sure you're a busy man. Would you follow me?'

Matron leads the way down the antiseptic corridors, her twitching butt drawing him forward. Flanagan avoids looking in the rooms, terrified of glimpsing a life nearing its end. His fear of death is matched only by his desire to *right* things, to place things in context, to act – always – for the greater good. Just so long as this quaint Irish utilitarianism does not involve his own death.

Matron turns into the farthest room to see Bronwen fussing with Iris's dresser. Bronwen's muffin face turns, shocked, and she slips her hands into her pockets, lowers her head and barrels towards the door, where Flanagan appears.

'Bronwen? How is Iris?' asks Matron.

'Fine, Matron, she's fine.' Bronwen keeps moving, heading for the door.

'Lieutenant Flanagan,' he says, extending his hand.

'. . . meet you,' mumbles Bronwen, and keeps going.

Bronwen and Flanagan jam each other in the doorway and Bronwen rubs against him, trying to free her bulk, rubbing her stomach hard against his. This sudden intimacy surprises them both and they stare at each other, blushing. A laugh rumbles in Flanagan's gut but Bronwen's face pinches with embarrassment as she hauls herself free. With a grunt she trots down the corridor, buttocks swinging.

The lieutenant pauses on the threshold, breathes deeply, tries to prepare himself for the sight of dimmed eyes and liver spots. What he does not prepare himself for is the sight of Iris's stump, pink and shiny at its tip, exposed as she sits in her nightdress in her chair. He turns to the window to compose himself as Matron introduces them.

'Iris, this is Lieutenant Flanagan. Lieutenant, this is Iris.'

He turns back, his hand extended, a smile on his face, a smile that disappears as he realizes he's held out his right hand. No matter what, he cannot bring himself to touch the remains of Iris's arm. But Iris ignores his gesture.

'So what're you? In the army or what?'

'May I sit down?' He lowers himself gingerly on to the bed, staring at Iris's face, not wanting to look at her ancient wound. 'No, no, I'm not with the army. I'm a police officer.'

Iris flicks a look at the matron. 'What d'you want with me?'

'Nothing, Iris. Just to talk, that's all.' A struggle rages in the lieutenant's barrel of a heart as he fights the impulse to run from the damaged, dying woman, and suppresses the desire to alleviate her suffering, to befriend her.

'What about?' snaps Iris, her lips pursed, beak-like, on this sunny day.

'Now, Iris,' coos Matron, 'the lieutenant here is a friend of mine and I was telling him the other day about the conversation we had, y'know, about Charlie Kane and everything. He was real interested, just on a personal level, about Charlie being a genius. Remember? Because' – an unusual flash of inspiration courses through Matron, unusual because she has a void where her imagination should be – 'because he has a child who is also gifted.' Matron smiles conspiratorially at the lieutenant, who still stares fixedly at Iris's eyes.

'What's he called?' Iris asks.

'Declan,' blurts the lieutenant, wondering where on earth he plucked that name from.

'Hmm.' Iris is not convinced, chews on her tender lower lip. She wants to like the lieutenant, wants to like him because he has big hands and he looks tired.

'Can I show the lieutenant the photograph of Charlie Kane? Can I, Iris? Y'know, just so he knows who we're talking about? So he can put a face to the name? Is that OK?' Matron moves to the dresser, aware of her sleek, seductive silhouette against the shattering sunlight.

Iris frowns. Her head is making noises, squeaks and groans. Small splintering sounds. She wants to think about them, wants to consider this new evidence of her body decaying, but she knows she must watch Matron, whom she does not trust.

'Where *is* that wonderful picture, Iris?'

'It's right thur, where it's alwiys bin. 'Nd I'm not share I want it pussed around fer anyone t'look it.' Iris listens, puzzled, to her own voice and language breaking down, collapsing.

'It's not here, Iris. It's not on the godda— on the dresser. Have *you* got it?' Matron spins round to glare at the sly, dissembling bitch. 'It is not here, Iris. It's not here.'

As she watches, something – the sweep of a malignant hand, perhaps – passes over Iris's face. The woman shrinks before them, deflates, dies a little. Flanagan moves forward, extends one of his huge paws towards Iris. 'For God's sake, what's the matter with her?'

Matron walks coolly to a red button set in the wall by Iris's bed, pushes it, and the lieutenant hears a bell ring faintly, endlessly ringing. From the other rooms come muffled shrieks and cries as the other dying cry for one of their own. Matron pushes Iris back in her chair and undoes the button at Iris's corrugated throat. She looks at the ruin of her face, dripping like wax. 'Looks like she's had a stroke,' she snaps, as the door swishes open and a doctor and nurse rush in. 'Shit. I'm real sorry, Lieutenant. I don't know where the photograph is, and I have a feeling we may never know.'

He looks at her appraisingly. 'Frankly, I don't think it's a concern right now.'

Iris thrashes feebly as she feels the doctor open her nightdress, violating her, pressing a cold cup on her chest to listen to her life ebb away. She looks in her eyes, tries to manipulate her one good arm.

Matron taps the young nurse on her arm. 'Iris is becoming distressed. Please fetch Bronwen, the Welsh nurse – she works with Iris and she may be able to calm her down a little.'

The doctor glances up, her fingers cold on Iris's wrist. 'Bronwen's just left. She gave notice this morning. Don't ask me why, she never said.'

Matron's relief at Bronwen's departure – another wage packet dispensed with, no more monologues about the weather – does not last long. For that afternoon, as Iris lies in a bed in the clinic, trying to wrest words from the chaos that lies between her mind and her mouth, Matron, who has asked a nurse to trip down to the mall and fetch her a fifth of vodka, realizes (indeed, knows even before she opens the drawer) that not only has busty Bronwen disappeared but so has four thousand dollars of petty cash.

Malibu, CA – February

M –

Two days later: I'm moving on. I still haven't heard from the guy in LA and I feel like a static target. I had a weird feeling the other day. I was lying in the hammock, staring at nothing, and I had the feeling like someone was reaching into me and stealing something. Nothing material, nothing bloody, just something of me. Something that's been dormant, and the only reason I know it was there is because it no longer is.

I'm going to keep writing to you, now I've got in the habit. But I guess things might be more difficult and maybe I won't be able to write so often. Seems like the lac of writing calms me, makes me feel I'm having a conversation with you.

Do you believe you can run out of luck? I do. I wish so many things. I wish I knew how this would end.

Yours,

C

IRIS

Iris Chandler was a dainty girl, so small, so petite, that her mother had to make her clothes, themselves so small that they were always being mislaid. Iris's mother was a seamstress, a mistress of gathering and tucking, of hemming. Sometimes Iris felt as if her mother had gathered her right up and tucked her in so that she became insignificant. Mrs Chandler worked in the back room of a house in Hoboken, New Jersey, in light dimmed by the shadows of other buildings. She sat bent over the treadle of an old Singer and played away her life to the staccato chatter of the needle dipping in and out, the clicking of bobbins, the tack-tack of needle and thread. The room was always full of lint, giving a bluish hue to the light, dulling it even more. Mrs Chandler spent years gathering in yards and bales of fabric. Spent her life tutting and stitching, loosening seams, opening tucks, edging buttonholes, turning up, letting down. She fingered the baptism frocks, the lengthening trousers, the seductive blouses, the maternity frocks, the increasing waistbands, the stiffness of the last suit to be sent to the undertakers. All life passed through her hands, and perhaps that is why she did not notice Iris's life passing, insignificant as she seemed.

Iris would go to her mother's workroom when she got back from school, her tiny feet dragging on the threadbare rug of the hallway. She would open the door, with difficulty because it was heavy, proofed against the sound of the treadle, and look for her mother in the mist of lint. And always her mother would be bent over, her shoulders hunched with concentration and something resembling fury.

'Hello, Mom. I'm home.' Iris sounded shy, her voice breathy, falling against her mother's back.

'Is it that time already?' Every day her mother would say this, every day she would sound surprised and pick up swags of material only to drop them, as if they were unmanageable. 'Iris, I won't be finished for a while. Why don't you go into the kitchen and get some milk? Don't forget your vitamins. I'll come in when I can.' This speech hardly varied in the years Iris came home and shoved at the door to the workroom. When she finished speaking, her mother would turn to smile at Iris, indistinct in the hazy room, and Iris would to her seem elf-like as she leaned against the lintel.

The kitchen was worn bald in places where hands and hips had rubbed over the years. The flooring curled at the edges, the glaze of the sink was mazed, the enamel of the range dulled by a thousand scratches. Iris would open the door of the pantry, each day hoping to find something more than the day before, a delicacy, a fragile dainty that would fall apart deliciously in her diminutive palm. Always she was disappointed. She would stretch up to the shelf to reach the cracked jug of milk, terrified of spilling. Then she would fetch the vitamins from a bottle by the range, pour a glass of milk and lift herself on to a chair at the table, her feet swinging above the linoleum. She would force the vitamins, large and coarse, past her throat, gagging on the yeasty taste, swigging the milk to force them down.

Then came the silence. Always the raw silence, always and every day. The sitting in the silence; waiting. Rubbing the shiny tabletop with agitated hands as the milk and pills dragged through her stomach. Waiting. Waiting for what? Not her mother, who would stay in her workroom, tutting and muttering. Not even for her father. It was not that the Chandler family did not love each other: it was simply that they all appeared to be waiting for something, comfort, security, height, whatever. All just waiting. And Iris, all the time Iris knowing that these were the good days. These days, these late afternoons, were supposed to be the best days, days you remember when you're old and shapeless, swinging on a porch. These were the sun-days, Rockwell days, spent shucking corn, playing tag, baking cookies, running round the yard, tobogganing, skating.

Sometimes, as her hands rubbed the table, she closed her eyes and tried to imagine the city of Peking, tried to imagine the compact emptiness of a cube, the act of playing a violin; thoughts sparked by the words of a teacher. Iris tried to free herself from the kitchen; imagined herself walking the streets of Peking, pictured chickens in the street, unspeakable food on plates, tiny, wizard-like men trotting under yokes. But she couldn't spawn hope from this and the pictures melted away. Something might happen but not in Hoboken, New Jersey. In Hoboken, New Jersey, you sat with your feet swinging and waited in the silence, waiting for something to happen. Waiting to grow. Fighting – if she did but know it – the canker of determinism flowering in her guts.

Always the evening slipped in as Iris waited and heard the

screen door slam behind it. Her father trod the hallway and came into the kitchen to cross to the sink, gently touching the crown of her head with callused fingers as he passed. He washed his hands with the cracked lump of carbolic kept there and dried them methodically, never able to clean the oil from his nails. He shucked off his blue overalls, and threw them on to the back of a chair before sitting opposite Iris and smiling distractedly. 'Mother, I'm home!' he shouted, startling Iris, even though he shouted the same greeting each night as he sat opposite her. Then he would put his head in his freckled hands and rub his eyes, dragging the reddened lids, stretching them.

Iris watched his nails as they moved, coarse and square, stained with the eternal black tattoo of the grease monkey. She knew her father was fastidious, that he washed and scrubbed, scraped and brushed, trying to present a cleansed face to an uncaring world. Iris did not know how she was aware that the world did not care. She sat at the kitchen table opposite her father and watched him getting old.

Iris grew in ways that her parents did not see. In ways that very few people saw, for she remained tiny. Mrs Chandler still saw the elf in the lint, Mr Chandler still saw the feet swinging above the linoleum, and they forgot that years were passing. Mr and Mrs Chandler spent their lives urging machines to stay alive – she as the treadle on the sewing machine stiffened, he as he tinkered with the cars in the impoverished neighbourhood. Both tried to swallow the indignation of poverty over and over until it stuck in their throats, leaving them little able to speak to each other.

One frozen December afternoon, as Mrs Chandler cursed the cold stiffening her rigid, frigid fingers, muttering a mantra of injured pride, she counted the years and knew Iris was older. She was ten years older than when she had arrived. It was Iris's tenth birthday and she, Mrs Chandler, her mother, had done nothing to prepare for it. She stood and pushed away the chair, allowed the treadle to grind to a halt, swirling the lint in the air. She stood and blinked, tapped the silver thimble against her teeth. '. . . forty-eight, forty-nine, fifty. Oh, Lord.' It was 1950. 'Oh, Lord.' She twisted the dress in her hands and heard the front door close as Iris came home from school.

Mrs Chandler squared her rounded shoulders and went into the hall, opened her arms and cried, 'Happy birthday, Iris!' Iris was shocked to see her mother outlined against the enormous door, dusty and pale with the fragments of cloth she had sewn. 'Come here, honey.' Mrs Chandler crouched down and held out her arms. Iris came to her and they hugged each other tentatively, quietly. Iris could hear the whorled calluses of her mother's thumb and forefinger rasp against the collar of her dress. Her mother sat back on her heels and smiled at her. 'Come on, let's have something to eat.'

Once in the kitchen, Mrs Chandler fought the desire to sweep Iris up and put her on the chair. She turned and watched Iris climb on to the seat and juggled memories as she tried to decide if Iris had grown. Perhaps a little, an inch or so. Perhaps. Mrs Chandler sighed as she opened the cookie jar, then fixed two hot chocolates and sat next to Iris, putting her arm around the bird-wing shoulders. 'Now honey, I've been racking my brains as to what to give you for your present. But the way I look at it, you're a big girl now' – Iris smiled at this – 'and I reckon you should pick it out for yourself.' Mrs

Chandler crossed the room and opened a worn, cracked-leather purse. Unzipping a hidden pocket she carefully unfolded two dollar bills, snapped them flat. She looked at the electric blue snow outside, dyed by the cloudless, darkening sky. She looked back at her little elf perched on her chair and tried to imagine her walking alone in the snow. For Iris had never been allowed out on her own, had always walked with the sureness of a girl who has a parent's hand swinging inches away.

Was this the time for her to step out alone? Mrs Chandler looked back again through the window, in time to see the streetlights flare and shadows hurl themselves across the snow. A few houses on the street had fairy lights strung out, sizzling and winking with the flickering electricity supply. She tried to imagine her daughter walking alone through this, how long the journey would take without a guiding hand, how many hazards she might encounter. She snapped the bills once more and reached a decision.

'Here, honey, here's two dollars. It's all yours. You can spend it or keep it, whatever you want to do with it.'

Iris held out her hand and took the bills, folded them carefully. 'I can spend it on anything I want?'

'Sure you can. Or you can keep it and save it for some other time.' Mrs Chandler smiled at her, hoping that that was what Iris would decide. Hoping that she would choose to put the bills in a tin and wait. But Iris had been waiting for ever in Hoboken, New Jersey. She slipped from her chair, kissed her mother, thanked her and walked into the hall to put on coat and gloves, wondering all the while what she would buy and what it would be like to hear only one pair of feet crushing the snow.

For years, whenever Mrs Chandler handled dollar bills, she remembered Iris walking out of the kitchen, her feet tapping on the linoleum, her back turned to her mother. Iris walked away, and some might say she never looked back.

1997

M –

I've been driving for a few days – some crazy route you'd never think of if you had something to do, somewhere to be. I'm happier now I'm moving. Malibu really got to me by the end. Non-place, nothing much happening except the talk of money. So I hitched into LA and bought a car.

Montana's a weird place. Shit, sometimes I think this whole country's a weird place. I'm writing this sitting in a motel room in some place in the middle of nowhere. Can't even remember the name of the town. You go into a bar here and everyone stops talking and turns their back. Which I guess suits me. So I bought a bottle of bourbon and came back here.

It's getting easier to write now, I'm doing it so often. Hope you don't mind. I can't talk to anyone else. Trouble is, I'm beginning to think a lot because of that. Because of the silence. I really don't want it coming back. I don't want it coming back. Any of it. Found myself thinking of Gödel's Theorem the other night when I was lying in bed. I'd done a couple of lines and it suddenly seemed crystal clear. You know, like I was thinking as if I *were* Gödel. I guess that's what the dust does. I'm hoping it's the dust because otherwise it *is* starting to come back.

Yours,

C

Bronwen does not have much luggage to take in the taxi to the Greyhound bus station; a small case and a large wallet are all that's needed for her purposes. As she boards the bus, anxiety and excitement broil inside her capacious guts, causing her to belch. She blushes and her head drops. She squeezes down the aisle, counting the seat numbers, and sees as she gets to her seat a woman so large that she, Bronwen, is dwarfed. Her fellow passenger spills on to Bronwen's seat, overflows her clothes, floods of flesh rippling. Bronwen blinks.

'Excuse me, is this seat fifty-one?' Bronwen points to the small remaining patch of grey and blue material.

The woman turns her head on her bloated neck and looks Bronwen up and down, like judge, jury and victim. 'Sure is.'

And when Bronwen hears her voice she knows why this woman has allowed herself to come to this. For her voice is like morning dew, like smoky brandy, like honey from the butts of bees that have gorged themselves on pomegranates, star fruit and nectarines. Her voice takes the listener from the Greyhound bus station to anywhere they wish to go. Bronwen stares at her, mesmerized, trying to think of something to say, anything to say, some question that this woman will have to answer.

'My ticket . . . it says this is my seat.'

Bronwen is startled by the cackle that rises from the back seat immediately behind her. She turns as quickly as she is

able in the confines of the bus and sees three women of the
night, as her ma would have said, lolling about on the seats,
laughing like drains.

The Voice-woman sighs and says, 'There's no way, honey,
there's no way you and me gonna be able to sit here together.
You sit here and we're gonna have four buns of jelly ten feet
wide.'

This is not what Bronwen wants to hear but as long as this
woman talks Bronwen is happy.

'Excuse me?' Voice-woman leans forward and taps the
shoulder of the man in front of her. 'Excuse me, sir?'

The man turns round, wiry of aspect and acerbic of face.
'Yeah?'

'Sir, we have a problem here.'

'Yeah?' His tapeworm-thin, elastic neck swivels his head
round to peer between seats. 'What's the problem?' A stoaty
tongue flicks out and licks his lips.

'Well, sir, how to put this delicately?' The Voice-woman
shifts slightly in her seat and the hydraulics of the bus beneath
her groan. 'This young lady here has the seat next to me and
we are neither of us nymphs, shall we say, hmmm?' The passengers fall silent; indeed, Florida itself seems to fall silent as
the Voice rolls like velvet through the bus. 'Seems to me it
would be a nice idea, in fact a service, if you would exchange
seats with her. You and me, we make maybe two seats
between us.'

The man moves as if in a dream, slowly, delicately, like a
Siamese cat attempting a castellated parapet. 'It would be my
pleasure, ma'am,' he says, and slips into the Giacometti-seat.

Bronwen is happier than she can ever remember being as
she bounces north to New York City. She can hear the Voice-

woman behind her, can hear nicotine-scratched laughs from
the back seat as the hookers (from Reno, she discovers) snort
their lines and disapproval, can watch the American Dream
made flesh as she passes through Orlando, Jacksonville,
Savannah, Fayetteville, Richmond, Washington, Baltimore,
Philadelphia: a cornucopia of revisionist delights if she did
but know it.

Montana – February

M –

Well, I've had it with this place. It's like a fucking
magnet to every crazy in the US – no one looks at you, no
one speaks, no one makes any contact. I don't know what
they think. Maybe that we're all aliens. Maybe that we're
FBI, CIA, KGB, IRA, IRS – who the fuck knows? And
it's so frigging cold. I tell you, if you spend any time out
here you realize that the hills aren't peopled with the
Waltons. Instead you got a load of bearded losers hunched
over bags of fertilizer and barrels of diesel fuel, with visions
of a country-wide federal conspiracy sparking in what's left
of their brains. I know I sometimes feel that the state isn't
doing all it might and that's why I do what I do. But these
guys are wild-eyed madmen planning Armageddon,
imagining they're one of the horsemen of the Apocalypse.
I tell you, you stand close enough to some of them and
you can hear the hoofs pounding.

It is beautiful, though – endless dryland and skies as blue
and wide as dreams. But no clouds means nights are cold,
winds coming down from the Arctic and blowing away all
my notions of staying round here. You drive and drive and
all you see are badlands dotted with the ruins of

homesteads. Maybe you've been here. I don't know. If you have you'll remember it – it's the fucking pathos of it all that kills me. All those poor bastards coming here thinking it would be all right. Just about the saddest thing you can see, a home someone built in the middle of nowhere rotting to its bones. And you know the people who lived there stayed and stayed waiting for something – sun, rain, hope, love. But always waiting for something that never comes.

Like I say I think they're all crazy bastards round here. It's not a refuge it's an asylum.

And yet, and yet . . . I was driving yesterday and heard something on the radio about a convict down in Harrison Penitentiary, Florida, who was killed while he was doing time. Addis Barbar – wonder if you heard the name? He'd just started a five-life sentence. Apparently someone called a local radio show and offered $1000 reward for Barbar's death. So, of course, another convict obliged, a guy called Ray MacDonald. Addis Barbar was inside because he killed a woman and then sexually tortured her daughter – who was only six years old – for nearly three days before killing her too. So maybe you feel like raising a glass to Ray MacDonald, maybe you even feel like he should be given a medal or a pardon or at least the $1000.

But – and this is a big but – it's not that easy. I've been following old Ray MacDonald's life-story for some time now. He doesn't know it, but I'm watching him. He's a real nice guy – white, forty-five years old, family man. Ray MacDonald was finally sent to Harrison (with an existing record of two rapes, and violent sexual assault for which he'd served seven years) because he repeatedly raped and

subsequently killed his own daughter. Read that again –
his *own* daughter.

So what d'you do then? Well, first thing I did was try to
work out how MacDonald even got near Addis Barbar –
Harrison Pen is twenty-three-and-a-half-hours solitary –
and I still don't get it. So I kept rolling along some
nameless road and switched radio stations to calm myself.
And then what happens? I heard a developer wants to
build a supermarket at Auschwitz.

Yesterday as I was bouncing along some frozen mud
bath by the Missouri the figure 0.6180339 came dancing
into my head. But everything's rusty and I can't remember
its significance. I will. I know I will.

Yours,

C

Lieutenant Flanagan squeezes behind his desk in his office, his
stomach dislodging the papers there, sweeping them to the
floor in a disgraceful arc. 'Shit.' He tries to bend down, scrab-
bles at the heap of information but his frame is too large, too
generous to move in such a pernickety space. 'Shit.' He shuffles sideways, tries to move his chair on its rollers but the back
of it is lodged against a window catch. 'Shit.'

Lieutenant Flanagan is stuck, jammed between a photocopier and a view of downtown Miami, whatever that is. He
wants more than anything to roar and rise, to flip the desk on
its back and break free, but resists the urge. He glances down
at the mugshot of Addis Barbar, which lies on top of the pile of
papers on the floor, and sighs. He looks at the telephone and
considers calling for help; chooses to leave the telephone
untouched. His only companion is Addis Barbar. The

lieutenant looks into the lunatic eyes staring back at him from the floor and thinks of them dead, lying in the morgue on a table, in the pitch dark, not needed any more. Serving no purpose. Simply sitting in the sockets, blind, glaucous marbles. He looks away, discomfited by the stare. He wonders what, exactly, the fuck he is supposed to *do* about Barbar. This case, for Chrissake, involves the investigation of the killing of a child murderer, paedophile and violent psychopath by a violent psychopathic multiple rapist, who has abused and killed his own daughter. Flanagan knows that he will have to investigate thoroughly, follow up the claims that the radio show producers incited violence, write reams of reports and triplicate them over and over. And for what? All he wants to do right now is push the desk over, drive to Harrison Penitentiary and blow Ray MacDonald away. Put a bullet through his brains. Then he could holster up, drive home and go to bed knowing he'd done a good day's work. Because he knows what will happen: he will be called to testify in the case brought by the relatives of Addis Barbar against the state for not protecting him; or the case they will bring against Ray MacDonald for murder in the first. He sighs heavily – not because he is anticipating the paperwork that will shower down on him but because he wishes he'd killed Addis Barbar himself. When he'd had the opportunity, when he'd had the excuse – resisting arrest. Instead he'd cuffed Addis Barbar and taken him to the station, having to endure his drug-crazed taunts along the way.

The lieutenant watches the traffic glide and stutter below him. Something other than constriction is gnawing at his pinioned stomach, for in a rest home a hundred miles away lies the broken Iris, babbling and burbling about her son. And the only person listening to her is the drunken, sexy matron. Lieutenant Flanagan thinks it is possible that inside Iris, somewhere in that ruined body, lies a key. A word, a message, a key. Iris does not know that she owns it, will one day spit it out, rusty and unused, and he, Flanagan, will not be there to catch it. Iris can – perhaps – resolve the puzzle of Mr Candid, who has apparently been running riot for years now. The lieutenant knows this and can do nothing. He is helpless. He is pinned between a photocopier and a view of Miami.

Lieutenant Flanagan also knows – without doubt – that Mr Candid would indeed drive directly to Harrison Penitentiary, slip inside there somehow and blow Ray MacDonald away.

Matron sits by Iris's bed and fires herself with another swig of vodka from her monogrammed silver hip flask – a present from her mother, who would be horrified to see her daughter come to this. For now Matron drinks on duty, at home, at night, in the day, in the car. She has even glugged from a bottle in the shower as water spattered around her. The thought of the delicious, bear-like Lieutenant Flanagan has prodded the teetering matron into the abyss. It was not until he left to return to Miami that the matron realized how much she had been hoping that the lieutenant would crush her against the hot curvature of his proud belly and hold her close. And now he has gone.

'What's he doing in Miami that he can't do here?' She surprises herself each time she speaks out loud, not expecting it. She takes another swig and gazes blearily at the palm trees dying outside. The gardeners have all gone – unpaid for two months now. The beds are emptying. As those without hope die she can find no one desperate enough to replace them: the rest home itself is dying around her. She consoles herself with frozen firewater as doctors, nurses, janitors complain and leave.

She hauls herself to her feet and paces the room. When did this start? When did this malaise infect her? She stops in front of the mirror on the dresser and looks at her ravaged face. In the glass she can see Iris inhaling shallow, yipping breaths as she, too, waits to die, waits for death dreaming of Charlie Kane.

'Bitch,' mutters Matron. She turns to the woman in the bed. 'This started with you and it will end with you. You started something with that photograph. It should have been here – I should have been able to show him it and then he would've stayed.' As she hears her own words Matron grimaces with the memory of Bronwen. Pushes the thought aside with a bolus of vodka. Salvation: that is all Matron seeks. And she knows this will happen if, and only if, she can lay an offering at the feet of Lieutenant Flanagan. Then he might return and save her.

She sits once more by the bed, looks with distaste at the stump of arm lying on the coverlet. 'You and me are going to talk, Iris. You're going to tell me things you never told anyone.'

IRIS

Iris closed the door behind her, shut her mother in the house with only her fear for company. Iris pushed her tiny hand into a pocket and fingered the dollar bills. These, she thought, these pieces of paper can get me what I want. She took the bills out and held them up in the sodium lights of the street, noted their dimensions and texture. I can swap these for something better, something different. She folded them carefully and put them back into her pocket.

Looking up the street she saw the fairy lights, the kerb bordered with slush, the trees drooping low with snow. Must have seen this a thousand times, but never like this, never on my own. She smiled her odd, crooked smile, strangely knowing, and stepped out on to the sidewalk. Another thought struck her and she stopped again. I can swap these dollar bills for anything I want. I can take hours choosing. I can *choose*. I can choose something bad for me and no one will stop me. Is that freedom? Is that what freedom means? Is that what the slaves wanted?

Iris began to walk once more, swishing her feet through the sludgy runnels on the sidewalk. She tried to marry her new-found notion of freedom to the lessons Mrs Gerrink had been teaching about Lincoln and the slaves, tried to imagine being a slave on a plantation, or a slave anywhere. Would a dollar bill make a difference to her then? Iris frowned, watched the grey slush stain her boots. Maybe choosing wasn't the most important thing. She sighed and looked up from her petite feet.

And what did she see?

What was it that Iris saw that cloudless night as the fairy lights dyed the snow? What was it that she saw in that town square, by the light thrown from a tall, feathery Christmas tree, as she wondered what difference the act of choosing could make to someone's life?

She saw a man so louche, so self-possessed, so sure he looked damn fine as he stood sparkling in the lights that she stopped dead and stared. He held a glass in one hand, an astrakhan coat draped over square shoulders, as his other hand rested on slim, tapering hips. The cloth of his suit hung just so, just just so, razor sharp and yet soft, cut on the bias. His hair was swept back in a jet-black swoop and his blue eyes crinkled as he guffawed, emptied the glass and let it fall on to a pillow of crusted snow, where it lay unbroken. One elegant, leather-shod foot rested on the fender of – what? The most desirable, the most luxurious, the sexiest car she had ever seen.

Iris left the safety of her mother's arms and ran straight into Luke Kane.

1997

Bronwen isn't sure about New York, hasn't made up her mind. She walks the streets of the frozen city and wonders how to feel about this walking, about this city, about the mound of crinkled dollar bills deposited in the safe at the hotel on West 32nd Street. Never has she felt so alone, never has she been so content. Ever since the jouncing, blubber-bouncing ride on the Greyhound from Miami she has been at a fever pitch of nervousness. The Voice-woman had talked and talked as the bus rolled north, away from the sun into winter, soothing Bronwen with her honeyed tones, complimenting her, even, on her own lilting accent. And yet, when they had arrived at Port Authority, the Voice-woman had melted away; even a woman as substantial, as awesome, as corporeal as the Voice-woman had disappeared into the city.

Bronwen found an oasis of calm, a fleck of the past, in a women-only hotel, the staid and musty air instantly familiar to her from her days in nurses' accommodation. She moved into a single room, paid two weeks' rent (startled by the amount of money she was required to hand over to the crone behind the reception desk for this privilege) and unpacked her small case. Then she sat on the sagging bed and counted out the bills remaining from the nest egg she had raided in

Matron's drawer: $3646. 'A tidy sum,' she announced to herself, as she slipped the money into an envelope and licked the seal.

Bronwen came from a meagre island of glaciated lakes, spare mountains and bare, flinty fields. They spoke a different language there, a language tortured by the absence of vowels, spoken by a people tortured by the absence of money. It was possible, if a person felt so inclined, to walk from one side of the island to the other in two days, seeing no one. It was an island swimming helplessly, pointlessly, in the Straits of Menai, so insignificant that the castle built for its defence had never been finished. Ynys Môn – a half-forgotten thought. Indeed, Bronwen has thought little about it in the months since she has left. Florida, New York, America itself are so alien that the Bronwen she was before she left Ynys Môn no longer exists. Certainly, the Bronwen she is now, the Bronwen who visits the delis and coffee shops around West 34th Street, who trawls through Macy's every day, who rides endless clambering escalators, who watches the skaters in Rockefeller Plaza, who wolfs down rock-hard pretzels; why, she cares nothing for the old Bronwen, does not mourn her. For the old Bronwen would never have taken the money from Matron's drawer, would have stayed and toiled at the rest home earning her keep. But *this* Bronwen, the Bronwen who one day drifted by mistake into a cinema off Times Square, who now sits every afternoon in darkened theatres with a bucket of popcorn on her lap, crunching greedily as she watches pornographic films, doesn't give a damn about Matron or the rest home. This Bronwen – strong, indomitable woman! – certainly doesn't give a damn about the fresh-faced girl who left Ynys Môn to find her fortune, her man, her place in the world. Why, she has found it all – she has the money in the safe, she keeps the photo-graph of Charlie 'Chum' Kane next to her heart and she has her seat in the XXX Cinema on West 41st – and doesn't that all amount to the same thing?

One bone-snappingly cold afternoon, as the sky broils yellow and grey with cloud and snow, Bronwen waddles into the cinema, greets the man in the ticket booth and sweeps into the warm bowels of the theatre. She settles into the seat she thinks of as her own, tears open the wrapping of one of many Baby Ruths crammed into her pockets and stares expectantly at the screen, waiting to be entertained. Moments later a penis, engorged and vascular, appears in retina-blasting close-up and a finely manicured hand slides down the ripened shaft as Bronwen swallows the last unmasticated lump of chocolate and shifts in her seat. She watches the screen intently as lubri-cated pink skin slithers back and forth, framed by coarse, curling hair. Bronwen has seen this particular film before, recalls enjoying it enormously. So why can't she concentrate? She finds her mind is wandering from the sibilant soundtrack, the heaving, sweating shanks.

Bronwen is worrying about money, her muffin-like face creased with concern. Each day she is raiding the notes in the envelope and the pile is growing smaller. What is she to do? What *can* she do? She can nurse. Bronwen watches dispas-sionately as yet another overwhelming breast sways into focus, and tries to imagine herself ever nursing again. The girl from Ynys Môn could care and nurture, nurse and pamper. But what of the woman sitting in this cinema? Can she? Bronwen is suddenly nauseated by the sound of grunting and rhythmic stroking of flesh in the seat behind her. She swings round to remonstrate, only to discover a man so deep in the swoon of his lust, so profoundly moved by what he is watching, by what he is doing, that his eyes are slammed shut as his breath rasps and squeezes between tightly clenched teeth. Bronwen thinks it rude to interrupt such an intensely personal moment but she's so irritated by the sounds that she heaves herself from the seat, showering the floor with candy wrappers, and leaves.

The sky has darkened even in the short time she has been inside and Bronwen stands in the shabby foyer uncertain what to do. The street swirls with litter, lights blur, the cars spray acid sludge on to the sidewalk.

'You didn't enjoy the movie?'

Bronwen starts, looking around suspiciously.

'You usually stay for the full programme.'

Bronwen is unsure where the voice is coming from, or if, indeed, the question is intended for her. It has been too long since she's had a conversation.

'Hey, over here.'

Bronwen turns and looks at the ticket booth, and the ticket-seller smiles at her, tipping his hat. 'How you doin'?'

'Very well, thank you.'

He slides out of his seat and emerges from the ticket booth, coming over to where Bronwen stands, rubbing his hands and blowing out warm air from his smoky lungs. 'Not much business right now. Always gets quiet around this time.'

'Yes, I expect it does.' Bronwen frowns.

'Cigarette?' The man holds out a tattered soft-pack of Winston.

'No, thank you.'

'So, you didn't enjoy the programme today? I mean, you left early, before it finished.'

'No, no, I like the film.' Bronwen frowns again. 'It's just that I've got a few things on my mind.'

'Know the feeling.' Sam the Weasel Man smiles, drawing his lips back from white, pointed teeth. He holds out his hand. 'Name's Sam.'

Bronwen looks at the limp paw stuttering in the flashing neon of the foyer. Gingerly she extends her pearly, dimpled hand and shakes the paw. 'Bronwen. Bronwen Jones.'

'Well, pleased to meet you, Bronwen. You bein' one of our best customers and all. Care for a coffee? Or maybe a shot of something? I got myself all set up in the booth here. You know, I got one of those gas burners and coffee, bourbon, whatever you need. It's real cosy in there.'

Bronwen glances back at the street. As darkness wraps its arms round the city, coaxing the night people from their lairs, fear edges its way around corners and leers. 'Yes, thank you, why not? I'd love a coffee.'

Sam's booth is indeed cosy, intimate even. Bronwen sits on a sagging, red-leather-upholstered armchair, pressed hard against the glowing heater. The combined scents of cigarettes, gas fumes, soured milk and bitter coffee transport Bronwen back to the staff room in Swansea General Hospital, where nurses hunkered against walls to ease their feet as they stole a few minutes' respite from the dead and dying. The walls of the staff room were covered in yellowing, torn posters of the urinary tract and inner ear. Bronwen looks around Sam's booth as he measures out shots of bourbon, and notices that the decoration here is not so different. She looks dispassionately at the photograph of an anonymous woman's vagina. The lens must have been so close as to chill the tender skin, so intrusive as to numb the woman's senses.

The effect, Bronwen decides, pursing her lips, is distinctly medical.

Sam passes her a coffee and a bourbon. 'Thought you might change your mind about the bourbon.' He gestures at the posters. 'They bother you?'

Bronwen shrugs. 'I'm a nurse.' She glances through the fleck-spotted glass of the booth as the man who sat behind her in the cinema passes. He's shucking on a coat, holding the handle of a briefcase in his teeth. He looks morose.

Sam settles on the swivel bar stool by the ticket machine and leans against the counter. 'So, where you from?'

'You wouldn't know it – it's an island off the north coast of Wales. Anglesey, or Ynys Môn, as it should be called.'

Sam's forehead wrinkles. 'Ynys Môn?' He shakes his head. 'That near London?'

'Nearer than here.'

Bronwen's mind takes an unexpected turn as she catches sight of herself in the glass door. She sees a fat Welsh woman with a face like a muffin sitting drinking bourbon with a pimp – for that is surely what Sam is? – in the booth of a sex cinema a block from Times Square in New York. A wave of doubt and revulsion sweeps through her and is gone: the last redoubt of the Welsh Puritan Methodist is overwhelmed and washed away.

'You got a lovely accent there, real pretty. Like another?' Sam holds up the Jim Beam and Bronwen nods. They sit in silence, already comfortable with each other, watching the hustling begin, the hard hustling on the sidewalk where everyone is fair game for the night hunters. Flyers fly, small, sealed plastic bags change hands, cabs stop for seconds as hands reach out and exchange dollar bills for one dream or

another. A man screams without drawing breath on the corner
of the block, a multicoloured hand-knitted scarf flapping at his
neck. Women appear, their faces angry with hate and makeup,
their legs wrapped in net to the crotch. Bronwen watches as
Sam smokes and hands over tickets for the show inside the
dank, warm theatre. She feels safe here, the most secure she
has been since she stepped off the bus.

'So how come you landed here? In New York?' Sam swigs
from the tannin-stained cup holding his bourbon and spills a
drop on his pristine shirt. He dabs at it fastidiously, frowning
at the spot.

'I got a job working in a rest home in Florida. A good job,
look you. Nursing, that was, looking after the old folk.'
Bronwen fills her mouth with bourbon, leaves it there, a
molten ball, until it burns her gums; then, and only then, does
she swallow. 'Actually, it was a fucking awful job.' Bronwen
has never said 'fucking' aloud before; she may have thought it
but she has never said it. She finds she enjoys it. 'It was fucking awful. Emptying piss-pots, swabbing bedsores, clipping
toenails, wiping their saggy arses.' Bronwen looks out of the
booth once more, watches the whores working their patches,
twitching tiny leather-clad butts, smoking with fury in their
mouths. 'And seeing their faces every day.' Bronwen recalls
Iris for the first time since she left the Emerald Rest Home,
recalls Iris's empty, collapsing face. Recalls the inertia of Iris's
life, the hollow at its centre; recalls what she, Bronwen, took
from her.

'So when d'you leave?' Sam watches Bronwen remembering and he calculates swiftly.

'Oh, about a fortnight ago.'

'You're not working now?' He picks furtively at a shred of

pastrami caught between two dazzling white teeth as he continues to calculate.

'No. No, I'm not.' Bronwen drinks deeply as Sam turns to the wire-meshed speak-hole and hands over two tickets.

'I guess you came up to see your boyfriend or something?'

'Well, no.' Bronwen readjusts the slack bun at the triple nape of her neck. 'He's away at the moment. He won't be back for a while.'

'How long?'

'Oh, I don't know. I mean, his plans are flexible.'

I bet they are, little darlin', thinks Sam the Weasel Man, whose musical taste runs to country-and-western.

Bronwen glances at him through the wavering heat of the pumped-up gas heater, through the wavering fields of cigarette smoke, and imagines she sees pity in his face. She turns away, fishes inside her shirt and pulls out a Polaroid photograph. 'This is him. This is Chum. Chum Kane.'

Sam takes the photograph and looks at it a while in the flickering light of the myriad neon bulbs burning in the entrance to the cinema. He looks at the car fender, at the bleached, surprised colours, at the cut of the jeans, and understands the photograph for what it is. This is not retro. This is the picture of a handsome man taken maybe two decades before. He holds it between forefinger and middle finger and offers it back to Bronwen. 'He sure is handsome. What d'you say his name was?'

'Charlie Kane. But everyone calls him Chum. Chum Kane.' Bronwen loves saying his name aloud. 'Chum Kane,' she says once more, needlessly.

Sam looks at Bronwen and nods. He rustles in the pack of bent Winstons and slowly withdraws a cigarette. What he sees before him is a woman unlike any other he has ever met, ever seen. Here is a woman who comes every day to watch the filth he shows in one of his many cinemas, who does not flinch from the beaver shots inches from her face, who watches the hookers with complete lack of interest. And yet he would be willing to bet a wad of bills that she sleeps with the door double-locked to keep dangers at bay, that she has a teddy bear on her pillow. To Sam's practised eye it seems that Bronwen has a vacuum where most people store their sense of prurience, of propriety. He also finds her strangely appealing. Not in a sexual way or anything, it's just that he likes dark-haired, large women; they remind him of Belinda. He nods once more as his calculations draw to a conclusion. 'You said earlier that you had a few things on your mind?'

'Huh?'

'You know, when you came out of the cinema you said you didn't enjoy the film because you were, you know, thinking. Had some things on your mind.'

Bronwen sighs as she remembers the emptying envelope. 'Yes, I have.'

'They to do with money? I mean, y'know, while you're waiting for your boyfriend and not working at nursing, maybe you're having a few financial embarrassments.'

'Well, I wouldn't say I was embarrassed.'

Sam the Weasel Man leans forward and drizzles some more bourbon into her cup. 'I got a proposition for you, Bronwen Jones.'

Seattle – March

M –

Things are beginning to shape up a little here. I feel real ecstatic today. Actually, I feel real, period. I'll tell you

why. I was sitting in a McDonald's yesterday and it came to
me, what 0.6180339 means. Or, rather, what it refers to.
I was sitting there on one of those immovable chairs eating
an immovable feast of an Egg McMuffin, staring at my
napkin and there they were. The Golden Arches. It was
like a handful of dice rolling across the table. They kept
rolling and all came up sixes. $x = (-1 + 5)/2 = 0.6180339$.
Or, if you prefer, point C on line segment AB if $AC/AB =
CB/AC$. In short, the Golden Section: a geometric
proportion in which a line is divided so that the ratio of
the length of the longer line segment to the length of the
entire line is equal to the ratio of the length of the shorter
line segment to the length of the longer line segment. I felt
I should state the case clearly. Forgive me. I picture you
trashing this and yelling Who Gives a Fuck?

I do. I do. It was the properties of the Golden Section
that enabled Pythagoras to discover incommensurable lines.
The geometric equivalents of irrational numbers, since you
ask. As you may have guessed, I've had a few bourbons
since I came back from McDonald's. I'm sprawling on a
bed in a shabby room on Virginia and 2nd and I'm
surrounded by sheets and sheets of calculations. It's weird,
it's like the old days. The Golden Section. The Divine
Proportion. The incommensurable line. The inexpressible
notion. The irrational drunk.

I just tried to read what I wrote last night and I can
barely make it out. I have to apologize for the scrawl but
I'm excited about the numbers. I guess it must never have
gone away, that desire to finish what so many have started.
To be able to express everything somehow. For sure it's

possible. Only now I don't think it's to do with the way anything is expressed. It's to do with trying to imagine it. Trying to be something else. Do you get what I'm saying? There're two Russian scientists in a back room somewhere in New Jersey sitting with a colossus of a computer trying to discover the exact value of pi. They came over here and instead of calling up a couple of girls or lying on a beach in the Virgins or gorging themselves on fruit and wine, they've locked themselves away in New Jersey. That's what I call dedication. I only mention this because it illustrates my point: some things which you can't see and you can't imagine are more important than anything you can express.

Yours,

C

Matron is hunkered down, resting against a wall in Iris's room. Between her knees her hands hang limp, their grip on a bottle of vodka loose and lax. Matron's appearance has suffered more than a little in the past weeks. She is still slim but it is the slenderness of the drunk, a tapering body seemingly filled with pellets of booze, a willowy bean-bag. Her skin is blotched, her cheeks crazed with rivulets of magenta arterioles which have burst under the heat of the ice-cold Absolut. Her clothes are creased, unsavoury. Her tights are laddered, her blouse flaps untidily, released from the waistband of her ash-streaked skirt. Her eyes have a film covering them, as if the vodka is leaking out, oozing from the full container of her guts. Matron looks up slowly from the dusty, food-spotted floor, looks up to the body of Iris on the bed. Iris is still alive: Matron can see the slight movement of greying sheets and blankets.

The Emerald Rest Home is otherwise empty. Beyond the confines of this room there are only empty corridors and empty beds. The surgery is soundless under a pall of dust; the laundry, the canteen, the offices, all empty. Machines clicker and hum, air-conditioning drips, mail falls on the mat but the phones remain silent. The mausoleum that is the clinic is gradually being swamped by the luxuriant, riotous swamp itself.

Matron is not quite so unbalanced as to imagine that she will be left always in peace. She knows that this time will pass, that other people will come to replace those who have left: police officers, inspectors, lawyers will all turn over the corpse of the rest home, looking for pickings, looking for blood, looking for culpability. It will not be long now. Surely it will not be long?

Matron gurgles vodka and stands up, stumbling awkwardly. Soon she will have to raid the kitchens for food. There's not much left – a couple of pizzas, a few tins of meat, a frozen turkey. She knows that this food is hardly suitable for the ruined woman on the bed, but what can she do? She is not a doctor. She administers drugs as well as she is able, but there are few of those left. She falls into the chair by the bed, assumes the position she always adopts when she is about to question Iris, lolling and vicious. Sometimes she forgets what the question is, or if she remembers the question she cannot recall why it is important.

'Iris?' Matron prods the stump of arm lying on the dirty blanket. 'Iris, wake up.'

Iris moans, trapped as she is inside a matrix of mental misinformation. That she is aware of this is to her the cruellest cut, the deepest incision. Every day this drunk wakes her and asks her questions. If Iris could answer she would. For all she wants is peace, peace in which if not to die then at least to think uninterrupted of Charlie Kane, of his slithering into the world. She tries to birth a word but only a gloop of sound emerges.

'Irish, Irish, tell me.'

Tell you what? moans the unfettered section of Iris's brain.

'Irish, where is Chum Kane?'

I don't know! screams Iris, unheard. If I did I'd tell you. God give me strength.

'Irish. Iris. Tut tut. You tell me something and I'll cook you the besht meal you have ever tasted.' Matron sits back in the chair, closes her eyes.

Suddenly Iris's head flies from the pillow, straining the sinews of her scraggy neck. 'Luke Kane!' she roars. 'Luke Kane, you fucking bastard!'

Matron's hands open in shock and the bottle drops to the floor, bounces, spurts vodka and crashes once more, spilling a lake beneath the bed. *Luke* Kane?

IRIS

Iris admired the sculpture before her of skin and bone, fur and cloth, larger than the town square, larger than Hoboken, larger than the world she has known. The dollar bills lay forgotten in her pocket, her thoughts of choice and freedom flew away as Luke Kane smiled at her. He lit a cigarette and Iris frowned as the flame washed his face and revealed such a symmetry, such perfection. He dropped the match and it sizzled in the snow, and then he turned and beckoned to Iris, smiling all the while. Iris swallowed and knew not what to do. Within her tiny, vulnerable body there was a tussle as the stories her mother had told, of wolves in the night, of the unknown, of unmentionable fates that befall those girls who are beckoned by strangers who rear their ugly heads. But surely this man, with his smile and his car, cannot be a stranger of that kind?

Iris crossed the square to its festive centre and stood next to Luke Kane, looked up at him, her face set and serious. Luke Kane crouched down, unmindful of the slush soaking the hem of his fabulous coat. 'Well, Merry Christmas, little girl.' The smell of eau de Cologne and cigarette smoke enveloped Iris and she closed her eyes and breathed deeply, rolling the scents in her lungs. 'What's your name?'

'Iris.' She opened her eyes and looked into his.

'What you doing, Iris? Are you out on your lonesome?'

'Yes. It's my birthday and I'm out to choose my present.'

'Your birthday!' Luke Kane jumped up and spun a pirouette, whooping, before crouching down once more, a long-fingered hand now resting on her shoulder. 'Well, ain't that something? But I guess it ain't so good to have a birthday so close to Christmas. Tough, really. Maybe you don't get as many presents as you would if you had a birthday in high summer, for instance.'

Iris fished in her pocket and brought out the tatty bills. She was suddenly, strangely, aware of their inadequacy.

'What's this?' he asked.

'It's to buy my present.'

Luke Kane sat back on his heels and appraised, noted the expert patching and restitching of her coat, the scuffed, dull leather of her boots, the righteous long-suffering buried deep in her eyes. 'Seems to me that a girl whose birthday it is, whose birthday is today, so near Christmas, needs another present.' Iris heard a wolf howl and chose – *chose* – to ignore it. 'Yes, seems to me that a present would not go amiss. What would you say to a drive in my car?' Luke Kane stood and slapped the car door, before opening it and waving her inside. 'You been in a car?'

Iris nodded.

'You ever been in a car like this?'

Iris thought of the coughing, sumping, rusting jalopies her father drove, that her father – grease monkey – fixed. She shook her head.

'Not many have, Iris. I have to be honest with you, there just ain't that many people that have ridden in one of these.'

He buried his nose deep in a red-leather-skinned seat and inhaled. 'It's so new, so fresh, it's still hot to the touch.'

Iris frowned. 'If it's hot how come the snow isn't melting?'

Luke Kane laughed. 'Good question. Good question, Iris. It's not actually hot, you know, it's just a phrase we use to mean it's so new it hurts. Look, I'll show you.' He reached out and took Iris's diminutive hand in his own and pulled her gently to the open door, placing her palm on the sheet metal.

Her petite fingers burned with cold and she winced, pulling her hand away fiercely. She looked up at his astonishing face and laughed. 'Gee, it's so cold!'

'So, what d'you think? Would a ride be a suitable present?'

Iris nodded shyly and smiled again as Luke Kane opened the door wide and waved her inside with a flourish. Iris slid on to the red leather, tucked her faded coat beneath her and folded her hands. She was so small that the sight of her nestled on the vast seat was surreal, disturbing almost. How old was she?

'How old are you, honey?'

Iris tried to stretch herself, tugging at the keyboard of her spine, trying to dilate the chalky hollows of her skeleton. 'I'm ten,' she said softly, aware of the inadequacy of her frame.

'Ten?' Luke Kane whistled. 'Jeez, you're practically an old woman!' He slammed the door, shrugged on the astrakhan and walked the length of the car to throw himself into the driver's seat. As the Eldorado fired and roared, two young, gangling men tumbled out of the liquor store, coats flapping around them, burbling and cawing. They spun in the snowscape, dipped and collected handfuls of snow, hurling explosive powder flumes across each other's shoulders. As they ran towards the car Luke Kane touched a button on the fascia and the red canvas soft-top inched back, gathering itself into flabby rolls on the shelf above the trunk. And as it rolled back, Iris watched the sky appear above her as the lights from the tree threw themselves in lurid shadows across her legs and arms.

'Don't mind the cold, do you, honey?' asked Luke Kane as he shifted into first.

She shook her head and tucked her hands deep into her pockets. The car rocked as the two young men thudded on to the hood, panting against the glass of the windshield as they tussled and shoved. Iris flinched and pressed her spiny stickle-back hard against the leather. Luke Kane stood up and bellowed. 'Hey, hey, watch the goddamn paint! Jesus!'

The two young men froze in mock battle and looked at him in awe, before noticing Iris's pale face, ghost-like against the seat. They shook themselves apart, slapping the snow-dusted cloth of their coats, pushing each other amiably.

'We moving on or what?' asked the taller of the two.

Luke Kane sat back on the seat with a whump and revved the engine. 'Sure we are. I'm just taking the little princess here for a drive. It's her birthday.'

Iris dared herself to look at them, tried to catch their faces through the clouds of warm, liquor-heated breath billowing from their iced, cherry-red mouths. She imagined – surely she had only imagined? – that she saw an aspect, a single aspect of fear, alien and unexpected, cross the face of the taller man. He glanced at Luke Kane and away, looked away, across the quiet square, away to look at something that was not Luke Kane's gorgeous face. He mumbled a vapour of misted air.

'What? Can't hear you!' Luke Kane bellowed, cupping his ear, rising satyr-like above the steering-wheel.

'How old is she?'

Luke Kane smiled and lit another cigarette. 'Why, she's ten years old today! This very day. So, if you'll excuse me, gentlemen?' He revved the engine hard, made it thunder in the square.

The tall man came to Iris's window and looked down at her. 'You have a good ride, y'hear. And don't forget we'll be waiting right here for you when you get back. Maybe we'll have a milkshake or something.'

The Eldorado fishtailed away from the lanky men wrapped in their concern. The car shot through the sludge, sliding, slip-sliding, careening a little. Perhaps, Iris wondered, a little out of control? Luke Kane fumbled in the glove pocket and brought out a bottle of whisky, clamped it between his thighs and twisted off the cap. 'I'd offer you a toot, but I think you're a little young yet.' Iris clenched her hands into fists the size of crab apples as the car swooped around a corner. 'So,' Luke Kane said conversationally, 'you live here?'

'Yes.' It was so cold that Iris could feel her jawbone for the first time in her life.

'Hell of a place.'

Iris watched streets flash past, watched the moon wheel. Luke Kane drank and drove as she wondered at the chill state of her bones, wondered at her inability to speak, to ask where she was going. The Eldorado crested a rise and slewed to a halt.

'There y'are, there's your birthday present.'

Iris looked for the first time at a city – and what a city! The mad necklace of Manhattan spangled on the neck of New York, the neon fractured by frost, by distance, by longing. Iris forgot her jawbone, forgot the pain in her fingers. Nothing had prepared her for this.

'It's New York City,' said Luke Kane.

'I know.' Iris inched towards the vision and her bones creaked. 'I know that.'

'You ever seen this before?'

'No. Never.'

'Best present you've had?

'Yes. Yes. Best present I ever had.'

A hand fell on the seat behind her, a hand heavy with money, burdened with privilege, sculpted by breeding; it moved to the nape of her neck. Iris welcomed the warmth, ignored the touch, too absorbed by the spangle before her.

Luke Kane was gentle that night. He did not lunge across the long, long red leather seat. He did not press Iris's fluttering, ever-cooling heart beneath his weighty hand. His fingers merely brushed her leg, his palm open and bare. He looked at Iris, flushed by distant lights, and took one of her doll-like hands in his. Luke Kane was gentle that night, but was that any excuse?

1997

Matron watches, shocked, as the lake of vodka spreads like a virus beneath Iris's bed. She starts suddenly and falls to the floor to scrabble for the bottle, rescuing the dregs. She hauls herself back into the chair and turns to Iris, whose face is etched with . . . what? Age, longing, disgust? Matron cannot tell which it is. 'Irish, Iris – who's Luke Kane? Your husband? Is that who he is? Your husband?'

Iris's head thumps back on to the pillow as the wave of fury passes. She knows now that she *can* speak, that all she has to do is to *mind* enough to speak. She slurs and mumbles but she can make herself understood. 'Yes,' Iris sibilates. 'Yes, my husband.'

'Was he Charlie's father? Was he Chum Kane's daddy?'

Iris stares at the ceiling a while, stares at it with her poor, tired eyes, tries to make sense of what this woman wants. Tries to remember why she, Iris, never wanted to talk about these things. But she cannot remember. The stump of her arm twitches on the coverlet. She cannot remember why it has been so important for all these years to say nothing, to lie, to dissemble. There is a reason – there must be. What happened? What *happened*? Something happened in a huge room with a cold floor. 'Yeth, he was Charlie's daddy.'

Matron moves in, closes in on Iris, puts her vodka-soaked face oozing its vodka-soaked breath so close to Iris's ear she could kiss it. 'Where is he, Iris?'

'Who?'

'Luke Kane. Your husband. Where is he?'

Iris cackles, a puff of age-soured breath bursting on Matron's nose. 'Luke Kane? Why he's gine. Ben gine long tame.'

Matron realizes that Iris is sliding again, sliding on the oil slick of her language. Suddenly she remembers the photograph of the fabulous confection of a gingerbread mansion on the water's edge. 'Irish, Irish, listen to me. Remember that photograph you showed me? The photograph of a house, a yellow and blue house, real fancy, with turrets and all? Remember that?' Matron realizes with a gush of nausea that she is clutching the pink, puckered nub of Iris's arm. She swoons and recovers. 'Remember that? Iris? Remember the house?'

'Yeth.' Iris remembers so many odd things, inconsequential things. It is the important events in her life that have fallen off the truck of her memory.

'Where is it, Iris?' Matron is exhausted by this, by excess, by worry. She relinquishes the stump and lays her drunken head on Iris's warm, rumbling stomach. 'Where's the house, Iris? Where? Is? The? Fucking? House?'

'Why,' says Iris, 'it's in East Hampton, Long Island.'

Which is the last meaningful sentence that Iris ever utters.

Portland, Oregon – March

M –

Couple of months ago, just before I left New York City

for Malibu, I sat in the Park and I made a promise to
myself. Actually, I made a few promises to myself. I
promised myself I'd stop doing what I've been doing. I
promised I'd stop doing the coke. I vowed I'd never take
another toot of bourbon.

There was one other thing. I sat in the Park and looked
at the Pan Am building, at all the cute moms with their
roller-blades and buggies and Walkmans scooting around me
at the South Side, at the sky punctured all around and I felt,
I don't know, sad? poignant? wistful? I really don't know.
All I do know is that as I sat there I thought of you for the
first time since I left you in Plymouth that night. Well, not
that I thought of you for the *first* time, but for the first
time I reckoned I had to contact you again, which is why I
write these letters.

And now I think of you every day. Lying here I
remember the first time we screwed. Fucked? Made love?
What the hell am I supposed to call it? Do you remember?
It was in that hotel in Provincetown. I'd thought of doing
it for so long, thought of being with you since the
moment I first saw you, if you want to know the truth.
And there I was lying on that bed, feeling like my scalp
was slipping down my back, like my hands were shovels,
never worthy, never worthy. You lay next to me, your jeans
on the floor, your breath in my ear. The winter light made
you look even more beautiful than I'd ever seen you,
shadowed by my body. You put your hand over my mouth,
stopped me. Stopped me dead. Your eyes even in the light
were dark. D'you remember what you said to me? I was
lying there with my balls bursting, a prick like a flagpole.
And you said to me, 'Can I trust you?' and I didn't answer

and you said, 'Can I trust you?' Then you put your mouth
inside my head and asked, 'Can I trust you?' And I said,
'Yes.' And you believed me. I'm writing this to tell you that
when I said, 'Yes,' I didn't mean it. I was lying. By which I
mean that what I felt right then, at that moment, lying on
that bed with your skin so close, I would have said
anything. Anything. But if you'd asked me later, if you'd
asked, 'Can I trust you?' I would have said, 'Yes,' and meant
it. But that would hardly have covered it. For by then what
I felt was inexpressible. I couldn't find the words to tell you
what I felt. I have never found those words. I left you never
having expressed anything at all. I'm so sorry.

    Yours,

    C

Lieutenant Flanagan is wedged once again, but this time his
bulk is squeezed behind a table in a coffee bar in Opa Locka
airport, Miami. Above him hangs a board flipping city names
back and forth, turning again and again like rows of domi-
noes. Flanagan sits with a hand wrapped around a cup of
coffee, dwarfing it, as the cities flutter above him, reminding
him of a flock of blackbirds. He sees that the flight from
Minneapolis has landed, bringing with it the parents of Addis
Barbar. As he predicted, the murderous meeting between the
two psychopaths ending in death has produced a flurry of
lawsuits, counter-suits and feigned outrage. It seems
Barbar's parents want blood, almost as much as – if not more
than – their son desired it. They want Ray MacDonald to fry,
to burn, to fizzle with electricity. But not, however, before they
have extracted as much money as possible from the state to
compensate for the untimely end of their beloved son.

Flanagan sighs, fingers the soft tip of his nose. He is
expected, as the representative of the Florida Department of
Law Enforcement who arrested their son, to greet them,
express his sorrow for the death of the murderous cocksucking
child abuser they contrived to raise, and then to escort them
across town to the offices of the FDLE. He will then liaise with
the authorities at Harrison Penitentiary and escort *les parents*
Barbar through various labyrinthine legal corridors, where
they will file their suit against Ray MacDonald, the FDLE,
Harrison Penitentiary, Bill Clinton, the federal government
and God-all knows who else. Lieutenant Flanagan is not
happy with this state of affairs. His pager bleeps and he
reaches for his taut belt, to find that he is being asked to contact Mrs Thackeray. Mrs Thackeray? 'Who the hell is Mrs
Thackeray?' he mutters. He sits with his cooling coffee and
wishes things were different, wishes that he lived in the world
his grandmother once described to him when he was a boy. A
world of hurling and Guinness, of shawls and peat squares, of
mean cottages on bog land. He resolves, not for the first time,
one day to visit Ireland.

To shake loose the images of a different Lieutenant
Flanagan, he picks up a paper left by a traveller, the *LA Times*
of two days before. This is what he reads:

DEATH OF JUSTICE ITSELF?

Justice is not a commodity to be traded on the stock market, it is not an object to be moved around between mobile goalposts, it is not a tangible asset. Yet it is still an asset to be coveted by all those who value democracy, by all those who have respect for the estates of State, Church and justice.

Justice comes in many guises, indeed may not even be immediately recognizable. The system creaks beneath the burden that is put on it and sometimes – not often – there are miscarriages. We can all think of occasions when the verdict has not been that which was expected by many (ex-professional footballers notwithstanding).

The means by which justice is handed out has always been problematic. Is capital punishment the answer? Is the electric chair, the lethal injection, the firing squad the answer? Should the state take a life in retaliation for another having been taken? These are matters for constant debate and reassessment.

But surely there are few people who believe that justice should be meted out by those who have themselves been found guilty of crimes against the innocent? Sounds a reasonable enough statement.

Yet the events that are taking place in Florida seem to point to the fact that many sane people are beginning to think that we should lock up all serious offenders in penitentiaries and leave them to sort out the problem of who lives and who dies. Leave them to run their own kangaroo courts.

THE FACTS:

In Harrison Penitentiary in February a 29-year-old convict, Addis Barbar, was two months into five life sentences, for the murder of Maria Sanchez, 24, and her daughter Christina, 6. Barbar raped Maria before slashing her throat. He then sexually abused Christina in a squalid coke-house for three days, before killing and mutilating her. Rather, it is hoped that the mutilation took place after death.

Also incarcerated in Harrison Pen was Ray MacDonald, 45, multiple rapist and murderer, who killed his own daughter. His other crimes are too numerous to list here.

One February night Mac-Donald heard a radio program during which the crimes committed by Barbar were listed and described in unnecessary detail. A man phoned in and offered a reward of $1000 for the murder of Barbar. Ray MacDonald obliged.

The $1000 is immaterial here. What should concern us is the thousands of people who have called the radio station, written to the papers, contacted the Penitentiary, marched in the streets, celebrating the death of Barbar, praising, almost, the part in it played by Ray MacDonald.

The days of the Wild West are long gone, yet we're back in bounty country. Where does it stop? Where do the acceptable limits of vigilante action end? Can we – as the world's greatest democracy – condone, even venerate, the actions of a convicted paedophile, rapist and murderer?

It seems the answer is yes.

Lieutenant Flanagan frowns. What should he do? Follow the endless paper trail that will lead the Barbars to court? Or act upon his utilitarian instincts, his investigative instincts? Which? He lowers the paper, knocks over his coffee cup. Scrabbling to avoid the spill, he wipes the table with the paper, sees a poor drawing of a face he wants to meet – there, above an article, is a police artist's impression of the face of Mr Candid.

SPEAKING CANDIDLY

So, you guys were kidding, yeah? You must have been, right? All those years, all those column inches, all those nights spent sweating over copy deadlines, and for what? Some weird notion about a twentieth-century Colonel Custer, Judge Dredd, Luke Skywalker, running around America righting wrongs. A guy who balances the scales, completes the circle, makes the difference. I speak, of course, about Mr Candid, The Scourge of the Criminal Classes (for which read Underclasses).

Be serious. This is wish fulfilment on a national scale. If people keep wishing so long and so hard it could become a global craving.

What do we have here?

We have some half-assed idea about a guy who saves Americans from themselves. If a drug cartel gets busted, it's Mr Candid who pointed the finger. If the New York Dons get blown away, it's Mr Candid who's holding the smoking gun. If the price of drugs rams through the roof, it's Mr Candid who's bought them up and trashed them. If drug barons are dumped handcuffed to their cars outside police HQ, if paedophiles are killed in their homes, if rapists are castrated in their own kitchens, it's Mr Candid behind these cathartic deeds.

There are some people who even believe that they have seen him – a grey blur, an enigma, the ghost in our collective machine. According to these concerned but deluded citizens, he's been hanging around in New York, Malibu, Montana, Seattle and even sad old Portland, Oregon.

I mean, get real. How can you identify a wishful thought?

Can't you just imagine him? An eagle-eyed, swash-buckling Errol Flynn, a Custer for the nineties. If Mr Candid had his way, Jackie O would still be with us, Marilyn would be seventy and hanging out with Roseanne. AIDS would be as virulent as the common cold, Jeffrey Dahmer would never have been allowed to die, Thomas Jefferson III would never have been allowed to live . . .

And as for the rest of us, we'd be swinging through the gates of our white picket fences, carrying apple pies for the little old lady down the street.

Wake up, America! These things are never going to happen. *There is no Mr Candid.* He is *not* going to slip through your screen door, or come down your chimney, and make everything all right.

I'm posting this as a reminder to Baby Boomers everywhere: Mr Candid will not save you. Keep buying the Mace, keep building the walls, keep taking the pills. And whatever you do, stay behind the barricades, because you're just dreaming, you're waiting for Clark Kent dressed *à la* Calvin Klein. He's not going to come because he doesn't exist.

The lieutenant looks once again at the faint charcoal drawing. *Could* it be Charlie 'Chum' Kane, smudged by newsprint
and coffee? If he'd seen Iris's photograph, he'd know. If the
matron had come up with the goods, he'd know the answer.

Across the years that have passed since he sat in a class-
room learning by rote, comes a verse, a half-verse, half
forgotten until now. Something about there being time, time
enough to prepare yourself for killing and creation. Time, too,
for a question to be dropped on your plate, demanding an
answer. The half-forgotten words bring him to a decision. He
rolls the sodden paper into a ball and deposits it in a bin. Then
the lieutenant turns and walks away from the coffee bar, away
from the arrivals gate, away from Miami airport. Away,
indeed, from the Barbars, who at that moment are collecting
their baggage, hearts singing with the thought of future
bounty.

Portland – March

M –

I guess I should have trusted my instincts, I should
always trust my instincts. Remember I said way back when
I wrote from Malibu that I thought they – someone –
were on to me, looking for me? Nothing to prove it, just a
feeling like an ulcer erupting, the turn of a hair, twitch of
a hackle. Well, I tell you, I have gotten too lazy. I opened
the goddamn paper couple of days ago and there it was.
The question and the answer. The sketch. It's a good one.
Justice and Mr Candid. And these articles have been
syndicated God knows where. Shit.

So I got rid of the car, bought some new clothes and
changed myself yet again. The chameleon emerges or

disappears, depending which way you look at it. All you have to do is change your walk, the way you stand, eat, breathe, sit at rest, change everything. Let your face go, fall slack, and then set it in a different mask. Hair is easy, even height. But it's more than that. Now everything about me says loser, lost loser.

I'm sorry. I never meant to bring all this into these letters. I never thought Mr Candid would come into this but it seems like he has. You asked me once if you could trust me. What I didn't say was that I always knew I could trust you, which is why I write to you.

When I read what that guy wrote in the paper about Mr Candid not being real I got madder than a wet moose. I know it's crazy – after all, I spent years creating clouds to hide behind, making sure that doubt overrode everything else, yet when I read that Mr Candid's existence is actually being denied . . . Well, that's no good. I know he exists because I made him. He *does* exist. I'm Mr Candid, as I'm sure you realized long ago. Maybe even before I did – given your perspicacity, that might just be the case.

I told you about all those promises I made to myself in New York. No more coke, no more bourbon, no more Mr Candid, and letters to be sent to you. One out of four is not good. But there's one more job to do. Just one more, and then I can put Mr Candid away with the other childish things.

Looks like I'll have to go to back to LA in person to arrange some meeting and then I'm heading east. Maybe I'll be heading towards you. I don't know. Maybe you live in Portland and you're sitting around the corner waiting for this. Maybe you're married and your kids are giving

you a hard time. Maybe you're your own idea of
perfection. Maybe you're not. Maybe you're lonely too. I
miss you.

 Yours,

 C

Lieutenant Flanagan sweats as he packs a suitcase, crumpling
shirts, bunching socks, bending shoes. A single case will be
enough to carry all the worldly goods he needs for this quest.
That, an address book, a fat wallet and an incalculable amount
of patience. It is as the neon flickers above a spotted mirror in
his bathroom, as he sees his pouched, tired face sputter in
front of him, that he remembers who Mrs Thackeray is. He
trots to the phone, throws himself on the protesting bed and
makes a call to the station. 'Harris? That you?'

 'Yeah, this is Lieutenant Harris.'

 'It's Flanagan.'

 'Where the fuck are you?'

 'The chief hasn't told you?'

 'No – told me what?'

 'I'm owed a couple of weeks' vacation and I'm taking them
now.'

 'What, you got a burning desire to sun yourself or something? I mean, this isn't a bit sudden?'

 'Yeah, I guess it is. I got some business I really need to
attend to before I can . . . before I can, y'know, whatever.'

 Harris grunts and Lieutenant Flanagan imagines him
throwing his feet up on to the desk the two of them share and
slowly, systematically beginning to pick his nose. 'What is it?
Pussy problems?'

 Flanagan flinches. 'No, nothing like that.'

'OK, OK. So how can I help ya?'

'I got a message that Mrs Thackeray called, and I need her number. I haven't been back to the station and I guess it must be on my desk.'

Harris grunts once more. 'Like I said, pussy problems.'

'Just get the goddamn number.' Lieutenant Flanagan hears Harris's feet thump to the floor and the rustling of paper.

'Got it. Six one eight zero three three nine.'

'Thanks, Harris.'

'Hey, Flanagan, she give good head?'

Sighing, the lieutenant replaces the phone and redials.

The situation at the Emerald Rest Home has not improved. The grounds have been daily sinking into swamp as the drains clog and pumps fail. Cultivated flowers rot on their stems; mould and decay encroach, sliding up the walls of the home as grasses proliferate. In quiet pools and stagnant puddles deposits of mosquito eggs hang suspended, a film of slime waiting, with the patience born of centuries of waiting, to hatch and fly. Only the palm trees have survived, thriving, now, on a cocktail of mangrove sludge and chemicals, growing in spirals, their leaves tinted magenta.

Matron has retreated permanently into Iris's room, hunkered down on her haunches, tugging at her nails with yellowing teeth as she waits for Iris to die, waits for Lieutenant Flanagan to call. Waits, too, for the police to arrive, because even Matron's vodka-damaged brain, loose with hunger, rolling in her skull, knows that this will come to an end. That is certain. She raises bleary eyes and looks around the room like a wounded sheep. There is no more food: the carcass of the turkey has been stripped and the bones gnawed. There is no more vodka, only a trail of emptied bottles, and she has no more cigarettes. Matron dare not leave the Home for fear that Lieutenant Flanagan will call, so she waits in this room with the dying woman because she is scared, now, to be alone. The two of them subsist on instant coffee and industrial-size bags of Oreos, bloated like pillows full of coal.

The telephone that she has brought into the room suddenly shrills, causing Iris to groan and mumble. Matron's walnut-brain swims a little; she is unsure what to do. The telephone rings once more and she picks it up.

'Hello?' she croaks.

'Ms Thackeray? Could I speak with Ms Twyla Thackeray, please?'

'Hello?' she croaks once more, unable to think of what else to say.

'Is that you, Ms Thackeray? It's Lieutenant Flanagan. Don't know if you remember – we met a while ago, at the Police Benefit Ball in Naples. Then I came to the rest home one after-noon. Do you remember? It seems you left a message for me. Is that right?'

Matron nods, clears her throat. 'Yes, that's right.' Her voice sounds like broken glass, splintered wood, shattered dreams. It has been so long since she has spoken that her larynx seems set in amber. She coughs uncontrollably as the phlegm of a thousand cigarettes rises in her gorge.

'Ms Thackeray? You OK? That's quite a cough you have there.'

Matron draws in a foul breath and speaks at last. 'Thank you for returning my call, Lieutenant.' If the voice is indeed a conduit to the soul then Lieutenant Flanagan may have a sense of Matron's life turning ever slower, its intricacies unravelling. She is fading to grey, leaking away. 'Lieutenant, I called to tell you that I found out where Iris lived. No doubt Chum Kane lived there also.' On the 'also' her voice cracks and she coughs once more.

The lieutenant waits, barely breathing: Iris *has* dropped the rusty key. As the sound of coughing echoes in the room of the dying woman, echoes down the phone line, the lieutenant waits.

Matron draws a saw-tooth rasp of breath. 'I wanted so much to tell you. You know? I wanted it so much to be me who told you, and now I can't remember why it matters so much. I think I wanted . . . I think I wanted you.'

Lieutenant Flanagan frowns. 'I beg your pardon?'

'Nothing. It's nothing. East Hampton, that's where the Kane house is. It's in East Hampton, Long Island.'

'Thank you, thank you. Ah, Jesus, thank you.' The lieutenant smiles and slaps the suitcase on the bed. 'Matron, can I trust you?'

Matron laughs, the sound of chalk sliding on slate. 'Why not? What am I going to do? Why not?'

'Matron . . .'

'Excuse me – director of healthcare if you don't mind.' It is the last shot.

'I must apologize, Ms Thackeray. I plain forgot. I was wondering if I could rely on you to keep this conversation between the two of us. For various reasons it would be best if you told no one about it.'

Matron looks at the wasteland of a bump on the bed that is Iris Chandler, her brain scrambled like half a dozen eggs lashed with milk over a slow flame. She smiles, splitting her lips. 'I shan't be telling anyone, Lieutenant. You can trust me.'

'Well, Ms Thackeray, I cannot tell you how much I appreciate that.'

'You're welcome.'

The lieutenant shifts on the bed and rolls gently from side
to side. 'Perhaps, if I may, I'll call you when I'm next down
your way?'

'You can try.'

'Well, I'll do that. Look after yourself, Ms Thackeray. I'd
get that cough looked at – doesn't sound good.'

Matron replaces the receiver gently and stares at the closet
in the corner. She stretches her legs, crossed at the ankle,
unwinds a little for the first time in what seems like weeks.
Through the window she can see the spiralling palms, stark in
the midday sun. She watches them for hours, pondering the
problem of food. She wishes, now, for this to end, wishes the
police would come. That *someone* would come.

Night falls sudden as a slap and she focuses her pained
eyes on the closet. Realizes that she has been in this room for
days and has barely looked at it, has certainly never looked
in it. She is filled with urgency, knows that her time is
running down, so she drags herself, emotional paraplegic,
across the dusty floor, accruing runnels of grey fluff in the
creases of her skirt. Opening the closet she is met by
the waft of . . . what? The smell of an ageing woman's life,
the smell that is the essence of years doing what? A few
clothes and shoes, sad scraps of bird-wing paper cut from
magazines, snake-knots of tights the colour of cappuccino,
cracked plastic compacts, the mirrors spotted, the foundation
powder gathered in tiny spheres rolling on tin bases. The
geological samples of a life. Not much really, thinks Matron,
to show for a life, even as damaged a life as the one Iris

appears to have led. Matron slumps against the wall and waits as shades of silver nitrate and Kodachrome play on the stroke-shattered walls of Iris' mind. The ghosts are moving.

IRIS

Iris Chandler stood outside the rackety fence enclosing the faded yard around her parents' house and tried to smile as her father hugged her close, his paper-thin skin no cushion for his box-boned hips. A camera clicked and a little of Iris's soul was snagged for ever at that moment. Her smile was faint in the photograph, no more than a suggestion, a whisper, but her lips were full and near-curling. When she saw the photograph she smiled once more, for only she knew what had caused her lips to curl: Luke Kane. She carried his scent everywhere with her, carried the touch of talc-fine, firm skin with her. Carried the memories to school, to the corner store, to pyjama parties; carried them to her bedroom.

Iris Chandler had spent her first decade waiting for poverty to end, for the boredom to melt away, waiting for change. Then change came at the exact end of that first decade and changed Iris. She had leaned against Luke Kane in a car, looking at the distant theatre of neon-dripping Manhattan, and everything had changed.

Still Iris did not grow tall; she barely grew at all, remaining a perfect miniature. Her skin was fair, her hair the rich cinnamon of a wolf's amber-angry eye. There were those at high school who taunted her, calling her pygmy, dwarf, runt.

But they did not call her these things often, for each was silenced by her composure, by the turning of her blue eyes, hard as glass, upon them. The boys became shy of her, desiring to touch her but afraid to lay their hands on a frame so fragile. Instead they became buffoons, jesting for her, fooling and clowning, becoming ridiculous. Pratfalls and slapstick cut a swathe behind her as she moved inexorably towards graduation.

The girls, with their wasp waists and bobby socks, thick ankles and padded breasts, whispered among themselves, mocking Iris because they feared her. They did not know it but what they feared was her independence. Because Iris did not need the clothes, the gum, the cigarettes, the stolen bourbon. She did not need the code of violation to which her high-school classmates adhered religiously, did not need to wonder if now was the time to allow a Cologne-soaked youth to squeeze her nipples in the back seat of his daddy's car. Iris needed none of these things, and because of that lack of want she was soon wanted herself.

Mrs Chandler marvelled at her daughter's serenity, her beauty without fault. As Mrs Chandler aged with the passing of years in the back room of the house, the treadle of her sewing machine running ever slower, her hands failing as joints inflamed, she marvelled. Often, as she tacked yet another curtain, christening robe, sundress, she wondered where Iris had found her composure. Where could she possibly have found it in that drab house with its cracked linoleum, frayed carpets, windows iced in winter? Where had she found her contentment? For surely it was not there in that house where two parents had let their lives slip away, hamstrung by honesty?

Mrs Chandler was right: Iris *had* found her self elsewhere. For years, through the years of adolescence, she kept locked in the velvet purse of her mind a secret – or, rather, an omission of telling. She never told her mother about the night of her tenth birthday; she told no one. She had come back that pin-prick-lit night in 1950, as America turned over, sighed and began to love itself, and locked away the time she had spent with Luke Kane. The reason that she was able to do this was because she knew with certainty that she would see him again. She had held his hand like a talisman in her own diminutive one and known, even then (perhaps especially then), that she would see him again.

The days and seasons passed, the summers in a haze of sweat and yellow-jackets, the winters wrapped in grey-streaked snow. Hoboken spread amoeba-like away from Manhattan as Iris waited; cars grew fins and sharp, slanting angles to the disgust of her father, music became sweet and ever-present, clothes pinched and tucked, confusing her mother. America tried to sweep through South East Asia like bleach through drains, fired by its new-found self-adoration. Thousands of days, each much the same as the others, as Iris sowed the seeds of her life, listening to her father mutter as the radio spat the never-ending list of the changing facts of life around them.

Iris graduated from high school and moved into the back room with her mother to learn the arts of threading cotton back on itself. This was an almost monastic time, a breakfast eaten with her increasingly silent mother, a brush of lips from her father, before she stepped into the lint-dusted room. The treadle marked the hours before and after lunch, as needles darted through the woof and weft, sharp and silver. Iris's tiny hands were deft and young and gradually her mother relinquished the fine work to her daughter, who was paid a pittance for the hours she spent with one knee crossed over the other, bent over cloth in a halo of unnatural light. Iris cared not one whit that she had nothing but her thoughts and a few dollars, for she knew that this time would end.

One day, when she was eighteen, sitting on the front porch, her dress soaked in sweat, her hair wild-slapped in strands across her glistening forehead, Iris fanned herself with a newspaper as Hoboken baked and cracked in fearsome summer heat. Her mother had thrown down a pair of drab woollen pants and retired to her bed to escape the cauldron of the sewing room, releasing Iris for the afternoon. And as the wires hummed and telegraph poles gasped, Iris heard it. She put the newspaper on the dusty wooden planks of the porch floor and dragged back her hair, peeling it from her neck. She could hear it clear as a rabbit scream. It was a way off yet, streets distant, and she closed her eyes to imagine that distance being shrunk to nothing. When she opened her eyes the car slid, roaring, around the corner.

And there he was, Luke Kane, at the wheel of the open-top Cadillac Eldorado. He pulled up to the kerb, cracking grit, and smiled, stretching his arm over the back of the seat. Iris and Luke Kane looked at each other for minutes, watched each other through the haze of Tarmac-heated air and petrol-perfumed fumes.

'Been looking for you,' he said.

'I've been right here,' said Iris.

'Hell of a place.'

'Hell of a place,' she agreed.

Luke Kane leaned over and pushed open the passenger door, which swung with its own satisfying weight. 'Ready to leave?'

Iris looked down the worn porch steps into his beautiful face, finer even than she had remembered, looked back at the blank windows of the only home she had known, imagined her mother lying, panting slightly, on her hump-backed bed. Iris remembered the small pile of wrinkled, greasy dollars folded into a tin under her bed. Twenty-seven dollars in all. That was choice?

'Sure I'm ready.' She stood and brushed down her cotton sundress and walked to the car. She sat sedately, her knees pressed into each other, her hands trembling on her thighs, as the car rolled away, taking her with it. Hoboken flew past as she tried to recall the last words she had spoken to her mother. She feared that they were 'I'll go get the scallions later.'

1997

M –

Sorry I haven't gotten around to writing you for a few
days. I spent a while driving down from Portland, and all I
could think, as the tyres thrummed, was how much I
would have liked you to be there. I don't know. I say that
but I guess I don't know what you'd be like now. But I
reckon maybe I do. Maybe there can be universal truths?
Absolutes? If there are then I reckon you must be one of
them. When I'm driving, I imagine what it would be like
if you were sitting there with me. I do that pitiful thing –
you know? – of having whole conversations with someone
who is not there. I mean, not speaking out loud or
anything, just in my head. But *you* know what the inside
of my head's like. It must contain every pointless idea
alongside every important notion. One minute I'm
sitting there trying to find some concrete correspondence
in reality for any hypothetical construct you care to
mention, and the next I'm trying to picture you across a
restaurant table. So I guess I could say that you're a
hypothetical construct.

But in some ways that's what it comes down to now:

restaurant tables. I guess I'm getting to the age when
sitting in a restaurant anticipating – what? Maybe some
clams, or breast of Barbary duck, or blackened bluefish, the
tablecloth so white and sharp, the sea close enough to
jump-start a life – all that seems like a fine notion. I've
spent seventeen years, God, nearly eighteen, eating pizzas
in cars, noodles from cartons, Big Macs in motel rooms.
I'm getting tired of it. Sure, I could always afford to eat in
Morton's, in Quatre Saisons, wherever, but I never had
time. Or, rather, if I had the time I never had the
inclination. Always so many other things to be done. Like
I said, this hankering after restaurants and clean sheets, a
home of my own, time to eat what I want, time to maybe
be with people – that feeling just keeps growing.

I have business here, in Venice Beach. The call I was
waiting for finally came through and they've got the name
and number – Mr Candid will have his logistical
ammunition. I don't know how much to tell you, but I
guess I've already told you so much that caution seems
inappropriate. I don't know if you'll understand any of it
but I want to tell you, then maybe you'll understand a little
of what I've been doing since the last time I saw you. And
more importantly, why. For instance, today I'm meeting
with some kid from the 21st Street Gang. You know
them? Well, who doesn't? Last time I was here, a few years
ago, I met him outside a bar. He must have been about
twelve years old. Skinny as a coat hanger and so hip he was
practically falling over. And so unhappy he was practically
falling down. To cut it short, we made some kind of deal
over some smokes and he's inside and trusted and he's now
my man when I want to find out what's going on

someplace, usually the streets out here in the west. I mean, he's just a runner – too out of it most of the time to be making any sense – but he's a good runner. He carries information and, no doubt, a number of viruses. But he has access to a whole load of stuff, including information about people inside. And not only that but DAs, screwed courts, corrupt lawyers, internal affairs, that kind of thing. AT&T has nothing on these kids – they can get you anything, sell you anything, find you anything, tell you anything you need to know, put you in contact with anyone. They could probably even find you. And they can make me very scared. A lot of people think the gangs out here – and everywhere else, come to that – are just a bunch of murderous, drugged-out kids, which in some ways they are. What they don't realize is that these gangs are locked into so much criminal activity that they're the first line of defence. These kids are out on the street carrying information, drugs, blowing people away. But it isn't their choice. I mean, they don't make the decisions. Other people do. But if the kids get caught they go down – they're expendable. The runners are the lowest form of life in this set-up – they don't know anything.

This kid, the one I'm meeting, the runner, is sixteen years old now and he makes me want to cry. He's got the tattoos, the bandanna, the walk, the arm shadows, and fuck all else. I'd like to give him something tomorrow because I'm not going to see him again. What *can* I give him? Love? Hope? He wouldn't know what to do with them. So I called a college and found out what the fees are and I'm giving him three years' worth. A chance to run. I have to give it in untraceable, used bills and he'll watch me walk out the door and look at a pile of thousands of dollars. And then do what? I don't know. I wish I could ask you.

Apologies for the length of this. I haven't had a drink in four days — I always stay straight when something's coming up. Problem is, I tend to ramble.

Yours,

C

The Upper East Side is, Lieutenant Flanagan decides, a little too discreet for his tastes, a little too decorative, a little too *rich* for his tastes. Understated should mean precisely that. As he passes yet another doorman flicking at invisible fluff on gold-tasselled shoulders, Flanagan hunches his own shoulders, feeling like an interloper here among this wealth. He is cold, his feet near numb, sloping through the ageing snow of another too-long New York winter. He reaches a brownstone decorated with ornate stonework, its doorway protected by a long candy-stripe canopy, and fumbles in his pocket to loose his bear-paw of a hand from its glove. He pushes the icy brass button on the wall and waits for an answer, watching the taxis hiss past, scattering steam billowing from grates.

'How can I help you?' a voice rasps from the metal box.

But Flanagan has forgotten himself for a moment. He is watching a woman on the sidewalk, treading cat-gentle in the snow, a deep-blood fur hugged about her. The woman is framed by yet another canopy, this one mint-julep and magnolia; framed by the promise of summer at the edge of a winter. A newspaper slithers from the grip of her elbow and carefully she comes to a halt, her tapping heels ginger on the icy sidewalk. Flanagan watches her as she stands and agitates.

The paper is sodden, made heavier by the unravelling of crystal flakes. But she cannot leave it, cannot litter so substantially. She flusters around the wet grey pile and eventually bends – gracefully, her knees boxy, shyly turned aside – to try to scoop the paper with ungloved hands. But its weight is now so great that it tears in two, like mush, like cattle feed, like grey, opinionated gypsum, leaving half of itself embedded in slush, opinions melting, the other half dripping weightily in her hand. Flanagan senses her embarrassment, her difficulty, and wants to help her.

'Can I help you?' The unbodied voice floats from the wall again, grating in the air.

Lieutenant Flanagan starts and reassembles his concentration. He turns to the wall, feeling foolish, and mutters, 'Bill Casey is a wuss.'

'What? Can you repeat that?' the wall replies.

Flanagan coughs, clears his throat, and barks, 'Bill Casey is a wuss.'

The heavy, ornate doors glide open, swinging back to reveal a long, burgundy hallway, the walls covered in heavily gilded frames, swags of velvet and chintz swooping low. The carpet is so thick and soft Flanagan sinks a little as he steps on to it. He begins to slough off his coat and a pale, manicured hand reaches for it. 'May I take your coat, sir?' asks the butler, taut and stiff in formal tails.

'Sure.' The lieutenant wrestles with the arms of the coat, which have rucked round his gloves. He feels young and childlike, wants to run but stays. The butler slips behind him and eases off the crumpled gabardine. 'Thanks.'

'You are here as a guest, I assume, sir.'

'Yes, yes, I am.' Flanagan tries to smooth his hair, adjust his cuffs, again aware that he is, among this finery, this luxuriance, a mere intruder.

'May I ask who you are meeting, sir?'

'Sure. I'm, um, I'm meeting Edison Keeler.'

'Ah, Mr Keeler. Yes, he is already here. Just step through the doors at the far end.'

'Thank you.' Flanagan moves away from the butler with a surge of relief, feeling like a child who has deceived an adult, a child who has contrived a deception and survived. He walks the length of the hall, awed yet irritated by its opulence, and pushes open the double doors, having no idea what may lie behind them. A storm of sound breaks over him as a cumulus cloud of cigarette smoke belches through the doorway. He steps back, blinking. Sleek, brass-blasted calypso pushes him back yet another step, until he feels a hand in the small of his back, propelling him beyond the doors. 'Just step through, sir, I think you'll find Mr Keeler at a table on the left,' the butler hisses in his ear.

The lieutenant feels the doors close hard against his shoul-der-blades and breath rushes deep and hot through his nose. He has seen many things he wishes he had not: the aftermath of highway accidents, dogs left to die and rot in baking trail-ers, a child with both hands crudely removed by a pair of shears, a cop snapped back puppet-like as a bullet slammed into and burst through her skull. But these were events that happened, events that balanced the fulcrum of what we can expect from others. But now, standing in this room, the lieu-tenant is shocked. The calypso rages around him, hammering at the delicate membrane of his eardrums; lights swivel and fade, burn and linger, turn crazily overhead as a porcupine ball of bulbs rolls and flickers along a mirrored pole. On a matte-black, featureless stage a naked woman stands in a beam of laser-sharp light, rolling her greased breasts in her hands, pinching the nipples, grinding her hips. This slow grinding bunches her buttocks, makes the sculpted muscles of her legs slide. All around the huge room there are tables set with crystal and silver, dainty flowers arching from vases that glitter in candlelight. At each table sit men in tailored suits, their faces content and ungiving, their movements made lazy by power. Flanagan recognizes faces as he scans the room, the scions of banking dynasties, political arrivistes, dealers, traders, merchant men, gubernatorial aspirants and incumbent senators, foreign despots and fading heroes. He had thought it was the music, the heat, the breasts rolled invitingly before him that made his breath falter, made his chest shrink. But now he knows that it is the weight of power which is squeezing him.

He looks back to the stage, looks back to the woman as being something he can understand. Her face is razor sharp, birthed by a whetstone, devoid of emotion as her hips roll. She reaches forward and picks up a blood-red dildo the size of a baseball bat.

'Sweet Jesus,' whispers Flanagan.

A hand thuds on to his shoulder. 'Hey, Flanagan! How you doing?'

'Huh?' Flanagan drags his eyes away from the stage, sees Edison Keeler beaming at him.

'I been watching you watching her. Reckon I had to come and getcha, otherwise you'd be standing there with your dick hanging out all night.'

'Keeler, hey. How's tricks?' Flanagan holds out his hand, crushes Keeler's delicate, office-shaped fingers. He smiles, slaps Keeler's shoulder, aware all the while that behind him there is a naked woman with a dangerous weapon. He wants to turn and look but does not because he knows his reasons would be misunderstood. He wants to check because he is worried for her. He glances at the men facing the stage but their faces register nothing, neither ecstasy nor disgust. They are unmoved.

'C'mon.' Keeler steers the lieutenant through the maze of men. 'I got us a place over here.' He leads Flanagan to a table and the lieutenant selects the chair turned away from the stage. He tries not to imagine what is happening to the woman, what she is doing. Keeler pours him a whiskey from a bottle on the table and drops in ice from a silver bucket. He holds the bottle out to Flanagan – eighteen-year-old single malt Bushmills. 'See? I remembered.'

Flanagan smiles. 'Jeez, it's been some time since I drank anything so sweet. Seems like these days all I can afford is garbage.' He raises the glass. 'Cheers.' He sips a cold marble of malt, rolls it on his tongue and swallows. 'Aah, that's grand.'

'So, how long's it been?' asks Keeler.

'Eight years? Nine, maybe. The Kowalski kid. Remember?'

'That's right, that's right.' Keeler's balding, buffed pate gleams magenta as the lights change overhead.

'What happened at the end of that?'

'You don't know? Of course, you moved down to some shithole place to work – Miami, was it?'

'That's right.' Flanagan draws down the malt fire into his belly, aware that the room has quietened a little, the atmosphere has frosted. What in God's name is that woman doing behind him? 'So what happened? How was it?'

'I don't know how much you know – most of it didn't make

the media. He admitted to eight similar. Fuck that – he didn't admit to them, he bragged about it. They were all mutilated, all of them had their hands cut off, some with a penknife, some with a breadknife. Shit, he even used a pair of shears on one of them. You know, like shears you use for trimming grass? When I was interviewing, he spent a long time telling me how he searched for something that was blunt, but still had enough of an edge to tear flesh. He talked me right through it so I'd understand the physics of it. That's what he kept saying, "so you understand the physics of it".' Keeler seems to dim with the memory.

'So he did all nine? I mean, you found them?'

'Yeah, we found them. Jesus, Flanagan, I had to be there each time. Each fucking time they said I had to be there. We'd go to some wasteland and dig and dig, and then we'd find them. Eight times I went and looked down some hole at a kid without any hands and by that time not much else either. And you weren't there.'

Flanagan throws his mind back and recalls the evening when they found the first child, Katarina Kowalski. Keeler, about whom his colleagues would remark 'The Ice Man Cometh' when he arrived at a scene; Keeler, whose nickname was the Yeti, because he appeared to come from a land so frozen that no emotion would survive; *that* Keeler had gone that evening with Flanagan to a small, sad beach and they had found the little Kowalski girl buried in a shallow, shifting grave. It had not taken them long to hand-shovel the damp sand away from her face, and then from her body. Flanagan had knelt by the grave, ignoring the salt water oozing through the cloth of his pants. He had looked up to Keeler, needing Keeler's impartiality, his automaton efficiency to anchor himself, only to find Keeler falling apart. He was weeping silently, his face – so young, so self-righteous then – crumpled with misery. As Flanagan watched, Keeler sank down, his hands clasped, his head slowly falling forward until it touched the sand. And he cried, he cried ceaselessly, as if tears were drizzling from him, as if he would never smile again. Flanagan watched Keeler for minutes, waiting for the Yeti to come back. But he never did come back, the Yeti; he walked away and left Keeler crying on the littered beach, watched by a curious crowd. It was the muffled laughter of a small boy, who pointed at Keeler and turned to a friend to say something, that galvanized Flanagan. He stood and walked round the makeshift grave to Keeler and knelt once more. Flanagan gathered Keeler to him, gathered him to his broad, bountiful, heart-thumping chest, and he held him close, smoothing his hair, listening to the sticky breaths. He held him fiercely as the sirens blared and the blue strobe lights turned, reflected in the reedy, scum-lined water, he held him as Forensics and the media arrived. He took him home and held him, smoothing his hair, rocking him gently, until Keeler slept, weeping through the night, the tears leaking from beneath his lids. And in some way Flanagan held him still, would not now let him go until one of them died.

Keeler pours each of them another whiskey. 'It wasn't right, sending me out to all those places after they posted you. Maybe I could have handled it better if you'd been there. I often think of them – the kids, I mean. Often. They were all so, y'know, small.'

Flanagan frowns. 'What happened to the case? I mean, I don't remember reading anything much about it after I left. *Nine* kids – I should remember that.'

Keeler looks at Flanagan sharply. 'The guy who did it? He was a politician's son. Some fucking state governor's son. Governor Thomas Henderson Granby Jefferson the second. People were climbing greasy poles to get round that one. I sat in the interview room with that bastard for weeks, listening to him playing games, making out he's a cross between Caligula and the fucking Archangel Michael, not knowing whether to give me the run around or come on strong about how *bad* he is. And I'm sitting there knowing that outside there're people busting their asses to plea bargain, to make him disappear, to offload him somewhere else. And then Jeffrey Dahmer came along and blew us all out of our seats. And you know what? I heard someone saying that it was the best thing that could have happened, that it would make the Kowalski case tame in comparison. "The best thing that could have happened." And I thought of the kids and their hands, and I listened to this guy explain how the media could be persuaded – that's what he kept saying, "persuaded" – to handle this.' Keeler falls silent, falls into a different space.

'Is that when you crossed over?' Flanagan fills his mouth with Bushmills, lets it sit on his tongue.

Keeler sighs and turns his sweating glass in his hand. 'Yeah. That was what made me go. I mean, I knew the Bureau was interested in me, always had been, but I reckoned – shit, I look back on that now – I reckoned the Police Department was, what? Straighter, y'know? More direct, out on the streets, more proactive.' He rubs his shiny pate. 'But in some ways it's the FBI that's more direct. That's not what I mean. I mean, it's more effective. It deals in macro-situations rather than inci-dents.' He smiles, looks at Flanagan. 'You think this is bullshit.'

Flanagan begins to speak, shouting as the calypso dies, his

words hanging on the cigar smoke as he hears movement on the stage behind him. He blushes and swigs from his whiskey, fighting the impulse to turn to the woman, to assess her, to check that she has survived her humiliation. He coughs and speaks. 'You were always the best, Keeler – always. You were the best cop I ever met. The best investigator. I mean, no detail was safe, nothing and no one could hide from you. You perused, you studied, you dug deep. You could analyse something into or out of existence.' Flanagan shifts in his seat, settling his bear-like backside more comfortably. 'You're right, I think what you said is bullshit, but if you believe it, if you act on that belief, then, yeah, the FBI is the place for you. And before you ask, no, what happened when we found the Kowalski girl did not make you unfit to be a detective. It made you a better one.' Flanagan sighs and shifts again. 'It was all a long time ago, wasn't it? And at least now you can buy me one of these.' He picks up the bottle and tops up the glasses.

Keeler smiles tentatively, reminding Flanagan of the young man hunkered by a sandy, handless grave. 'Thanks.'

'Hell of place to suggest we meet.' The lieutenant waves his glass at the walls, the tables, the faces. 'You said it was a club. Call me naïve, but this looks more like a meeting of the Union of Rome or a world summit to my unpractised eye.'

Keeler shrugs. 'Happens. Like attracts like. There's more business goes on here than on the Hill.'

Flanagan eyes him, anticipates him. 'So what about the floor show? I mean, what's that about? Some woman has to rearrange her internal organs so the finer points of NAFTA can be hammered out?'

Keeler smiles again. 'Oh-oh, that great big bleeding Irish heart. I forgot how it beats. Flanagan, it happens. It just happens. The girls are well paid, they're safe, they're not on the streets. C'mon. Get serious. It happens everywhere.'

The lieutenant's Irish-lime eyes narrow. 'You're telling me that these guys,' he swivels round in his seat, marvels yet again at the faces he sees, 'you're telling me that these guys need someone's fanny in their face to close a deal?'

This time Keeler laughs, sits right back in his seat and laughs. 'Hey, don't keep things to yourself. I mean, why don't you come right out and tell me what you think?' Again Keeler laughs, the skin on his skull crinkling a little. 'OK, OK. Look, it's very simple. This is no two-bit operation, as you may have guessed. The Bureau rents this place and its . . . its attractions from a guy who knows everyone and everything. He practically owns the city.' Keeler sees Flanagan squirm, sees him twitch. 'Look, I'm not saying it's right, I'm just telling the facts. This guy's a businessman, that's all, and in his line of business he's wiped his ass with the great and good. They trust him. The Bureau trusts him. Shit, next to Santa Claus he's New York's favourite sugar-daddy. Don't ask me why. I can't even begin to guess who he is. Came out of nowhere a few years ago. Look, there are always deals being done. We use this club as a sounding place, a conduit, a place to hear things, keep the finger on the pulse. So he rents out the building and insists on throwing in a little action for profit. Suits everyone.'

Flanagan squirms and squares his shoulders.

'Hey, c'mon, Flanagan, it's just sex and politics. The same old cycle, the same old story. Sex and politics. Even *your* heart ain't ever gonna to beat loud enough to drown that one out.' Keeler watches Flanagan, watches the man who held him close and saved him, watches him wrestle with the facts of life. Keeler wishes he had arranged to meet in a bar, in a pizza parlour, anywhere but here. But he had wanted to impress, wanted to flaunt the fact that he moved along the corridors of power. Why had he ever thought that? Why had he thought that Flanagan – of all men – would be dazzled? Keeler shoots a look at the stage and is relieved to see it empty, but he is aware that there will be another woman waiting in the wings. 'So, why did you call? I mean, it's great to hear from you, but I'm wondering why you called.'

Flanagan focuses on Keeler, pulls him into his eyes. 'I need some information. But I have to say right now that this is way out of line. I'm on official vacation, this is not police business. If you don't want to answer I'll just drop it.'

'Why d'you need to know?'

'It's personal.'

Keeler looks absently at the next table, watches the VP of an oil conglomerate cut a couple of lines on a bespoke mirror set. 'Well, try me. Can't hurt.'

'I want to know about Mr Candid.' Flanagan's voice rumbles across the table to reach Keeler's ear.

Keeler flinches. 'Mr Candid?'

'Yeah. I really need to know about him.'

Keeler looks away, drums a tattoo on the table with manicured fingers, and Flanagan remembers that Keeler has always done this, tapped the same rhythm, the same story, all his life. Keeler exhales a long breath. 'Mr Candid. You want to know about Mr Candid. Shit, Flanagan, I can't tell you about that. It's real sensitive.'

'So the Bureau *is* interested.'

'Flanagan, he's a ghost, he's a dream. We can't chase that. We can't even begin.'

'But *you* know he exists.'

'If you're asking official policy, then no, he doesn't. The media invented him, wants him to save the world. He doesn't exist.' Keeler picks up a spent match and begins to push dead butts around the ashtray. Anything to avoid Flanagan's eyes. 'If you're asking what do *I* think, then, shit, I think he's out there. Sometimes' – Keeler draws breath – 'sometimes I think he's where I am. Know what I mean? Like he could be here, watching me. Sometimes I think he's the guy who steps out of the elevator and brushes past me as I step in. Sometimes I think he's the janitor in my apartment block.'

'And that's what the Bureau thinks too?'

'Unofficially, yeah. We know he's around, but it's like hunting a chimera. Look, I really can't elaborate.'

Flanagan sips his whiskey and judges the moment. 'I can give you a name.'

'What?'

'I can give you his name.'

Keeler sits very still, calculating.

'I'll give you the name after you tell me what you know.'

Keeler raises his dainty, pale hands, palms upwards. 'Hey, c'mon. Where's this name from? What status does it have? I mean, is it corroborated?'

'Never mind about that right now. Tell me what you can and I'll give you the name.'

Keeler calculates once more, the memory of falling into Flanagan's wide, warm chest nudging him towards a decision. He leans forward, pushing aside the ashtray and the flowers, and rests on his angular elbows, inviting Flanagan to draw closer. His voice drops, rasps a little, like starched linen on delicate skin.

'It started maybe sixteen, seventeen years ago – not that

we knew it then. I mean, all this is what we've put together since. As far as we can make out it started in Vegas. Four paedophiles were found dead in a house. At the time it was thought they'd been killed during some ritual or something. So no one thought anything of it.

'Then, a couple of months later, an undercover cop in Vegas, working on a narc bust, said the streets had gone crazy. Stuff was coming in, y'know, it was reaching Vegas and then it was disappearing. It never showed up on the streets. The price of smack went through the fucking roof and none was coming in to supply the market. Thing is, it never went anywhere else, either. Someone was in the loop and was buying it up and trashing it. All of it – smack, coke, poppers, everything. There was nothing left to push, nothing to hit the kids with. Which is, y'know, a good thing, but *we* weren't in control of this, the Bureau couldn't act on it, couldn't capitalize. Then the same happened in Portland, in San Diego, in Miami, in LA. He even tried it here, in New York, but there's so much shit around here no one can control it all.

'Then we began to notice a pattern. Wherever the narc scene went seismic, the body count grew. But these weren't bodies that anyone much cared about – rapists and child sex abusers, kiddie pornos, y'know the sort of thing. Then a couple of people got hit on the inside – again they were child rapists. There was a major internal investigation because those institutions were not running open house. I mean they were high-security, Grade A One security penitentiaries. But all the investigation turned up was the fact that no one inside was responsible for those murders. So someone had walked in from the outside, killed the motherfuckers and managed to walk right out again.'

Keeler pauses, stretches his forehead tight with his finger-tips. 'That's when we started to get real worried. It's also when the rumours started about some guy who could walk through walls, through locked steel doors, through computer screen-ing, everything. The rumours started in the pens and every time someone got paroled they took the rumours outside. Then the media got hold of it and the fireworks started. You know the rest – that there's some guy out there, the Bogey Man, who'll come and getcha if you're bad.'

Flanagan's lime eyes are fixed on Keeler's face. 'I read in the papers that he's killed Mafia, intercepted gun runs, blown away whole street gangs. That true?'

'No. No, he just goes for the sickos. Sickos – child rapists, child killers – and drugs. He can jam the operations of an established Colombian cartel for months. It's fucking up the balance of things. We don't know what's happening next or where it's happening, we can't *anticipate* him.'

'What's the charge sheet?'

'More than ninety murder ones that we know of, probably many more. Shit, Flanagan, ninety. There's never been any-thing like this.'

'What else you got?'

'Sweet nothing. We know he works alone, that he moves around a lot and very quickly. He's good at disappearing, no one ever remembers the face, or if they think they've seen someone, the descriptions never match each other. So he's not only a ghost, he's a chameleon, a shape-shifter.' Keeler lights a cigarette, blows a plume of smoke skywards, where it fires crimson and indigo as the lights spin. 'We had a profile drawn up by a psychiatrist. She says Mr Candid's probably white, late thirties, articulate, imaginative, all that shit. Also that he's exceptionally gifted. We paid thousands of dollars for that assessment and it's what they say about all of them. She did say one interesting thing, that his behaviour is not obsessional – that is, he feels compelled to do these things but she doesn't think he's obsessive about it. Which sounds like a pile of crap to me. One other thing she said was that a trauma may have started this. I mean, you gotta ask, why? What kick-starts something on this scale? But the shrinks say it could have been anything. The scent of his mother's clothes, the shadow on his bedroom wall when he was a kid. Anything.

'I don't know, I've been working on this for a couple of years and I haven't understood squat. I haven't got a picture, I don't feel like I know him. If we could put enough of the bits together, enough of the pieces, then we could move on. People are out there, speaking to him, looking at him. People know him, they just don't know he's Mr Candid. OK, most of those people are street people but we've always managed to tap in on them in the past. Look, we've got a body count of ninety and the Bureau's going crazy. We can't go public because that will only light the public fire. We'll have every politician in Washington on our backs, fanning the flames. Thing is, the shrink said because he's not an obsessive he could stop any time. Just stop dead and we'll never find him.'

'Where does he get the money?'

'Huh?'

'Where does he get the *money* to do this? The money to buy drugs in those quantities?'

'We don't know. He hasn't been linked, as far as we know, to any fraud, larceny or bank heists. There's certainly no pattern to any major market activity or bank losses to match the drug upheavals. We just don't know. These are major sums of money that seem to appear and disappear.'

You're lying, thinks Flanagan, you're lying to me. You gave me the clue minutes ago and now you're denying it. The gaming tables of Las Vegas spin in Flanagan's mind. 'So, what's happening now? I mean, d'you know anything?'

Edison leans closer over the table, his voice drops, seeming to come from a distance. 'The last I know we think he's in LA. We think he's travelling with someone, which is a deviation from the norm. But these are just rumours like they always are.' He stretches his forehead once more, runs an ivory finger across his sweating upper lip.

'Right. Right.' Flanagan sits back, knowing he will get nothing more, knowing that a kernel of panic is beginning to burgeon in Keeler's chest as he realizes how much he has divulged. 'One more thing – where's the name come from?'

'Huh?'

Flanagan pours more whiskey. He needs Keeler for few minutes more. 'Mr Candid – where's the name come from?'

Keeler smiles. 'Oh, that. It was years ago. During a debriefing session some agent started to talk about *Candide*, y'know, Voltaire's *Candide*, the best of all possible worlds and all that shit. When the transcript of that meeting arrived, there was a spelling error. So he became Mr Candid.'

Flanagan frowns. 'But that was inside the Bureau. I mean, that's where the name was used. How come it's in every paper?'

'Ah, come on, people talk. They always talk.' Keeler finally moves away from the lieutenant. 'Shit, listen to me tonight – I've given you ten years of the Bureau's time. And as far as I know this conversation never took place, OK?'

'Sure. Don't worry about it. Like I said, this is not police business, I'm on vacation.'

'So why d'you need to know? You said it was personal.'

'I'm interested. I have been for a while. I read the papers, listen to the news. I'm interested.'

'Bullshit. What's going on, Flanagan?'

Flanagan sighs and looks away from Keeler. He scans the room and wonders why he was awed by the power brokered there. What would Mr Candid make of it? What would he do if he were there? 'I can't work out if he's right or not.'

'Come again?'

'I can't work out if what he does, the way he does it, is right or not. I just want to ask him how he lives with himself – if he feels any guilt, if he sees himself as a saviour or something. I've stood behind some guys as they're being cuffed, my gun resting at the base of their skulls, and I've thought about what they've done – maybe to some woman, maybe even to their own wives or children – and I've wondered whether I should just blow them away right there. And sometimes I've found out that one of those men that I had in my sights has done his time, come back on the streets and done it all over again. Or maybe his attorney got him off on a technicality. And I think about whether I should have done it, whether I should have squeezed the trigger.'

'C'mon, Flanagan, everyone feels that way, every cop has thought that. You're no different.'

Flanagan has not even heard him. He is talking to himself, for himself. 'That guy you were talking about? The governor's son in the Kowalski case? Thomas Jefferson? Mr Candid would simply find him and kill him. Simple. No doubts, no questions. No court case, no reasonable doubt, no plea bargains, no technicalities, no temporary insanity, no psychological fitness tests. Mr Candid would simply ensure that that guy ceased to exist. And would you stop him ensuring that?'

Keeler looks at Flanagan, pauses a long minute as a keening wail sounds and voodoo drums hammer out a tattoo, signalling the next surprise to arrive on the stage. Keeler lowers his eyes. 'No, I wouldn't stop him. I'd help him any way I could.'

'Well, then, don't you see? Keeler? Don't you see? It cancels us out. We've done *nothing* for the past seventeen years. All we've managed to do is to serve these assholes up to the courts where all the games of jurisprudence are played. We've done nothing. But if he's right' – Flanagan frowns and clasps his hands – 'if Mr Candid's right, if what he does is right, then all the faith I ever invested in the system was misplaced. You say every cop feels like that as if this is not important, but it's important to *me*. I want to do the right thing. That's all. All those times when we could have done something, could have stopped something – shit, could even have stopped something happening again – we didn't. So you got ninety bodies in the morgue. So what the fuck? You think someone's crying over them? They were shit and we both know that.'

Keeler leans forward, his face set and sharp, angered by so many things. 'Christ, Flanagan, what do you think the Bureau's been doing? It's turning itself inside out, if you want to know the truth. It's tying itself in knots over this one. Most of us wouldn't give a flying fuck if the files on Mr Candid disappeared and we had to start all over again. Y'know, give him time to knock off a few more crazies. But too many people know about it, it can't be shut down. Ninety bodies so far. And I've seen them all. I've stood in those morgues and looked at them, watched the men in white coats slide them out the wall and turn back the sheet and I've looked at them and I haven't given one good goddamn about them. You know why?' Keeler is wild now, he's so enraged that he's hissing, spittle flying as his forefinger jabs the table, bending on each strike. 'You know why?' Of course Flanagan knows why, knows exactly what Keeler is going to say. 'Because every time I visit a fucking morgue and look at one of those bastards I think of that night on the beach, I think of Katarina Kowalski lying in the sand without her hands. We never found their *hands*, Flanagan. We never found any of their hands. And as I'm standing in the morgues looking at those dead men, all I can think is that somewhere there are eighteen hands, eighteen fucking unburied hands.' Keeler draws a slippery, salty breath, as if a salmon is being drawn deep into his lungs. 'I know that as I look at them lying on the slabs I'm supposed to think, Hey, this is some mother's son, this guy deserved to be tried, deserved justice. But I can't. I can't because Katarina Kowalski was some mother's daughter.' Keeler rubs his eyes viciously, sucks down a draught of whiskey as the lieutenant remembers looking dispassionately at Addis Barbar's mutilated body. This thought is replaced by the image of Iris sitting in her chair as the blood flooded through her brain – some mother's son. 'Like I said, the Bureau's official line is that Mr Candid does not exist. What else can we do? What else can we say? I lied – it's nothing to do with Washington. It's to do with everyone *outside* Washington. If we say he exists and we find him, then what? What do we do then, Flanagan? What do we do then? Do we tell Middle America that we caught the guy who cleaned up the streets? That we caught the guy who managed to destabilize the entire narcotics industry? That we're

incarcerating the man who dealt with more rapists and paedophiles than we ever fucking managed? Who's gonna tell
them? Who's gonna tell the people who fought to legislate
Megan's Law that we're locking up Mr Candid? *No one will do
it.* I wouldn't do it. No one in this club would do it. Clinton
wouldn't do it. Shit, maybe even *you* wouldn't do it.'

Lieutenant Flanagan looks down at the hands that have
held guns so close to the skulls of so many men. Slowly he
raises his head and looks at Keeler. 'So you understand why I
need to find him? You know why I'm doing this? Why it's
personal?'

Keeler nods once. It is an admission of sorts. He gathers
himself, rearranges himself, becomes a bureaucrat once more.
'I have to ask, I'm sorry but I do have to ask – what's the
name?'

'Sorry?' The voodoo drums have moved up, are beating
loudly now, causing the lieutenant's chair to rumble, to shake.

'You said you'd give me a name.'

Flanagan pauses. He could say anything, could contrive a
name, and Keeler would be satisfied. But that would not be
truthful, would not be right. 'Chum Kane.'

'What?' Keeler cups a hand around his ear as the drums
grow louder.

'Chum Kane. Or Charlie Kane. That's what I hear.'

'Chum Kane?'

Flanagan nods.

Keeler's face empties. 'I have to ask, I'm sorry, but I do. Do
you have any other information relating to this matter?'

Flanagan looks at him across the table, dusted now by ash
and pollen, and thinks of Iris, thinks of the matron in the rest
home, thinks of the house in East Hampton, Long Island.

Imagines the FBI reaching Mr Candid before he, Flanagan, finds him and the furies that would be unleashed. 'No,' says Lieutenant Flanagan, 'I have no other information relating to this matter. And now I have to go to the bathroom.'

The lieutenant stands and sidles through the tables, his bulk brushing the shoulders of the great and good. The floor is buzzing, vibrating with the bass rumble of drums, and reluctantly the lieutenant looks over to the stage. A woman emerges from the wings, naked but for a G-string. Folds of blubber bounce jauntily as she sashays across the floor, her knees and elbows dimpling, double bracketed by flesh. But for her breasts, vast mammary pillows, she could be a colossus of a baby. Flanagan stands and stares, his breathing shallow, stunned, as slow recognition dawns. He has brushed against this woman's stomach – Bronwen Jones is on stage, dancing her life away, staring right back at him.

Matron is lying on the floor by Iris's bed when they come. Her hair is matted, her clothes sullied and crumpled. She's dehydrated, half crazed by thirst, and her stomach feels brittle-thin as a scraped plate. She lies on the linoleum, inert, her eyes closed, as she listens to them moving through the rest home. She picks out sounds of disgust and imagines they have found the turkey carcass. She hears doors banging open as they check the corridor of rooms and finally she feels the rush of air eddying the dust and filth as the door to Iris's room opens. 'Oh, my God,' she hears. And 'Jeez, wouldja look at this?' Followed by the sounds of someone retching.

Matron knows Iris is still alive. She has spent too many days with her in this room and would now feel her death as an absence. Matron begins to slip away, slip deep into oblivion, knowing that others will move in to provide, will move in and take the decisions. She opens her yellowed, bloodshot eyes a crack and looks through the curtain of her own lashes at the pitch-black mirrored surface of a pair of boots moving towards her.

Iris can hear, too, although she can do very little else; she can barely summon the will to breathe. The breathing that she does is done only because she is waiting for Charlie, she is waiting for Charlie 'Chum' Kane to come so that she can say goodbye. 'Goodbye,' she practises, in the furred cauldron of her mind. 'Goodbye.' Iris reckons that her traitorous tongue can manage that simple word.

Iris feels hands pulling back the greasy, sweat-dampened coverlet, and then the sheet is peeled away from her. If it were possible she would control the blush she feels rising on her face, for she knows that the sheet is caked in excrement, that it is stiff with a bloom of urine. But if Iris could have controlled the flood of blood through the delicate brachiate deltas of her wasting body then she would not have been lying there help-lessly. Instead, as the hands lift her, trying to find purchase among the bedsores, she slips away to her secret place: her past life, which is hers alone. No one else has lived it. No one else, perhaps, would have done.

LUKE KANE

Picture this: it is 24 October 1929 in America. It is, indeed, 24 October 1929 everywhere, but America seems unaware of this, for depression has taken hold and she is not thinking. Elsewhere, nations till the soil, gather the harvest, cut the jacks and salt the finnan, cull the deer and bless the stones; they suckle babies, bury the dead, raise the flag, worship the gods. The rhythms of the nations beat. Winds still howl over the islands at the edge of the world: over the wastes of the Hebrides, the skank grass of Chatham, the vast, arrogant profiles of Easter Island. But the winds keep moving, whipping over oceans to arrive in America, bowling through the states, stripping them, turning bushes into cartwheels, fields into dust, cattle into carcasses. Then they turn away, the winds, wheel away to Zanzibar, to Madagascar, the Balearics, the Azores, simply bowling along in the pursuit of happiness.

America sulks, like the young child she is. She has been laid bare, then stripped of her skin. In the excoriated dust-bowls aggrieved families stand alone in acres of barren land, wishing things had been different. In the cities men stand by tickertape machines and wonder what these families are doing as miles of punctured paper slip through their numb fingers. The world watches America's aching turn, for she is new to this, this stillbirth of hope. The Incas, the Egyptians, the Romans all turn and shrug. The dynasties of China permit themselves a tight, barely perceptible smile. Deep, deep in Africa, so long dead their names will never be unearthed, lie the outlines of cities buried beneath the lush, spreading petticoats of an even older forest. The rulers of these cities, the demi-gods of their day, turned now to dust, grimace keenly, for they knew first how fragile power is.

America, however, is a plump little child with plenty of reserves. As the steel mills slow and the cereals crumple to the arid earth, life fires. New York begins to dance underground as the Black blues take hold. In Los Angeles the light transforms liars into stars, joiners into craftsmen, madmen into moguls. Citrus fruit breathes easy in the never-ending drought. A vintner from Sicily ruminates as he rolls a mould-frosted grape between callused finger and thumb. America may be depressed, may indeed be throwing a tantrum, but for the few the money keeps rolling in.

Two crops burgeon in that year, 1929, over which no one has any control. One is the firewater, the gut-rot, the splash from the rural stills that serve the speakeasies, the farmhouses, the tenements, the country homes. Stills bloom like the pox, spreading without fear, dangerous and rural, hand-cranked Molotov cocktails. The second crop is less substantial, spun with words. It is a mythology of gangsters and molls, of towns wreathed in gold, of a land of milk and honey to be found over the next crest, the next ridge, the next mountain. The jalopies roll, creaking and unbalanced with their loads of scuffed furniture and hope, only to find more of the same. Men's feet carve new tracks, new roads across the continent, as they walk from place to place looking for things they will never find, the hollows stark in their cheeks where the teeth are missing. Children's hearts cease to beat under the assault of rickets, TB, diphtheria, anaemia, malnutrition, as cholera rages in the bayous.

And yet there are those whose lives still sparkle, touched by diamonds, untouched by misery. Look here, in this private hospital in Manhattan, look through the amber-tinted windows on this Christmas Day – so welcoming, so safe – and see the blonde woman lying between satin sheets, a cloud of imported gardenias around her, as her husband nuzzles her neck, whispering endearments. They are warm, they are safe. They are rich. The woman turns to her husband and smiles. The hushed light suits her, flushes her dimpled cheeks and throws her pert nose into shadow. What man would yearn for molasses and midnight, gumbo and spice, heat and life, when faced with this dainty? Her hands are fine and unused, her face unlined by poverty. She is simply delicious.

'The best Christmas present we could have had,' Lucinda lisps prettily to her husband as she gazes at her breast, where wisps of ebony hair spatter Luke Kane's soft-boiled skull.

'Why, honey, what more could a man want?' Theodore's voice cracks appropriately as he fires a discreet glance at the clock.

'Isn't he beautiful?' She touches the butter knob of Luke Kane's nose and squeals a little with delight.

Theodore, substantial and beefy, well groomed in his tailored suit, looks at the child as if for the first time and is startled to see cobalt-blue eyes staring back. He watches the blood pulsing through his newly-minted son and smiles. 'My God, but he's a handsome one.'

Which is an echo of the thought running through the mind

of the midwife, settled now in an office down the hall. Why, then, she wonders, did she stifle a moan as Luke Kane slipped between his mother's legs? Why did she fumble with the child and drop him as if he were a handful of lava, hastily scooping him up again from the sheets? Why – if the little boy was the most beautiful baby she has ever delivered – did she rush away with an almost indecent haste, glad to savour the air and light between them?

1997

Lieutenant Flanagan has emptied his urgent bladder and returns to Keeler's table, brushing against senators and congressmen in his haste, bumping them with his backside. He throws himself into his seat and tries to order jumbled thoughts. Bronwen, the nurse from the Emerald Rest Home who pinned him in a doorway with her massive stomach moments before the brain sitting snug in Iris's skull had expanded and burst its banks. Bronwen, who knew Iris when she was whole and could speak. He turns towards the stage, dreading what he will see, yet compelled to look. There is Bronwen Jones of Llanerchymedd, every fold and crevice, every dimple and pucker, exposed to the scrutiny of the audience. They sit wreathed in cigar smoke, their minds bamboozled, reeling with bourbon and ecstasy, fine wine and coke, heat and light, watching her. For Bronwen dances beautifully, rhythmically, sexily, her hips thrown this way and that on the borderline of each beat as she swivels on the hard balls of her long-suffering feet. The voodoo drums drive her, make her skeleton jig and canter. The room grows hotter.

Flanagan turns back to Keeler. 'Can you arrange to meet the women?'

'What?' Keeler asks, his eyes following Bronwen's fabulous breasts.

'Can you – can *I* arrange to meet her?'

Keeler finally looks at Flanagan and grins. 'Well, lookee here. I wouldn't have taken you for a meat and potatoes man. Oh, no, something slim and cool – that's what I've always pictured you with.'

Flanagan bats this away with a wave of his huge hand. 'So what do I do?'

'Hey, don't get too eager – it ain't easy is what I hear. I've never done it because I can't afford it. Kids' orthodontist, new car. But I know some guys have. You have to ask the butler – y'know? The English asshole in the lobby. He may fix up something. Then again, he may not. He gets picky, like he has the right to dictate who does what. He's a pain in the ass.'

The drums crescendo, swallowing Keeler's words and laying them at the now-still feet of Bronwen. She shudders to a halt and curtsies deeply, before exiting stage left.

'Shit, I gotta get going.' Flanagan pushes back his chair, downs his whiskey. 'I'll be seeing you.'

Keeler stands and wraps his arms around the lieutenant, hugging him. 'Hey, it's been great to catch up.'

'Yeah.' Flanagan moves away, anxious, driven to find Bronwen.

'Flanagan?'

'What?'

'Hope you find him before we do.'

'So do I.' Flanagan begins to weave through the tables.

'Flanagan?' Keeler has raised his voice a little, pushed it into Flanagan's head.

'What?' He is annoyed now, wants to be moving.

'If you do, will you call me? Y'know, to tell me what his answer is?'

'Sure I will.' Like fuck I will, thinks Flanagan, as he throws open the double doors which lead into the lobby. The butler is there, by the door, fetching coats from the cloakroom as a small crowd mills and murmurs. Flanagan waits for the men to leave and strolls up to him.

'Your coat, sir.' The butler holds it as Flanagan shrugs into it, fighting a blush, wondering what to say.

'I was wondering.' He stops, searches for a phrase, a word, an escape route. 'I was wondering.'

'Yes, sir?'

'I was wondering if I could arrange to meet one of the performers.'

'I see, sir.'

'In fact, I was wondering if I could meet the one who's just finished.'

'I see, sir.' Flanagan's skin feels as if it is being seared from the bone, burnt with shame. He knows the butler is imagining the two of them together, Bronwen and the lieutenant, naked, on a bed, together. More flesh meeting than on an Irish hog. The butler smiles faintly. 'I'll see what I can do, sir. If you'd like to wait here.'

'Maybe you could tell her Lieutenant Flanagan is asking.'

The butler does not miss a beat, but the skin round his mouth tightens a little. 'Of course, sir.'

He returns a little later to find the lieutenant perched uneasily on a spindle-bundle of a gilt chair.

'Everything is arranged, sir. There is a car outside waiting for you.'

'Thank you.'

'You're welcome.' Flanagan knows that he will never be welcome here again.

The lieutenant steps out, allows the frosted air to cool his skin before opening the door of the limo and sliding in. He finds he is sitting next to a slight man with a sliver of a moustache razoring his upper lip. The man's clothes are nondescript but spotless, a soft packet of Winstons crammed into his shirt pocket beneath a drab overcoat. 'Pardon my appearance, Lieutenant, but I'm heading off to inspect some other corners of my empire and I've found it's always best to blend in with the natives.' He smiles, exposing a fine set of virgin teeth, unsullied by caffeine or nicotine. It is Sam, Sam the Weasel Man. 'I'm a – how to put it? – a friend of Bronwen's and I've just come to check out that you're on the level. I mean, I have to take care of everyone.'

Flanagan looks in amazement at the scrap of a man on the seat next to him. *This* man, with his thinning hair and the face of a skinned rabbit, owns the club? Also something else: he looks familiar; Flanagan is sure he's seen him somewhere before.

'For instance,' Sam continues, 'you said your name was Lieutenant Flanagan. Would that be lieutenant as in NYPD?'

'No. And I'm on vacation.'

'OK.' Sam watches as another limo pulls up, collects its cargo and swishes down the street towards the Park. 'You were the guest of Edison Keeler – nice guy, but he drinks too much, owes too much money.' Sam turns his lupine eyes on the lieutenant. 'I just want to make sure that you know the rules. I like Bronwen a lot. I mean, she ain't my kinda thing but I have a great deal of respect for her. So no fucking around, OK? Treat her well, give her a good time, pay her the money and send her back like a kid with a whole summer vacation to look forward to.'

'How much do I pay her?'

'Twelve hundred.' Flanagan watches absently as Sam lights a cigarette and flicks the match in a phosphorescent arc on to the slushy pavement. 'So, you got that?'

'Sure.'

'What I mean is, you understand what I'm saying? Everything's gotta be sweetness and light.'

'No problem,' mumbles Flanagan. Good Christ, where's he going to get twelve hundred dollars?

'See ya 'round.' Sam slips out of the car and steps across the road. Flanagan tries to watch him but it is as if he fades into the sludge. The car rocks and groans as Bronwen fills the still-warm seat Sam has left behind.

'Well,' says Flanagan, 'I didn't—'

Bronwen's voice rides rough-shod over his as she taps the driver on the shoulder and says, 'The usual.' She turns fast as a krait and Flanagan sees her brush a finger to her lips. He slumps back, nestles into his overcoat and watches Manhattan fly by.

Venice, LA – March

M –

　　Like I said in my last letter, I wish I'd been able to ask you what to do about that kid. I'm sitting in my room at some crazy place they call the Cotel on Ocean and Windward. From here I can look out the window at the palms moving on a blue sky. If I looked out on the street, sorry, boardwalk, I'd see acres of tanned flesh, moving and admiring itself, preening and flirting, see the market selling

its trash but in such a good-humoured, down-home way
no one cares. And the temperature is just fine, warm and
fresh, coming into my room off the ocean.

So, what was wrong today? What could possibly be
wrong with this particular version of Paradise? Plenty, as it
turns out. I asked the kid – the one I wrote about, the one
from the 21st Street Gang – to meet me in the Sidewalk
Café just down from here. I reckoned it was a good place
because it was right out of his patch, full of tourists,
travellers, all eating and moving on. I figured we could stay
a while unnoticed with all the traffic. He turns up – I call
him Gideon, don't know his real name and I think he's
forgotten it – around an hour late, which pisses me right
off because then I've been sitting there with the waitresses
coming over every five minutes busting a gut to earn their
fat tip, looking into my pretty face and asking if I want
anything. So Gideon comes in, slouching like an old man,
sneer fixed with glue, in the costume of white vest, baggy-
ass jeans, hi-tops and bandanna. He slumps in the chair
next to me and I can see he's got ghosts moving in his
eyes, still running on the last visit to a crack house. But
he's all I've got, so I order a four-hit espresso for him and
wait for him to get me in focus. Which takes some time.
Eventually he seems to shift a little and come towards me,
so we start talking.

And that's when I began to wish that you were there,
sitting in the seat next to me, with maybe a diet Coke or a
beer or whatever it is that you drink now. And maybe
you'd be wearing drainpipe jeans and one of those grand-
daddy shirts like you used to when you thought you were
going to be the next Patti Smith. That, even when we

were still trying to accommodate the first Patti Smith.
(Remember that dickhead in college who used to holler
out her lyrics in the bar? He thought she was singing, 'Go,
Rambo, go, Rambo . . .'?) Anyway, I wanted you there,
bringing some balance to the day, counteracting the
desolation at my other elbow.

Gideon could barely speak, and when he did the first
thing he asked for was a beer, so I called for a pitcher, and
he sits there looking at everyone like he's sucking a lemon.
Watching the women pass by with his ghost-filled eyes,
hissing breath through wet lips. I call him Gideon, he calls
me mothafucka. Nice. I try to talk to him, try to bring
him back into the world where sitting in a cafe is an
ordinary thing to do, but I begin to get worried that he's
floated so far down the river that I'm never going to reel
him in. So I ask him things that I never asked before –
about his family, where he lives, what he does every day,
that kind of stuff. And something happened to him.
Maybe it's because I'm in and out, because I'm white but
not regular. (Sometimes I think he thinks I exist only
when he's watching me.) Whatever, something gets to him
and he begins to talk. At first he's fierce and so angry his
sentences are like Mexican beans strung together, jumping
everywhere. Then the crack starts to slip away, its structure
breaking down in the tidal wave of his blood, and he
begins to soften. He's not happy with this, with this
softening, like there are two of him blurring at the edges.
Folding into each other.

He talks about his mother, which doesn't take long.
Gideon's sixteen years old. His mother ('fuckin' ho') died
when he was just two years old. He was born with a habit,

awash with the heroin she sent down the cord that joined
them, so he craved things he couldn't control, that he
couldn't have, even in the womb. He says that she died
overdosing on some mixture of filth, some H cut into
some other powder over and over until no one knew what
they were buying into. And I sat there and listened as he
told me that his daddy had said to him that around that
time people on the streets couldn't get hold of anything so
they jacked up with any shit they could find.

I sat outside the Sidewalk Café and counted back the
years. Fifteen years ago I bought up a stash coming in from
Venezuela, a stash big enough to leave the entire world
without reason, and then I hired a fifty-two-foot yacht,
weighted each bag with lead, sailed out into the Pacific as
far as I could bear to go, waited until it was so dark that I
couldn't see the hand I held in front of my face, and then I
launched those bags over the side. It took some hours to
haul them from the hold and over. I remember sweating as
the boat bucked, wondering how far Hawaii was because I
was drifting so far west. And I remember when I finished I
sat on a pile of rope, coiled like a rattler, lit a cigarette,
cracked open a beer and smiled. I thought it had been a
fine night's work.

Fifteen years later Gideon's sitting there telling me that
his momma's dead because she was reduced to shooting up
phosphates and agricultural fertilizer, glass and salt cut in
with pure smack. What am I supposed to think? I try
telling myself that the woman was in way too deep, that
she would have died anyway. That there should have been
somewhere she could have gone for help when the supply
dried up. I can't say this thought did me much good. So

what do you hang on to? I'll tell you: the happiness of the as-yet-unborn.

Then Gideon starts mumbling about the place he lived with his father – some public housing out near Culver City. If Gideon's telling it straight then his father's on welfare, looking after four kids. Only he's not looking after them because he's on the street most of the time trying to cut another deal, pass along another package, set up another supply line. So he's gonna be at home warming the milk and making sure the kids get their shots? There's dog shit in the elevators, piss on the stairs, gangrene in the ice-box, age-old come crusted on the sheets. And we want these kids to grow up to be doctors? Then Gideon meets some kid when he's ten years old and the kid takes him along to some place where the gang hangs out and there he finds everything he's been looking for: a place to go, as much company as he needs. Because that's what he said got him the most – he was always lonely. When he was a kid, he was always lonely. Ice-blue-cube.

At this point he's folding over on himself so fast that it's like watching the waves break. One minute you're watching him sneering and leering, every sentence punctuated with the words 'know 'm sayin'?' and the next minute his eyes are swimming and he's breathing very, very deep to stop a cry stone dead in his chest.

I order some chicken, fries and salad and he gets punchy, pushing the salad away as if to say to everyone, 'Look, look, I'm so macho I'm going to die of vitamin deficiency,' and he wolfs down the fries and eats a little chicken and then says he has to go. I ask him where, exactly, he has to go to, and he gets cagey. But it's the cagey like I don't want to know, like I don't need to know. Like he's protecting me by his silence. Which I can believe.

All through this I've been feeling in my jacket pockets, where I have two envelopes. In one of them is five hundred bucks, in the other thirty thousand. One is fair exchange for the information I want, the other is the money to get him through college. I don't know which I'm going to give him, because I know I'm only going to give him one.

I ask him for the contact. That's all, just the name and number of a prison guard. The guy works way out of state but I know the gang can find the name; like I said, they can find anything; they have some network. But, for once, Gideon says they can't do it. But he does give me something – a slip of paper with a name and a phone number. Apparently this guy knows everything that happens from Maine to Florida, anywhere the Atlantic breaks. Sam the Weasel Man. But this comes as no surprise, because I've heard of Sam the Weasel Man for maybe seven, eight years now.

That's the end of it. I stand up, knowing I won't see him again, knowing that this is the last time we're going to meet, Gideon and I. I look down at him, sitting in his chair, legs jiggling, fingers laced in his lap, brushing his prick. He's flexing his crazed adolescent muscles, bunching them up outside his T-shirt, squinting up at me, trying to block out the sun. And he looks so young and black and handsome it could break your heart because the odds on him reaching twenty are so slight you could slide them under a closed door. And I'm thinking of when I was sixteen, and wonder how two members of the same species can have such different experiences. I stand there almost paralysed by the desire to mention your name and to ask him to find out where you are, but I can't. I have to leave and I can't let him know that I won't see him again; I've exposed him enough as it is. Way I see it, he's in too much danger already just getting from one day to the next.

I put my hands in my pockets and rub the envelopes there, one fat, one thin, between my fingers. Five hundred, or thirty thousand. If you'd been there I would have given them to you and walked away. Would have allowed you to choose which envelope was given to Gideon and I would have walked away knowing that whichever you chose was right. Shit, I couldn't make up my mind. I thought about his mother. And then I thought about me bucking about in that fucking yacht throwing kilos of uncut heroin to the fishes and I dropped both envelopes on the table and walked away.

Love,
Chum

Iris is lying in a clean bed, which stands on a mirror-like floor in an antiseptic room speckled with splashes of cut flowers. Beside her there is a jug of fresh water and a bowl of fruit – mere tokens, since Iris cannot move in any co-ordinated way. This is the first morning she has opened her eyes and she looks about in wonder. She has splintered memories of people lifting her and carrying her away from that room, which was full of nothing but nightmares, heat and questions, and a foul odour which she knew to be wafting from her own body. But now she is washed and powdered, her hair is lying dry and stripped of grease on a gleaming, scurf-free scalp. Iris closes her eyes again, allows herself a screwed, lopsided smile. Now things will be different. Now she is away from the Emerald Rest Home, away from the stick-thin harridan who badgered her with questions, asking why? where? when? who? over and over. Iris tries to remember how much she had said in her delirium but there are veils of net floating down between her thoughts and she worries she perhaps said too much. For she has always known, although nothing was ever said or written on paper, she has always known that Charlie 'Chum' Kane does not want to be found. It has been seventeen years now since she set her eyes on his lovely face, and for seventeen years she has wondered where he is and what he does. So many absences in her mind. Worse now. Void after void; pure, oxygen-free vacancy. But Charlie will find her in good time. He'll come, she thinks, when he's good and ready. He'll come bowling through the door with a book and some story. For sure. He'll come before she dies.

What has always surprised her, saddened her during these seventeen years, as she waited and wasted away, is that she can't remember the manner of his leaving. Where there should be a picture of waving hands and tears, of a car disappearing round a corner, there is nothing. How, Iris wonders – and not for the first time – did Charlie 'Chum' Kane leave her? How did he say goodbye? But, try as she may, she cannot conjure up a picture.

Iris snuggles down a little between the clean, crisp sheets, snuggles as much as she is able, what with her bedsores, her aching stump of an arm and the snakes of green catheters writhing over her body. Why is it that she can recall in such clarity the burning day she walked out of her mother's house, down the worn porch steps and across the scorched verge to step into Luke Kane's car, worrying about scallions, and yet the moment of Charlie's leaving is lost to her?

Iris sighs and turns her head, only to open her eyes and see across the aisle in the neighbouring bed the sallow face of her interrogator, the creator of her misery. For there is Matron, wan and wasted, greedily sucking up the plasma and salts being pumped through her as her kidneys groan and her brain calls out for vodka. Iris simply stares at Matron, her hands twisted to claws, her mouth working soundlessly. Why is *she* here? Why is the bitch-harridan from Hades lying next to her?

A memory bursts into Iris's ragged mind, of Matron lying on her in that room, questioning, questioning. It is settled: this woman knows too much about the things Iris cares about, the things Iris was supposed to protect. Iris will have to see about that. And soon. But first she must summon some strength, some purpose, some lifeblood; must garner those things that are coursing through the catheters. Iris closes her eyes again and concentrates on ordering her pitiful muscles and reordering what is left of her mind.

It had been an odious but understandable mistake on the part of the team that had eventually swept through the Emerald Rest Home. They had found the matron and Iris in the same room, both rotting away, both near-inhuman, and had mistaken them both for patients, close friends even. So, when the money cascading into Iris's bank balance was discovered, the powers that be had decided the two friends should share a room in the most exclusive club in Florida – Diamond Days, the dandiest geriatric nursing home in the US of A; *the* place, if you like, to take a Terminal Tour.

LUKE KANE

Luke Kane, as the baby born that day in 1929 became known, was a child blessed by many things. His mother, Lucinda, began to fuss with him – touching his cheek, curling his fingers, his toes, combing his hair with her dainty, pale fingers – from the moment he was placed, swaddled tightly in white knit, on her blue-veined, bloated breasts. She never ceased to fuss with him, always touching and feeling, cuddling and hugging. If Luke Kane reached out, from the cradle, from the bed, from a car, from a swimming pool, his mother would be there, soft and fragrant, her mind vacant.

Lucinda was a fool, too foolish even to realize how the world worked. Beyond Long Island at that time was a world falling apart at the seams. The Crash had emptied cupboards and banks, the wind had scoured the land and the droughts had cleared away any survivors. Her fellow Americans were dying of hunger but for Lucinda these things might as well have been happening in Sumatra or Melanesia. Oh, she realized that occasionally a cocktail party was more sparsely attended than had been originally planned, a hole blown in the guest list by the suicides of financier acquaintances. And for these she was sorry, in a small, private, rather confused way. When stories were told – of men locking the doors to

their offices and burning papers before resting the muzzle of a
.32 against their trembling, furred tongues – she faded a little
for a while, her eyes dimming and her head lowered. She was
imagining what she would do if Theodore, her husband, the
father of Luke Kane, were to drive his car into a wall, leap
from an open window, hang from a rafter in the stables. But
then she remembered that this would never happen and her
countenance would clear.

Theodore Kane was a wise man, wiser than many knew.
His money, birthed on Wall Street from the mountainous pile
of notes left to him by his father, had been spirited away long
before. His money, some in soiled notes, some in fresh-cut
blocks, in bullion, diamonds and Krugerrand, was spilled all
over the world as if the winds of change had carried it to
Zurich, Jersey, the Bahamas. Indeed, Theodore was a very
wise man – he kept his opinions to himself. He read the papers
and talked in his clubs over Havanas and cognac, he spoke
with senators and busboys, he called the bankers of Zurich
and spent afternoons in the Jewish back rooms of the West
Forties, watching diamonds perform their angular tumble
from small leather sacks as voices murmured.

When he had finished reading and writing, speaking and
thinking, he had formed three opinions: that Europe would
soon go to war, that a massive investment in steel would be
prudent, and that his wife was an imbecile. In all three of these
he was proved right, with one minor amendment: it took far
longer than he had imagined possible for Europe to face down
the Austrian bully-boy. By 1937 Theodore Kane was known as
Mr Steel, a sobriquet he relished in private but affected to dis-
like in public.

The combination of these three realizations caused

Theodore Kane to withhold himself from his wife. Oh, he would pass inconsequential conversations with her over the dinner table, would sometimes spend a weekend at the Hamptons during the dog-panting days of August, would ensure that her accounts were flush with cash. But of himself he gave nothing. He would buy cars and horses, crates of moonshine, hire gardeners, fire chauffeurs. He would, in fact, do anything to keep her happy, for when she was happy she was undemanding of him. He would even slip into her bedroom occasionally and crawl between her legs, slightly revolted by the extreme paleness of her skin and the patches of freckles. But she would writhe and give him dry, powdery kisses on his neck and so he supposed she was satisfied. The one thing he would not give her was his seed; always he pulled away so that it spilled on the laundered sheets. Theodore Kane wanted another son, for he disliked Luke, but he would not have another until he was certain of this world.

Perhaps it was this deep, curved hollow Lucinda felt at the centre of herself that caused her to turn to Luke for comfort; perhaps she would have loved Luke too much even without the cold splash of her husband's indifference washing over her. She sought Luke as a heliotrope seeks the sun, with certainty, each morning. Perhaps if Luke had not had the face of an archangel, this would not have happened; if, perhaps, he had not been so complaisant in this love affair, Lucinda would have tried to seduce her husband rather than her son.

Luke Kane was protected from so much during his childhood that he should not have been expected to understand the word 'danger'. Yet he did, simply because he himself was dangerous. Visitors to the Kane mansion in the Hamptons shied away

from him, as he lay in the cradle, as he sat in a pram, as he tod-
dled from room to room during the endless cocktail parties.
Henry Ford knelt to speak with Luke Kane, looked into the
child's eyes and stood hastily, searching for a distraction.
Governor Roosevelt stepped aside so that Luke Kane would
not brush against him, would not touch him. Even his father,
Theodore Kane, was wary in his son's company, although he
could not have explained why, had he been asked.

The only person who adored Luke Kane unreservedly was
Lucinda. She would call him into her swagged, ruched bedroom each morning and would coax him on to the plush
four-poster bed where she would lie with him for hours, marvelling over his every word, his every motion. In turn he
marvelled at her childlike hands, her clear skin, her lisping,
high-pitched voice – why, she was hardly more than a child
herself. He would help her dress, selecting shifts and petticoats, silk blouses and tight skirts. Lucinda encouraged him to
roll sleek stockings over her elegant legs, tapping his wrist as
he reached the softest part of her thigh, smiling a peek-a-boo
smile and dimpling lusciously – a mixture of apparently innocent humour and sensual licence. Often the two of them
would lie like vixen and favoured pup on the rumpled sheets
in shafts of afternoon sunlight, Luke Kane resting on his
mother's naked breasts, a pudgy hand kneading the soft flesh,
to both their satisfaction. His father would appear at the door
and look at this scene, to be reminded not of Madonna and
Child but of Morgan Le Fay and Mordred, occasionally of
Romulus and Remus, with himself cast as Faustulus.
Theodore would move away from the picture, unsettled, his
groin sparking, his heart aching, his mind undecided.

*

At seven Luke Kane was sent by his father to a private school, housed in a charmless building of solemnity and solidity, which claimed to instil the virtues of diligence, integrity and a sense of civic duty in its wards. On the day of Luke's admittance to Christchurch Prep Lucinda wept and held him close, running her hands over his face as a blind woman might. Luke Kane stood motionless through this, neither pushing his mother away nor returning the affection. Theodore eventually pulled her away, shook hands with Luke and propelled him through the door. Throughout the tear-stormed journey back to the Hamptons Lucinda refused to speak to Theodore, refused to cease sobbing and when they reached home refused food and drink, retiring to her room to savour her sorrow.

When Luke Kane walked through the gates of Christchurch Preparatory School the other boys were awestruck, although none would have admitted it. The most masculine, the frailest, the stoutest, the saddest of boyish hearts leaped when confronted with Luke Kane. Yet none would go near him, hampered either by shyness or by a sense of self-preservation. Luke Kane excelled, of course, in each subject, in each sport. He was the golden boy cast in fool's gold. As the other boys in his dormitory slept through the long fall nights dreaming of Luke Kane, he would lie with his hands cupping his penis, awake, his eyes shining, thinking of lying on a vast bed with his petite mother, imagining the cat-fur-soft skin on the swell of her tiny breasts.

Each vacation when Luke Kane returned to the house at Long Island Theodore looked for change, searched his son's face for signs of diligence, integrity and civic duty, and each time he was disappointed, for in their place he saw an indolent languor, a shamelessness, a disdainful indifference to others. Luke Kane was shrewd. His vacations were spent with his mother, shopping in New York, sailing out of Long Island, horse-riding and swimming. They played together as adolescent friends, with Theodore looking on, unable to disturb this balance, this status quo. For Luke Kane rarely spoke with his father, and when they did meet Luke Kane was unfailingly polite and reserved. But Theodore knew, always knew, exactly what Luke Kane was.

The first time Luke Kane brushed his pubescent palm over his mother's nipple, watching in delight as the skin puckered and a pulse began to jump at her throat, it was Lucinda who looked away, unable to accommodate this. Luke Kane watched her as she closed her eyes and watched her as she moved away from him. She curled into herself, a tiny woman in the middle of a ruck of silk sheets rippling around her, as if she were a stone thrown into an unfathomable well.

At eleven years old Luke Kane returned to his school with a knowledge that he should not have possessed, and this knowledge imbued him with an assurance which sat unusually easily on his shoulders. It was this assurance, this braggadocio, which was to be his undoing, for it attracted the attention of those who were least able to imagine that things could be otherwise. A supple youth, who before Luke Kane's arrival had been himself the subject of many tortured dreams, spent hours cold in his bed, sleepless, imagining what it would be like simply to brush Luke Kane's lips with his own. So it was that he crept one night into the room Luke Kane shared with one adenoidal other. Luke Kane was awake, lying between the sheets waiting to grow older, waiting for time to pass so that he might do the things he wished to do, as the gilded youth slithered over him, caught Luke Kane's mouth unawares, and pressed his taut, exquisite thighs against Luke Kane's groin. The gilded youth groaned and spurted as the room-mate snored through an adenoidal ganglion.

Two weeks later Luke Kane found the youth in a glade not far from the school, reading in a knot of trees visible from the principal's office. Luke Kane sprawled next to the smitten boy and smiled. He shook the book loose from the boy's fingers and leaned forward until he hung over the boy's adoring face. As Luke Kane pushed himself between the white, clenched buttocks, he glanced over his shoulder at the windows of the principal's room, finding himself disappointed that there was no appalled face to be seen watching him. Minutes later, as he beat his fists time and again into the boy's fragile, fine-boned face, he was smiling still.

It is possible that Luke Kane would have contented himself with his mother, would have been content to stroke and probe her soft yet strangely cool body. He might have continued to do this to both his and his mother's delight until he discovered other diversions. He might even have been eventually redeemed if Yugoslavia had not fallen to the Balkan blitzkrieg, pounded by Stukas and Messerschmitts, the echoes of which bombardment sent the scions of Wall Street scurrying home to their cabals. For if Yugoslavia had not fallen then Theodore would have stayed at his desk, would have eaten in his club, would have spent the Easter weekend in his hotel on East 85th trying to persuade those who would listen of what he had known for years: that Europe was tearing apart at its fragile seams and that the signs had been there for all to see for years, for as long as his son had been alive. But no one listened, believing that he wanted war because he would be a major player in the race to arms, supplying the munitions industry with his own steel. No one believed that he thought the cause just, no one believed that he thought that America was obliged, morally bound, to act. When he spoke, all they could hear was the sound of money pouring into the Kane coffers. So they turned away from him, too concerned with convincing each other of the honour that lay in appeasement and isolation to listen to his arguments.

Theodore Kane sprawled on the supple black leather in the back of his car as his driver whispered him out of New York and east to the Hamptons. The car rolled and bucked, lulling him into a near-sleep as the city drifted past. Theodore was overwhelmed by a sense of black destiny as the car rolled along the strangely empty roads. As his head rocked against the leather he felt the cancer of historical certainty buried deep in his guts and in a half-dream he imagined he saw the fields of Europe splashed with gaudy patterns of blood. He imagined he saw Yugoslavia turn in on itself and fall silently, unloved, unmourned. He tried to crawl away from these images but it was not until the car glided to a halt in front of the house that he succeeded.

Theodore opened the door, looked around the hallway, lined with oils and tapestries, peppered with flowers, its polished floor covered with Turkish rugs, and sat on a chair he had not even noticed before, a delicate Chippendale, ornate and fine, which cracked in surprise at his weight. In his hand he still held his briefcase and daily paper, still he wore his heavy coat and scarf. He leaned forward, allowing the case and papers to slide to the floor as he dropped his head into his hands and so he sat for the next hour, compressed by grief for things he could not change. It was the telephone ringing on the table next to him that broke his pose. He reached for it and answered, speaking for minutes before standing, shucking off his coat and roaring, into the startled silence, 'Luke!'

Luke Kane was home for the Easter vacation, and at the moment that his father's roar flew across the hallway he was lying in his mother's bed, smiling lazily as his mother's tiny, hot, dry hands caressed him, slipping between his legs, as the roar raced up the stairs and scattered against the door. Lucinda's china-blue eyes slammed open and her tongue became dusty with terror. She had no time to dissemble; she had no time to turn the hands of the clock back to the day when Luke had first brushed her nipple and she had, with her silence, acquiesced; she had no time to recast herself as mother rather than harlot, no time to claw back the opportunities to change this, to make things other than they were. She scurried backwards on her haunches, feral and fearful, catching her feet in the stained sheets as the door flew open, crashing against the dresser, shattering the glass on its top, turning over scent bottles which leaked their contents in oily drops on to the carpet.

Lucinda was never again able to wear the perfume of Chanel, was unable to encounter its scent without recoiling as if from a blow. The smell became for her the signifier of that night, its fragrance became a stench. The stench of silence. Because Theodore said nothing, as if the bellowing of Luke's name had emptied him. He stood, colossal and awful, in the doorframe, his face shadowed by a terrible knowledge. He stood and looked at his wife and his son caught in a pose so crude, so *unlikely*, that his anger was held, for a time, in abeyance. He stood and watched his wife gather the sheets around her in tiny, ineffectual motions, as his son's tumescence subsided. He watched as Lucinda slipped awkwardly away from the bed, away from her son and her husband, to go into the bathroom, closing the door gently. Theodore and Luke Kane looked at each other across the room for minutes, stoking their hatred for each other. Theodore looked at his son and saw depravity, saw the son of Laius; Luke Kane looked at his father and saw impotence.

Theodore's anger finally burst its dam and thundered across the shapely body on the bed. He grasped Luke Kane's still-forming wrist and dragged him from the mattress, as his son howled and screamed for his mother, hoping she would come and divert this fury. But Lucinda was standing frozen in her bathroom as she listened to Theodore beating his son, shouting about the telephone call that had broken his grieving. The young boy whom Luke Kane had raped and beaten so savagely had finally broken his silence, telling his mother in tear-broken sentences what had happened as the two of them took tea in a café in Boston. The mother had called the principal of Christchurch Prep who in turn had called Theodore. Luke Kane was no longer welcome at the school and was fortunate not to be facing a court case. The only reason he had been spared this was that the mother had not wished her son to face the taunts that would surely follow.

In the decades that followed Theodore would often think of that afternoon, when Yugoslavia fell and Luke Kane was exposed. He thought of it when he was old and alone, and, like Lucinda, he would imagine turning back the hands of the clock, the pages of the calendar, so that he, too, might make things different. But as he sat with a blanket over his knees, hands trembling, he could not imagine how he might have made things different, how he might have made his son *right*. And all the old man that Theodore became could imagine having done differently was not to have conceived Luke Kane at all. Often he thought of how he had sat in his hallway on the Chippendale chair, his aching eyes closed, his head snug in his palm, thinking of Europe fracturing as the telephone rang. While the principal spoke it had never occurred to Theodore that Luke Kane might not have done those things because Theodore knew that he had, could only too easily imagine the smile on his son's face as he raped and destroyed.

Lucinda waited in the bathroom for hours, until the sounds of male pain and fury disappeared. When she could hear only her own breathing she stepped into her room and the stink of Chanel roused her gorge and she retched, throwing up on the pale peach rug in front of the dresser. She sank down, a wan, diminutive Jocasta in her makeshift toga of satin sheets, and bowed her head. Later, when she looked up blearily through the miasma of vomit and perfume, she saw her husband lying naked on the bed.

'Luke,' he said, his eyes fixed on the ceiling 'has gone. I have sent him away to a place where he will be fed and housed, where he will be educated and contained. In the vacations he will stay in that place. He will not return here. If we are asked about him we will say he has gone to California to stay with an aunt. You may, if you wish, say that he has been evacuated in case of America becoming involved in the war. You will say nothing about this evening. We shall not speak of it again.

'I will not forgive you. I will not pardon you. I will not help you try to explain or excuse what you have done. It is unforgivable and you are culpable, as if you even know what that means. Neither will I throw you out, as I possibly should and as many men would. In exchange for this uncommon indulgence, I expect another child, another son. Some might remark upon the reasonableness of the request.'

Elizabeth Kane was born at twenty-two minutes past two on 7 December 1941, as the tapes on the teleprinters began to spew and chatter in New York. Two and a half thousand men died in the flames of Pearl Harbor as Elizabeth was blown into the world by her mother's reluctant convulsions. The Kanes had marked yet another of America's rites of passage.

1997

As the limousine, black and discreet, engineered to within a whisker of perfection, murmurs its way south past Central Park, Flanagan watches Bronwen light a liquorice stick-thin More cigarette. She presses a button on the door and the window whispers down an inch, smoke snaking out frisky as a unicorn's tail. Her white, babyish hands, coruscated with rings, cushioned with excess flesh, flash pale in the neon that leaks into the back of the car. Her hair, hanging, now, in tailored ringlets, is lustrous and thick. Her lips glisten with pearly Tahitian Tint and her eyes have been made large by deft brushes of chestnut powder. An artist of maquillage has managed to tease the suggestion of cheekbones from the doughy moon that is her face. She is sheathed in a Vivienne Westwood creation, moulded to her startling form, corseted, bustled and bristling with epaulettes. Bronwen Jones has changed; she has become, the lieutenant decides, quite magnificent.

The limousine floats to a halt, the difference between motion and inertia all but denied by its buttered wheels. Bronwen flicks the embers of the cigarette on to the sidewalk of Fifth Avenue and waits for the driver to open the door. 'I'll call when I need you again,' she says, sweeping past the chauffeur and into the lobby of the hotel.

Flanagan is mesmerized by the velvet-bustled backside as it sashays down the halls to the elevators, and meekly he follows the vision. The elevator battles with the laws of physics as the two of them are whisked, considerable stomachs lurching slightly, to the penthouse that is now Bronwen's home.

The doors open on a suite so large, so lavish with its bounties, that Flanagan is dismayed. He steps backwards and is nearly pulled into the vortex as the elevator doors close. Bronwen slams her pudgy fist against the call button and he is reprieved. He steps out cautiously, unsure of himself, as Bronwen throws her purse down on a sofa and eases off her high-sheen, high-heeled shoes. Not knowing what else to do Flanagan looks at Bronwen's feet, watches the toes, which have been pinched to the shape of a viper's head, separate slowly and open petal-like. Bronwen groans with relief and heads for the open kitchen. 'Will you be wanting a cup of tea? Or something else?' she asks.

'Tea would be just fine.'

'Sit yourself down. I won't be a moment.' Bronwen moves round the Carrera-marble-wrapped kitchen, then waddles off to another room.

Flanagan walks around the suite, which has a three-sixty-degree view of Manhattan, the elevator rising in its centre like a mushroom stalk. He is mesmerized by the view, by the spangling neon atoms jumping in their glass cages, just as Iris was forty-seven years before when she watched the Manhattan skyline dance on her tenth birthday. Flanagan, made slightly dreamy by the Irish whiskey moving like mercury in his veins, walks twice around the suite, made childlike by delight, naming buildings, trying to place streets and bridges, delighted by the size of the cars, by the sight of the foreshortened pygmies scurrying below. It is five o'clock in the morning and Manhattan is still jive-dancing, pulling the pygmies back and forth across its map, jerking their strings, making marionettes of the night-people and their desires. Flanagan sighs and his breath clouds the glass, makes obscure the picture of two cars colliding silently. The windows are so thickly glazed that the bedlam of eight million people yawning and brawling, screaming and snoring, the sounds of revving juggernauts, klaxons and planes howling overhead are all rendered impotent. As the mist of his breath clears he sees a pale reflection of Bronwen in the window. He watches her go to the kitchen and pour tea, not wanting to turn and acknowledge her, not wanting to move away from the vision that has entranced him since he was a child.

'Sugar?' asks Bronwen.

'Huh?'

'Do you take sugar in your tea?'

'No, no, thank you.' Flanagan sighs and moves away from the window, sits on a sofa, an island floating in a beige-carpeted sea.

Bronwen gives him the tea and sits opposite, her chubby legs pulled neatly beneath her in a movement so deft that Flanagan is reminded of her dancing that night and he blushes. 'I have to say, it took me a while to put two and two together when I was told your name. Then I remembered – we bumped into each other at the rest home. So, Lieutenant, what were you doing in the club tonight? I wouldn't have imagined it was your cup of tea.'

'My cup of tea?'

'You know, not your sort of thing.'

'It's not, it's not. I've never been anywhere like that.'

'So why were you there? Were you looking for me?' Bronwen's piggy eyes narrow as she remembers the money she took from Matron's desk, the money she had guarded jealously in a tattered manilla envelope. A mere four thousand dollars – a bagatelle, a trifle. Bronwen smiles slightly at the memory of her having thought it a fortune, great scads of money. For now she knows it is nothing, that it bought her nothing but the fear of losing it. Since meeting Sam her notion of how things should be, of the worth of things, of the worth of her *self* has changed. But she is aware that the lieutenant might not take such a worldly view.

'Looking for you? No, not at all. Why would I have been?'

'No reason.' Bronwen shrugs. 'So it was a coincidence that you were there?'

'Sure. I was just meeting a friend, y'know.'

Bronwen looks at him appraisingly, and it is this look that amazes Flanagan, because it is so calculating and cool, so measured, that it is itself the measure of how far Bronwen has moved from the dumpy naïf, tightly wrapped in a white uniform with flat shoes and an unformed mind, whom he saw fleetingly in the Emerald Rest Home. He calculates how long ago that was – ten, maybe eleven weeks in the city has wrought this change.

Flanagan heaves himself forward on the sofa, tries to order his thoughts, which have been jumbled by a startling night. 'Look, Bronwen, I swear I just saw you in that club. It was coincidence, nothing more.'

'So why did you ask for me? Don't tell me it was for old times' sake.'

'No, no, not for that.'

Bronwen leans forward to collect her cigarettes and lighter from the coffee table, her alarming breasts bunching and growing beneath the stiff, scalloped dress. The lieutenant blinks. 'Then for what, Lieutenant? You want to fuck?' Ever since the afternoon when Bronwen discovered that she could say 'fuck' and not be struck down by a bolt of electric blue God-fury, some might say that she has been overusing the word.

'Oh, Lord, no.' Flanagan's blush grows deeper. 'Not that, well, no, I . . . That wasn't the idea.'

'So, if it's not your sexual desires, Lieutenant, that brought you here, what can it be?' Bronwen lolls back on the cushions like a bloated Tallulah Bankhead.

The lieutenant stands and crosses to the window, trying to clear his mind. 'You were in the room that day when I went to the rest home, d'you remember? I came in one afternoon to talk with Iris.'

The smile on Bronwen's face disappears and she becomes wary. 'Yes, I remember.'

'And she had a stroke and couldn't speak? D'you remember that?'

'No, I didn't know. Poor Iris.'

'Did you talk to her at all? I mean, y'know, before that? When she talked sense?'

'Well, yes. I talked to all the patients. I was a good nurse. I was a *good* nurse.'

Flanagan's heart tears a little as he hears the plaint in Bronwen's voice. He looks down at Fifth Avenue, sees the cars still tangled from the crash minutes before. Men are standing in the street gesticulating, waving matchstick arms and pushing each other as a woman in sleek ivory silk leans against one of the dented hoods, her head in her hands. 'I'm sure you were, Bronwen. I'm sure you were an excellent nurse. Did Iris say anything about her family?'

'A bit, not much.'

'Did she mention her son?'

'Yes.'

Two hundred feet below the men have begun to swing their little twiggy arms at each other. One man falls in the slush, his legs sliding from beneath him, his coat fanning out in the snow. 'What did she say about him?'

'Nothing much.'

The whiskey in the lieutenant's veins begins to thin and he remembers that questions can turn corners. 'Why did you leave the home so suddenly, Bronwen? What are you looking for?'

He can hear the faint creak of a cigarette being smoked behind him, a sound so faint it could be a leaf growing.

Below him he can see the blue strobe lights of police cars approaching the crash. The cars are blocks away from the scene but he, Flanagan, knows they are approaching. This knowledge gives him a misplaced, drunken sense of omnipotence.

'If you must know, I'm looking for Chum Kane.'

The lieutenant lurches a little, puts his hands against the glass to steady himself. He turns and looks at the vision of violet and rust velvet, organdie and chintz on the sofa. 'What do *you* know about Chum Kane?'

'Enough.'

'Enough for what?'

'Enough for me.' Bronwen blows a tight cone of smoke heavenwards and stubs out the slim brown butt. She looks at

Flanagan, her lips forming a plump *moue*. 'You don't have twelve hundred dollars, do you, Lieutenant Flanagan?'

'No.'

'How much money do you have?'

The lieutenant fumbles in his pocket, draws out a battered billfold and counts the few limp, much-thumbed notes. 'I have fifty-three bucks.'

'You didn't come here to fuck me, did you?'

'No.'

'I didn't do well at school, didn't like it, if you want to know the truth, but I'm not such a fool as people think. If you came with no money, having met Sam, either you think I'm going to give it away or you want something else.' Bronwen stands and smooths the crumpled velvet round her butt. 'All you've asked me is stuff about Iris. When you came to the rest home it was to see Iris.' Bronwen walks to the window, stands next to Flanagan, and the two of them watch a police car slew to a halt, headlamps lighting the fight in the road. 'Now, Iris is a sick woman who has probably led a blameless life, as me mam would say. The only interesting thing about Iris is her son.'

'Why is he interesting?'

'Oh, come on, man, you think he's interesting, don't you? Otherwise you wouldn't be here.'

'Maybe.'

The reverie of the woman in ivory silk has been broken by the blue strobes and she looks up to see cops in uniform striding towards her.

'How are you going to find him?' asks Flanagan, as his eyes follow the developments below, watching the woman straighten her dress and rearrange her hair.

'I'll find him.'

'How? You don't know anything about him.'

'No. But *you* do, I should think. I mean, you're a police-man.'

'So? Maybe I know a few things. So what?'

'Well, you're looking for him too, aren't you? Seems that way to me. Maybe we can help each other.'

Flanagan frowns. This is not what he expected. He is being boxed in, forced to move from one point to another in an ever-diminishing area. On Fifth Avenue the traffic is backing up as a tow-truck arrives. The cops stop, unholster their guns, hold them easily in their hands. 'Bronwen, what do you know? What do you know about Chum Kane?'

'Like I said, enough.'

'Enough for what?'

'Enough to know I want him.'

Flanagan finally realizes what she is saying. '*You* stole the photograph. You've got that photograph. That's why you left. Shit, you know what Chum Kane looks like.'

Bronwen smiles.

'Bronwen, can I see it? Please can I see the photograph?'

'Of course not.'

Flanagan looks out of the window once more, breathing heavily. What to do? His heart has been set racing like a hare before hounds by the thought that there is someone who can point to Mr Candid in a crowd and say, 'That's him.' And that person is standing right next to him, dressed not unlike Mary Queen of Scots. He knows that Bronwen will not give him the photograph, will not let him see it. What to do? What does she want?

'What do you want?' he asks.

'I want to come with you.'

'Where? Where am I going?'

'Well, how the hell do I know, man? If I did I'd be there by now. My guess is you're going to the last place that you know he's been. Am I right?'

Flanagan is still watching the ivory-silk woman. She is moving towards the gun-toting cops, her manner easy, confident. He can discern that much, even from such a height, and he frowns slightly, knowing that her money and power will iron out this problem. Flanagan thinks how cold she must be without a coat.

'Am I right?' Bronwen asks again.

'What?' Flanagan turns to look at her.

'Did Iris say something, give you any clues?'

'Yes.'

'Then let me come with you. I know what he looks like and you don't. You need me.'

Flanagan sighs as he realizes that she is right. 'What about all this?' He gestures around the penthouse.

'It's not mine. I can leave it. Have you got a car?'

'Yeah. It's in a garage.'

'I'll call the desk and arrange for someone to fetch it.'

'Bronwen, I have to ask – why do you want to find him so bad?'

Bronwen laughs. 'If you'd seen the photo, you'd know why.'

Keeler is sitting in an unmarked car across the street from Bronwen's apartment, the boredom of his vigil broken by the succession of wailing police cars that have been passing, followed by tow-trucks. So busy is he speculating about the reasons for their passing that he nearly misses Lieutenant Flanagan and Bronwen Jones climbing into a dull, grey car, which is brought to the apartment block's entrance. He nudges the driver and gestures for him to follow. 'At least she ain't difficult to spot,' he mutters. 'Wake me when anything happens.'

Las Vegas – April

M –

Dawn this morning: I'm on a plane flying LA to Reno. The plane taxis and takes off and you look out and think there can't be anything much more beautiful as you fly over the desert. I mean, there's the sun, there are the Sierras, and nothing. No water, nothing. Then I see some strange lake below and ask a stewardess what it is. Her face is like a blank screen. I mean, she's not picking up any signals. Seconds pass. She smiles a deranged smile and says she's got no idea, she'll ask the captain, so off she goes and comes back, still smiling like a mad woman, and she tells me he doesn't know either. So I thank her and look back out the window, and for God's sake, there's Half Dome and Grand Capitan. So it's got to be Mono Lake, right? I mean, for Chrissake, it's just one of those things you know. Eventually we bounce out the clouds and skitter along the runway at Reno, swimming through warm air so arid that you can hear your skin creak. I get in the airport and everyone's playing the machines, just playing the machines, punching and jabbing at those buttons, hoping one of them will unleash a dream. And outside is the desert, just rolling away, but I guess they don't think much about that. So I hire a car and drive to Vegas.

You may be wondering about the intelligence of flying hundreds of miles north to hire a car and drive hundreds of miles south. The reason I did it, in case you're wondering like most normal people would, is because I didn't want to hire a car in California and drive it out of state. Same as I've always done – zigzig backwards and forwards in crazy lines that no one would guess at. It took seven hours to drive here through places like you'd never believe existed. Why does anyone live in Nevada? What's the point? The car's on cruise control and so is my mind.

And I start to think of you. Like I always do when there's nothing on the horizon. I feel like I've been blocking you out for years. I don't know why I thought I could do that for ever, although seventeen years has sometimes felt like for ever. I'm heading for Tonopah and I've got the map flapping on my lap and I realize that if I don't stop, if I just keep going, then that road will take me straight to Mexico and maybe *that*'s where you are. And maybe not, because you could be anywhere. You might even be back in Harvard, which is a weird thought. I can imagine it easily, though. You just sliding along the corridors of academe with your hair flying and men hanging off you like ticks. Which would be nothing new.

Remember the time we had that fight in some bar on the Square? I can't remember the name of the place, but I see it real clear – had half a '47 Oldsmobile sticking out the wall. You'd been to a religious-education class that morning and you were rattling away about the Gnostics, how seductive their theories were, you know, about how we're born with a divine spark but then dropped into a material world where we're going to be spun about by fate,

kismet, karma, life and death. And the Gnostics believed
that only those who achieved mastery over esoteric
knowledge would be reunited with the Creator, with the
spirit. I can hear you saying it now – 'esoteric knowledge',
in your strange, cracked voice, saying it like you had
something valuable in your mouth. And I started to piss
you off, asking questions about who, exactly, was going to
be able to acquire this knowledge if it was only for an
initiated minority, and who chooses the minority, and –
this was the killer – where the fuck did you get off getting
romantic about something defined as a 'divine spark'? I
said all this as only a rampant, egocentric behaviourist
could. You picked up your beer and threw it at me, glass
and all, and I watched you walk out, wanting to run after
you.

I think of myself sitting there in the bar, so dogmatic, so
opinionated, as if I were the fount of all axioms, and I
want to shoot myself. Because now I'm lying here on a
motel bed off the Strip in Las Vegas and all around me
people are spinning the wheels of fate in the most venal,
avaricious society on earth, but now I know that there *is* a
divine spark, or something like it, and you had it. Is that
the esoteric knowledge that I was supposed to acquire?
And will it save me?

I did follow you after a while, from the bar, I mean. I
never told you, but I followed you across the Square to
Halls and watched you walk up those echoing stairs. You
dropped some books and when you bent down to pick
them up I could see that you were so sad.

Love,
Chum

Iris Chandler has not walked for six and a half thousand days. For years she has lain in bed and defied the medical authorities to diagnose her complaint. So many diagnoses have been offered that it would be a miracle that she is still alive had any of them been accurate; indeed, if she were to throw aside the bed sheets and skip across the room, her healer would be hailed not so much as a miracle-worker as a necromancer. Doctors, specialists, consultants, quacks, herbalists, homeopaths, surgeons, sawbones, psychiatrists and alienists have all examined her, their fees paid by the infinite bubbling of the pelf-well dug by an anonymous hand. She has been cauterized, poked, stabbed, prodded, X-rayed, manipulated, poulticed, bandaged, venesected. Earnest young men have questioned, coaxed, quizzed, interrogated, examined and grilled her. However, even medics have their limitations, and after a deal of informed argument between the representatives of the various august bodies of the profession, they agreed to differ – Iris was suffering from a neurological complaint, nerve sclerosis, a neurone disease, a complaint of the thyroid, a complaint of the mind – and then they went their own ways, wallets bulging. Iris was left to her bed and her memories of what it was like to walk out into the day.

Now, however, Iris wants to be able to walk, wants to cross the slick linoleum aisle between her bed and the matron's. Iris may flubber and gibber, may now be unable to speak as well as being bedridden, but her mind, trapped behind the web-like portcullis of her brain's burst veins, can still construct simple scenarios. She imagines herself climbing silently from her bed in the dead of night, walking across to Matron, smothering her, then walking back to her bed and lying down for the last time. Iris's memory banks are all but empty, some handfuls of loose change all that is left rattling about in them, yet she remembers enough to know that Matron cannot live because she knows a lot about Charlie Kane and no one must know about Charlie Kane. Iris still cannot remember why, exactly, this is so important but she knows that it is.

So each night she tries to flex her muscles – pitiful little strings of hope, thin and flexible as spittle, hanging loosely from bootlace tendons. She bunches her five fingers into a fist, squeezes tightly and releases it, over and over, worried that she may not be strong enough to hold down the pillow with her stump. She tries to sit up without help, raises her legs beneath the sheet and flexes her knees. She practises pulling out the catheters in her arms and replacing them. And all the while she imagines crossing the floor and placing the pillow, pushing against it. Occasionally she near-cackles with delight, for it will be the perfect crime. After all, Iris has not walked for seventeen years: the perfect alibi.

Flanagan is sitting in his car on the forecourt of a gas station in Queens, trying not to burn his crotch with scalding coffee, which leaks from an insubstantial styrofoam cup. He is waiting for Bronwen to change her clothes in the restrooms. As they drove out of the city at dawn, across Queensborough Bridge, Bronwen's *haute couture* became increasingly outlandish the higher the sun rose, the colours of the velvet growing more garish with every passing mile and Flanagan eventually pulled over and suggested a change of costume.

As he waits he considers rummaging through the case Bronwen put in the trunk, to search for the likeness of Chum

Kane, but he knows it will not be there because Bronwen will always carry it with her. Flanagan sighs wearily, sips the coffee, which tastes only of heat, and scrubs at his eyes. He is weary. He looks around at the chrome-flashing slip-stream of cars beginning their journey into the city. He is surrounded by a jumble of hoardings and stop-lights, shabby shops and neon. What is he *doing* here? He should be in Miami, trying to shoehorn the prickly Barbars through the legal system so they may take their revenge on the state for the death of their son. Instead he is sitting in a cold car at a gas station, his body aching with a surfeit of whiskey and lack of sleep, travelling in search of a myth with a two-hundred-pound woman whose idea of discretion is to dress high-camp sixteenth-century.

The restroom door slams open behind him and he looks with consternation in the rear-view mirror. He sees Bronwen heading for the car, her face scrubbed, her hair tied back, wearing jeans and a sweatshirt, and he sighs once more, this time with relief.

'I need something to eat,' she says, as she thumps down on the passenger seat.

'Sure. No problem. We'll stop at the next place.'

Keeler, sitting in the unmarked car in the forecourt of a Japanese restaurant opposite, is feeling as shabby as Flanagan. He hates Queens, does not want to be there.

'Follow them,' he says to the driver, as Flanagan pulls out in search of breakfast. He reaches for the radio and calls headquarters, and so he begins to cast the net around Flanagan and Bronwen, who are themselves casting their own nets.

Las Vegas – April

M –

Sorry to write again so soon but I've got some time on my hands here, waiting for a flight to New York. I just had a day like you wouldn't believe – like no one would believe. I strolled around town, dressed down, still crushed, like a loser, like every salesman from Minneapolis who's ever gone to Vegas for a good time and found only bafflement. I walked into every bank where I had money saved, every deposit box where I stashed chips, promissory notes, IOUs, rings, deeds, car keys, house keys – you name it. It's amazing what people will throw on the table at three in the morning with the whisky half gone, the battle half done. You've got them then, whether the cards are with you or not. You just nail them with a look, like it's half pity, half admiration that they'll give away anything, *anything*, just to win the next hand, just to pull off one big win in all the years they've been trying. People always ask – what do you look for when the guy has raised you $250,000 and you've got a pair of threes and a pair of sixes and you know, you just know, he's running two jacks and three kings? Well, you don't look for anything, you simply calculate. At least, that's what I did.

I came back to the motel room and spread it all out on the bed, and guess what? I'm one rich bastard. Turns out I got houses in Palm Beach, Houston, Santa Monica, Old Greenwich, London and East Orange (I'll pass on the last). I've got apartments in Paris, on the Grand Canal in Venice and in Manhattan. I've got Ferraris, Porsches, a Jag, two '64 Mustangs and a few Harleys. Not to mention an island off the Caymans, the leasehold of an atoll in the Maldives and a villa on Capri. And that's without the cash. So I'm walking round Vegas with more money and assets than anyone here dreams of and because I look like a foozler no one takes any notice of me. I walked around with drafts and cheques for more than fifteen million dollars, along with three million in cash (my substantial assets of stocks and shares are banked elsewhere) and even the jive talkers and hustlers ignored me.

I guess you may have been wondering where the cash comes from to support me in the life I lead – you know, buying cars, moving around, hotels, houses, flights all over the place. Well, that's where. Remember I told you that when I went to Harvard that first semester, when I was thirteen, the first class they moved me into was pure math? I can still picture walking into that lecture room for the first time. It was cold and there were those huge arched windows with lots of panes of glass, a long, sloping bank of seats, full of guys with long hair, beards and glasses, all looking at me like I was shit. I sat on my own in the front bench, with no one near me, and I felt like crying. I just wanted to be back home with Lydia and my mom. But I guess I also wanted to know everything, I wanted to know everything so much that I didn't care that the other students were such assholes. Of course, now I know they weren't assholes, they were just scared, scared that I'd make them look dumb. Which, of course, I did without breaking sweat. Not right away, because I wasn't sure of myself. But while I might not have been sure of myself, I *was* sure about probability theories. So I'm sitting there, shaking, and the professor starts in on distribution, random variables and associated probabilities. Before I know it I'm arguing about the derivative slope of F and the impossibility of zero skewedness in empirical exemplar. Maybe I shouldn't have; I don't know all these years later if I should have maybe just sat there and kept my mouth shut, but all the other students were shitting bricks because they had no idea about what I was saying. After a few weeks the hostility got so bad that I had private tuition for pure math.

But the point is that that lesson started it all. I learned my theories of Gaussian distribution, threw in a little sidewinder of Poisson theory and worked out a sure-fire numbers game. In the evenings I used to play around with cards and dice and counters, just messing about sorting out theories. Fact is, people like me are supposed to understand the theories and then go on and learn some more. Maybe postulate some more. But others never think that people like me take those theories and go into the world and use them. Not in casinos, anyway. I wouldn't have done it, either, if I hadn't needed the money. It's like taking candy from a baby if you have a memory that can carry over a thousand integers and images and perform mental tricks with them at the same time. All the gamblers I've met wear the same tie or the same jacket or carry a shamrock or a monkey's paw or something when they hit the tables. All I take with me is $f(x) = (2\pi^{-1/2}\exp(-1/2x^2)$ with a little $\lambda^n e^{-\lambda}/n!$ thrown in along with a memory like Deep Blue and I do just fine.

Maybe I would have been a chemical engineer or a statistician or a psephologist if that night hadn't happened. Maybe I would have been all of those things that people wanted me to be. Maybe I would have been a futures trader on Wall Street. The way I look at it, that's what I do anyway: trade futures.

Love,

Chum

LUKE KANE

Luke Kane was sequestered in a Jesuit school in east California for the rest of his childhood, or what passed for childhood in his case: he arrived when he was eleven years old and left when he was eighteen. Luke Kane never discovered what his father said to the scholars, never heard what passed between his parents the night he and Lucinda were discovered, and he was perspicacious enough to realize that to ask would be futile. He spent his adolescence in an institution where all else but thought was dismissed. And so he thought when he was asked to, slept when he was told to and ate when food appeared. He seemed, to the delighted Jesuits, to be the perfect scholar, an ascetic whose life was blameless, whose room was spartan, whose mind was focused on the pursuit of knowledge.

Luke Kane had, of course, discovered long before how to dissemble. His life was not as eremitical as the priests believed, although it could have been argued that he was an aesthete, a scholar hunting down the notion of pure beauty. He hunted only those boys who were vulnerable, docile and acquiescent, those who were fair of face and full of grace. He remembered, too, the youth at Christchurch – his one error of judgement, his only miscalculation – and always he kept in his mind the picture he had constructed of that youth's tearful exposition of the events of that day. He remembered his father's promise that he would end Luke's life if there were any more scandals, and that promise was one of the few things that Luke Kane believed without qualification.

He was not incarcerated without respite, without relief. There were visits to other schools, there were many trips to the Salinas Valley, to ranches, to museums and theatres in the city, to the beach. There was the annual visit to Yosemite, to Mammoth Lakes, to Mono Lake. It was during a trip to Mono Lake – to conduct experiments on the salinity of the water, and the concomitant carbonate suspensions – that Luke Kane encountered eyes he could not turn, a heart he could not break. He had wandered away from the crowd of young boys, feeling old, feeling tired, when he saw a young priest alone at the edge of the cobalt shore. Luke Kane drifted, like scent, like feathers, towards the priest, his groin gathering, his hackles twitching. As he neared the priest he smiled, his blueberry-soft lips curling, eyes zaffre-smudged, his hair greased ebony. The priest reached out and pulled Luke Kane into the shadow of a tufa pillar, kissed him violently, touched him without tenderness, without care, and released him, never to speak to him again. Luke came, eventually, to admire the priest for his actions, but that afternoon in the light and shadow of the bleached Californian sun he wept. For what, exactly, he was crying he could not have said.

Theodore Kane lived alone in a house in Westchester once he had taken the decision that even if he wasn't going to divorce Lucinda he certainly wasn't going to live with her. Often, as the years passed, he stood in his study, looking over his deer-spotted

land, its immense lawns dotted with ponds, and remembered
his colleagues whispering his nickname behind his back,
remembered the column inches devoted to Mr Steel, and he
would grimace. For now he was made of shale, of sand, of
driftwood. He was a sack of skin filled with bones, shame and
regrets. He had been impregnable, tempered by resolution,
and yet Luke Kane had found the chink in his steel-plating,
glimpsed the red, beating heart within the armour, and had
pierced it. As Theodore stood at his study window in the
empty, echoing house, in the evenings of spring, summer,
winter and fall, watching leaves change, watching the deer
grow old, he watched his reflection in the window age with
them. And the thought that could make his pierced heart
bleed a little more was that he had waited for so long, had
judged his life so finely for so long, only to exact a revenge on
his wife who had left him with a daughter born on the very
day that America threw itself into a war.

Some might ask what difference that made to him, for he
rarely saw Elizabeth Kane, only occasionally visiting the mansion in East Hampton where she lived with her mother.
Theodore would arrive there on birthdays, at Christmas,
during sun-baked August days, and sit with the girl on the
beach, at the table, in the car on trips to Cape Cod. He tried to
talk to her, tried to celebrate the passing of her life, marked by
birthdays. He sat with her and tried to love her but he found
he could not. Elizabeth, who was known by everyone but her
father as Sugar, was not the son he had craved to replace Luke;
in fact, she was Luke's mirror. She shared many of his features
but they were softened, difficult to place, like an image
moving through glass. Theodore found it increasingly hard to
talk to her, to touch her, to love her at all, and so his visits

became fewer over the years until eventually the birthday presents arrived with the mailman, and in place of his being there, Theodore sent cheques.

He knew this to be wrong, knew it to be another failure. Yet each evening in his darkened house he sat and watched the deer, his mind chasing forever the image of Luke Kane in his mother's bed.

Lucinda lived the life of the indulged dim-witted. She banked the cheques, she ate at the finest restaurants, she attended the season's parties, sailed the Sound, mirrored the prejudices of whomsoever she found herself with, wherever that might be. She railed against Roosevelt, Hitler, rationing, the poor, the rich, the dispossessed, the powerful, the unfortunate, in a snake-twisting ganglion of contradictions. She simpered, she pouted, she pressed into everything. She considered herself popular, oblivious of the fact that it was the lure of money which attracted the feeding frenzy of attention that surrounded her. She would rise at noon, fuss with Sugar, dressing her in frothing organdie, and have the driver take the pair of them into Manhattan to shop, for shopping was the only thing she did well. Lucinda Kane could shop long enough to break a bank, long enough to break a heart. Carpenters arrived at the house each month to build more cupboards to house the clothes, the glassware, the ornaments, the pictures, the trophies of wealth.

Lucinda loved Sugar, loved dressing her and pampering her plump little body. She could look at Sugar and think of Luke without pain – why, they were siblings! They were her children – of *course* she might think of them. It was only when she was holding Sugar Kane that she could think of Luke at all. At other times she could not picture him. When she was in the bath, when she was in bed or being driven – alone, as ever – to a party, sitting elegant and fine in the back of a top-range Cadillac, the image of Luke Kane escaped her, slipped from her hands, the thought capricious as a live fish. Lucinda was fortunate: she had so little imagination that she was not troubled by thoughts of what might have been.

Since the night when she had sat on her bedroom floor in a smear of Chanel-scented vomit, she had managed to obliterate the events that had brought her to that. She had convinced herself that Luke Kane had been sent away for his own safety, which was, of course, true. Theodore had forbidden her to see him at school and she obeyed, for the price he would exact if she saw her son was one she could not imagine paying, because then she would no longer be indulged.

So Lucinda held Sugar close and waited for Luke to finish school. She shopped and partied, she crooned to her daughter and drank bourbon, flirted and slept alone, aching for company.

Luke Kane left the Jesuits' school with a small case of books, an acceptance from Harvard and one hundred dollars in cash. As the other students raced into the arms of their waiting parents, he walked away brimming with a sense of destiny. He set down the case and sat on it, his thumb extended, hitching a ride to San Francisco, knowing that the first car would stop to pick him up. He spent the night in the bars around Market, drinking beers, spilling froth down his crisp shirtfront, wailing and yahooing with whichever men crossed his path. As he spilled late out on to the sidewalk, his case lost, his tie long gone, he scented prey nearby. He found the house off Market, paid for three women and bucked the night away through to the hour of dawn, his buttocks bunching, his shoulders rising like a wounded bull's. While he slept the women stayed, smoking, saying nothing, simply watching his face as he dreamed of meeting his mother.

Luke Kane arrived home five days late that summer of 1947, the chauffeured car sweeping to a halt in front of Lucinda and Sugar, who were waiting to greet him on the steps of the Hampton house. Luke Kane woke slowly in the back of the car, his hair greasy and lank, his clothes grimed and crumpled, his skin the white-grey of the unwashed. He yawned, stretching his back, which was stiff from hunching over too many bodies, for by the end of his stay in San Francisco the women had desired him more than they wanted money. Luke Kane opened the car door and eased himself out, shading his eyes against the sun. He looked at his mother in silence. Where once she had been petite and demure she was now bloated with bourbon, her face wrecked by excess. He turned away from her and saw Sugar, her baby-dumpling fat melted away, her face open with hope and admiration, her tight little dress hugging her just so. Luke Kane looked at his sister and he smiled.

1997

Sam the Weasel Man is sitting in his booth at the XXX Cinema on 42nd. The gas fire hisses and rivulets of condensation roll down the spotted glass, making the street waver. Sam is picking between his remarkable teeth with a piece of folded card torn from the flap of his pack of Winstons. It's seven o'clock in the morning and the garbage men, green and grey, sweep the sidewalks and hose the gutters, a frothing wave of scum and paper, bottles, condoms, half-eaten pizzas and hot-dogs racing before them. The men work round the derelicts on street corners, in doorways, on benches. The sun shines on this daily ritual for the first time in months and Sam squints as the wet sidewalk glistens, stares at a tag-covered hydrant, unseeing, working a piece of debris from between his teeth. Sam likes to visit this cinema, one of the seediest outposts of his business empire. He finds that it is here, in the steamy booth, that his mind can roam, undistracted.

A wreck of a man comes to the booth, breathing heavily, his eyes swimming in rheum, his nails black with street filth. He fumbles in a pocket and pulls out a five, slipping it beneath the meshed glass. Sam punches out a ticket and slides it over to the man, holding his breath, trying to survive on the lungful of air he drew moments before, trying to evade the stench. Sam looks into the man's face, is saddened by the sores on his forehead, by the unstitched wound on his nose, left to scab and fester. The man shuffles away, into the anonymity of the theatre, and Sam rests his elbow on the counter, scrubs at his eyes. He has lost Bronwen. She hasn't returned. And, anyway, who the fuck is Lieutenant Flanagan? What is he to Bronwen?

Sam the Weasel Man is uneasy, twitchy. He can feel the puckered lips of the ulcer buried in the vascular, acidic walls of his stomach preparing to blow him a kiss. As he sits, unmoving, he notices the sudden, unlikely silence of the city. Where there should be horns and rumbles, shouts and cat-calls, there is silence. He can hear his breath blowing soft against his palms, can hear his stomach gasping. Where is Bronwen? Sam thinks of the extent of his empire – the cine-mas, the shops, the clubs, bars and casinos, spread ribbon-like along the Atlantic coast. Thinks of his customers, loathing all of them. Everything had been going so well, everything was in place, his revenge near done, near finished. The operation of a few nights before had passed off seamlessly. Sam had been anticipating one last joust with the establishment, had been relishing the thought of watching the establishment finally turn the sword on itself. But now there was this silence and the absence of Bronwen. In many ways it didn't matter – but something about the Welsh woman had touched him.

A pager vibrates against his thigh and Sam sighs. He picks up his jacket and closes the booth before slipping into the the-atre where he unlocks a box bolted to the wall in a dark corner, and picks up the telephone hanging inside. Sam the Weasel Man knows that the FBI watch his every move, knows they bug each line, each mobile. About this line they know nothing.

Sam turns his back to the screen, speaks quietly into the mouthpiece. 'Yeah?'

'Someone comin' in from LA. Been given yo' name. He'll be visitin'.'

'When's he comin'?'

'Dunno, man.'

'How will I know him?'

'You'll know him.'

'Who is he?'

'Fuckin' ghost, man. Don't aks me. He dangerous.'

'To me?'

'Not if you treat him nice.'

'What's he want?'

'What the fuck does anyone wan'? A favour, man, he wan' a favour.'

The line goes dead and silence rushes again through Sam's head.

The derelict who came in earlier brushes past Sam, mumbling, his flies unzippered, his coat hanging open. Sam steps back, bumps against the wall as Chum Kane slithers past and commits Sam the Weasel Man to memory.

The keen April sunlight illuminates the blemishes on Bronwen's scrubbed face as she checks her hair in the mirror of the car. She tuts and opens her purse, pulling out a lipstick, flicking it open deftly and applying it in sure strokes. Flanagan watches her, wishing that she could be prettier if that is what she wants.

'So, where are we?' Bronwen asks, dusting her cheeks with powder.

'East Hampton.'

'What are we doing here?'

'It's near where the Kanes used to live. I'm going to try to get some information, find out what I can.'

'How?' Bronwen teases the ringlets around her plump face.

'I dunno. Ask around.'

'Hmm.'

'Look, Bronwen, you'd be doing me a great service if you'd let me see the photograph . . .'

Bronwen snaps her purse shut. 'Not a chance. If I show you, why would you keep me around? After all, it's not my good looks that got me here.' She clambers out of the car.

Flanagan drums out a tattoo on the fascia, tries to order his thoughts. Bronwen taps the window and he lowers it. 'How long do you think you'll be?' she asks.

'Few hours.'

'I'm going shopping. I feel just dreadful in these clothes and this seems like a nice place to look around.'

'I'll see you here around two.' Flanagan fires the engine and backs out of the space.

'Good luck!' calls Bronwen, flapping a wave.

Flanagan pulls out of the car park and hangs a right, back to the police station they had passed back along the boulevard. Because he has not realized that a car has been following him since he left New York City, neither does he realize that it is no longer following.

Keeler watches Flanagan drawing away, slipping out of sight into the blessed, gilt-lined streets of the Hamptons, watches as he listens disbelievingly to the voice of his superior on the closed-band radio.

'Keeler, get your ass back here, and like yesterday. We have a situation.'

'But, sir, I'm tailing a lead.'

'Fuck that, d'you hear? *Fuck* that, Keeler. You're out there on a chase to nowhere and you know what we've got here? We've got Governor fucking Jefferson's wife shot on Fifth Avenue by two cops. Shot by two fucking cops, watched by fucking hundreds. Get back here, Keeler.'

The radio hisses static as Keeler stares at the driver. 'Governor Jefferson? Shit.' Keeler's bowels flex. 'Shit.' His fingertips freeze, feel numb. 'Christ, forget Flanagan. Let's get going – c'mon, *move!*'

The unmarked sedan squeals away from the car park, horn blatting, and noses back towards the city.

New York City – April

M –

Been in New York a few days now. Every time I come back I get a zing. Remember that first time we came down and stayed over the weekend? In some really funky place near the Park. Belonged to a friend of yours, I think. Can't remember too clearly, it was so long ago. I do remember getting into Grand Central late Friday night, walking through that lobby, surrounded by people who didn't know us, watching that extravagant clock turn as people waited around it. We caught a cab to the apartment and laughed all the way up in the elevator, nervous, waiting to be found out, feeling too too lucky. Ah, shit – and then the apartment, the carpets so lush we tripped on them. So soft we made love on them. Remember *that*? In front of that fireplace covered in cherubs and harps, grapes and figs. We lay and looked at it for hours.

And do you remember that when we stopped admiring

each other and we went out it was so late, maybe two in
the morning, and we caught a cab down to the Village and
found some back-street bar that wasn't a bar at all, just a
Chinese store with a table on the sidewalk and he sold us a
couple of bottles of Kirin and sat, unsmiling, and watched
us as we drank it, like he was worried we'd steal the table?
Then we walked round to Bleecker and Christopher and
found a club with a queue snaking for a block, and you
sashayed up to the gorilla on the door and smiled at him,
breaking his heart. He lifted the chain and let you through
and you grabbed me and pulled me inside too and broke
his heart a little more.

I want to do those things again. I want to walk through
a train station with no fear. I want to drive to the beach. I
want to laugh and go to see movies and eat in restaurants. I
want to do what everyone does. And I want to do these
things with you.

Love,

Chum

At Diamond Days Iris is restive. It is as if she can feel her first-
born drawing nearer, can sense him approaching. Still she
does her exercises, lifting her arms, stretching her legs, clench-
ing her fist under the cover of darkness. The matron has not
moved, has said nothing, seems stillborn beneath her sheets.
Iris watches her all day, as the tropical sun slews across the
sky, angle-slashing through the ward. Iris has nodded and
smiled to thank the staff for putting her in with her friend, has
flubbered for policemen when they have come asking questions. Iris does not want the matron moved, wants to be able
to watch her, to stifle her, to suffocate her.

Yet today Iris is restive. Perhaps it is the exercise that has awakened her, perhaps it is the sense of her own imminent death – who knows? Today she wants to see her photographs, wants to look at Charlie with his foot on the fender of a car, and the house in East Hampton, wants to tie herself to this earth with more than catheters. But when she asks a nurse – which takes Iris a long time – to bring her photographs, her scraps of memory, the nurse scurries away and calls a doctor. The doctor, high of brow and low of sentiment, informs Iris that everything in the Emerald Rest Home that was not bolted down has been burned. Mattresses, sheets, blankets, towels, beds, furniture, papers, files, disks, photographs – all have been incinerated.

'The place was a microbiologist's dream,' the doctor remarks. 'There were viruses and bacteria you never even heard of.'

Iris turns her face to the wall, turns away from the matron for the first time in days. She will not cry because she cannot waste the energy. She will not cry in front of this man in a white coat who is younger than Charlie Kane must be now. She will not cry because she has cried enough. She stares at the wall until the doctor sighs, shrugs and walks away. Iris lies in her bed, only fifty-seven years old, a ragged collection of memories and bones, and remembers the day she ran down the steps and into Luke Kane's car, remembers the bunch of scallions she never bought for her mother. Iris knows, now, that this time, a few days by her own reckoning, is the only time she has left to balance the scales, to remember events that only she ever experienced. When she ran down the steps into Luke Kane's car, into Luke Kane's arms, she thought she was making a choice.

'You were,' she mutters, 'you were making a choice.' Iris speaks to herself for the first time in years. Speaks to herself in a room lit by a sun harsher than she had ever known when she made that choice. Her voice has changed so much she barely recognizes the sound. 'It's just it was the wrong one.' She sighs. Remember, she thinks to herself, remember Charlie walking in the garden, remember Charlie holding Lydia. Remember Lydia. Iris coughs and Matron stirs. 'Remember, remember, remember,' she mumbles.

The evening passes with Iris straining to recall all the days she has forgotten, straining her life through a fine sieve, aware that she has lost too many pictures, lost too much information for the pictures to flow, to coalesce. In one moment she sees Charlie looking up from a newspaper, smiling, as she walks towards him, in the next she sees Luke Kane's hand, his palm, in such detail that his life-line, the whorls on his thumb are as clear as the contours of a map. In the next moment she sees Lydia, her cracked-cup grin fired inappropriately, as she sits on the potty, passing soft yellow turds. 'Lydia never worked,' Iris mutters, 'never worked.'

The sun twists itself around the world, slipping away from Iris's room, as she tries once more to remember Charlie Kane's leaving, and yet still there is nothing but a white nothingness. Something happened . . . something dark steals into the edge of her mind. But when she takes a mental step towards it, the darkness moves away. This saddens Iris more than anything else – that she cannot remember what Charlie looked like when he left, when she last saw him.

LUKE KANE

When Luke Kane tumbled from the car in front of his mother's Hampton mansion, razzled by the debauchery of his days in San Francisco, Lucinda had to shade her eyes against the sparkling sunlight to see him, her trembling hand shielding bloodshot eyes. For seven years she had not seen her son, remembered him as the tousled, olive-skinned man-boy, tetchy as a cougar, who had shared her bed. The man she saw climbing the fan-steps leading to the portico was someone unknown to her. His face, she saw, was hard and gorgeous beneath the streaks of grime. She watched as his eyes flicked over her, cringed for the years that had passed and flinched as she saw his smile break when he looked at Sugar. With one of the few truly instinctive maternal gestures she was ever to make, Lucinda pulled Sugar close and tried to summon a smile for her son as she swallowed a rivulet of bile which welled up from her stomach. Lucinda might have felt estranged from the man walking towards her but she recognized that smile well enough. Luke Kane gathered his mother and his sister in his arms to hug them and the smell of stale alcohol, mingled with a scent Lucinda recognized, swept over them, displacing the salt air washing in from the ocean.

Lucinda drank less in those summer months than she had for years because she was maintaining a vigil, guarding Sugar against the wolf. Her skin freckled and burned as she sat in the dunes watching Sugar play. Her hair frizzled and broke as she swam again and again in the heavy salt water and bounced out into the Sound on power-boats, the lurching terrifying her as Sugar screamed with delight. She attended the children's barbecues, took Sugar into the city, sat in the sun watching as Sugar had tennis lessons, riding lessons, swimming lessons.

Each night Lucinda read to Sugar, lulling her to sleep, and tucked crisp sheets around her. Once Sugar's eyes closed, Lucinda would close the shutters, fetch herself a glass and a bottle of bourbon and sit by Sugar's bed, watching the light fade from powder-blue to black between the wooden slats. As she waited each night for Luke Kane to return she would think of her husband sitting in his house in Westchester, alone and righteous. She had not seen him for years. The cheques arrived, the presents came, the bills were paid. As he had promised, he never did leave her, never did desert her entirely. And when Lucinda had seen Luke Kane smile as he looked at Sugar, she had known, finally, that Theodore had always been right. He had been right to send Luke Kane away, had been right to refuse to see him. It seemed that Luke Kane was everything his father had feared he might be.

She waited each night until she heard Luke Kane return, until she heard the crash of his door closing, until she knew he slept. Then and only then did she pick up her glass and bottle and go to her lonely bedroom. Even late at night she was aware of his body, as she skimmed the fields of dreams,

skimming over them, never lying down in the long, whispering grass to sleep. She floated in the space between bourbon
and disquiet, listening for the sound of a door opening.

Theodore Kane's money and his status ensured that his son
was welcomed back into the society of the Hamptons without
question. No one thought to ask why Luke Kane had been
gone for so long, why he had not visited his parents. Instead
the sons of the banking families fought for his attention, awed
by his composure, his startling looks, his arrogance. They
fooled for him, fought for his attention, followed him everywhere they could. Luke was aware of these antics and
accepted their adulation as his due. Invitations arrived daily,
to parties, fishing trips, for weekends in Nassau and Cape
Cod, to barbecues and ball-games.

Luke Kane wanted nothing more than to be older, to be
away from his mother, away from the Hamptons, away from
the endless beer-drinking and fatuous empty boasts of the
boys around him. The girls and their mothers he found insipid
and sexless. He preferred to spend the days alone in the sand
dunes, lying under the August sun, sand gritting in his mouth,
growing hotter and hotter, his groin boiling, until he could
stand it no longer and he would race to the sea and throw
himself into the waves. Each morning he threw a towel on to
the back seat of his car and drove miles to empty, private
beaches, where he lay watching the sun turn his skin dark
brown, thinking about what he might become, what he might
do in the world, what he might do *with* the world. When the
sting went out of the sun he drove back to East Hampton,
hungry and stiff with salt. Arriving home he often found the
house apparently empty, and he showered and dressed in

silence. In as much as these things his days were as monastic, as ascetic as they had been at the Jesuit School.

At night he sat a while on the deck in an old rocking chair, his feet on the rail, looking out over the ocean, his hair slicked, skin free of salt but slightly tender to the touch where the sun had burned him. In his hands he held a glass beaded with ice-melt, filled with vodka. He sat so still that Lucinda often did not notice him as she moved from room to room behind him. He could hear her pacing, hear the floorboards creak as she walked back and forth, agitating. Luke could have stilled her anxieties, could have said to her, 'Sugar is of no interest to me, she is too young,' but he didn't because he couldn't be bothered.

Some nights he sat for hours, refilling his glass, listening to the waves when they had become too dark to see. Sometimes he would drive to a party, train his blue-blue eyes on a wide-eyed woman and take her to a beach or a roadside car park, where he seduced her. These encounters bored him, as the women would affect either to misunderstand what was happening and then weep as he pressed them into the rear seat of the car, the damp towel from his daily swim knotted beneath them; or they would relent too soon, their plump, fragrant limbs lying dumbly acquiescent beneath him. Sometimes he slapped the women, knocking their faces into the seat leather, and was gratified to hear the moans that followed. He decided, that summer, to limit himself to women, because he wanted nothing to interfere with his departure from that house, despite the fact that there were many solitary men who lingered in the dunes every day, eyeing him longingly.

On a few occasions during that long, hot, silent summer, Luke Kane and Lucinda spoke, at the breakfast table, at a cocktail party, when they met on the beach; spoke like strangers, with an odd formality. Lucinda knew her son was biding his time, waiting to leave, that he was in the house simply because he had nowhere else to stay. Luke Kane knew that Lucinda did not care what he did, where he went, which women he saw, as long as he stayed well away from his sister. They had ceased to love each other, mother and son.

It seemed that only moments rather than months had passed since Lucinda had stood on the porch waiting for her beloved Luke Kane to arrive, and yet here she was willing him gone, watching him pack cases into his car for the drive to Harvard. She pulled Sugar closer, held her tight as Sugar waved and blew a kiss to her strange, silent, handsome brother. Luke Kane winked and blew a kiss right back, staring straight at Sugar, willing her to do something, to say something. Lucinda frowned and waited until Luke's car had disappeared from view before she let Sugar go.

1997

Lieutenant Flanagan is being given the run-around by the police in East Hampton. He has been told to wait and someone will see him. He has sat on a hard bench in the lobby for over an hour and watched officers pushing pens, clicking mice, answering phones and wondered what the hell they're all engaged in – the place hardly seems the epicentre of violent crime. In fact, the station seems like a two-bit operation. In his guts a whirring snag of fury grinds into action as he heaves himself from the bench and walks to the desk. 'Excuse me?'

A young cop, who Flanagan swears must be sixteen years old, looks up in annoyance. 'Yes, sir? How can I help you?'

Flanagan heaves his weight from one foot to the other. 'I've been waiting over an hour. I was told someone would come to speak with me.'

'What is it you want, sir?'

'I want,' Flanagan battens down the spiralling mass in his stomach, 'I want to ask some questions about a family who used to live around here.'

'May I suggest you go to the library, sir? They have all that sort of information.' The cop's vacant, innocent eyes look into Flanagan's reddening face.

'May I suggest that you give me some fucking answers,' Flanagan says evenly.

The cop steps back, pushes her palms against the desk. 'With respect, sir, your attitude . . .'

Flanagan fishes in his pocket and pulls out his badge, something he wishes he did not have to do but time is passing and with each moment memories recede and future events grow nearer. 'Perhaps this will speed things up around here. Officer, I want to know about a family called Kane who used to live here years ago. Used to live somewhere in East Hampton. First I want to know the address of the place, and when I get back from checking it over I want you to tell me everything you know about it. Got that?' Flanagan is shamed by his belligerence, by his bullying.

'Of course, Lieutenant. One moment, sir.' The young policewoman swivels round and delves into a drawer of a cabinet, pulls out a file and browses through it. 'One zero seven eight Apaquogue Road,' she calls over her shoulder. 'Straight down the street and take the third right. Left, and then you'll see it a couple of miles on. Looks out over the beach. Down a driveway off the road.'

'Thank you, Officer. I'll be back in an hour or so and I'd appreciate it if you had any further information ready for me.'

It has taken Lieutenant Flanagan many miles, many weeks and plenty of dollars to arrive at 1078 Apaquogue. Indeed, it has taken him so long, by a route he could not have imagined, that he has near forgotten why he began this quest. As he sits in his car, hot, now, in the unusually strong midday sun, he remembers that when he began to think of searching for Mr Candid it was winter. He also knows that his own personal

hunt began years before, when he realized that Mr Candid
was no media construct, no journalist's wish-fulfilment, that
there was, in fact and not in fiction, a Launcelot, a *chevalier mal
fait*. Flanagan strains to remember what has brought him
here – why is it important?

'The question,' he mutters to himself. 'You have a question
you must ask him. C'mon, c'mon.' Flanagan pulls himself out
of the car and turns to look at the Kane house, 1078 Apaquogue
Road.

There is nothing but a carcass, a ruin, a blitz of a house.
Turrets have tumbled, decks sag and bag, windows are eye-
less, doors hang skewed on rusted, torn hinges. The roof has
tumbled and inched and slithered into the hallway three
storeys below. A vast plane tree has burst its banks and effortlessly lifted the east side of the house on its sturdy root system.
The grounds are matted with wild rye grass, raging kudzu,
and spindly shrubs, locked in an infinite three-dimensional
embrace, run riot across the remnants of lawns.

Flanagan stares open-mouthed at the shambles, oblivious
of the cars wheeling behind him; sleek, blonde women steering Porsches one-handed as they glide to the mall, to the
office, to their lover's bed. He has never seen a structure so
shambolic, so ravaged. Has never seen a building so
unloved still standing. He leans on the roof of his car and
gawps. He is amazed to find this *here*, this enormous plot of
land on the beach – right on the beach, so close you can
smell the salt – in one of the world's most expensive areas of
real estate.

'I can't believe it,' Flanagan is saying, as he walks once more
towards the young cop on the desk. 'I can't believe that house

has been left to rot away. What's going on here? Has anyone lived there since the Kanes?'

The officer holds up a soft, white palm in a gesture intended to stop Flanagan's progress. 'Um . . . could you – could you wait one moment, sir?' The young woman picks up the desk phone and mumbles into it, her back turned to Flanagan. 'Someone will be right with you, sir. Excuse me.' She turns and scuttles away, gently closing a door behind her.

Flanagan begins to sweat. He has no jurisdiction here, should not have waved his badge at the cop, should not have bullied her. He considers leaving, remembers the winter snows that lay on the ground when he started his move towards this moment, and holds his ground. A door slams many rooms distant and Flanagan knows that someone is approaching him and the sweat gathers on his palms. A door behind him opens and Flanagan turns to see a man so solid, so avuncular, that he wants to whoop with relief.

'Lieutenant?'

'Yes.'

'I believe you're asking questions about the Kane house.'

'That's right.'

'Can I see your badge?'

Flanagan gives the man his badge, sits on the bench he vacated an hour before.

The sergeant hands the badge back. 'Florida. You got no business here.'

'I know that. I *know* that. I'm relying on some brotherly feeling here. It's a case I'm working on and I was in the area and I thought, Well, why not?'

'You were in the area?' The sergeant raises an eyebrow.

'Well, I'm on vacation and . . . y'know how it is.' Flanagan is embarrassed by the inadequacy of his response.

The sergeant shakes a cigarette from a pack and holds it, simply holds it without lighting it. 'Gave up years ago but I still like to have one, y'know, just have it in my hand, like I could start again any time I wanted. Then it doesn't feel so bad.' The sergeant waggles the cigarette, taps his boots on the floor and turns to Flanagan. 'So, what d'you want to know?'

'I want to know about the Kanes, about the family who lived at one zero seven eight Apaquogue. I'd really appreciate it if you gave me everything you got.'

The sergeant sits down beside Flanagan and looks at his broad, open face. 'Those files were closed years ago.'

'Files? What files?'

'On the Kane family. Must have been seventeen, maybe eighteen years ago. About nineteen eighty would be right.'

'What files?'

'You don't know? Thought you said you were working on the case.' The sergeant frowns.

'Well, I am. I'm looking for someone and I think he may be wrapped up with the Kanes.'

'In that case, I wish you luck. Come to that, I wish *him* luck. We looked for the Kanes for years and never found them.'

'What d'you mean?'

'Just that. We never found them.'

'I don't understand.'

The sergeant shifts on the seat, folds his arms, leans back. 'OK. Like I said, it happened around seventeen years ago. One day the Kane family was living in the house on Apaquogue and next thing they'd gone. I mean, we didn't get over to the

house for a few days – no call to. It was Thanksgiving weekend, the help was off, so no one noticed. But . . . when we did
get over there – shoot. It was a bloodbath. I never seen anything like it. There weren't a patch of that kitchen that wasn't
covered in blood – floor, ceiling, everything. They found four
different blood samples – four people, two blood types. Strange
thing was, all their clothes, money, credit cards, everything,
was left. Nothing was stolen, nothing damaged. The only thing
that went was a car – amazing old car, y'know? A Chevy, a
Pontiac? Nah, what was it? An Eldorado, a nineteen-fifty
Cadillac Eldorado. Now that *was* found, a couple of weeks
later, in Missouri, if I remember right. Just left on a street, with
the keys still in it. Forensics dusted it down but all we got was
the same samples and some prints. But they don't match anything on file. 'Course, we put out APBs but nothing came of
them. We put tabs on the accounts but they never changed, no
money went in or out. Which is weird, I can tell you, because
there are hundreds of thousands of dollars there. We closed the
files, musta been seven or eight years ago. Had to, because
nothing was happening. No one saw anything, no one heard
anything. They just disappeared.'

'What about the house? No one ever bought it? I mean, it's
prime real estate, must be worth millions.'

'No one *can* buy it. It's never been for sale. Some legal
thing – gotta be twenty years before it's released. It's not like
there're any creditors or anything.'

'It's still owned by the Kanes?'

'Sure is.'

'Did you know them? Did you know the family?'

The sergeant frowns and taps the unlit cigarette. 'Yeah, I
did. Just about every cop on the Island knew them.'

'Huh?'

'It was not a happy home. Mainly it was him, Luke Kane.' The sergeant shakes his head. 'I never saw such a good-looking bastard. He had a fine wife, a couple of kids, more money than you or I will make in a lifetime and he was the meanest son-of-a-bitch I've ever met.'

'What d'you mean?'

'He musta been stopped a thousand times for drunk-driving, accidents, assaults. Got out of all of them somehow. Best lawyers, too much money. He ran around with women all the time. And a few men, some people said. Shoot, *they* chased *him* most often. A couple of the women filed complaints against him – you know, assault, rape, that kinda stuff. But nothing came of those either – after all, people had seen these women running after him. Might be different now, but this was twenty-five years ago. Lotsa people thought he hit his wife and she did go to the hospital and get fixed up a coupla times, but she always made out that she'd had an accident. I don't know, I reckon it was him.'

'You didn't like him?'

'You want to know the truth, he scared the shit out of me. He could be a real nice guy sometimes, real charming, but you were always thinking he might turn any time. I used to hate having to go out there. So did every other cop I know. Another strange thing – Luke Kane's sister lived with the family, always had as far as I recall. Now *she* was something, very beautiful. She used to be *the* woman to know, like she was royalty or something. All the women in town wanted her at their parties and clubs, y'know how it is. There was a lot of talk about the two of them, Luke Kane and Sugar Kane – that's what she was called, Sugar. There was something strange about them, the way they were together, like they were married and the wife was the sister. I wouldn't be surprised if there was something going on there.' The sergeant sighs, shakes his head, puts the cigarette back into the packet. 'I don't know – there were too many accidents, too many coincidences, too many complaints. More we investigated, asked around, interviewed, more we found out about him – Luke Kane. Like I said, it was not a happy home.'

Flanagan sits listening, his head slightly bowed, his hands squeezing his knees so tight he can feel his bones creak. 'You said there were a couple of kids.'

'That's right.'

'You remember what they were called?'

'It was a long time ago. Uh, what was it? I can look it up for you. No, wait. Charlie . . . Charlie and . . . and Lydia. That's it.'

'Did you know them?'

'No, not really. I always felt sorry for them, with Luke Kane for a father. Not, I guess, that he was there that much. Charlie was a nice kid, very quiet, very polite. He was real smart, a genius, they said. He went off to Harvard or some Ivy League place when he was young, thirteen, fourteen or something. It's a shame – he was such a good kid, you know, deep-down *decent* like some kids are. He would have done something special. I reckon he'd have left his mark on the world. Maybe been a writer or a scientist or something.'

'And he disappeared too?'

'Yup. He came up for Thanksgiving that weekend, that much we know. Never went back to Harvard, never came back here. Just like the rest of them. He was last seen somewhere in Massachusetts.' The sergeant stands and stretches, his plump belly hanging proud over his belt. 'That's it. That's all I can tell you. That's all I know.'

Flanagan stands and shakes the sergeant's hand. 'I really appreciate you taking the time, sir.' He thinks of Iris lying in her bed thousands of miles away in Florida, thinks of her face as the stroke struck and drops the sergeant's hand. 'One more thing: what do *you* think happened that weekend?'

The sergeant shakes his head. 'I dunno. I haven't thought about it in a long time. I don't know. I guess they must be dead, must have been dead for years. If Luke Kane was involved anything could've happened. He was smart enough and crazy enough and rich enough to do anything you can think of.'

Keeler's face is itching because sweat has beaded on his cheeks. He is standing in a room which is air-conditioned and ionized, its temperature a constant sixty-one degrees, and he is sweating. His superior, the chief, is sitting at his desk, his face impassive, yet fury radiates from him. This fastidious, bland man with an instantly forgettable face is scaring the crap out of Keeler.

'To summarize, last night at approximately oh five hundred hours a fifty-two-year-old Caucasian woman was shot, apparently by two officers of the NYPD, on Fifth and Fifty-first Street. You were in the area at the time.'

'Yes, sir. I was in an unmarked car, er, staking out a hotel.'

'You saw nothing?'

Keeler coughs, discreetly wipes his face. 'I, um, I saw some tow-trucks pass and I heard some sirens. That was it. My suspect came out of the hotel at that point and I followed him away from the area.'

'To return to the salient facts: the incident was witnessed by two hundred and seventeen people, all of whom say they saw an NYPD car arrive at the scene. The two officers got out, unclipped their issue firearms, and the woman in question began to walk towards them, talking. The officers said nothing. Instead they aimed their weapons and fired at her, hitting her four times in the thoracic area. One bullet passed through her heart and she was dead in less than a minute. At that moment two other cars arrived and the situation rapidly deteriorated. The victim was later identified as Jessica Millicent Jefferson, the wife of Governor Thomas Jefferson the second.'

Keeler is wishing that he had not drunk whiskey the night before, is sure that the room is being contaminated by the sour fumes boiling in his guts.

'This morning the papers are full of polemical pieces concerning the problem of police brutality and accountability. I have had the mayor over here screaming for the Bureau to step in publicly and sort this one out. I have had Congress and the Senate, Republican and Democrat, all screaming at me. This afternoon the President is phoning. What do you think of the situation so far, Keeler?'

'I think, sir, I think it's unacceptable.'

'Unacceptable? *Unacceptable?* Well, that's true, but I don't think it's adequate as a description of what's happening here. The city is, as they say, restless.' The chief slips silently from his chair and turns his back on Keeler to look at the view over Manhattan. 'I can see Fifth and Fifty-first from here, Keeler. Come and look.' Keeler swallows and wipes his face with damp palms. He wishes he had some gum to mask his whiskey-breath. He stands next to his superior and scans the skyline. 'Look, Keeler, down there, that's where it happened. If

I'd been here working late last night I could have watched the entire thing unfold. Could, perhaps, have stopped it. Or so you might imagine. But,' the man turns to Keeler and studies his profile, 'you would be wrong. I could not have stopped it, even as chief of the FBI I could not have stopped it. Because the gunmen were not NYPD cops. They were wearing the uniform, they had the car, they even had the demeanour of New York's finest, but they were not cops.'

Keeler frowns. 'I don't get it.'

'Apparently, two weeks ago a unit was stolen in the Bronx and never recovered. The uniforms are easy enough. It's dark, there's a fight going on in the street, a fender-bender to distract people. Two hundred and seventeen witnesses saw two cops shoot a wealthy white woman on Fifth Avenue. The gunmen never got back in the car. They simply walked away.'

'But *why* shoot her? What's she got to *do* with anything? Kidnapping maybe, but why kill her and walk away?'

'That is a question I have asked myself.'

Keeler is chewing a snagged nail, trying to galvanize his mind, trying to turn the wheels. 'Makes no sense.'

'Unfortunately she is in no position to assist us, so we must speculate. That speculation is made more difficult when we know that the car she was travelling in had five kilos of the finest-grade cocaine in the trunk.'

Keeler gawps at his superior. 'You shitting me?'

'I wish I were. The one positive fact is that the driver of her car is well known to us and is currently sitting in a cell awaiting questioning.'

'Did any of the officers who arrived at the scene see anything? Anything at all?'

'No, the situation was too volatile when they arrived.'

'Shit.' Keeler rubs his shining pate. 'Shit. This is way out of control.'

'As you say, way out of control. And we are in the business of control. I want you to interview the driver. You know what to ask – just get the information. We have to stop this. We have to start building walls, fielding questions. We have to have control.' The chief sits and pushes a file across the desk. 'This is all we got.'

Keeler fingers the file, feels how slim, insubstantial, it is. 'Sir, can I say something?'

'Go ahead.'

'I headed up the team that investigated the Jefferson murders eleven years ago. I am aware that Governor Jefferson's son was responsible.'

'Tell me something I don't know.'

'I just . . . I just wanted to make sure that you knew that.'

'Point taken. I also know that last night you were tailing a Lieutenant Flanagan, who, I believe, worked with you on the case for a time.'

Keeler stares at the chief. 'Yes, yes, he did.'

'Coincidence always surprises human beings. I'm not sure why.'

New York City – April

M –

I got to tell you about my flight to Newark. I get to my seat and there's this woman just billowing all over. I mean, she must have weighed in at four hundred pounds and she had two seats to herself, and even then the arms were buried in her sides. She was *huge*. But all the same, she had

an air of serenity. On my other side is a madman, a born-
again crazy who asks me if I've accepted God into my life.
So the next few hours were a delight. I mean, he's rattling
his mouth off, quoting chapter and verse, I'm wrestling
with my desire to ask for a large bourbon and a gag, and
Leviathan-woman's shifting about, trying to get
comfortable. The movie starts and the Madman decides to
pump up the volume, yelling about being raptured. You
heard of this? Apparently some Americans are being
raptured, that is, chosen by God to be blessed in the next
world. But he takes them any time – just dumps them in
Paradise on a whim. You could be sitting in a movie
theatre, for instance, ten minutes from the end of *Seven*,
and suddenly your Maker thinks you're all right and whips
you out of your seat. So as Kevin Spacey rolls his spacy
eyes and the head arrives in the box, you find yourself
inside the pearly gates. To substantiate his claim, Madman
cited the cases of people who have disappeared, never to
be seen again, unaware, it would seem, that sometimes
people just choose to walk away.

   Leviathan-woman began to laugh. She roared, she
whooped, she slapped her thighs as the plane trembled.
Then she turned to Madman and said, 'What a pile of
crap,' and began to laugh again. I've never heard a voice
like it. It was of hot chocolate and rare steaks, waterfalls
and woodsmoke. Everyone on the plane stopped to listen
to the echoes of that voice. Her laugh was like a hot
cinnamon roll, thick and sweet, almost too inviting. I
began to talk to her just so she'd speak. I was asking her
anything, anything at all, to keep her talking. She'd been
out in Vegas for her mother's funeral and as she talked

about it it was like you saw the pictures of her sorrow, felt the colours in her heart. Her voice made me see.

When I kissed you I smelt lemons. When I touched your face I drank champagne. When I was inside you I was raptured. I miss you so much.

Love,

Chum

Bronwen and Flanagan lie in silence on a king-size bed in the L-A-Zee Motel on the river at Hampton Bays. The bed groans as Bronwen rolls over to stub out her cigarette. She lies back again, folds her hands over her alarming breasts and sighs. 'So you didn't find out anything?'

Flanagan shakes his head. 'Not really.'

'Why not, man? What's the problem? If he lived here then surely someone knows about him.'

Flanagan sits up and groans. He is tired and dispirited. He is feeling pity for Bronwen, who wants to find Chum Kane so that she will be able to put her heart to rest. He is also feeling sorry for himself. He has been trying to catch smoke, trying to snare a shadow. He no longer knows if Chum Kane exists; has no evidence that he does. Neither is he sure any longer that Mr Candid is indeed out there balancing the scales for the misbegotten. He is disorientated by his new-found knowledge of Luke Kane's murderous character: *He was smart enough and crazy enough and rich enough to do anything you can think of.* He thumps back down on the bed, rocking it. 'Bronwen, how old is Chum Kane in the photograph you got?'

'I don't know. Twenty? Maybe. I don't know.'

'Does it have a date on the back or anything?'

Bronwen goes into the bathroom, locks the door for a few moments, then reappears. 'Yes, someone's written "Thanksgiving nineteen eighty".'

'Bronwen, please can I see it?'

'You know you can't.'

'Bronwen, Bronwen.' Flanagan's voice is breathy, weary. 'I know you think I'll take the photograph and leave you here, but I won't, really I won't. I'm a decent man. That's just about all I am, a decent man. I'm never going to be much else. I won't leave you. You don't see, do you, you don't see what this is about? It's all about decency. Or something like it. I need to have something confirmed and I think Chum Kane is the only person who can answer the questions I need to ask. That's why finding him is important for me. If he's who I think he is, I need to know how he cleans his hands. How he *lives* with himself. I need to work out if he's right.' Flanagan sighs. 'Please, let me see the photograph.'

'It's the only thing I've got.'

Flanagan twists round on the bed to look at Bronwen. She is perched uncomfortably on the edge of the bed, her head sunk between pudgy shoulders, her pale skin made wet by silent tears. 'Ah, Bronwen. Ah, I'm sorry. I didn't mean to bully you. And, anyway, what d'you mean? That it's the only thing you've got? That can't be.'

Bronwen's voice is sticky as molasses. 'It is. It *is*. I look at his picture and I think that if I knew him I'd be safe. That I'd be different. That I'd be, I don't know . . . that I'd be right. That's all. That I'd be right, 'cause I know that I'm not right. But he'd make things different, I know he would.'

'What d'you mean, you're not right?'

Bronwen doesn't hear the question. 'Some of the things I

did after I met Sam. Sleeping with men, that sort of thing. Well, I can't believe, now, in this room, that I did them. It was like I was someone else. D'you know what I mean? I'm lying here on this bed with you and we're both dressed and we wouldn't even think of doing anything, y'know, anything, and yet the things I've done. Strange, the things men want.' Bronwen pulls a clump of toilet tissue from her pocket and blows her strangely dainty nose. 'But when I look at him I feel like . . . like I know him? Like he's the answer to a question I hadn't even thought of. Like if I was with him then I'd be all right. I can't explain. I don't understand why you want to find him but I feel like I need to.'

'Bronwen, when I was in town this afternoon I went to the library and I found the high-school yearbook for nineteen seventy-one. I saw a photo of him. I know what he looks like.'

Bronwen's face crumples and she snivels snot on to her wrist. 'So you don't need me, then?'

'Bronwen, of *course* I need you. How else am I gonna have cookies fed to me while I drive? How else am I gonna have someone read the map and tell me where to go? Of *course* I need you.' Flanagan shifts across the bed and puts a huge, hairy hand on Bronwen's thigh. 'Bronwen, I want to tell you something. Do you mind if I hug you while I tell you this something? Would you like to lie down and I'll just hug you while I tell you? Would you do that?'

Bronwen looks at him, her eyes bleared with tears. She sniffs. 'Yes, OK, I'll do that. But no funny business.' She sinks back on the bed and rests her head on Flanagan's barrel of a chest, a chest so large it could mature a gallon of whisky, a lifetime of hope. He strokes her head and begins to speak.

'Years ago, Bronwen, years ago, when you would have been so young, living the life of a child in . . .'

'Llanerchymedd, Ynys Môn.'

'Yeah, uh, in Ynys Môn, that's when a legend began to grow in America. People began to believe that there was a man somewhere who would right wrongs, make everything right again, like you were talking about. Almost like Clint Eastwood as the Man With No Name. Someone who'd ride into town, solve the problem, count the bodies and ride right out again.'

'You mean Mr Candid, don't you? I watched something on TV about him, on *Oprah*. She said he didn't exist.'

Flanagan closes his eyes and breathes, breathes so deeply he could be breathing for the world. He decides. 'I think he does. I think it's just possible Chum Kane is Mr Candid.'

The L-A-Zee Motel was built but three years before and yet it shifts in that moment. A slight tremor, a twist of mortices and tenons. Nothing that can be seen. Bronwen looks at the splendid, bearded face that belongs to Flanagan.

'Bronwen, I went to see a local cop today and we had a long conversation. Thing is, thing is . . . ah, shit. The thing is, he told me Chum Kane disappeared seventeen years ago, along with the rest of his family. Thanksgiving weekend, seventeen years ago. November nineteen eighty. He also said that it's assumed Iris is dead but we know she's not, don't we? I have to tell you – I'm sorry, but it's also assumed Chum Kane is dead. Please can I see the photograph?'

'Why?'

'Bronwen, Thanksgiving is the last Thursday in November. You have the last known photograph of Chum Kane, taken the night before he disappeared. Don't you see? When I went to the library the photos were in the paper, in the yearbook, but he's only thirteen. He went to college then. He graduated high school when he was thirteen. I need to see the photo of the *man*.'

Bronwen breathes a gluey breath, presses harder into Flanagan's chest. 'He's so handsome.'

'Let me see.'

Bronwen reaches into her T-shirt, pushes inside her brassière and pulls out a Polaroid. 'I want it back,' she says as she passes it over to Flanagan.

The photograph is warm in Flanagan's hand, warm because it has been nestling against Bronwen's breast. Slowly, he turns it over to look at Chum Kane. And what he sees is a tall, blond man, easy with himself, easy with his limbs. His face is square, stubbled with a dark blond half-beard. His eyes are cobalt blue. He's resting a foot on the fender of a car, leaning on his elbow, near laughing. And you know, you just know, that the person taking the photograph has said something to make him guffaw soon. You can sense the smile of the photographer as the shutter slams open and shut.

'You can almost hear her,' whispers Flanagan.

'Eh?' Bronwen shifts, delicately touches Chum's face with a finger.

'The woman who took the photograph, you can hear her saying something that made him laugh.'

'How do you know it's a woman?'

'Because he wouldn't laugh like that for a man. It's obvious. I don't know how I know but I do.'

'Can I have it back now?'

'Sure.' Flanagan passes the photograph to Bronwen and she slips it inside her brassière.

'What are you going to do next?' she asks.

'I'm going home.'

'What? You're going to give up?'

'There's nothing more I can do. The cops have looked for him for seventeen years. I don't imagine I'll find anything they didn't.'

'But what about the woman who took the photograph? What about her? She'd know something.'

'Bronwen, the cops will have asked her everything they could. It's been so long she probably doesn't even remember him. You know the note on the back of the photo? Well, I reckon he dropped her off somewhere or visited her and then went home. The photograph is a Polaroid – they must have taken it on the way down. It didn't need to be processed, so the cops couldn't even have asked for the roll.'

'So that's it? You're giving up?'

'I'm tired, Bronwen. I ought to be getting back. I should get back to work.' Flanagan doesn't want to tell Bronwen what he knows about Luke Kane – that Chum Kane would have been no match for that privileged, powerful, twisted man, his father.

LUKE KANE

When Luke Kane arrived at Harvard he was not alarmed to
find himself surrounded by golden boys because that was what
he had expected. To be sure, none of the other boys' brilliance
quite matched his own: Luke Kane glowed with health, carried
with him a corona of danger, a corona which glowed bright,
attracting other night bar-flies. He studied as hard as he needed
to, avoided the braying youths from Long Island he had met
over the summer, and spent the nights prowling the streets of
Boston and Cambridge. For the years he was there he thought
of Harvard as a squat, crimson place, warm and comfortable,
blood-rich in flesh. He smoked, he drank, he fucked his years
away, learning all the while about finance and business.
Cheques were deposited every month in his bank account by
Theodore, enough money to keep him away from the
Hamptons, where Lucinda and Sugar grew older in their
beach-front house. Luke Kane invested a portion of the money
and spent the profits on women and men. He was polite to his
tutors, charming to his inferiors when he chose to be, irresistible
to all others. His money (the son of Mr Steel – who had, in the
end, made millions when the guns rolled out over Europe), his
square jaw, his tall, lean body, which boxed and rowed, swam
and played tennis effortlessly, made him a magnet. His college

life was one long Christmas, one infinite present, one door after another opening for him day after day. He barrelled through his college years, collecting straight As and accolades.

Temptation, when it came, was often in the form of an hourglass figure outlined against a light-filled, smoky background in a dark bar. Or perhaps at the beaches on Martha's Vineyard, where broad, tanned backs tapering to taut buttocks would catch his eye. He was discreet, he was restrained. If ever he felt his hands growing too heavy he recalled the fair-haired boy at Christchurch and the taste of salt at Mono Lake. There were men at Harvard who were more talented, who were indeed endowed with the diligence, integrity and sense of civic duty Theodore had craved for his son, but they did not fly as high as Luke Kane. He was mythologized by all but himself. And there lay the gilding of his young life: he accepted the homage but was aware of the hollowness of the myth. He had learned enough about himself to know the extent of his own frailty.

There was one mistake, however, one error of judgement which surprised him during his college years. In his final year he travelled down to New York City for the weekend and paid for the services of a tall, black Amazon. Obviously, he need not ever pay but the exchange of money always hardened the thrill for him. The two of them went to her room and there Luke Kane's hands did grow too heavy. As he stood panting, naked, by the window, looking at the bloodied woman on the bed, the door flew open and her pimp burst in: a huge Negro in a dark suit, his scarred face twisting when he saw the damage. Even as Luke Kane called the house in the Hamptons for the first time in three years, the barrel of a gun hard against his ribs, he was calm, his voice measured. Because he knew that Lucinda would pay to keep his name out of the papers. He and the pimp sat on the floor and smoked, shared a flask of bourbon and talked as they waited for the car to travel from Long Island. When the money finally arrived, in a small blue linen sack, the pimp allowed Luke Kane to dress and shook his hand as he left, saying it had been good to do business with him. The woman was dead but, hey, that was OK, he'd deal with it. Luke Kane stepped out into the dawn and shivered, not because of the chill in the air but because of the sense of having not been in control.

His mother wrote to him during his last summer before graduation, demanding that he meet her in a hotel in Boston. Luke Kane was dressed in pale chinos and a loose white cotton shirt when they met in the lobby and he felt pleasure when he saw that Lucinda was hot in a boxy Dior suit, her ankles puffed above slight, insubstantial shoes. The two of them were ushered to a booth in the bar, Lucinda ordering bourbon to his beer. Luke Kane sat with the sweating glass in his hand, looking at his mother. The three years since they had last seen each other had not been kind to her; indeed, they had been positively vindictive. Her hair was thin and brittle, her skin dried by sun, liquor and smoke. He couldn't imagine that he had ever reached out for her across the snowy sheets of her matrimonial bed.

'You graduate this semester?' Even her voice, which had whispered, now grated.

'Yes.'

'What will you do?'

Luke Kane shrugged languidly, his eyes flicking to a passing sophomore, who turned (having heard about Luke Kane) and smiled.

'Frankly, I don't give a damn what you do.' Lucinda brushed at a strand of pale hair, finished her drink and motioned for another. 'The only thing I ask is that you don't come back to East Hampton.'

'But, Mother, that's my family home.' He smiled.

'You may choose to think so but your family says otherwise.'

'How can you stop me?'

Lucinda's small, pale-blue eyes narrowed as she looked at him. 'I can't. But you're not going to come back. Theodore will see to that if I ask him. I'd rather not have to.'

'Disinherit me, you mean?' Luke Kane arched his perfectly arched eyebrows.

Lucinda shrugged, readjusted her hose. 'Maybe.'

He watched his mother guzzling bourbon like breast-milk, her mouth sucking at lifeblood. He calculated. 'He's done that anyway, hasn't he?'

'I wouldn't know.'

'Still the happily married couple, then? The perfect family?'

Lucinda looked over to him with something approaching indifference. 'Maybe not. But we have arrived at an arrangement which suits both of us. As for the money, I don't know and I don't care if he's cut you out or not. As far as I'm concerned there's enough to go round.'

Luke Kane watched his mother again, drinking and smoking, shifting uncomfortably on the banquette, sweat beading her pale, freckled face. He thought of his father – whom he had not seen since the day when Yugoslavia fell – a man of steel with a heart of stone. 'I don't suppose, Mother, that you've read anything of Ewald Hering's work?'

Lucinda's unfocused eyes fixed on her son for a moment. 'What was that?'

'Ewald Hering. He coined the phrase "genetic memory" –
absolute bunk, of course, since nothing he argues can be
proved in terms of genetics and heredity. But all the same.
Hering argued that because of genetic memory, spawn
"remembers" to grow into a frog.'

'What are you talking about?'

'I was just looking at you and thinking I must have forgotten to grow into you and Theodore.'

'You're not coming home.'

By this turn in the conversation Luke Kane was reminded
of the stubbornness of the imbecile. 'I haven't thanked you for
the money you sent to Manhattan a couple of months ago.'

'Don't bother. And don't tell me what it was for. I don't
want to know. I shan't do it again.' Lucinda beckoned over a
waiter and ordered yet another bourbon.

'No, I don't suppose you will.' Luke Kane sat forward, resting his elbows on the table between them. 'I guess we'd better
come up with a compromise, a treaty of sorts. Has it occurred
to you that I may not *want* to come home? That I may not
want to spend time in that sad, empty house? Why would I?'

'I know one damn good reason.' Lucinda stubbed out one
cigarette and lit another. 'That's why I don't want you there.'

'What, I wonder, would Hering make of that? Where does
that genetic memory come from? Remember to sleep with your
mother?' Luke Kane smiled, looking improbably handsome.

'I have some money of my own. I'll give you what you
want.'

'I don't think so, Mother. I don't think you can give me
what I want. But you can give me enough money to set me up
in the city. And I think a graduation present would be in order.
I shall, after all, be graduating *summa cum laude*.'

Lucinda gathered up her purse, stood and tugged at her skirt, which was stuck with sweat to the back of her thighs. She looked down at her son, said, 'Write me,' and walked through the lobby and out into the broiling sunshine of downtown Boston.

Luke Kane watched her wave a hand and step into a cab. He never saw his mother again. He did write to her, however; a reasonable letter which did not demand much, merely, as he had said, enough money to set him up in the city. The request for a white 1950 Cadillac Eldorado as a graduation gift was a caprice, the whim of a moment. He knew she would give it, as it was something that he could use to move away from her and Sugar. The day he drove away from Harvard, in the Eldorado, with two fellow graduates, travelling south through snow and frost, towards sun and heat, the dusty flatlands in Nevada were lit by nuclear fission and the bedrooms of Boulder City flashed blue-white as a mushroom cloud bloomed.

It was unfortunate that Luke Kane's desire to escape the winter ice of the north-eastern seaboard should coincide so neatly with Iris Chandler's tenth birthday. It was also unfortunate that his passengers asked him to stop, so they could buy a couple of bottles of Thunderbird, in a square in Hoboken, New Jersey.

1997

During the night at Diamond Days silence is king. The nursing-home is so quiet that it is possible to hear lives ebbing away; this ebbing sounds like ink drying on paper. Iris is lying in her bed, staring at the faint silhouette of her ex-torturer across the aisle. Iris's brain is pulsing very faintly, its electrical charges so slight that they no longer generate thoughts or memories (and certainly no genetic memories). The charges can only make Iris's body breathe and swallow, sleep and sigh. But tonight they are firing more wildly and she remembers that she has a task – she has to kill the matron.

Iris pulls the catheters from the thin, creased skin of her wrist. She pulls back the sheets and thinks – faintly – about what she has to do. She is hoping that the memory of walking, a memory more than seventeen years old, will come back to her. She is worried because although she can remember how to read, how to speak, she can *do* neither. She is also hoping that her bones are not so brittle that they will snap. Her feet touch the floor, which is cold and hard, and gingerly she transfers her weight from the mattress to her heels. She sways to her feet, holding the rail by the bed. Iris is vertical. She shuffles, achingly slowly, across the few feet of linoleum, her blood dropping to her feet, dropping like red stones. Were her brain worthy of the name she would feel faint. She stands over the matron, her shadow falling across the woman's ravaged face and remembers that she needs a pillow. Sighing, she retraces her faltering steps, wedges a pillow under her stump and returns to the matron's bed.

Iris wonders, feebly, if she should say something. A few words? A short prayer? It seems so impolite simply to suffocate the woman without some sort of valediction. But what could she, Iris, possibly say? So she holds the pillow in her hand and falls forward, trying to throw herself but instead slithering – much as Charlie 'Chum' Kane had all those years before – across the bed. She is half sprawled on the matron, her one elbow pushing the plump pillow into the woman's mouth. To her surprise Matron does not struggle. Iris experiences the oddest sensation, that the matron is relieved by being relieved of her endless craving. She knows when the matron is dead, can feel it through the down and cotton. Breathing hard, her arterioles popping under the strain, her lifeblood leaking into her skin and organs, Iris pushes herself off the corpse and shuffles back to her own bed. She sinks on to the sheets and sighs again. She pushes the needles back into her wrist, pulls the sheet back over her reedy, wizened body and listens to her mind exploding. Perhaps it is because of all the noise in her head that she can't remember *why* she has done what she has done. Why she walked for the first time in seventeen years. Iris's last thought is that she enjoyed it.

Genetic memory.

As Iris's brain flickers and finally dies, Flanagan wakes with a start in his bed in the motel. He can hear Bronwen's snores, which is hardly surprising since she is still lying with her head on his chest. Flanagan, energized, positively revitalized by his ten hours of slumber (or possibly by his proximity to Bronwen), eases himself away from her and she rolls on to her back, arms akimbo. It's as he's sitting on the white plastic seat, voiding his bowels, that the realization hits him. The car, in the Polaroid. The fender of the car, the bulge of its headlamps – it's a Cadillac Eldorado. No doubt a 1950 Eldorado. The car found in Missouri. He thinks of the ramshackle house on Apaquogue, thinks of the woman who made Chum Kane laugh. Flanagan no longer wants to go home.

'Ooh, sorry,' says Bronwen, blushing as she catches the lieutenant wiping himself.

Strange, Flanagan thinks, that a nurse can dance naked in front of a club full of strangers, yet be embarrassed by the act of excretion. 'Bronwen,' he says, zipping his fly, 'I'm not going home.'

'What are you saying, man? That you've changed your mind?'

'Yeah. Let's get some breakfast and move on.'

'Where to?'

'I don't know. I need to think about it.'

Bronwen and Flanagan have more than just their size in common. Unsurprisingly, they both also enjoy eating. When they eat they think of nothing else. As sausages, bacon, hash browns, scrambled eggs, tomatoes and wheat toast, preceded by cereals and milk, followed by triple scoops of ice cream, disappear from their plates, they smile shyly at each other, both relieved to be in the company of a fellow lover of belly-timber. Eventually they fall back from their empty plates and rub their stomachs. Flanagan belches quietly.

'Shoot, that was fine,' he says, picking a fragment of sausage from between his teeth.

'Now, if we'd had soda bread, it would have been perfect,' Bronwen observes. 'So where are we going?'

Flanagan sips coffee and watches cars streaming past, heading for the city, dazzling and flashing in late-April sun. He tells Bronwen about the car, about the woman. 'I can't get her out of my mind.'

'Who?' Bronwen asks, as a sizzle of jealousy burns her throat.

'The woman who took the photo.'

'I don't know why you're so sure it's a woman.'

'I just know it is. Can I see it again?'

Bronwen looks furtively round the diner, darts a hand into her cleavage and fishes out Chum Kane. She puts the picture on the red, scarred Formica table and the two of them stare at it.

'I still don't see why you think a woman took it.' Bronwen frowns, purses her lips and the lieutenant notices that she bears a resemblance, in some lights, to a muffin.

LUKE KANE

Luke Kane was twenty-one when he moved into his penthouse on the Upper East Side. He furnished the apartment, bought a secure garage for the Eldorado and found himself a job on Wall Street. This last was not difficult: he simply telephoned a Harvard man at Hunter-Philips merchant bank and was invited to dinner rather than interview, for Luke Kane's grasp of financial niceties was well known.

New York City, or rather Manhattan, suited a man of Luke Kane's sensibilities. He was, after all, one of those with money and breeding, good looks and good taste. The money could buy him time whenever he needed it. It could also buy him silence whenever he needed it. He revelled in the sight and sound of the city, its arrow-straight streets, the wide boulevards, the pinpricks of sky peering between spires. He accepted the weight and gravitas of the vast oak doors leading into Hunter-Philips bank as a personal compliment. He revelled in the atmosphere of discreet dining rooms and restaurants, their long windows swagged with heavy drapes, silver glistening on lily-white, thick linen. He liked to walk a few blocks before hailing a cab down to Hanover Street, so he might push his way through the crowds of those less fortunate. He had his hair cut by Luigi on Baxter in Little Italy, his

shoes shined by a Negro with a stall on the corner of West 43rd
and Madison. His suits were hand-tailored, his shirts came
from London. At weekends he filled the Eldorado with colleagues and their women and drove to Atlantic City to gamble
away the days. Or they would drive up to Cape Cod and sail,
drifting in and out of the small, provincial harbour towns.
Occasionally he drove out to Long Island, for cocktail parties,
dinners, summer barbecues and speed-boating. But he never
went to East Hampton, never visited his sister and mother. A
deal, he felt, was a deal. He'd taken his mother's money
(money which, like a virus, multiplied itself many times over,
seemingly without human help) so he kept the deal.

Luke Kane was the predator at the top of the human food
chain. He had in his armoury every weapon with which to
prise out and discard any woman's honour, any man's self-
confidence. So why, then, as he approached his late twenties,
was he aware of a lack? He'd sit in his apartment, tie loose,
hair ruffled, in the early hours of the morning, a shot of bourbon worming its way through his chest, and watch a square of
sky lighten at the window. And he would think about this
lack, this absence. How to detect an absence? How to grasp
something that was not there? Luke Kane had sufficient self-
detachment to know that if someone had a mind to tap him in
a certain way he would sound hollow. He did not regret this,
he sat alone in the early morning and simply wondered about
it.

One night as he sat in his opulent apartment staring at neon-
dyed sky framed by a window, a bottle of Jack Daniel's loose
in his manicured hand, an image came to him, seemed to fill
the glass as he watched. It was a picture of Sugar Kane

standing on the steps of the house in East Hampton, Lucinda's arm wrapped tightly round her. He pictured the perfect curve of Sugar's cheek, tanned by a summer's sun, remembered her shy smile and the kiss she had blown him. He probed the hollowness inside himself and wondered yet again how it might be filled. With a grunt, he hauled himself out of the chair, pulled off his tie and slipped on his astrakhan coat.

As he walked to the garage where the Eldorado waited, the crowds on the sidewalks parted for him. Even sharp-suited pimps – hats pulled low, faces wreathed with cigarette smoke and breath-mist in the cold night air, a scarlet-lipped woman on each arm – moved deferentially aside to allow Luke Kane to pass. He reached the garage and pulled the doors open, the metal rattling like gunshots across the rain-slick street. The bottle was still in his hand and he swigged from it before sliding on to the soft leather seat and firing the engine. He sat for a moment – a short, sharp moment – and considered what he was doing, considered the bonds of a deal, the strength of his word. And then he stopped thinking and he began to drive. North along Fifth and then east over Queensborough Bridge, heading along the Parkway for East Hampton, Long Island. When he arrived there, he parked the car in the shelter of a plane tree and walked along the beach until he reached the dunes in front of the Kane house.

The house, which he had not seen for seven years, had not changed. It faced the ocean blindly, shutters closed against sea-mist. The gardens were lush and the driveway tended, and in the pale pre-dawn light he could make out the faint outline of the rocking chair on which he had sat, feet on the railing, listening to Lucinda pacing the rooms behind him seven summers before. Luke Kane wrapped the coat tightly round him and crouched in the dunes, smoking and drinking, the sand seeping damp into his clothes as he waited for sunrise.

As the sky began to lighten he was rewarded for his patience. In the gun-metal dawn he saw shutters open to reveal a golden square of lamplight, into which Sugar Kane moved. She leaned out of the window, twisted to look at the sky, looked up and down the beach and then disappeared. Minutes later the doors leading to the deck swung open and she stepped out, wrapped in a thick white robe, a towel round her neck, deck shoes on her feet. She trotted down the steps to the beach, passing within feet of Luke Kane, who crouched in the sand behind clumps of couch grass. He watched her slip off the robe, push the shoes from her feet, and then run into the quiet, near-flat waves. He shivered as she split the water, imagining its ice-blue coldness. Eventually Luke Kane stood up, brushed the sand from his coat and pants and strolled down to the water's edge. The sky was changing each moment, the play of light first lightening then darkening both sky and ocean. Sugar's arms cut the water and it seemed to him that she left behind her angel's wings with each stroke. He picked up the robe and towel and held them out to her as she began to make her way to shore, knowing that the rich, glorious light which suddenly slammed out above the cloud line on the horizon would bathe his face, softening it. He knew, too, that his jet-black hair was tousled by the wind, his coat flying like a cloak. He knew, in short, he looked magnificent, god-like.

Yet even so Sugar Kane paused when she saw him, became a still, black, lightless silhouette, knee-deep in bubbling waves. She clasped her hands round her upper arms and took a step backwards. He could see nothing of her face.

'What do you want?' she called, her voice made thin by wind and fear.

'Well, just to say hello, I guess.'

Sugar took another step back and he imagined how cold she must be. He walked to the water's edge, careful not to wet his high-polished shoes, and held out the robe again.

'Hey, come on, come in.'

'What do you want?'

'You don't recognize me?'

Although he could not see her eyes, he could feel her gaze on his face. 'Luke?' Her voice quavered as a shiver ran through her.

'Sure it is. C'mon. Come in.'

Sugar waded out, rubbing herself, and took the gown. She towelled her hair and looked at him as he smiled. 'What are you doing here?' she asked.

'Thought I'd come and see how you're getting along.'

'But you're not supposed to come here.'

'I know. But I wanted to. Here, let me.' He took the towel and stood behind Sugar, rubbing ropes of wet black hair, releasing the smell of hard salt.

'But you *mustn't* come here.'

'Well, maybe. But seeing as I am why don't we have some coffee or something?'

Sugar turned, and finally he saw her face in the golden light. It was as if he looked into a mirror and his infinite hollowness was suddenly filled. The two of them, brother and sister, stood on the hard-packed, damp sand and stared at each other, each silently admiring what they saw.

Sugar looked away and took the towel from Luke Kane's hands. 'I can't. You're not allowed in the house.'

'I know that. But why don't you get fixed up and dress and I'll meet you out front? We can go into town and find something.'

Sugar stared at him again, a hand mindlessly rubbing the towel. 'I'm not allowed to meet with you.'

'I parked my car down the street. I'll wait for you there.'

Luke Kane smiled and walked away, digging his hands into his pockets, his polished shoes now stained by salt water despite his care. He waited in the Eldorado, the engine running, the heater blowing warm air over his feet. He looked, once, in the mirror and saw his chin was dark with stubble – he looked rakish, looked dangerous. As the last of the bourbon washed over him he dozed, his head resting against the window. So he missed his moment of triumph, the sight of Sugar Kane, dressed, now, in jeans and a dark, baggy woollen jumper which had been his own as a boy, walking down the track towards him. It was the sound of Sugar tapping on the glass that woke him, and he opened the car door, she slipped in and he drove away.

They drove in silence until they found a drugstore open outside Amagansett. It was still not yet seven o'clock in the morning and the man behind the counter was yawning as he tied his apron. He brought them coffee as they sat in a booth, looking out on an empty street.

'Looks like it's going to be a fine day,' he said, wiping the table with a damp cloth. 'You on the way somewhere?'

'Yeah,' said Luke Kane.

'Thought so – I know most people around here. Hey, wait a minute . . . you must be . . .' The man stared at Luke Kane and then at Sugar. The combined effect of their sapphire eyes drove him back behind the counter. Not knowing why, he found a pretext to go into the kitchen out back.

'So, how are you?' asked Luke Kane. 'I haven't seen you since you were . . . seven? Eight?'

'I was six,' said Sugar, stirring cream into her coffee. 'I remember you being home. I remember you leaving.'

'Did Mother ever say why I wasn't to visit?' He wanted Sugar to say no, because for the first time he felt shame about Lucinda – not for the fact of what happened but for the fact of her loss of beauty.

'No.' Sugar reached out for his cigarettes, lit one and sat back. 'I guess . . . I guess I never really wanted to know. I mean,' and she blew a plume of smoke towards the low-hanging lamp globe, the action making her seem older than her fifteen years, 'it had to be something really bad, right?'

'Maybe.'

'You're not going to tell me?'

'Just think of it as a young man going too far, going over the edge.'

'You're really not going to tell me?' Sugar smiled. 'Can't be *that* bad.'

'Maybe not, but I'm not going to tell you.'

'Ah, go on! Otherwise I'm just going to think of terrible things. Did you steal a car or something? Or perhaps, uh, perhaps you did something with a girl? Or . . .' Sugar bounced a little on her seat as she tried to imagine what her brother could have done that was so awful.

Luke Kane touched her hand and put a finger to his lips. 'Sssh. I'm not going to tell you.'

Sugar watched a truck pass, loaded with pumpkins, swaying dangerously with the weight.

'Do you see your father?' asked her brother.

'He's your father, too. Why do you say he's my father?'

Luke Kane shrugged, picked a flake of tobacco from the tip of his tongue. 'I haven't seen him so long I've kind of forgotten him. I don't think of him in any way.'

Sugar frowned. 'He sends cheques for my birthday and Christmas. He used to visit sometimes, come over to the house. But then he stopped and I didn't really care because he always seemed so sort of unhappy when he was there. I mean, even when I was really young I knew he was unhappy. It's funny, I still love him even though I don't see him. But I don't really know him. I guess I always kind of admired him.'

Luke Kane smiled. 'Yes, he was always an admirable man. His word was his bond.' He turned away from his sister and called for more coffee. 'Let's forget it. What's happening with you? How you doing at school?'

And as Sugar told him about the boarding-school outside Greenwich, Connecticut, a girls' college she had attended during the week since she was five, as she told him stories about teachers who hated her, parties in the dorms, bullying and success, Luke Kane watched her. Sugar was beautiful, even at fifteen, made poised and confident by money. Her face was haunting. As she talked, Luke Kane smoked and drank coffee, turning the cup in his hand, watching her smile and frown.

'D'you have a boyfriend?' he asked at last.

'Oh, God, no!' Sugar laughed and laughed.

'Come on, that's not such a crazy question.'

'Well, last summer there *was* a guy who I liked. He was called Rick and he was a guard on the beach? But it's so corny, y'know? The guard, all tan and blond? It was just so *corny*.'

Jealousy shot through Luke Kane and he clenched his teeth as the memory came back to him: of a priest laughing by the shore of Mono Lake. He was impotent in the face of this, because the memory of Rick on the beach in the summer of '56 would always be there for Sugar.

'So you don't have a boyfriend?'

'No. I guess I don't have time. Like, when I'm in school? All we do is work. And in vacations Mother's always around.'

'Maybe she's just worried about you?'

Sugar squirmed in her seat. 'But she drives me nuts. She's really over-protective, y'know? Even my friends notice. Like, they're embarrassed for me.'

Sugar reached out and took Luke Kane's arm, pushing back the thick coat to reveal the watch on his wrist. 'Gee, it's nearly nine. I'd better go or Mother'll go crazy. I mean, OK, she doesn't wake up till nearly noon or something, but today would be the day when she's up for breakfast.'

'She still drink as much?'

'Yeah, I think so. She's real sneaky about it but I know the signs now. C'mon, we better go.'

The man in the kitchen did not emerge until they had gone. He collected their cups, emptied the ashtray and stared at the five-dollar bill Luke Kane had left. As he wiped down the table, a white Eldorado rolled by the window, Sugar Kane leaning out of the window, laughing.

Before Sugar got out of the car, parked once more beneath the plane tree, her brother asked her if she'd like to visit him in New York.

'You live in the city?' she asked.

'Where else? East Eighty-second. I got a great apartment. Maybe you'd like to come in and we could see a movie and have dinner.'

Sugar sat back, trying to comb her hair with her fingers. "S'funny, for years you've been like the bogeyman? But you're not. You're just like everyone. You're like me.'

'So, would you like to visit?'

'Yeah . . . but I couldn't. Mother wouldn't let me.'

'Mother doesn't have to know. Can you get out of school any time?'

'Well, maybe. But it'd mean lying and stuff.'

'Look, it's not like I'm Rick or some college boy. I'm your brother. It's about time we got to know each other. And, like you say, I'm not the bogeyman.'

'Mmm.'

'Here's my phone number. Just call me if you want to come down, OK?'

'OK. I'd better go. Thanks for the coffee.' And she smiled back at him as she walked away.

Of course, three weeks later, during a dark October evening as the first snows of winter fell, Sugar did call Luke Kane. She had arranged for a friend to say that the two of them were staying with an aunt in Boston. So could she come to his apartment on East 82nd for the weekend?

1997

Edison Keeler is sitting in his office, rubbing his pink skull, while phones ring around him and e-mails appear on his screen. In front of him are a pad of paper and a pencil. The office is underground, lit by pinpoints of halogen light, which throw shades of grey into relief. Keeler has disappeared into himself, disappeared right into the skull he is rubbing. He is unaware of the phones shrilling, unaware of the ever-shifting monitor screen. On the pad he has written names, a spinning bundle of names which rolls like tumbleweed around his cranium: Mr Candid? Chum Kane? Flanagan? Gov. Jefferson? Jessie Jefferson? Bronwen? He underlines the last. <u>Bronwen</u>.

Lieutenant Flanagan did not lie when he said that Keeler was the best detective he had ever known; that Keeler could worry a fact into being. (<u>Bronwen</u>.) Keeler thought that Flanagan wanted a fuck when he left the club, nothing more. But now he knows there is something else: Flanagan thinks Bronwen has something he wants and it's not her body. But what can it be? The last thing Flanagan talked about was Mr Candid and as he spoke Keeler saw an almost evangelical glint in Flanagan's eyes, as if – God help him – he was in search of the truth.

Coming out of his trance, Keeler swivels his seat and begins to stab angrily at the keyboard in front of him, and eventually grainy black and white pictures flicker on the screen. A naked Bronwen sways on her callused feet, her erotic movements rendered comic by poor camerawork. It is the surveillance footage from the club, delivered by a multitude of hidden cameras. He freezes the film at a close-up of her face and downloads the image, snatches the disk from the computer and lopes down white-walled corridors until he reaches his goal. The techno-kids take the disk, upload the image and enhance it until Bronwen's resemblance to a savoury confection is undeniable. The image is printed and Keeler takes it to his superior's office, places it on the table in the air-conditioned office. The chief looks at Bronwen's portrait with something approaching distaste.

'Who is this?'

'I don't know her name.' Keeler is annoyed to find himself sweating again. 'I want to run a check on her.'

'Why? In my opinion you have more important things to do.'

Keeler wipes a hand across his brow. 'I think that she's in some way involved in everything.'

'Involved in everything? Be specific, Keeler.'

'I lifted this from the surveillance tape at the club – she was dancing there. She left with Flanagan and was with him when I tailed him. I can't explain.' Keeler looks into his superior's blank, pale-grey eyes. 'It's . . . it's a gut instinct. That's all. There are connections out there.'

The chief stands and walks over to the window, which looks out on the road where Jessie Jefferson fell, her heart punctured by NYPD-issue bullets. Keeler's reputation as a spinner, a weaver of facts preceded him. Keeler's gut was more prophetic a tool than a diviner's rod. But . . . but . . . but . . . The chief knows many things to which Keeler is not privy. For instance, Keeler does not know who Sam the Weasel Man is. Sam must be left alone, untouched; he must not feel threatened. The chief turns and frowns as he notices Keeler's sheen.

'I don't want you going to the club. Leave it with me. I'll have someone go there and ask around quietly. Meanwhile, I want you to get on with the Jefferson case. In,' the superior checks his watch, 'one hour I want you to interview the driver of her car. You may use any interview procedure you wish.'

'Yes, sir.'

'Get back to me.' The chief turns his back on Keeler and scans the mad, fractured skyline as if looking for answers.

As Keeler waits in his office to interview the driver, his mind wanders, wanders back to the Hamptons. Where, he wonders, is Flanagan? Nearly a day has passed since Keeler last saw Flanagan and he is no longer being tailed. Keeler reaches for the phone and calls the number he has for Flanagan in Miami and speaks to the feckless Harris.

'Ah, um, my name's Keeler, NYPD. Used to work with Flanagan years ago. Maybe he's mentioned me?'

'Nope.'

'Well, look, I'm a friend of the family and I really need to get in touch with him.'

'OK. This is what we'll do – give me your secure line number and I'll run a check on you and we'll talk. Y'know, I need to verify.'

As Keeler waits for the return call to be rerouted he stares at the wheel of names on the pad. <u>Bronwen</u>. The phone rings.

'OK,' says Harris. 'What can I do for you? I don't know where Flanagan is. Fucker's disappeared.'

'Are there any messages for him – or even from him? Or anything?'

'Well, uh, yeah. Some woman called him. If you ask me, he's taken time to sniff around some pussy.'

Keeler holds the phone away from his ear and stares at it with amazement. He tries to imagine Flanagan sniffing around some pussy and shakes his head. 'How long have you known Flanagan?'

'Shit, not long.'

'Right. Anyway, so who's this woman? You got a number?'

'Wait up . . . here it is. Some woman called Twyla Thackeray. She's on Miami six one eight zero three three nine.'

'Thanks, Harris. Appreciate it.'

'Look, I dunno who you are and I don't much care if you're a friend of his or not. But maybe you should know that there's a warrant out for Flanagan – he's considered out of bounds.'

'A *warrant*?'

'And an APB. He's disappeared and he's flashing his badge where he shouldn't be.'

'You telling me Flanagan's a wanted man?'

'Looks that way. So if you hear from him, ask him to turn himself in. He's got some woman with him and she's in deep shit, too.'

Keeler puts down the phone, frowning, and redials. Of course, he is told that he has reached the Emerald Rest Home, Naples, Florida, but that, unfortunately, it has been shut down. The Emerald Rest Home? Keeler jots down the name, sets it spinning in the wheel of other names. Keeler agrees with his superior – coincidences should not surprise. He glances at his watch. It's two in the morning and the time has come to talk to the driver of the unfortunate Jessie Jefferson's car.

New York – April

M –

Well, I'm still in NY – snow's gone and sun's arrived with a vengeance. I'm lording it up in the Four Seasons. I have to say it's been something to wake up in the same room, same bed, and piss in the same john every morning. Went down to the Village yesterday (deliberately taking a route which took me past that apartment we stayed in – still looks faded but not jaded) and just walked around, mixing with the crowds. It was full of crazies and Japanese and students and businessmen. I bought a *Times Atlas* from one of those bookshops off Washington Square and I've been lying on the bed in my room looking at it, retracing my journey of seventeen years. What a fine fucking madness – tens of thousands of miles zigzagging across a continent, my arm slung out the car window, or crushed in an economy plane seat, or numb ass on a Greyhound. Was it all worth it?

I also followed (with one of my inelegant fingers) the route we'll take across Europe. I reckon we should begin in Tromsø and finish up somewhere on the Turkish coast – just so long as we can linger in Italy. I always wanted to do that. We could get a donkey or something and walk across the Crete, dust flying behind us, black cypress trees in front, like Mary and Joseph or something. I guess I've been planning this trip all my life, or at least since I last saw you. Like I said, I have to see Sam the Weasel Man, then head down to Florida for a trip and then that's it. We have money, which will buy us all the time we want. We can go anywhere, do anything. I can't begin to explain how excited I am – I feel like when I was younger and knew much less than I do now.

Next day: I did try this once before. I gave it all up and walked away from Mr Candid – left him on a wharf in Bellingham, Washington. I tipped my hat, waved a hand and hitched the Caribou Highway to Prince George and then headed west to Prince Rupert and jumped on a ship heading up to Juneau. I drifted north for days, up the Clarence Strait and Stephen's Passage – I'm following that route right now, touching every fine line on the map. I remember the islands covered in pines, the logs tumbling, guided by tugs and nets. I remember a pod of orcas following the ship, cruising effortlessly, sharp black and white. Eagles swivelled overhead, sea otters floated by, hammering at the shells held on their chests, their faces registering eternal surprise. I stood by the rail every evening, my body used to the vibration of the engines rubbing at my heels, not even noticing it, and it felt like the whole world passed by. It was summer and there were banks of wild azalea on the slopes, splashes of colour on the banks of all the islands and inlets. I stood there with a beer and breathed deep – not mourning the man I left behind in Bellingham. Felt like I'd done it, I'd broken free, walked away. That coastline: dropped from a height on to an uncaring earth, shattering into a million pieces and then drowned. I didn't sleep that summer. I stood at the rail every night as the boat slipped past towns swaying on stilts, hanging over rivers silver with salmon, shades of grey in

the strange sunlight. Because, of course, the sun still hung
low at midnight. Midnight sun, which revealed more
shades of blue and grey than I ever knew existed.

I slipped off the boat in Juneau and stayed there a while,
hanging out in the Alaskan Hotel, then bought a car in
Anchorage and drove my usual looping routes for a few
weeks, setting up camp and burning driftwood fires every
night, lying on my back on the remnants of some of the
oldest rock on earth, watching the stars. Maybe it was
during those short, grey-blue nights – when I watched the
sun and moon slide and reappear between mountain peaks,
listening meanwhile for grizzlies which were loafing about
nearby, scratching themselves and lusting after the juiciest,
tastiest organs I carry with me – that I began to reconstruct
you, Cartesian-style, as we now know. (I think therefore
you are.) I began to put the pieces together, all the pictures
of you that I have in my mind: bending down to pick up
some papers, looking sad; naked in a car, your legs hanging
over the door; grinding coffee beans with your mouth set
in a way it never did at any other time, as I ground
numbers. I spent those nights lying with my shoulder-
blades rubbing against gneiss, trying to keep Peano's fifth
postulate, quantification theory and Leibniz's lunacy at bay,
as I repainted your face in my mind. I was very content
then; at peace in some way, like I was on my own at last.
I wanted to be in Alaska because there the people talked
about 'outside' – by which they meant everywhere that
isn't Alaska, as if there was a dingo fence running across
the continent like they have in Australia. There's even an
island on the archipelago called Unalaska, as if when you'd
had enough of the real thing you could go to that island

and do the opposite, whatever that might be. But all that
was fine, that was what I wanted, because Mr Candid was
on the other side of the fence.

And now my finger's walking up the page, crossing
mountains, valleys and glaciers, heading for Denali. One
late summer's day I took myself in my battered 4×4
towards the National Park. The sun was high and there
were moose rummaging and rumping by the roadside, the
road itself swooping like an arrow shot into a high wind,
wavering and curving across scenery like I'd never seen.
Cowboy Junkies' 'Blue Moon' was playing on the radio,
which seemed appropriate because I could see it right in
front of me, riding high in a white blue sky as I sang along.
I swooped around a slow bend and there was a line of cars
backed up on the two lane highway. Maybe half a mile of
them, both ways. And in the middle of these two polite,
fine lines was a crash by a roadside hut, a police car's blue
strobing light and smashed chrome flashing in the bush. I
waited like everyone else, waited for something to happen.
Waited maybe thirty minutes, drumming my fingers on
the dash, fiddling with the radio. But then I had to go to
the bathroom so I stepped out of the wagon and headed
for the hut. It must have taken me ten minutes to walk up
there, up a gentle slope. As I got nearer to the cops and the
crash I heard a noise like I never heard before or since –
although I have heard something *very* like it: it was the
sound of a father watching his daughter die. He was a
bear of man, with a bushy blond beard, and he was
bawling, crying, *screaming* for someone to do something,
while we all waited for the chatter of chopper blades that
never came. As I edged round to the john, I could hear

another sound. It was the other guy, whose car had
slewed across the road and slammed into the father and
his daughter. The guy was bowed over his steering-wheel,
blood running down his face, the door so smashed up
they'd have to cut him out. And he was crying. Not
crying like you and me but like a young child. He kept
calling, 'Help me, help me,' and there was this cop trying
to talk to him, but you just knew the guy wasn't listening.
And I could tell from his voice that he was out of it.
Beyond this world. The guy was flying on coke or speed
or liquor or a combination. He wasn't even feeling
anything except self-pity. I went into the hut and tried
to piss but I couldn't. When I got back to my wagon I
turned round, headed towards Denali a different way.

That night, as I sat with a beer in the old train wagon
they use for a bar there, the radio was playing and I heard
that the little girl had died of multiple injuries and that the
other driver had survived. The girl's dog, a Labrador, had
died as well in the impact. The dog was called Tinkerbell
and when I heard that I put my head in my arms and I
cried and I couldn't stop and I tried and I couldn't stop
and when I looked up, snot and tears running down my
face, there was Mr Candid, leaning against the bar looking
back at me, unsmiling.

The point is, I thought he was outside the fence – I
thought he was Outside – and he wasn't.

Anyway, I guess the reason I've told you all this is
because I want you to know that I have tried to leave Mr
Candid. I have tried to walk away. But this time I mean it.
I'm going to leave Mr Candid on another wharf, or in a
bus station or a departure lounge somewhere. Anywhere. I

know I can do it because this time I'm going to walk towards you. I'm going to find you. I may even go back to Gideon. He'll know how to.

Love,
Chum

'Gideon. That's all I fuckin' know.' The driver of the dead Jessie Jefferson's car is sweating in the airless room. Keeler is sitting on a desk, skinny legs swinging, his eyes focused on the driver's face. 'That's all I fuckin' know, man,' whines the driver.

Keeler frowns. 'Gideon? You shitting me? Gideon like the Bible?'

'Yeah, like the fuckin' Bible.' The driver's hands are dancing in his lap, pushing at the denim of his jeans, fiddling with a worn Zippo, reaching up and dancing in his hair. 'Got a smoke?' Keeler nods to a colleague and a pack of Salem appears on the table. The driver has difficulty lighting the cigarette, what with his hands making unmatched movements.

Keeler clears his throat as the smoke curls. 'OK, facts: you are driving Mrs Jefferson along Fifth at Fifty-first at five a.m. Your vehicle is involved in a collision. You exit the car and an argument begins between you and the other driver involved. Mrs Jefferson gets out of the car and stands nearby. A fight erupts and you are knocked to the ground. At that moment a police car arrives, with two officers. Mrs Jefferson begins to walk towards them while you're lying on the sidewalk. The cops shoot the unarmed Mrs Jefferson four times, then walk away as more cops arrive. After you have been arrested and Mrs Jefferson declared dead by paramedics, five kilos of coke are discovered in the trunk of Mrs Jefferson's car. Correct so far?'

The man nods, the cigarette now crushed between thumb and forefinger, and swallows, his epiglottis closing with an audible click.

'Doesn't look too pretty for you. How long have you been driving for Mrs Jefferson?'

'Uh, I don't. I mean, y'know, I haven't before. Yesterday was the first time. I stood in for her usual driver.'

'Why?'

'I dunno. Look, I done nothin'. I don't deal, I don't touch that shit. I just get a call tellin' me to turn up at the Jefferson place, drive her to some fancy party. Then I gotta take her uptown about five in the morning. There'll be an accident and I gotta start fighting. Then I'm supposed to walk away. Just fuckin' walk away. That's what was supposed to happen. I didn' know about the coke and I didn' know what was gonna to happen to her. Shit, if I did I wouldn'ta taken the job. Thousand bucks for this shit? I don' fuckin' think so.' He crushes the cigarette butt in an ashtray and his hands begin to dance again. 'I wanna fuckin' lawyer.'

Keeler leans forward. 'Did Mrs Jefferson know about the coke?'

'I dunno. I don' think she knew anything. She was shit-faced. She'd had a few martinis by the time I collected her. She was flyin', man.'

Keeler scans the man's face, his mind snapping shut on possibilities. There is, Keeler feels, no reason for the driver to lie. 'Did she say anything? Anything that kinda caught your attention?'

The man frowns, looks down at his hands and laces his fingers. 'I wanna lawyer.'

Keeler smiles. 'You'll have one. Don't worry about it. You

help me and I'll try to help you, maybe come to some arrangement.'

The man stares into Keeler's flat eyes. 'I dunno nothin'. She was jus' a drunk rich bitch. I mean, y'know, it was difficult to even understand what she was sayin'.'

'What exactly did she say?'

'I wanna lawyer.'

'What did she say?'

Still the man stares at Keeler, shaking yet mulish. 'I wanna lawyer.'

'I'll tell you something. If this is anything like I think it is, you don't need a fucking lawyer, you need a different *life*. That's something a lawyer can't give you. But I can. I can even get you a different face, different prints and a bigger dick if you want it.' Keeler's colleague smiles at this. 'Who's Gideon? Where's that name come from?'

'It's the only name I got with this. Some guy called up, like I said. Sounded kinda old to me, and he said somethin' about Gideon.'

'So who is he? Who's Gideon?'

'I used to know him in LA. It was Gideon got me my work here.'

'Your *work*? What, did Gideon check over your CV and write a glowing reference for the head-hunters?' Keeler slips from the desk and stands in front of the driver, bends down until his face is mere inches away. 'You seem to forget we know you already. You're a piece of shit – I know that and you know that. You're a bit man. You take the shitty jobs no one else wants. This being a prime example. Who the fuck is Gideon?'

'I wanna lawyer.'

'Well you ain't gonna fucking get one. Who is Gideon?'

The driver lowers his head, breathes hard.

Keeler leans even closer, his spittle spraying the driver's face as he says, 'You're beginning to really fucking annoy me. C'mon . . . c'mon. You going through all this shit for a thousand bucks? Who is Gideon?' The driver mumbles and Keeler cups his ear. 'Can't hear you.'

The driver swallows hard. 'He's just a homeboy. He ain't anyone. Hangs out with the Twenty-first crew; does the running for them. Lives out in Culver City. He's jus' a fuckin' runner.'

Keeler stands up swiftly and leaves the room. He trots down the corridor, trying not to think how long it is since he has slept, trying still to push the images of small, unburied hands from his mind. Reaching his office, he picks up a phone. Ten minutes later he reappears at the door of the interview room and beckons his colleague, who joins him outside.

'We got lucky for once,' says Keeler. 'You're not gonna believe this. LAPD picked up a young black male this afternoon, a Winston Luther Gibson, otherwise known as Gideon. He was arrested after a drive-by. He's got two previous. He also had thirty thousand bucks in his pocket in an envelope. Apparently, he says he was given it and he's gonna use it to go to college. Go to college.' Keeler and his colleague smile. 'He's a known Twenty-first Street homeboy. Anyway, they're putting him on a plane. He'll be here by eleven, maybe twelve.'

Keeler's gut is firing now, as if holding its own, private pyrotechnic display. Keeler feels he's getting closer to something but he's still not sure what. He wonders how close Flanagan is to feeling the same way.

LUKE KANE

The night that his son seduced his daughter, Theodore Kane was enjoying a casual supper at a friend's house, just outside Westchester. He was laughing, raising his glass for another bloody half-inch of St Émilion, when his fingers cramped, crushing the lead crystal, at the moment Luke Kane entered Sugar. Theodore's friends rushed to help him, as blood and wine mingled on his palm. He stared blankly at the starched white tablecloth while the carpet stained red, knowing that something was happening. That it was *happening again*. His friends, worried by his pallor, drove him home and helped him to bed, having called a doctor. The doctor, a sensitive man who could detect with his fingertips not only the frequency of a pulse but also the degree of a patient's will to live, shook his head and told the friends to prepare for the worst. So they drew up chairs and sat with Theo through the night.

Theodore Kane had been born in 1880, into the age of gold in a billion-dollar country run by robber barons. His father had fought in the Civil War, Theodore himself lived through the Indian wars, the Spanish-American war, the Boxer rebellion, the Great War, the Second World War and Korea. His life had been lived in violent times during which he amassed a fortune. Mr Steel lay on his deathbed, aware of his friends'

quiet breathing, and thought about this life. He had had ambi-
tions to found a dynasty to match that of the Astors, the
Vanderbilts, Morgans and Carnegies but he had failed. Instead
he had contrived to spawn the unthinkable. If only he had
had the courage, he could have stopped it all.

Theodore survived that night, wishing he had not. But
having lain down, a broken man, he took then to his bed, leaving the phone unanswered, letters unopened, meals uneaten.
Months later, at two in the morning, a time when hearts stop
beating, Theodore died. There was no one with him, no one to
murmur prayers or stroke his brow. Mr Steel simply rusted
away.

Luke Kane rocked on his sister and thought of his father, his
mother, thought of silence, of feeling whole, and he laughed. It
had taken a matter of hours, once Sugar had arrived at his
apartment – her cheeks reddened by the freezing wind and the
flush of deceit, having lied to her school principal – to take her
to dinner, ply her with wine and then manoeuvre her into a
supine, vulnerable position. But what heightened his pleasure
was that Sugar laughed, too. It would seem that she wasn't
vulnerable at all. In fact, Luke Kane and Sugar came together
in a welter of sweat and laughter; the first time of many.

For the next year, as Sugar turned sixteen and Luke Kane
twenty-nine, they met often. Sugar would catch a train into
Grand Central, where Luke met her. The two of them dined in
opulent restaurants – the waiters smiling indulgently as they
served the older brother and younger sister – and then they
returned to the apartment on East Eighty-second and spent
the night together. The extent of their self-absorption grew as
they stared into the mirror of each other's faces. Neither felt

shame, neither felt that their world was awry; indeed, both felt that the world had righted itself.

One night, as they lay naked on Luke Kane's bed, smoking, wordless, he remembered years before sitting on the crest of a hill in New Jersey, looking over the neon necklace of Manhattan, a delicate, pale hand in his lap. That girl had been tiny and pliant, worshipful. Endlessly grateful, even. She would, he knew, forgive him anything. And if he could picture so clearly the small, heart-shaped face of that girl after such a long time, perhaps he should have her?

'I may get married,' said Luke Kane.

'Why?'

'Because it's expected.'

'Who will you marry?'

Luke Kane told Sugar about Iris, describing their meeting of years before. Sugar laughed.

'You're not jealous?' he asked her.

'Why would I be? She sounds like a ghost. How will you find her?'

'I'll find her.' Luke Kane ground out his cigarette and reached for his sister's body. 'I wouldn't be seeing you for a while.'

'That's OK. This isn't over.' Sugar's eyes were bright.

'No.'

Sugar turned in to her brother, into his arms. 'You've done this before, haven't you? That's why you're the bogeyman.'

(Genetic memory.)

The next day Luke Kane drove the Eldorado to Hoboken, New Jersey. He circled the streets, vulpine as ever, closing in on a grey, shingle house. Eventually he turned a corner and saw Iris Chandler sitting on the steps of a porch, waiting for him.

1997

Bronwen waits for Flanagan in a bar on Harvard Square in Cambridge, shivering in the too-cold conditioned air. The tables around her are full of students, most of them reading silently, cramming for exams. Bronwen adjusts her bra strap, picks her teeth, stares at the shell of half an Oldsmobile car sticking out of the wall. She is bored. Flanagan has been gone for hours, had disappeared into the bowels of the university library hours before. Bronwen shifts in her chair, which creaks audibly. Each time the door opens dazzling light bounces in from the square outside, blinding her. She lights yet another cigarette, her furred tongue protesting, as the door slams open and Flanagan stands in front of her. Bronwen shades her eyes.

'Well, man? Any luck?'

Flanagan orders a beer and a burger, sits opposite Bronwen. 'Some. Some.'

Bronwen watches admiringly as he wolfs down the burger, drains the glass and orders the same again.

'I found all the yearbooks and the archives. They didn't tell me much that I didn't know already. Chum Kane was a genius, *is* a genius. I flashed my badge and got access to some of his records. He was born nineteen fifty eight in New York City. At the age of three he was solving complex mathematical questions and reading. That's when the Kanes moved to the family house in East Hampton. He went to local school and had some home tutoring until he was thirteen, when he graduated and came here, to Harvard. Because he was so young he lived with a tutor until he was eighteen. I tried to trace the tutor but he died eleven years ago.' Flanagan pauses and bites into the burger, spilling dill slices on the table.

'So? What else have you found out?' Bronwen fidgets, bored by the details she's being given.

Flanagan swallows. 'Well, thing is, Chum Kane graduated in 'seventy-six and began his doctorate, living in Halls. Three years later he defended his thesis, and at the age of twenty-one he was a full research fellow, began teaching. Incredible, just incredible. Then, Thanksgiving weekend, nineteen eighty, he went home for the weekend and was never seen again.'

Bronwen looks at him sceptically. 'So? I thought you already knew most of that.'

Flanagan leans back in his chair, smiles expansively as he rubs his belly. 'It's always reassuring to have your hunches confirmed.'

'Bully for you, man.' Bronwen scowls, and scans the bowls of chips on the counter.

'When I'd finished with the archives I took myself on a walk. I went to Chum's dorm house and I asked around. One stroke of luck, that's all you need. There was a janitor there, an Irish guy, maybe sixty-three, sixty-four. He's been doing that job, cleaning those rooms, for more than forty years. Happens that his family come from the same town as mine.'

Bronwen's eyes move from the chips to Flanagan's face.

'So we went outside and sat on a wall for a while, reminiscing about things I've never even seen. Then I asked Fergus about our friend Chum Kane. Turns out he knew him, knew him very well. Liked him a lot and cleaned his room for a coupla years. You clean someone's room that long, seems to me you'll be knowing everything about them.' Flanagan smiles.

'And?' Bronwen is holding her heart, holding the picture of Chum close to her skin.

'Seems Chum was a real nice guy, quiet, hard-working. Unassuming. He stayed out of people's way, he wasn't arrogant about his achievements. Fergus said that Chum was always generous, always ready to take five minutes to talk. And one of the things he talked about was his girlfriend.'

Bronwen's heart spasms beneath Chum's face.

Flanagan shakes his head. 'You should have seen his face, Fergus's face, when he thought of her. It was like it was *him* who loved her. Said Chum and her were together maybe two, three years. She used to stay over in his rooms when he was still there, before he bought an apartment, and Fergus knew her well. Her name was Marilyn.'

White skirts fly in Bronwen's mind, curves and breathlessness wheel around her.

'Marilyn, it seems, was a petite, dark woman with strange green eyes. A theology student. She and Chum were inseparable. In fact, they made such an impact on Fergus that he even remembers the two of them leaving for Thanksgiving seventeen years ago. He remembers walking home that morning and Chum's Eldorado pulled up across the street, outside Chum's apartment, and Marilyn got in, carrying some luggage. The two of them were laughing and she called over to Fergus, waved as they left. He never saw either of them again. Apparently Marilyn lived in Plymouth, Massachusetts. Seems we were right. Chum must have dropped her off at home, after she took the photo of him, and then he drove on to the Hamptons.'

'And then?'

'That's the problem. And then? What happened that night? What the fuck *happened*?'

'What happened to her? To Marilyn?' Bronwen's piggy eyes are narrowed.

'I can't imagine. I tried to call the number that was on her files but there was no answer. She dropped out when Chum disappeared. Dropped her studies and then disappeared too. Left home, so Fergus says, and lost all contact with Harvard. It was seventeen years ago. It's a long time. It was Marilyn who called the police to say she was worried. I guess she must have been waiting for him to collect her after the weekend, to bring her back here. But he never arrived.'

Bronwen suddenly slams her hand down on the table and the silent students around them look up as Flanagan belches softly with shock. Bronwen leans forward, resting her startling breasts on the table. 'Whatever happened must have been awful. Chum Kane was a professor or whatever, he had a girlfriend, he had a place in the world. He was safe. It was Thanksgiving and he was going home, to his family. It can't have had anything to do with him. He can't have had a choice.'

Flanagan looks at Bronwen sharply. 'Going home to his family.' In his mind the picture of a key, glittering and sharp, appears, spinning in space. Chum's family – Iris's key. Iris would have been there that weekend. She was, after all, Chum's mother. She would have been stuffing the turkey, trimming the pumpkin, fixing the table. Iris would know what happened that Thanksgiving weekend. She'd already spit out the East Hampton address. Perhaps if he asked long enough, if he asked nicely enough, well, what else might Iris regurgitate? He knew that Iris had liked him, had warmed to him. She'd have recovered a little by now. Flanagan pushes back the chair, scraping it on the scuffed, stripped floor. 'Come on, we've got a drive in front of us.'

'Where're we going?'

'Back to the Emerald Rest Home. Way I look at it, no one else has realized that Iris is Chum Kane's mother, apart from the matron – but I can handle her. *That's* our advantage. Iris has known the answer for seventeen years. C'mon, let's go.'

It's as the two of them are trawling the aisles of the A&P, throwing chips and Coke, cookies and wraps in a trolley, that Flanagan scans the national papers, sees that Jessica Jefferson has been murdered on the streets of New York. He stops dead, a family bag of Animal Crackers in his hand. Skimming the piece, he sees a small item, bottom right, about the fugitive status of a Lieutenant P. Flanagan of Florida Department of Law Enforcement.

New York – April

M –

It's all set up. I called the man and we're meeting tomorrow in the Battery to talk, me and Sam the Weasel Man. He says I'll recognize him by his teeth – 'the dandiest teeth in the state'. Didn't like to tell him I'd already checked him out in the cinema. Strange – then he seemed like a sad, wrinkled sack of a man. Hard to believe he's mixing it with the powers that be. But I guess I should know better than most what deception and stage make-up make possible. I'm

going to sort this last chore/task/job/kill/whatever and then I'm coming for you. Will you recognize me, I wonder, when you open your door to find me standing there?
Love,
Chum

Keeler has slept for six hours when his alarm sounds, dragging him from the sleep of the dead. He is lying on the black leather couch in his office, one foot dangling from its edge. Before he thinks anything else – before he remembers his own name, works out where he is, remembers that he is a father – a wheel rolls into his mind, the wheel of names. One has been added: Gideon.

Keeler throws himself from the couch, strips and heads for the shower attached to his office. Fifteen minutes later, dressed in a fresh, sharp suit, he is at his desk reading the files on Gideon. An hour later he walks into the room where Gideon sits, cuffed, at a bare table. Keeler sits next to a colleague, puts a coffee in front of Gideon. As Gideon stretches his hands out for the cup, Keeler throws down the envelope containing thirty thousand dollars. Gideon pauses, looks at Keeler with filmy, bloodshot eyes as his hands fall back into his lap.

'Coffee's for you,' Keeler says softly, but Gideon doesn't make a move. 'Take it,' he says, nudging it towards the black boy, noticing – just as Chum had done – how Gideon rubs his crotch mindlessly.

Gideon stares at him, reaches for the drink. 'Smoke,' he says. It's not a question. Keeler motions to his colleague, who slides a pack of Salem across the table. 'Fuckin' menthol,' Gideon remarks, as he lights up.

Keeler clears his throat. 'Winston Luther Gibson? That is your name, isn't it?'

Gideon rubs his eyes with the heels of his hands, right leg jigging, always jigging.

'OK. So your name's Gideon, then. Well, that's what I'm calling you, Gideon.'

'An' I'm callin' you mothafucka.'

'Where's the money come from, Gideon?'

'Fuck you, mothafucka.'

'Thirty thousand bucks. Lot of money for a homeboy like you. Where's it come from?'

'You got no charge, mothafucka.' Gideon's right leg is dancing a solo tarantella.

'Got news for you, Gideon: we don't need one. We're not the cops.'

Behind the milky film of Gideon's eyes something flashes. But, then, it has been fourteen hours since he had his last hit. He's coming round. 'Not the cops?'

'You're in trouble.'

'Fuck you.'

Keeler stands and stretches, crumpling the shoulders of his newly pressed suit. He perches on the edge of the table, swinging an elegantly shod foot. 'I've read your files – it's not pretty, is it? The picture of your life? Not pretty at all. Born with a habit, mother dead when you were two. I've read it all – all the welfare reports, all the school psychs' reports. I know everything about you. I wasn't expecting to feel pity but I find I do.'

'Don' need yo' pity, mothafucka.'

'Oh, I think you do.' Keeler swings off the table, sits opposite Gideon so he can look in his eyes. 'Your mother died because she injected herself with cut heroin.'

'I kno' that.' Gideon is staring at Keeler, challenging him to make life worse.

'Of course you do. But did you know that the cutting was deliberate? I mean that someone wanted to destroy the dealers by destroying their stock. A man sat down and worked out what it would take to make the heroin fatal. He bought up all the smack he could find so the dealers had to cut it, stretch it out. What I'm saying is that effectively it was murder.'

Gideon says nothing but his mouth works. The film over his eyes is clearing. Keeler's insides begin to spin, just like the wheel of names in his head. It's his gut instinct cutting in. He chances his arm with nothing to lose.

'We have some idea of who it might have been. We're trying to get him, Gideon. We've been chasing him for years and now we got some kind of picture. Where d'you get the money?'

Off balance, Gideon says, 'He give it to me, man. I din' take it. He give it an' tell me to go to college.'

Keeler looks at the young man. 'What's his name? This guy who hands out thousands of bucks.'

Gideon's eyes narrow, his leg dances. 'The fuck I'm gonna tell you, mothafucka. I ain' done nothin'.'

'Gideon, Gideon – how can you say that? You're implicated in two drive-by shootings, five forced entries and three serious physical assaults. And you're sitting there telling me you're an angel?' Keeler looks at Gideon's hands moving and sees other hands, small and white. He shakes his head. 'You're bailed to appear for the drive-bys and you're already way past three strikes.' Keeler stops and lets the sentence hang in the dead air. Gideon may not yet have been to college but he has survived for years on feral streets.

'You can do somet'in' bout that?' Gideon asks.

'Maybe.'

'OK, mothafucka – what you wan'?'

'Does the name Jessie or Jessica Jefferson mean anything to you?'

Gideon moves his head side to side, loosening his neck, stretching time. 'Yeah.'

'What? What does it mean?'

'She was messed up in somet'in'.'

'You telling me she was dealing?'

Gideon sniggers. 'You crazy? She a rich white bitch – why she gonna be dealin'? She was fitted up.'

'Why?'

Gideon shrugs. 'How'm I gonna kno'? She annoyin' somebody.'

'Who?'

Gideon shrugs again. 'Fuck should I kno'?'

'Gideon, you live in LA – two thousand friggin' miles away. How could Jessie Jefferson be annoying anyone?'

'*Here*, mothafucka, she was gettin' to someone *here*, in New York.'

'Who?'

'Fuck should I kno'?'

Keeler sits back, his fingers drumming a tattoo on the table-top. He appears alert but it's a façade; he's retreated into his mind. Something is jarring here: pieces that should be tumbling into place are still whirring around like electric birds. He looks at the young black man, handsome and doomed. Keeler rubs a temple. Speaks softly. 'Gideon, I want you to listen to what I'm going to say. I don't want you to speak. Just listen. But I want you to remember all the time I'm talking, I can help you. We know a little about the operations of the gangs, that they're linked to many other organizations. We know that there's a lot of money out there, a lot of deals and contacts between these organizations. We know that none of these organizations is legal. There are guns being bought, drugs being bought and sold. Names and contacts being passed around, contracts being agreed. We know that some of these names are lawyers or cops or whatever, guys who are giving the gangs information. We know the gangs buy names – or get them other ways – and sell them on. We know that this is a sophisticated operation – do you know what I mean? We know that the gangs use cellphones, e-mail, drops. That they use runners. That they pass information on and they don't care who to as long as it pays a few bucks. Do you understand me?'

Gideon is frowning, his hands still working. 'Huh.'

'What do you know about all this? Do you know anything? And, remember, I can help you.'

'I don' kno' fuckin' nothin'.' Gideon's eyes are flicking around the room. This is not what he had expected.

'What do you do, Gideon? I mean – how d'you spend your days? What d'you spend your days doing?

'Runnin'. I'm a runner.'

'What does that mean, Gideon?'

'Fuck should I tell you?'

'I can help you, remember?'

Gideon squirms a little, rocks his head on his shoulders; squares those shoulders. But he's sixteen years old and he's scared of the thin man. 'Like, I'm given a name or somet'in' an' I meet a guy and tell him. Or I wait some place for a call, or a pack-pack-package. In a place. Y'know. Sometimes I have to pass over like a . . .' Gideon gestures 'a . . . envelope. With numbers and names and shit.'

'What kind of names and numbers, Gideon?' asks Keeler.

'I dunno.' Gideon's head drops, he stares at the floor as his hands fall still.

'You telling me you never check it out? Look at the papers? Maybe for a bit of private insurance in case anything goes wrong?'

Gideon shakes his head and Keeler knows why.

'Gideon, you can't read or write, can you?' Gideon doesn't move. Keeler glances at his colleague. 'Tell me about the guy who gave you the money.'

Gideon sits back in his chair suddenly, hands locking as he tips the chair backwards. 'He white. Look the same to me, know 'm sayin'?'

Keeler's colleague kicks Gideon's chair and he flips on his back, his head thudding on the tiled floor. 'Sorry,' says the colleague, as he hauls Gideon to his feet and pushes him back in the chair. The unexpected has loosened Gideon's tongue. 'He's like, thirty-five? I don' fuckin' kno'. Blond. Kinda skinny. Blue eyes. Uses smart-ass words – y'know, like a real college boy.'

'What's his name?'

'Never gave me one.'

'How come you meet with him? What can *you* give him?'

'Anythin' he want, mothafucka – don' you see? We can do anythin' we wan'.'

Keeler's jaw works. 'And what does he want? What did you get for him?'

'Names and numbers – that all he ever wan'. Jus' names and numbers. Shit, he paid.'

'He gave you thirty thousand dollars for a *name*?'

Gideon looks away, fumbling with the memory of sitting in the sun outside the Sidewalk Café, drinking cold beer and talking with the white guy. It feels like a different life. 'No, wasn' like that.' Gideon frowns. 'He give me five hundred for the name. He give me thirty thousand for college. It was like a presen' or somet'in'. He jus' give it me. Like he was sayin' sorry for somet'in'.'

Gideon falls silent and Keeler hears the clock tick for the first time.

'What was the name you gave him? Gideon, what was the name?'

But Gideon is lost in the fantasy of going to college – maybe sitting in a bar talking about lessons, or just walking round the streets with books tucked under his arm. Maybe he'd learn to read and write. Gideon forgets where he is, turns to Keeler. 'He wan' me to go, man. I reckon he really wan' me to go. Thass why I kep' the money, din' throw it aroun'. I wan' to go to college.'

'And maybe you will, Gideon, maybe something can be arranged. But first you got to give me the name.'

Gideon sighs, lowers his head. After all, these are not the cops. 'Sam the Weasel Man.'

Bronwen and Flanagan are on the I-95, heading south, heading for the Sunshine State. The footwells of Flanagan's old, rusting Camero are full of Cellophane wrappers, styrofoam cups, crushed cigarette packets. Bronwen shifts in the passenger seat, her rump numb.

'How much further?' she asks, rummaging in an Oreo bag.

Flanagan laughs. 'Hundreds of miles, Bronwen, hundreds

of miles.' Flanagan stares at the black-top, his mind whirring
in tandem with the whirring of passing barricade posts. He's
a fugitive and Jessie Jefferson's dead? What, in God's name, is
going on?

LUKE AND IRIS KANE

Luke Kane and Iris Chandler were married in Las Vegas in 1958. Luke Kane had decided many years before that he would marry before he was thirty, and as he and Iris walked up the garish aisle in the Cococabana Motel off the main strip, Luke Kane was a year shy of that birthday. As the two of them stood at the makeshift plastic altar, decorated with dusty, perished roses, Iris looked up at her husband and smiled, squeezed his arm. Luke Kane was seething with humiliation at the tawdry affair. But it had been his choice – it was yet another barb sent flying over the horizon to pierce Lucinda's complacency as she rocked on the gallery of the house in East Hampton.

(A photographer, who suffered from disfiguring psoriasis on the left side of his face, took a picture of the two of them flanking the Reverend Smith, and Luke Kane posted a print to East Hampton. Lucinda opened the envelope on a morning when the sea could not be seen from the window of the drawing room because of the fret. She looked at the photograph of her son and his wife and her fractured heart tore a little more. Because Iris, in a simple, pale, knee-length dress, reminded Lucinda of herself, of herself as she had been when she was younger. In fact, Iris looked exactly as Lucinda had when Luke was a child, when he had shared her bed. Tiny, strawberry-blonde, with a dusting of freckles. Lucinda tore the photograph in half, crammed it in a bin and poured herself a bourbon, careful to avoid the reflection in the mirror above the drinks' cabinet.)

Iris Chandler, who had spent her life waiting in Hoboken, New Jersey, wondered at the speed with which that life had changed. She had never had any money and so had never developed the habit of spending it. She had never spent the dollar bills her mother had given her on her tenth birthday, choosing instead to preserve them as a reminder – of what, she wasn't quite sure. She had left the bills and the few possessions she owned in her parents' grey-shingled house. Not that it mattered because Luke Kane was rich – her *husband* was rich.

Iris's life changed in other ways. For years her evenings and nights had been spent sitting in the shabby parlour in her parents' house, listening to the wireless, her hands always busy – unpicking stitches, removing buttons, tacking hemlines. But now, during this, her week-long honeymoon, her evenings and nights were spent in other ways. All day Luke Kane would sit at the tables, playing roulette or baccarat, throwing wads of bills on the baize in exchange for chips. For hours he would sit in the smoky, dark casinos, weighing chance and probability against luck, his elegant, jewelled fingers playing with fat cigars, shaping the ash. When he was done, he would appear in their room, where Iris was watching the black and white television with unmasked awe, lying on the bed, surrounded by unwrapped boxes and unopened bags from stores around town. Luke Kane would flick the television off and join Iris on the bed. On their first night together Iris had gasped when Luke Kane first entered her and he had looked at her sharply, angrily. So since then she had swallowed the pain and smiled. Now, as Luke Kane came again and again inside her, she opened her eyes to look at his improbably handsome face and the pain would diminish.

Iris was eighteen when she spent her honeymoon week in Las Vegas. She had no means of articulating what she wanted, what she expected, how she *felt* about this experience. She couldn't believe that Luke Kane wanted her, and she certainly couldn't imagine why. She changed her wardrobe, she changed her hair, she tried to change the way she spoke, the way she walked, subtly altering herself until Luke Kane looked approving. On the last day of their honeymoon, Luke Kane rented a soft-top car and they drove out into the desert. Iris was enchanted by the relentless, barren landscape, free of cars and billboards, streets and houses. She took her hat off and raised her face to the sun but Luke Kane told her to cover herself – he didn't want her freckles to spread. It was that afternoon, after Luke Kane had lifted Iris's flared, flowered skirt on the back seat of the car, under a cloudless sky, deep in the shadows of the badlands of Death Valley, that Charlie 'Chum' Kane was conceived.

When the honeymoon was done, the married couple returned to New York City where Luke Kane bought a large apartment in the East Sixties. He placed large amounts of money each month in Iris's home-keeping account and he returned to Hunter-Philips bank to receive the back-slapping congratulations of his colleagues on his new-found happiness. He never told Iris that he had kept his penthouse in the East Eighties – why would she need to know?

The evening Iris told him, smiling tremulously, that she

was pregnant, he digested the information in much the same way as he was digesting the steak and beans he had eaten at supper. He folded the newspaper, kissed Iris's pale cheek and left. He walked to the corner of the street and called Sugar at school. Later that week he met Sugar in the penthouse and it was as if he had never been away, had never been married, was not a father-to-be.

For three years the lives of Iris and Sugar and Luke Kane ran on rails. Her husband spent enough time with Iris to make her feel loved, even if she wasn't. Sugar spent enough time with her brother to move away from her friends at school, the very people who might have saved her. Luke Kane spent enough time at work to amass a fortune and earn the respect of those who should have known better. He appeared to be a devoted husband and caring brother, a good provider for his child. The rails on which their lives ran seemed to narrow, disappear uninterrupted over the horizon.

One evening Luke Kane turned the key in the lock of the apartment and stood stamping his feet free of the snow that had settled on his shoes. Iris rushed down the hall to greet him, grabbed the sleeve of his coat and dragged him into the kitchen.

'Luke, he's reading! Charlie's reading!'

At the table, on which, Luke Kane was annoyed to see, lay the unprepared ingredients of his supper, Charlie sat, scanning the paper. The child's legs were still plump, slightly bowed. His blond hair was tousled and fine, swept into a comic point. Charlie looked up. 'Hello, Daddy.' His blue eyes returned to the page.

'Charlie,' Iris said, kneeling by the boy's chair, 'read Daddy something.'

Charlie frowned, swiped at his hair. 'OK.' He looked back to the print. '"After a night of uncertainty John Fitz-Fitzgerald Kennedy emerged as the new President of the United States by a nar-nar-narrow margin."'

For the first time in his self-assured life Luke Kane did not only not know what to say, he didn't know what to think.

Iris smiled up at him. 'Isn't that something? I mean, Charlie can *read*.'

Luke Kane ignored her. He, too, knelt by his son. 'Read something else.'

'OK, Daddy. "Early returns fav-favoured Kennedy and shortly after midnight the several thousand Repub-Republicans waiting in the Los An-Angeles ballroom feared the worst."' Charlie smiled at his father with two spit-glistening teeth.

Luke Kane stood up, his briefcase still held in his hand, snow-melt dripping on the linoleum. He smoothed his own black hair, then stroked Charlie's soft head. 'Goddammit. Goddammit.' He didn't know whether to feel proud or threatened. 'He's three years old – how can he be reading?'

Iris rubbed Charlie's plump knees. 'I guess he must just be a little genius, is all.'

Luke Kane breathed deeply. Charlie – the gurgling boy in the high-chair – had suddenly assumed a personality. Looking at the paper Luke Kane saw Jackie Kennedy gazing at her husband, a straining coat tight over her bulging stomach.

'Luke, honey,' Iris said, standing up, her hand still resting on Charlie's leg, 'I've got some other good news, too.'

'Hmmm?'

'I'm pregnant again.'

1997

Charlie 'Chum' Kane wakes up in a fat, luxurious bed in the Four Seasons, East 57th Street. He lies between the sharp white sheets and stares at the cathedral-like spires of commerce he can see through the window. As always he has woken early, before the alarm clock rings, and he turns on his side, curls into a ball, his eyes open. Chum is thinking – but, then, he is always thinking. It is as if his mind is beyond his control. There are times when he wishes he could stare blankly into the distance, thinking nothing, imagining nothing. He sees people doing this everywhere – in convenience stores, in airports, in offices – and he envies them. Because he cannot *stop* thinking. Perhaps he remembers the lecture theatre in Harvard, where he sat as an uncertain thirteen-year-old, aware of the discomfiture of other students. Or he pictures his room in Halls where he lay on the bed with Marilyn, laughing and talking. Often he considers predicate and propositional calculus or the derivatives of functions and integration, mentally attempting to disprove their inverse operations. Sometimes he even imagines what it would have been like to teach at university, to have got tenure, to have lived with Marilyn in a house that was their own. He constructs towering fantasies around a possible life he might have had, revolving around tending the yard, washing the car, shopping at the market; a life cushioned by the mundane: dirty laundry, cooking, watching TV, making shelves, making love. But on this morning, the sky blue and the sun already risen, his mind is solely occupied by two people: he is conducting his daily internal argument with Mr Candid, and he is preparing himself for his meeting with Sam the Weasel Man. Chum realizes that he is shaking slightly beneath the sheets, his limbs trembling faintly.

Fear kicks him out of bed, into the bathroom, and in the mirror he sees a worried man. As he shaves he thinks of Marilyn – standing by a white Eldorado on a snowy track – and he pays the price: a nick in the soft skin of his neck. He swears and staunches the blood with a blob of tissue. As he dresses he notices his hands are unsteady. Unusual. He also notices that he is too thin – he must eat more. Chum tries to throw his mind forward, to the meeting with Sam, in order to calm himself, but the attempt fails. At breakfast he spills coffee on the starched linen cloth and drops his silver-plated butterknife. He feels better once he is out of the hotel, walking along Fifth Avenue, pushing through the crowds heading south and north. He decides to walk to the Battery. It will take a couple of hours but he has all the time in the world.

Sam the Weasel Man is sitting on a bench at the south end of the Battery. It is his favoured spot, from where he can see the dying wharves, the yellow ferries scattering scummy water on their routes to other islands. Sam blends into his environment, looking shabby, fretful and forgetful. In his hand he has a bag of torn bread, cut crusts, which he scatters at his feet for flocks of pigeons. Nearby a scrawny cat lashes its tail in the debris of the night before, sending an empty bottle spinning across Tarmac. Sam feels, rather than hears, someone sit at the other end of the bench. He turns to look at the arrival: a blond man with blue eyes, tall and rangy, clean-shaven. On his neck is a tuft of tissue, stuck to the skin by a bright spot of blood. The newcomer looks as if he has been bigger, stronger, as if he has lost weight. Indeed, Sam has seen a twenty-year-old photograph of the man looking stronger, wider, more substantial. Sam is stunned – he did not expect Bronwen's heart throb to appear. He closes the bag, gets up, walks to a nearby waste bin, dumps the remnants of the bread, and sits down next to Chum.

'You're early,' Sam says, fishing a Winston from a squashed soft-pack in his shirt pocket.

'Yes.' Chum shifts, turns to look at Sam, crosses his legs. Sam smiles and Chum says, 'I see what you mean about your teeth.'

'I take care of 'em. Got a phone call telling me you were coming in. Not exactly a recommendation, I have to say. It was a warning, more like. What d'you want?'

Chum squints into the bright sunlight as a ferry hoots nearby. 'I need information.'

'Obviously.'

'I need to get into Harrison Penitentiary, Florida. I was given to believe you might know someone there who could help. Guard, lawyer, whatever. I was told you know everyone on the east coast.'

Sam stares at Chum, notices that his hands tremble slightly. 'Harrison Penitentiary? May I ask why?'

Chum watches the ferry churning away, chased by urban gulls. His mind races and he comes to a decision. 'I need to get to someone.'

'Who?'

'Ray MacDonald.'

'Again I have to ask, why?'

Chum clenches his fists without thought, explains about MacDonald and the death of Addis Barbar. Explains how MacDonald became a hero for a day, for a night. 'But the thing is, MacDonald raped and killed his own daughter. He's famous, he's notorious – not for that but because he killed another rapist.' Chum is still watching the ferry.

Sam takes a toothpick from a silver case, begins to dig between his teeth. 'What's that to you?'

'He's no hero, is he?' Chum's eyes are bright. 'His victims were girls. Young girls, most of whom suffered from Down's syndrome. One of them was seven. That one was his daughter – she was seven. And he'll be strutting around the yard like a hard man.'

'You done this before?' Sam's toothpick is still.

'Maybe.'

The two of them sit in silence for a moment. Sam thinks a while, makes connections, snaps the wooden pick and drops it on the ground. 'I know who you are.'

'No, you don't,' says Chum, too quickly, as if the speed of the statement will make it true.

'You're Mr Candid. Don't take a genius to work that one out. I've read the descriptions, talked to a few guys.'

Chum shoves his hands in his pockets. 'Can you help me? I mean, do you know anyone?'

'Yup, I just might be able to help you, Mr Chum Kane.'

For the first time in as long as he can remember Chum's brain freezes, empties. He doesn't know what to think. His mouth is dry, his hands shake violently in the depths of his pockets. He hasn't heard his own name spoken by someone else in years.

'Hey, look, don't worry about it,' Sam says. 'I ain't gonna be telling anyone.'

'How the fuck d'you know my name?' For seventeen years Chum has constructed a world within a world in which no one knows him.

'Friend showed me a photograph of you, told me your name.'

'Who? *Who* told you?'

'Like I say, wouldn't worry about it. Picture musta been twenty years old or something. You got your foot on the fender of some old car.'

'A nineteen-fifty Eldorado,' Chum says automatically.

'Nice car. You still got it?'

Chum interrupts: 'What she look like? The woman who showed you the photograph? What did she look like?'

'Young, big girl. From Ynys Môn, wherever the fuck that is. She's not the one you're looking for.'

'How d'you know what I'm looking for?'

Sam shrugs. 'We're all looking for something. And she ain't it.' He stands up, shakes his coat to rid it of crumbs. 'I know a good deli near here. You want some coffee or something?'

Chum nods and the two of them walk out of the park, in silence. They turn a corner and there's a long, black stretch limo. Sam nods at the car and Chum stops walking.

'What's the problem?' asks Sam.

'I don't know you.'

'You don't want to get in the goddamn car?' Sam smiles. 'What d'ya think I'm gonna do?'

Chum stares at him.

'If I wanted you any way other than you are right now, that's how you'd be. You want the contact name or not?'

Still Chum stares at him.

Sam sighs and gets into the limo, leaving the door open. 'I'd walk with you if I could, but it's too far at my age. Mr Kane, I don't know how to persuade you to get in here and ride with me.' Sam sighs again, rubs his eyes. 'What can I say? I've waited years to meet you. Past few years I've *dreamed* of meeting you. I almost feel like everything I've done, everything I've worked for, comes down to you. I've made my plans, and they're good plans, but they're not good enough. I need you. I need you to help me. You and me, we have the same, the same . . . priorities.'

Chum looks at the old man's face and something familiar is etched there. A minute later, having weighed his options, Chum joins him. It is the same limo that delivered Flanagan and Bronwen to the penthouse suite. If Chum had a more acute sense of smell, he would be able to detect a trace of Bronwen's perfume.

As the two of them sit over Danish pastries and coffee, Sam watches Chum's movements: precise, economical. 'I've always admired your work,' says Sam.

'*Admired* it?' Chum is aghast. 'I don't want to be admired. I don't think it's admirable.'

'Oh, but it is. Each time there's a story about some asshole being found dead, you can practically hear the roar of approval going up. Y'ever told anyone about what you've done? How you did it?'

Chum's eyes narrow slightly and his hands stop shaking. He scans the street outside, scans Sam's face, his clothes. He reaches out without warning and strokes the old man's chest.

Sam is startled. 'You think I'm wired? Hey, don't worry. *I* wire other people.' Sam leans forward. 'Look, if it makes it any better, I'm not so different from you.'

Chum looks into Sam's watery eyes and believes him. Doesn't know why he does. 'So, you admire me?'

'You ever told anyone about what you've done?' Sam asks again, lighting another cigarette, motioning for more coffee.

'No.'

'Tell me. Tell me what you *want* to tell me. Tell me what you *can* tell me.' Sam settles in his chair, his small hands wrapped around the steaming mug of coffee.

So Chum tells Sam about the first hit he ever made, in Las Vegas. How he had heard that there was a porn ring in the city, circulating a new form of entertainment – the snuff movie, starring the under-fives. Chum went into a trance-like state when he heard that, as images of violence wheeled in his mind. When he emerged from the trance he went out on the streets and asked around, pretended interest in the mutilated genitals of infants. What appalled him almost as much as the fact of the movies existing at all was the ease with which he could move into the orbit of the porn ring. He was given an address on the edge of town, a fly-blown shack set back from the roadside, with cracked windows and two rusted cars in the driveway. Chum drove out there, walked up to the door, not bothering to hide or dissemble. He knocked and shouted a password through the torn screen door, went in and saw a dim room, drapes drawn, with two settees, four men and a television. The men glanced at him but remained sitting, one waving a hand at a hard-backed chair in the corner.

'We'll do the business later,' the man said. 'Ya should watch this.'

On the screen a small blond boy, looking not unlike Chum when he began to read, was strapped over a bench. Behind him stood a man, naked from the waist up, holding a pipe of some sort. The man's face registered nothing as he inserted the pipe into the boy's anus. Chum realized that the rapist was the man who had spoken, which was why Chum chose to shoot him first. The gun jumped a little more in his hand than he had expected and he made minor adjustments to his aim as he fired the bullets into the bodies of the other men. The silencer gloved the sound, made it chunky and plump, satisfying. Chum stopped the video, removed it from the machine. Considered, for a moment, shoving the muzzle of the gun into the offender's own anus but rejected the idea. Instead he placed the handle in the man's hand. After all, Chum was rich – he had spent months gambling at the tables; he would buy another gun. He took the video into the kitchen – a bare, scratched room – found a canister of lighter fuel and burned the tape in the sink. The fumes were foul, and when the tape had buckled and melted he doused it with water before washing his hands and walking out.

Chum has not spoken of this before, indeed, has not had a conversation in years. And now he finds he cannot stop. For an hour he talks, almost in a monotone, about the things he – or, rather, Mr Candid   has done. The men he has killed. Always swiftly, sometimes deviously. He even tells Sam about the time he sailed out into the Pacific Ocean and fed heroin to the fishes. When Chum has finished, when he falls silent, head bowed, Sam looks older.

'You can't feel guilty,' Sam the Weasel Man says. 'What you just told me . . . you *can't* feel guilty. It's OK. It's OK. I still admire you.'

'How can you?'

'You're thinking right now of the people you killed. Why don't you think instead of the people you saved?'

Chum looks up at him with thin, watery eyes. 'I wrote someone once that I think of myself as a futures trader. I trade one future for another.'

'That's a great way of putting it. That's *exactly* what it is.'

'Tried to stop once. Went up to Alaska. Thought I'd be safe there, but I wasn't.'

Sam scans the younger man's face. 'Y'know, seems to me you must be lonely.'

'I'm . . . I'm going to stop soon. I want to stop. I just need to get to MacDonald and then I'm going to disappear.'

'Where you going to go?'

'I don't know.'

'Look, you told me everything already. What you're telling me now don't mean anything compared to that.'

Chum's eyes have cleared. 'You said you've done similar. What d'you mean?'

'Not the same way. Not the same way at all. Always at one remove. You read about that woman, coupla weeks ago, shot on Fifth Avenue?'

'Yeah – the sirens woke me up. Some governor's wife?'

'That's right. Jessica Millicent Jefferson. I set it up.'

Chum slumps back, frowning. 'You set her up? What d'you mean? You can't shoot unarmed women on the street. You can't justify that.'

'Let's go.' Sam stubs out his cigarette and stands, walks out of the deli without paying. Chum goes to the checkout to pay, but is waved away. He follows Sam and the two of them begin to walk east, the limo crawling the kerb ten yards behind. A cold wind has kicked up and the two of them button their coats.

'I'll help ya,' Sam says. 'I *do* know someone in Harrison, who is – sympathetic? – a supervisor on Block C who'll shield you if you can get inside. That bit I leave up to you – I know you can do it. But I need you to do something in return.'

Chum is frustrated, raging in his head. He is appalled by what Sam has done and yet wants to end all this, wants to get to MacDonald and end all this. Wants to get rid of Mr Candid and *end all this.* 'What?'

'There's someone else in Harrison I want you to visit.'

'Who? What's he in for?'

'Oh, you need to judge the case, do ya? See if it fits in with your idea of what's right? Is he *bad* enough?'

'Something like that.'

'Mr Kane, I've said I admire what you do. I just want to suggest something to you. You get rid of child rapists and sex abusers and I think that's a good thing. But there are people, Mr Kane, who do other things that maybe don't have to do with sex and they don't have much to do with anything else, either. And maybe you should pay some attention to them – they are equally worthy of your attention.' Sam stops on the sidewalk, puts his hand on Chum's sleeve. 'My name is Sam the Weasel Man. That's what I'm known as. But it ain't my name.'

'I know that.'

'Hardly anyone knows my real name. I've told you your name and in a minute I'll tell you mine. I come from the Bronx. Lived in a shit-hole there till I was twelve and then I left, walked away from my mom and step-dad and never seen them since. I came here, I worked and then I worked some more and then I got very rich, selling radios and shit off Times Square. Then I worked some more and made even more money. Always legal, always right side up. Married a woman who worked in one of the stores, Belinda was her name. She was comfortable, y'know, comfortable to be with. We had a good life together but she died twelve years ago. I miss her. I miss her a lot. We were happy. Didn't want much – just a good family, vacations in Florida, Virgins, Hawaii, maybe Europe, y'know? And we had that. I used to go play cards every Thursday and when I got home, there she'd be.' Sam stops, looks down at the sidewalk.

When will he get to the point? thinks Chum.

'Like I said, I have two different names, two different lives. These days I'm known as Sam the Weasel Man. But I wasn't always. We had a girl, Belinda and me, a little girl called Katarina. She had real pretty hair – black and curly it was – and big blue eyes. Would be her eighteenth birthday next week. ' Again he stops.

'What happened to her?' asks Chum, swallowing hard, because he knows something must have done.

'My name, Katarina's name, is Kowalski. My girl was Katarina Kowalski.'

Again, Chum frowns. Kowalski? He knows this name. From a long time ago. His mind kicks into action, throws the switch of his memory and a headline comes back to him, from nine years before. His eyes widen. 'The kids with the hands.'

'Without them, you mean. Katarina was the first. They found her on a beach, buried under some sand. He'd cut off her hands. First there was me, Belinda and Katarina. Then me and my little girl. And then just me. That's when I became Sam the Weasel Man. That's when I started using my money to do things. Meet the right people, find out who has the power.'

'But they got the guy. Thomas Jefferson the Third. They got him and they locked him up so deep even I can't find out where he is.'

Sam begins to walk again and the limo glides forward. 'You know, it took eight more kids dying to get him. A governor's son. Governor Jefferson's son. Also Jessica Jefferson's son. He was judged to be insane. Well, of course he was fuckin' insane. But what difference does that make? He still fuckin' did it. And his parents had the luxury of pulling strings and spreading money so he's still alive and kicking in Block C, Harrison Penitentiary, Florida.'

LUCINDA KANE

As Chum Kane waddled on his podgy, bowed legs around the apartment in Manhattan, pulling books from the shelves, crumpling newspapers as he learned to decipher signs, his grandmother passed her bourbon-sodden days in the old Kane house in East Hampton. Lucinda was now in her sixties, a bloated ghost, wan and dry. Her skin itched, flaked away, and she scratched at it mindlessly as she tried each evening to muster her thoughts, tried (much as Iris would do years later) to remember what had happened.

Her days followed a pathetic path: the purgatory of each morning as she crawled from her solitary bed, on hands and knees, wrecked by dehydration, her head pounding, to draw a bath. She lay in the scalding water for an age, resolving to change things, to pour the bourbon down the sink once she was dressed, to do good works; in short, to change. But once she hauled herself from the water the demons began to mutter. As she towelled herself dry she caught sight of herself – no matter how hard she tried to hide – in the mirrored wardrobes. Her thighs rumpled like tidewater sands, the wrinkled skin hanging beneath her arms, the opal-shot stretch marks on her sagging stomach. Her toenails were yellow and ridged, her neck folded, her face paunchy. Beneath her eyes were the bags holding the disappointments of her life. Despite herself, she would move to the mirror, stand inches from it, staring into her eyes, the sclera scored with fine, bloody lines, despising herself as the demons yowled. The weeks and months she had spent protecting Sugar from the big bad wolf, all those days spent lying on the beach or speeding across the water as the sun blasted down, had sucked the life from her skin. Theodore, she thought, would be pleased that she had, after all, paid a price.

Once she was dressed, in loose flowing clothes which left her flaking skin to itself, she went down to the kitchen, her swollen ankles protesting as she descended the stairs, to pour away the bourbon. Each day she opened the bottle, moved to the sink, only to be overwhelmed by the sweet fumes, which made her throat ache. Hating herself, she'd snatch a glass from the drainer and pour herself two fingers, swilling it down, without ice, without water, without thought. Only then did she begin to feel better.

Juanita, the maid, and José, her husband, the gardener, would move ever more cautiously around Lucinda as she sat in the magnificent drawing room, or on the scrubbed deck, in the same chair as Luke had rocked years before, depending on the season. Lucinda was cunning with herself. She eked out her mind through the daylight hours, keeping herself afloat on the surface of the bourbon, floating just enough to be safe.

It was when Juanita and José left in the late afternoon that Lucinda began to mutter to herself, then that she began to drown. Every evening she paced around the house gathering together her memories. She recalled the glittering cocktail parties of the forties, when women wore long, flared skirts gathered at tiny waists, tight angora high-necks, and drank highballs. When cigarettes were smoked in pearl or jet holders and diamonds glittered. Whenever she pictured herself at those parties, Lucinda was always centre-stage, flirting, laughing, surrounded by admirers. She poured more bourbon and acted out past glories, leaning on the piano in the drawing room, conducting conversations with people who were not there. Garland, Hayworth and Garbo joined her, Dior dressed her, Astaire danced for her – all there, in her drawing room. Communists were chased out of Hollywood, Truman arrived. Anyone looking through the windows of the house would have seen Lucinda gesturing, smiling, talking to herself. She played old gramophone records, stumbled round the floor, tripping on rugs, to the scratched strains of 'Slow Boat to China', 'Baby, It's Cold Outside' and 'You'll Never Know'.

This euphoria lasted an hour or so, before the alcohol dazed her. Then her thoughts darkened as the memory of Luke Kane re-emerged. She imagined she could smell the odour of vomit and Chanel No. 5, and with this smell came the loneliness that haunted her. She had lived without a husband for more than twenty years, yet was still married. Always, it was when she had sunk into blackness that she reached for the telephone and called Theodore. The first time this happened he had talked to her, tried to soothe her, convinced her to go to bed. But as she called more often, as it became a nightly lament, Theodore ceased to answer the call, left the phone to ring endlessly, and eventually changed his number. Once he had died, she retreated into her damaged self and left the world outside well alone. Some nights Lucinda managed to climb the stairs on hands and knees and fall on to her bed, still dressed. But most mornings Juanita found her lying on the sofa, or on a rug, her eyes blackened by damp mascara. Juanita would call

José and the two of them, frowning and speechless would haul Lucinda's heavy body upstairs.

This state of affairs could not continue indefinitely. Lucinda knew it – which was why she made her daily resolutions – and Juanita and José knew it. But none of them did anything to break the cycle. Instead, it was brought to a close by a phone call, coincidentally another phone call from a school: Sugar's boarding school, in Connecticut. Fortunately, Miss Caulkin, the principal, called early in the morning, catching Lucinda as she was dressing, before she went down to the kitchen to empty the bottle. Lucinda stood in her bedroom, surrounded by chintz and organdie frills, and listened, ankles aching, as the principal listed the dates on which Sugar had been absent from her dorm. Weekends during which she had claimed to be staying with friends but, it had now been discovered, she had not been. Sugar, it seemed, had been spinning a candyfloss of lies.

'Do you . . .' Lucinda cleared her throat. 'Have you found out what she's been doing?' But Lucinda already knew the answer. All those days spent bobbing on the sea as the sun sucked the life out of her had been for nothing – the big bad wolf had snatched Sugar anyway.

'Yes, we have. It seems she's been spending weekends with her older brother in New York. Is that right?' The principal's voice was concerned.

Lucinda thought rationally for the first time in a long time, balanced her options. 'Yes – sure that's right. I'm surprised she didn't tell you straight out. There's nothing wrong with that, is there?'

'No, of course not. He's a family member and a responsible adult, so it's not a problem. And Sugar's a very self-possessed

young woman of eighteen. I'm simply surprised that she felt
unable to tell the truth about the matter.'

'I have no idea myself. Will she be punished?'

'Well . . . she'll be grounded for a month. But since she graduates next semester, I see no reason to jeopardize her record
further.'

'Thank you, Miss Caulkin, for taking such an enlightened
view.'

'You can understand why we were so worried? There are so
many more temptations, these days, than there were in our
time, Mrs Kane.'

No, Lucinda thought, the temptation never changes. 'Quite
so.'

'Well, thank you for clearing up that detail. I'm sorry to
have bothered you.'

'Goodbye, Miss Caulkin.'

Lucinda replaced the handset carefully. Walking down the
stairs, her hand supporting her on the rail, she did not bother
to pretend to herself that she was about to throw away the
bourbon. Instead, she went straight to the drinks cabinet and
poured herself a tumblerful. Juanita, who was mopping the
floor, saw this and raised an eyebrow. All day Lucinda drank,
remaining strangely lucid and apparently sober. In the afternoon she sat in the study, writing page after page in an untidy
scrawl, eventually tearing each sheet to shreds. Once the help
had gone and she was left alone, she opened a second bottle
and took it out to the deck, even though it was October and
the sea breeze was up. She sat and rocked in the chair, watching the waves, drinking from the bottle. As usual she thought
of how things might have been different, but this time her
thoughts were hard-edged, clear. She thought of Theodore's

funeral two years before, of the hundreds of people who had come to mourn, how his praises had been sung, the paeans of international praise – all played out in the absence of his son. She recognized that she was to blame for what had happened, because Theodore – who had been a *good* man – would have stayed if she had not slept with her son, and then she wouldn't have been lonely since his leaving. Lucinda knew she wasn't smart but – sighing – she thought that even she could have been smarter than that. She was surprised that Luke Kane had broken his promise, broken the deal not to see Sugar. Perhaps he thought, because his sister was eighteen, the deal was void? As Lucinda sat there, bleached by moonlight, she realized that, for once, her skin wasn't itching.

Astaire, Garbo and Garland stayed away that night; there was no singing and dancing, no cocktails and laughter. Instead her only company was the grey, thin cloud cover, that shifted across the sky. It occurred to her that she had very few life-long memories – she couldn't remember her childhood, her parents, her schoolfriends with any clarity. She should have memories of the Great War, when ten million had died, the Russian Revolution, the first time she heard 'Rhapsody in Blue', Coolidge being re-elected, the days when she secretly practised the Charleston with girlfriends. She knew that she was alive when these things had happened but the first event in her life she remembered clearly – could see it as if the event were unfolding in front of her – was the nurse in the maternity hospital recoiling when she saw the newborn Luke Kane.

Lucinda sat on the deck until she could drink no more, and when she stood up she was taken aback to find herself stumbling, because her mind was still so clear. In her bare feet she walked off the deck, across the gravel drive to the garage, unmindful of the cold. It was José who found her, the next morning, when he opened the garage door to fetch a hoe. Lucinda was hanging from an exposed beam, hanging neatly, hands by her sides, her white and red house robe delicately folded round her thighs.

1997

Sam Kowalski is walking away from Chum, his shoulders hunched in his raincoat. The reliving of the day Katarina was found on the beach has made him older, smaller. Chum catches up with him, falls into step.

'What do you want me to do?' Chum asks.

'Whaddya think?'

'Is that the deal? I get to know the contact if I agree to get rid of him? Jefferson's son. I get the contact if I finish this for you?'

Sam shrugs. 'There're no conditions. It's up to you.'

'I get to choose?'

'You get to judge.' Sam smiles a thin smile. He waves for the limo and it glides to the kerb beside him, blocking the traffic. A traffic cop sees this, walks over, flipping open a pad. Chum forces himself to relax, to breathe. The cop readies his pen, checks the plate and stops, closes the pad and walks away. Sam ignores this and opens the limo door.

'The contact in Harrison – he's called Troy, Junior Troy,' and Sam gives him a slip of paper with a telephone number.

'Thanks.' Chum is aware of the cop lingering nearby. 'I'll let you know what happens.'

Sam pauses, scans Chum's face, ignoring the cars hooting

in the jam behind. 'I gotta ask – what started this? You talk like a college boy and what I hear is that you were Ivy League or something. I hear you're very, very smart and this ain't exactly a white-collar profession. What happened to you?' Sam watches Chum's face close: it empties like a building on fire, becomes blank as a white-out. 'Look, it ain't no big deal or anything. I'm just interested. I just can't imagine what would do this to you. I told you what happened to me, what happened to my Katarina. That's my reason, my only reason. Revenge. But I can't even begin to imagine yours. What I do – it's personal. What you do ain't.' Sam sees that his words aren't even registering; his words are hitting the blank screen that is Chum's face and sliding away. The sound of klaxons and shouts from the cars and buses backed up behind the limo begin to register with Sam. 'I gotta go, Mr Kane. Forget I asked. If you ever want to talk, you know how to find me. Here.' Sam fishes in a pocket, draws out a card. 'You can always reach me here.'

'In the cinema on Forty-second? The phone locked in the box?'

Sam frowns, then extends his tiny hand for Chum to shake. 'Why am I surprised? Good luck.' Sam slides into the limo and closes the door. The car glides down the street as the cop begins to direct the traffic, trying to free the snaggle of cars. Chum pulls up his collar, lowers his head and walks away.

Bronwen is restless. Flanagan's car is old, the air-conditioning and heating malfunction, on occasion confuse each other, resulting in blasts of oily air hitting her face as a freezing wind bathes her ankles. She feels smoked out, as if one more cigarette will close her larynx. Yet she lights another.

'How much longer, man? How much longer are we going to drive?' She kicks out at the mass of garbage at her feet – candy wrappers, cardboard Wendy's boxes, empty M&M packets, twisted like small turds.

Flanagan glances over at her. 'Maybe a half-hour. There's a HoJo twenty miles down the road. Why doncha listen to the radio or something?' He flicks the switch and twists the dial.

A tomato-fat voice bursts out: 'Feeling lonely? Feel like today's world is too much for you? Feel like no one under-stands? Make friends with the Lord! He'll help you through loneliness, illness and stress. He'll guide you to happiness! Grab a new life for yourself – live with God! Accept him into your life. Friendship packs just thirty-nine ninety-nine, includ-ing post and package. Credit card charges applicable.'

Bronwen snorts. 'What is wrong with all of you? I mean, just listen to that!' She snorts again. 'Arsehole preachers in white suits running up and down the country, yelling and screaming, taking everyone's money. What is *wrong* with you? You know, I watched some TV when I was staying at the hotel in New York. It was ridiculous! Boys of ten dressed up like Liberace, putting their hands on women old enough to be their grandmother. The audience jumping up and down, screaming. I mean, what is all that about?'

Flanagan smiles weakly. 'Well, it's our constitutional right.'

'What? You have a constitutional right to look like com-plete twats?'

'I guess that's not a compliment? All I mean is Americans have a right to pursue happiness.'

'Strange you should mention that, because I noticed that everyone in those programmes looked as miserable as sin.'

Bronwen fiddles with the radio as Flanagan attempts to explain. 'Thing is, we're a God-fearing people. We believe in God. Or at least, most Americans do.'

'What I want to know, man, is do you all believe in his forgiveness? Because it seems to me that that's what you need more than his love.'

'What you getting at?'

'I've never understood how you Americans can say that you have a right to happiness, and at the same time you carry guns everywhere.'

'The right to bear arms is so we can protect our family and our property.'

Bronwen looks at him with her little piggy eyes narrowed. 'But what about the right to happiness of the people who are killed by those guns?' She is perspiring with the effort of thinking so deeply.

'It's a difficult one,' concedes Flanagan.

Bronwen snaps off the radio and sits back, unties and reties her hair. 'Tell me again why you want to find Chum.' She says his name shyly, as if she feels she is taking it in vain. 'You said you wanted to know how he lives with himself.'

They sit in silence, as Flanagan thinks. The expressway rolls into the night, trucks and cars speeding by, an endless stream of white and red lights. They are passing a port on a river where tall silver chimneys, decorated with neon insignia, belch steam. The sky is dark orange.

Flanagan clears his throat. 'Like I said before, I think Chum Kane is the person they call Mr Candid. I think he's responsible for the deaths of many people. But everything I've learned about him makes me believe he's fundamentally a good person. Sounds crazy, doesn't it? How *can* he be a good person? I've been told that he's known to have killed more than ninety people. But they reckon it's more than that. They reckon it'll be in the hundreds.'

Bronwen is agitated, keeps trying to interrupt. 'But Oprah said that this Mr Candid was supposed to only kill bad people – even though she doesn't believe he exists. He only kills, you know, rapists and people like that. He *is* a good person.'

Flanagan rubs his forehead. 'Bronwen,' he says gently, 'he can't be a good person. He's a serial killer.'

'But if he gets rid of filth like that, it's got to be a good thing, right? I mean, I know lots of criminals get away with things. Either they're not caught or maybe they get off in court. Like, just before I came here and me mam was on jury service? Well, she had to do a case of a rapist. The woman said he'd raped her and he said she was a slut anyway, but that she'd agreed to have sex. And I don't know why, but the jury let him off. But when the case ended the judge told them he'd been in jail twice for rape and been accused eight other times. The man laughed. Me mam came home that night and cried and cried. But the point is, he should never have had the opportunity to do it twice, let alone another eight times. How does that *happen*? And, you see, if someone killed him – who'd care? It would be a good thing.'

'Bronwen, that's a failure of the legal system. Doesn't mean we can go round shooting anyone we think is guilty.'

'But he *was*!'

'Not according to the courts.'

'Maybe not, but I know you think he was too. You're a policeman, what if you'd arrested him and then, and then' – Bronwen is near tongue-tied with fury – 'you know, then found out that he'd been freed? And then maybe he did it again? What would you *think*?'

Flanagan slows and pulls off on to a ramp. He drives into the parking lot by a vast, glassy mall. 'I need to buy some fresh clothes. You want to come along?'

'Answer the question, man. What would you think?'

Flanagan turns suddenly, rocking the car, wedging himself behind the wheel, facing Bronwen. 'I can tell you exactly, but exactly, how I'd think because I've done it a hundred fucking times. I've gotten to scenes where maybe the mother's lying on the floor, bleeding to death as her kid watches, and the guy's so out of it that he didn't even think to get out of there. So I cuff him and take him away and maybe he walks because of a technicality. Or maybe the scene's different. Maybe there's a drive-by and a seventeen-year-old boy's lying on the side-walk with half his face missing, but everyone caught the plate, so I go round and arrest two suspects. Then I find out months later they plea-bargained and got a year's community and a pledge. Or I get the guy who tortured a little girl to death after raping her and raping and killing her mother, and he does get sent down. But then I find out he's killed another prisoner and people think he's a fucking *hero*.

'Or maybe,' and Flanagan draws a shaky breath, 'I get to a beach and I dig in the sand and I find a little girl nine years old, and she's so pale, and her skin's grey. And, dear God, she doesn't have any hands because someone cut them off. And maybe I find out later that they were cut off when she was still alive. But that time I don't get the guy, someone else does – but only after he's done the same to eight more kids. Then, nine years later, I find out that he was judged criminally insane and he's serving out his time in a secure unit. He's in a building feeling secure, enjoying *security*, which is more than any of those kids are.'

Flanagan looks away from Bronwen's shocked face. 'The kids were buried without their hands. They never found them and he never said where they were. I just found that out a few days ago.' Flanagan sighs a shuddering sigh and the car rocks again, gently. 'And what about their parents? If I feel like this after nine years, how the fuck must they feel?'

Bronwen stretches out a plump, warm hand and rests it on Flanagan's. 'I'm sorry. I shouldn't have asked.'

"S'OK. You're right to ask. Thing is, sometimes I've been standing there with some asshole, my gun against his head and the room's been empty. I mean, I could have blown him away and no one would have cared. I could have argued self-defence. I could have changed things. And sometimes I think if I knew how to clean my hands afterwards, if I was sure I was *right*, I'd do it. That's why I need to find Chum Kane.'

For minutes the two of them sit watching cars pulling in and out, watching neon signs flicker, fade and flicker as Bronwen holds his hand. 'Come on,' she says eventually, so softly he barely hears her. 'Let's go and buy some clothes.'

New York – April

M –

I just got back from my meeting with Sam the man. I called Room Service the minute I hit my room and now I'm sitting at this writing desk, drinking too fast and looking out the window at people going about their business.

I was scared today – this guy I met, he knew who I was.

He knew my *name*. He knew my name. Mr Chum Kane, he called me. I thought the only people who knew my name were you and my mother. But he knows it too. And looks like other people might. Apparently some woman showed him a photograph of me and told him my name. You know which picture it was? The last one you ever took of me, when I was dropping you home for Thanksgiving. Remember it? He described it and I knew straight away which it was – I had my foot on the fender, just looking at you. And you pulled it out of the camera and waved it around, waiting for it to dry. The wool on your gloves stuck to a corner. I remember that.

And I remember something else, too: as you stood there, peeling the backing off the photo, I asked if you were sure you wanted to marry me and you said yes. I was so happy I could hardly speak and you wrote on the photo so we'd always remember it. As if I'd ever need reminding.

Later now. I been lying on the bed thinking, drinking. I gave that photograph to my mother. She thought it was so wonderful, and she was so unhappy when I got home that night, I gave it to her. I reckoned she needed it more than we did. She put it in her dress pocket and kissed me, told me thank you. How did this woman get hold of it?

One more thing. Sam asked what happened to me, why I'm like I am, why I do what I do. I couldn't answer him and why would I? I haven't even explained it to you. And it seems to me that you need – no, deserve – an explanation more than anyone else. After all, I asked you to marry me and left you smiling at your parents' door and I drove away waving and you never saw me again. It didn't happen because I didn't love you. I did. I do.

Later: when Sam asked me what happened I wanted to tell him about Tinkerbell. I wanted to explain, but I thought he'd reckon I was crazy. I don't feel crazy.
    Love,
    Chum

Keeler is standing outside the door to the chief's office. He is staring at the beige wall opposite, trying to order his thoughts. If anyone were standing next to Keeler, it might be possible for them to hear him ordering these thoughts, hear the various mental filing cabinets slamming. Bronwen, Gideon, Jefferson, Flanagan. Mr Candid. Chum Kane. And now Sam the Weasel Man. Keeler's gut fluxes and spasms, an instinctual thrash. Something – or, rather, someone – links these names. He knocks on the door and the hatchet-faced man behind it barks a command. 'Come.'

Keeler walks into his superior's office and is dazzled by the sunlight streaming through the windows, the first natural light he has seen for nearly two days. The man behind the desk looks up at him. 'Sit. What can I do for you?'

'Sir . . .' Keeler shakes his head, clears it. 'Sir, I have a few questions. I think there's something going on but I need a piece of information to put it all together.'

'What?'

'Remember what you said about coincidence? That it shouldn't surprise us? Well, I agree. But I'm tripping over too many of them at the moment. I have a list of names—'

'What happened in the interview, Keeler? Just tell me that.

Stick to the facts. I don't have much time.' The man is clicking a pen over and over, snapping it open and shut with his thumb.

Keeler outlines the interviews, both with the driver of Jessica Jefferson's car and with Gideon, the homeboy from the 21st Street Gang.

'So, what name did Gideon give you?' the chief asks, faintly bored.

'Sam the Weasel Man. It's a name I've heard before and, sir, I know that there's a connection here. If I can get to that, get to that connection, I think . . .' Keeler pauses, choosing his words, near-overwhelmed by their import '. . . I think I'll be that close to Jefferson's killer, but, more than that, I'll be able to put a name and face to Mr Candid.'

The chief is looking at him with an expression the like of which Keeler has never seen on his face before: frozen panic. The chief stands up, walks to the window, turns, turns a ring on his pinkie, walks away from the window. If Keeler didn't know better, he'd say the man was agitated.

Which is exactly how his superior is feeling. How has Keeler made the connections? But then . . . but then, Keeler is known within the Bureau for precisely that: making connections. 'So,' the chief says, 'are you postulating a scenario?'

'Uhh, I wouldn't go that far.'

'Try.' It's an order.

'OK. The Bureau knows, despite statements to the contrary, that Mr Candid exists. I have reason to believe that his name is Charles Kane, otherwise known as Chum Kane.'

The chief looks up with ice-cold eyes. 'Have you informed anyone of this?'

'Well, no, I haven't. The source is dubious.' Keeler

apologizes without words to Flanagan for describing him as dubious.

'Nevertheless.'

'Uh, I think the source is linked to Kane in some way.'

'What way?'

'Well, Bronwen Jones – the woman in the club video? – she's now with the source.'

'So Flanagan is the source?'

'How d'you know that?' Keeler begins to sweat, just as he always does in his superior's company.

'Be serious.' The chief smiles thinly.

'So – Bronwen Jones is with Flanagan; Flanagan knows Kane's name; Gideon describes the man who gave him the money – sounds like a lot of the descriptions we've gathered for Mr Candid over the years. Gideon knows about Jessie Jefferson – that she was hit because she was annoying someone – and I quote. Then he mentions this Sam guy; that was the name Chum Kane wanted, the one he paid for, the one he wants to meet. And that's the weak link for me. I've heard of Sam the Weasel Man but I can't see the connection. I guess I asked to see you because I thought you might know.'

Yet again, the chief stands and fingers the ring on his pinkie. He is weighing two things in his mind: Sam's anonymity and the protection of which he has been assured by the highest office in the land, balanced against the necessity of finding Mr Candid and stopping the roll-call of death. He comes to a decision swiftly, which is precisely why he is everyone's superior. 'Keeler, I'm going to say this once. You will not question me, nor will you pass judgement on what I say.' Keeler nods. 'Sam the Weasel Man's full name is Samuel Kowalski.'

Keeler is still nodding faintly in agreement and then the import of the name hits him. *'What?* Sam Kowalski? Katarina Kowalski's *father?'*

'Yes.'

Keeler swallows convulsively as the picture of the body on the beach swims into his mind. 'Sam Kowalski?'

'He owns the club, he runs a lot of business up and down the coast. Nothing exactly illegal, but he runs close. But we leave him alone. That's the deal.'

'The deal? What deal?' Keeler is foundering on the banks of incomprehension.

'You remember Thomas Jefferson?'

Keeler nods because he cannot speak. He spent days in a room with Thomas Jefferson, listening to how the blunt edge of garden shears cut just so.

'It was a delicate situation, as you'll appreciate. He *is* Governor Jefferson's son. So the Governor wanted some kind of plea bargain, some accommodation. The deal we worked out, Thomas was certified insane and Sam Kowalski got our protection in return. The other parents were dealt with, too. A payment if you like, a *quid pro quo* to drop a civil case. Sam set up the club and we bought into it.'

'You bought his silence?' Keeler is puzzled.

'If you like.'

Keeler does not like, but says nothing. He cannot imagine Sam Kowalski's silence being so easily bought. Keeler was there when Sam Kowalski was told that his daughter's body had been found. Keeler had watched the man fall apart, become infant-like, his grief overwhelming. Indeed, it was the trauma of that meeting that had driven Keeler into the Bureau. But wait . . . wait—

'Sam Kowalski killed Jessica Jefferson, didn't he? He arranged for the crash, for the guys in NYPD uniforms. He arranged for the coke in the trunk so it would cover his traces. Just one more drug-related crime.'

The chief is stunned, impressed by Keeler's inexorable logic. 'Keeler, the event was unpredicted. We never thought Sam'd do anything like this. He's been clever. He waited nine years, so long we weren't even watching him. Goddammit, we've been helping him, keeping him safe. As you can imagine, Governor Jefferson is not in good shape.' The chief is pacing now, back and forth, in front of the window.

Keeler is still calculating. 'I assume you haven't arrested Sam yet?'

'No. Of course not. He knows far too much and he has too much insurance. If we take him, a lot of things will blow up in the air. We can't touch him – one, because he knows too much and, two, he's covered his traces. The only people who can finger him are – shall we say? – unreliable witnesses. A home-boy and a serial killer.'

'I can also assume that Chum Kane has already met with him, given Gideon gave him the contact weeks ago.'

'Mmmm.'

'In which case, sir, I would speculate that, given Sam Kowalski and Mr Candid appear to be playing the same ball-game, they have come to an arrangement.'

'Like what?'

'Well, Sam Kowalski's got rid of the wife. I guess he'll be going after the son next. Not Sam himself, of course. But it's possible he's hired the most successful serial killer we've ever come across. Or, rather, not come across.'

'You think Mr Candid is going to get to Thomas Jefferson?' The chief is incredulous. 'In *Harrison*?'

'Yes.' And Keeler smiles, because if there's one thing he would love to happen in this world, it's that Thomas Jefferson III should suffer a little before he dies too soon.

'What's funny?' the chief asks.

'Nothing.' But Keeler can't stop smiling.

LUKE AND IRIS KANE

On 20 January 1961, the day that John F. Kennedy was sworn in as President, the remains of the Kane family moved into the old Kane house in the Hamptons, which Lucinda had left to Sugar in her will. As the removal men struggled past him carrying boxes and furniture, Iris directing them into various rooms, Luke Kane sat with a bottle of beer in his hand and Charlie on his lap, watching the young President speak on television. He pondered the idea that he should ask himself what he could do for his country and snorted. Charlie slapped him with a book.

'Daddy, read.'

'Daddy not read,' said Luke Kane, putting Charlie on the floor and standing to stretch. He walked into the kitchen, where his wife, bloated with pregnancy, eight months gone, was sitting at the table, resting her back. Luke Kane opened another beer, leaned against an old dresser and looked at his wife of four years. Her pregnancies had been difficult, they had aged her. And looking at her now, in the flat grey light coming in off the sea, sitting in the familiar kitchen, she looked a great deal like Lucinda. Lucinda, whose ghost Luke Kane was trying to expunge from the house.

Iris looked up from a list she was making and smiled

vaguely. 'Luke, honey, d'you really want to throw out the bed-room furniture? I mean, it's still in very good condition and all.'

Luke Kane watched the way her mouth crinkled as she spoke, faint lines already beginning to appear on her upper lip. Her hands, too, were beginning to wear, acquiring a soft sheen. 'Throw it all out. I don't want anything of hers left here.'

'Luke, I don't get it. It's just so wasteful.'

'We're not keeping anything.'

Iris sighed and returned to her list. The screen door banged and in walked Sugar, her cheeks flushed by a long walk on the beach. She shook her black hair out of a scarf and walked over to Luke, who put his arm round her as she leaned against him.

'Hey, it's great out there.' Sugar laughed and poked his stomach. 'You should have come with me instead of sitting round drinking beer.'

Iris looked up, again smiling vaguely. The Kanes looked so alike, so at ease, that for a confused moment she thought they were twins. Charlie's cry rolled out of the drawing room and Iris stood, steadying herself against the table before walking out. Luke Kane kissed Sugar's cold, rosy cheek.

Perhaps it was the years she had spent in Hoboken, New Jersey, waiting, watching her parents being worn down by genteel poverty, that had stifled Iris's imagination. Who knows? The fact was that apart from her moment of passion, her moment of recklessness, when Luke Kane appeared out-side her parents' house, stole her away and married her, she had acted always in a rational manner. She didn't smoke, she drank in moderation. She liked her apartment, her house, her entire environment to be ordered, tidy. She was grateful that her husband was rich and handsome – these qualities seemed more than she deserved. And yet all her childhood she *had* dreamed, she had had imagination then. For some reason she had known that Luke Kane would return and he did and she had had her moment. But she had never even tried to imagine what would happen *after* that moment – what married life would be like, what her husband would be like. How he would behave. So she thought nothing of his absences, knew nothing about his apartment in the city, which he had kept after his marriage.

Iris also did not consider it strange that she never met any of Luke Kane's family other than Sugar; after all, Iris never introduced Luke Kane to her parents. She wrote them once she returned from her honeymoon, promising to visit soon. But the thought of returning to that house, with the sad tin of dollar bills hidden beneath her bed, was too stifling, so she deferred the visit until she forgot to make it. Their world was so removed from the Hamptons, it was a distinct and separate entity, unapproachable.

Her first months as a wife in the apartment in the city were a revelation. Luke Kane gave her an allowance and went to work each day expecting her to spend it in his absence. The stores were full of new electrical devices, Formica and sharp-angled furniture. Iris dressed each morning then launched herself on to the streets of Manhattan to spend, spend, spend – overwhelmed almost by her ability to choose. But after a few months she wearied of this, weighed down by her expanding belly. The pregnancy was difficult – Iris suffered bouts of nausea, pain in her lower legs which became oedema, inflamed joints and fragile teeth.

The arrival of Charles Madison Ewald Kane, newly minted and blameless, saved Iris from the boredom that had threatened to swamp her. She loved her son unreservedly, without stint, and she devoted her life to his care. Perhaps it was the degree of her love for Charlie that blinded her to Luke Kane's increasing absence from her life. The afternoon when Charlie picked up a paper from the kitchen table, smearing the print with juice-sticky fingers, and read aloud, Iris felt as if her life had, for the past twenty-two years, rumbled along to reach that moment. She forgave the students who had taunted her at school, she forgave the teachers who had bullied her, she forgave Luke Kane his indifference, she even forgave her parents their austere Methodism.

But the move to East Hampton shook her new-found complacency. She was only four weeks short of giving birth when the move was made, and the decisions she had to take, the size of the house, the logistics of changing place, wore her out. Also, the house was owned jointly by Sugar and her husband. It was then that she became aware of how much time brother and sister spent together – she would see them sitting in the dark of the drawing room when she struggled down the stairs in the middle of the night for a glass of water. Each morning she walked into the kitchen to find Sugar already sitting at the table, reading the paper, a cup of coffee at her elbow, and even that early in the day Sugar looked fabulous, clear-eyed and lithe. Sugar bought pieces of furniture and scattered them through the house, bought curtains, carpets and crockery. Because of her pregnancy, because of Charlie's demands, it took Iris a long time to work out what was happening: she was being usurped by her sister-in-law.

One night, as she shifted uncomfortably in her bed in the

early evening, she thought about this. Downstairs she could hear Luke Kane and Sugar laughing over dinner, a dinner Iris had felt too nauseous to eat. She heard the dull hollow thunk of yet another bottle of wine being opened. Another record was slipped on to the turntable. Iris switched off her bedside light, hoping that the darkness would soothe her aching bones. She tried to turn on her side, rolled back on to her back. Her ankles were swollen, her tongue probed a loose molar. But she could not sleep because the music was too loud. And then there was silence, as there was every night. Something – pain? intuition? – stopped Iris heaving herself from the bed and going to the landing to call down to her husband.

Hours later the bedroom door opened and Luke Kane came in, humming, slipping the belt from his chinos.

'Hello, honey,' Iris said quietly.

'Mmm. You're not asleep yet?'

'Not yet.'

Luke Kane went into the bathroom, stripped and show-ered, stood wrapped in a towel at the mirror, brushing his teeth. Iris watched him, noticed a slight thickening about Luke Kane's torso. 'Honey?' She addressed his back.

'Mmm.'

'When's Sugar moving out?'

He turned from the mirror, his face thrown into shadow. 'What?'

'When's Sugar going to move out?'

'What makes you think she is?'

'She's not going to live here permanently, is she honey?' Iris's voice was rising.

'Of course she is. It's her house, too.' Luke Kane turned back to the mirror, slicked back his black-black hair with a pair of old-fashioned gentleman's brushes.

'Ah, come on, Luke. We've only been married four years. We got a son, we're expecting another. We should be living as a family.'

'Sugar *is* family.'

'She's not my family. I just want to be with you and Charlie and Baby.'

Luke Kane walked over to the bed, switched on the bedside light and stood loose-limbed, expressionless, his eyes glittering in the light. 'What are you saying?'

Iris heaved herself up on to the pillows and her nightdress shifted, flapped open to reveal her full white breasts, the swell of her body. 'All I'm saying, honey, is that I'd like some privacy.' She looked at him and smiled, but his expression didn't change. Iris began to babble. 'You know? She's here every morning, every day, every night. She chooses what we eat, what we sit on, everything. It doesn't feel like my house. Doesn't feel like *our* house.' She reached out for his hand and he withdrew. Tears gathered behind Iris's eyes. 'And every night you stay up with her. You stay up late, like now. It's one in the morning – and you have to go into the city to work tomorrow. I mean, you must be exhausted.'

Still Luke Kane said nothing. Iris suddenly beat the mattress with her tiny fists. 'I'm exhausted. Every night I have to listen to you two partying. The music gets louder and louder and I can hear you laughing and dancing. You never do that with me – you never *did* that with me. And then in the morning there are so many bottles, dirty glasses. You two keep Charlie awake as well, he has broken nights, he cries during the day, he doesn't eat so good. Don't you care?'

'Shut up,' said Luke Kane.

'What? What? What did you say?' Iris was shocked, con-fused. Her husband had always been unfailingly polite.

'Shut up.' His voice was like frozen water.

'Luke, honey . . .' Iris struggled to keep the tears dammed.

But Luke Kane ignored her. He slipped the towel from his waist and, with his back turned, slipped into the bed, pulling the blankets around him.

Iris mulled over these events in her mind, as her blood pulsed and she felt the baby lash out with a foot. Iris didn't even flinch when that happened, she was too angry. 'You can't talk to me like that, Luke. You *can't* talk to me like that. I'm your wife. I'm trying to tell you how I feel. All I'm saying is I think you should spend more time with me. You need to spend time with *me*, not with Sugar. You can't just tell me to shut up. I'm fed up with the noise and the drinking and you never being with me. I mean, what do you two do down there? What do you do when you go into town or for a drive? What do you *do*? I mean, some people might think it's strange that a man – a father – spends more time with his sister than his wife!'

It was the first time that Iris had argued with her husband, the first time she had criticized Sugar. It was also the last, because Luke Kane reared up next to her and made two swift movements. The first was to slap Iris with an open palm, split-ting her lip. (This was also the first but not the last time that Iris saw the whorls and life lines of his hand so closely.) Luke Kane's second movement was to bunch his fist and slam it into Iris's bulging belly.

1997

Keeler still cannot wipe the smile from his face, a smile prompted by the thought of Thomas Jefferson III dying at the hands of Mr Candid. His superior is walking back and forth in front of the window.

'OK, Keeler. This what I want you to do: get a team together here, including two units, intelligence. Arrange with the Bureau to have three units, two undercover, ready in Miami in two hours. Sequester whatever transport you need. I'll clear that. I shall contact the governor at Harrison and clear security passes. You and the teams are inside and out, both armed, civilian and undercover. You get there, you burrow down and you wait for him. The briefing of everyone involved I leave to you. After all,' the chief allows himself a twitch, 'you claim you can recognize Mr Candid from the descriptions. You can tell people what they need to know.'

Keeler's smile fades. 'Sir?'

'What?'

Keeler swallows hard. 'Sir, you're asking me to *protect* Thomas Jefferson?'

The chief's bland face with its empty eyes scans Keeler's. 'I'm ordering you to arrest Chum Kane, also known as Mr Candid.'

Keeler's nose flares as fury burns through him. 'Sir—'

'Keeler, it's an order.'

'Thomas Jefferson is responsible for—'

'I know exactly what he's responsible for, Keeler. That is not our concern. We are the FBI. We are committed to protect and serve. We are not Supreme Court judges.'

The Ice Man, the Yeti, is so far away now that Keeler can't even remember him. 'Thomas Jefferson killed nine kids.'

The chief roars. 'And Chum Kane has killed more than ninety men. Move it, Keeler.'

Keeler bows his head, remembers the absence of hands, remembers the smell of the beach in New Jersey, remembers the sound of Flanagan's heart beating. 'Sir, can I ask you a question, sir?'

The chief looks at him, shakes his head and sighs. 'What?'

'Do you think he's right?'

'What're you talking about, Keeler? We're wasting time.'

'Do you think Mr Candid's right? That he's doing what we'd all like to do? I mean, if you thought you could get away with it, wouldn't you do it, too?'

The chief sighs again and Keeler catches a glimpse – but only a glimpse – of the son, the father the chief is when he is not standing in this room making decisions. 'Keeler, I didn't want to appoint you. I can tell you that now. I didn't want a washed-up NYPD detective on my staff. But I was persuaded that you were the man for the job. And I have to say that you have proved me wrong. You are an accomplished operative, the most accomplished that I have ever encountered. I stand corrected. But I feel that in this case your judgement is becoming clouded. You are allowing emotions to compromise your professional objectivity.'

Keeler thinks of Flanagan once more: an Irish-American bear of a man who is currently embarked on a quest. The best, the most decent, man Keeler has ever known. 'Sir, I'll ask you again, if I may. If you thought you could get away with it, would you do it? Would you blow Thomas Jefferson away?'

The chief stares at Keeler, unblinking, for moments, for what seems like minutes. 'I have a deep-seated aversion to importing personal lives into a working environment. For that reason, I have not informed the people with whom I work that last week Gloria, my granddaughter, who is five years old, was approached by a man as she was playing in a park and he exposed himself to her. He called to her and opened his coat. Beneath it he was naked, his penis was erect and he began to rub it vigorously, moving towards her. Fortunately Gloria screamed and her mother and every other adult was there in seconds. They caught the man, restrained him until the cops arrived. I was not there, but even the imagining of my granddaughter being in that situation keeps me awake at night. The man's name is Scott Graves.'

'Would you kill Scott Graves if you thought you could get away with it?' Keeler asks, for once not sweating under his superior's scrutiny. The chief stares at Keeler. Time stretches. Keeler walks to the desk, leans against it. Looks at the man. 'Would you give Mr Candid his name?'

The chief shakes himself a little, loosens his bones. 'Agent Keeler, I have ordered you to perform certain duties. I should, perhaps, review your appointment as the head of this particular surveillance team. However, I am prepared to overlook your possible deficiencies on this occasion. To give you, if you like, the benefit of the doubt. Agent Keeler, assemble your team and shift ass.'

Keeler is trying to read the man's face but nothing is written there. 'Yes, sir.' He swivels on his heel and walks to the door.

'Keeler?'

'Yes?'

'Can I trust you? Will you get him?'

Keeler looks at the chief, realizes for the first time that he is older than Keeler had imagined. He is a grandfather. 'Yes, sir, you can trust me.'

LUKE AND IRIS KANE

Iris's waters broke at the moment that Luke Kane's hand made contact with her pale cheek. The foetus wondered what was happening, why there was this gushing sound, this sliding away, as Luke Kane's fist intruded on her territory and spun her slowly round in the blood-rich chamber. The umbilical cord, like a bloody marshmallow candy twist, swirled, looping itself round the foetus's neck. The foetus moved her neck, trying to loosen the noose, but movement was so difficult in that confined space.

Hours later, in the operating theatre of a hospital, a doctor released the foetus by slipping the noose free with large, clumsy fingers. Hours later. The foetus fell through space, clutching at bloody walls. Hours later. The foetus became a baby and lurched into the world to fall between Iris's thighs. Hours later. Too many hours later, it transpired. As Lydia launched herself into the unknown, Minuteman, the world's first intercontinental ballistic missile, blasted into space. Lydia was unaware of this.

Oh, to be sure, Iris carried home a baby with the large, zaffre eyes of the Kanes, with the smooth, pale skin of the Chandlers. A beauty. She was a beauty. She was bouncy, she was engaging (she was also damaged, but no one realized that for months). When Iris reappeared at East Hampton, carrying her swaddled baby, Luke Kane was waiting for her at the door, waiting to escort her to the nursery he had had decorated. Iris realized that this decoration was his apology and she forgave him his lone punch.

It was Sugar Kane, hanging one day over Lydia's cot, smoking a cigarette, a beer in her other hand, who noticed that Lydia's eyes wandered. 'Hey! Iris, c'mere,' she called.

Iris was sorting Charlie's clothes, folding piles of T-shirts, rolling his socks. 'What?'

'You gotta see this.' Sugar watched as Lydia gurgled and her familiar eyes jiggled left to right.

Iris came into the nursery, pushed Sugar aside. 'What? What is it?'

'Her eyes.' Sugar took a swig of beer. 'Look, they're not focusing on anything. They're just about all over.'

It was 1961. It took many months for the extent of the damage Lydia to become apparent. Iris spent days in clinics, in the surgeries of paediatric specialists, in the car driving between one and another. Iris fought every doctor she met, every specialist. Why, Charlie was a genius, so how could Lydia be any different? But Lydia *was* different.

'So what does it mean?' Luke Kane asked one Friday night, when he returned from Hunter-Philips merchant bank. 'What's wrong with her?' he asked, as he poured himself a bourbon, dressed, still, in his suit and coat.

Iris was sitting on an opulent, newly upholstered sofa in the drawing room, rubbing Charlie's toes through his socks, as Charlie slept, his thumb in his mouth. 'Lydia's brain-damaged. She'll be able to walk but not very well, able to sleep, to eat and breathe. But she'll never speak properly. You see, she can't think.' Iris lowered her head. She was not crying, she was beyond that. She was defeated. Sugar was still there and Lydia was not. Or, rather, Lydia was there, but locked away in a place Iris would never be able to reach.

'*Fuck!*' Luke Kane shouted, and slammed his glass on a cabinet, shattering it. Charlie shifted in his mother's arms, yawned and fell asleep again.

As it turned out, Charlie was the only human being who ever made contact with what was left of Lydia. The moment he saw his sister he fell in love with her – with her tiny hands, her perfect skin, her eyes. (Genetic memory?) He stood peering between the bars of Lydia's cot and watched his sister gurning and giggling, reaching for her plump feet with plumper fingers. Charlie loved her and he read to her, talked to her, played with balls and toys she couldn't catch, couldn't even focus on, without ever becoming bored. He loved her without question, without thought. She was the reason he woke every morning, the reason he learned nursery rhymes, the reason he read children's books. He did not know there was something wrong with her: he thought she was slow and forgetful but utterly lovable.

When Charlie was six and Lydia was three he tried to teach her his name. 'Charlie,' he said, over and over. But Lydia was unequal to the task of saying two syllables and so Charlie became Chum – to Iris's annoyance. Chum Kane was reading the *New York Times* and Lydia couldn't even say her brother's name.

Iris spent years watching Chum and Lydia at play and offered some god thanks for Chum's patience. Because her daughter wore her out, made her old. The Kane house was too big, too cluttered, too *dangerous* for Lydia. But when she was with Chum, Lydia was fine. She would watch his mouth and his hands, try to ape him and fail magnificently. The two of them would sit with books open in their laps as Chum read aloud and Lydia tore out page after page, sometimes eating them, sometimes tearing them to shreds. In the late summer evenings, Chum would lead Lydia outside, to the garden. He'd grab her hand and drag her, as her stout, sturdy legs worked asymmetrically beneath her, to the play-frame. He would force her, lard-like, into the seat of the swing and she screamed and yelled and laughed aloud as he pushed her ever higher. Sometimes she would tumble from the seat, fall spinning in an arc through the hot evening air to land with a whump on the scrubby grass. But she never cried out, never wept as blood blossomed from her knees, because Lydia did not understand that pain was bad, that pain hurt. Perhaps she couldn't feel it. Occasionally on those childhood summer evenings, as the sun fell behind the house, Iris would look out and see her children playing on the swing, the grass glowing in the yellow light, the white picket fence behind them stark against the ocean, and she could believe for a moment that all was well with the world.

The balance of their lives was disturbed on the first day that Chum went to school and the authorities discovered the extent of his scholastic abilities. It was then that the educational psychologists appeared, all of them desperate to test him, to calibrate his infinite mind. These professionals questioned him, interviewed him endlessly, and arrived at the conclusion that he should be put on a fast track to success, sent to a dedicated college. They suggested to Iris that he should go to an institute for the gifted but she refused – if Chum went

she would be left alone with Lydia and what would they all do
then? So Chum stayed at home, being tutored privately in the
morning in science, math and literature, and attending a local
school in the afternoon to socialize with other children.
Although the psychologists disappeared, they had left their
mark on Chum. Because he now understood how different he
was, he became aware of how different Lydia was. He knew
then that she didn't work. She couldn't read or calculate. She
couldn't even speak properly, couldn't learn words, and
Chum knew, somehow, that she never would.

Iris spent the next decade fashioning a life for herself, a life
which was bearable. She gradually assumed responsibility for
the running of the house as Sugar lost interest in it: Sugar
would rather spend her life drinking cocktails than shopping
for groceries. Iris drove her husband to the station most mornings and collected him most evenings, if he didn't stay over in
town. During the days she would supervise the help, maybe
read a little, perhaps prepare menus. She had lunch with Lydia
and Chum, and when that was over she would take Chum to
school, collecting him a few hours later. Occasionally she
played bridge in the afternoons, with a group of other mothers
who lived in the Hamptons, as Lydia rolled on the carpet at
her feet, drooling and missing her brother. Those long afternoons, punctuated by the murmuring of 'doubled' and
'redoubled' and the sipping of iced tea, were awkward. The
other mothers did not know quite what to do about Chum and
Lydia. They talked of their own children, laughed about the
usual, common, *normal* escapades and trials of parenthood,
and then would fall suddenly silent as they thought of the
genius that was Chum and the idiot that was Lydia. More

than that – once Iris had picked up her purse, dusted Lydia down and left – they put the cards aside and speculated about Luke Kane and Sugar. Despite their wealth, despite their breeding, these women were bored and liked nothing more than to dissect others' lives. They pitied Iris her trials and tribulations – her strange children and absent husband – but they also laughed at her accent, her clothes, her manners. After all, Iris was from Hoboken, New Jersey; not exactly East Coast blue blood. (And it should not be forgotten that most of these women had spent time, years before, on the back seat of Luke Kane's car, acquiescing or crying.)

Iris retained Juanita and José and over the years she grew fond of Juanita, a quiet, unhurried woman from Puerto Rico. An understanding grew between them and often Iris would sit with the maid over a cup of coffee. Slowly Iris put together a picture of Lucinda Kane, her husband's mother. She found out about Lucinda's drinking, her lack of love, her lonely death. She also discovered that Luke had been banished from the family house when he was a boy and she wondered why. Late one night she asked Luke Kane the reason and once again she saw his hand in detail as it flew out and knocked her off a chair. Iris learned not to ask questions but nevertheless the slaps and blows fell on her. The rousing of Luke Kane's anger became an increasingly casual affair, but Iris was too isolated to know whether or not all wives suffered this, so she tried to ignore it.

Luke Kane and Sugar spent the sixties running around like trash, having a ball, living it up, drinking, smoking, trying cannabis. Luke Kane grew his hair and forgot how to jive; he switched from bourbon to beer and and his waist thickened. He threw parties most weekends, inviting colleagues and their wives to the house for barbecues and cocktails. He and Sugar dominated these affairs, Luke Kane flirting with every woman, Sugar playing the role of the lady of the house, as Iris sat with Lydia, trying to calm her daughter, who didn't like strangers, who screamed and fretted when the music grew too loud.

Chum sat on the window-seat in his room during these parties, looking out over the garden, his eyes following his father and Sugar as they trawled their guests. He'd hear Lydia in her room, listen to his mother trying to calm her, and he wondered if every family was like this. He hardly saw his father, who worked in the city and filled his home with strangers every weekend. Sometimes, during the long evenings, Luke Kane would open Chum's bedroom door and peer in at his son working at his desk, wrestling with mathematical conundrums.

'Hi there, soldier. OK?'

Chum would look up, his eyes unfocused. 'Yeah.'

'Good.' And Luke Kane would close the door and disappear to find Sugar.

Chum graduated high school when he was thirteen. He could have done this years before but Iris slowed him down, anchored him to the house for as long as possible. But even she couldn't disguise his talent for ever and so when Chum was thirteen he went to Harvard to study pure and applied math and physics, a transition which was reported in the newspapers, causing leader writers to speculate as to the effect of this move on such a young boy.

Luke Kane drove his son up to Boston because he realized that this was a rite of passage he should oversee. It was, after all, Luke Kane's Alma Mater. The journey of six hours was the longest period he had ever spent alone with his son, and he found him a reserved, thoughtful boy. Luke Kane had always felt threatened by Chum's prodigious intelligence, yet was nearly suffocated by pride each time he mentioned Chum's achievements to colleagues. Chum spent the hours in the car worrying about Lydia: what would happen to her now?

1997

Flanagan and Bronwen, dressed in new, clean clothes, are back in the car, skirting Wilmington, having picked up the I-95 once more. They have spent hours heading south in the ever-rising heat, yet still have more than a thousand miles to travel. An intimacy is growing between them, born not of the nights they have spent together, sharing king-size beds; rather, it is the hours spent in the car, especially in the ever-shortening evenings, as the sun falls and the car becomes a world of its own, with its softly glowing lights and whispering radio, that have created their bond. They spend their days commenting on other drivers or the ugliness of the outskirts of the cities they pass: New York, Baltimore, Washington, Richmond. But as the light dies their talk becomes more personal. Bronwen talks about her childhood in Ynys Môn, about how cold, how bleak, how *small* the island is: the distances she and Flanagan are travelling seem endless. When she had travelled north on the Greyhound, from Florida to New York, the Voice-woman had distracted her from the length of the journey but now she is aware of every passing mile. Flanagan talks about his family – his grandmother from Ireland, his one short, failed marriage. He even talks about why he became a cop, what his motives were, all based on utilitarian principles, based on moral grounds.

On the third day they cross the state line into Florida, and to celebrate their arrival they book into the Saltspray Hotel on Fernandina Beach and spend the evening on their balcony, eating mountains of seafood, looking out over the Atlantic. Now they are in Florida, heading for the Emerald Rest Home, they feel that they are closing their jaws on a problem. Bronwen, however, has another problem.

She wipes her mouth clean of butter, dips her fingers in a water bowl. 'Flanagan, I won't be able to go in with you. To see the matron, I mean.'

'Why not?'

'When I left, I stole something. I stole the petty cash.'

Flanagan sits back, his chin greasy. 'You *stole* it?'

'I didn't have any money and I really needed to get away.'

Flanagan sighs. 'Well, OK. But I think you should give it back. How much d'you take?'

'Four thousand dollars.'

'That's petty cash?'

'That's what was in there. But you're right, I should give it back.'

Later that night, as Flanagan brushes his teeth in the bathroom, Bronwen sits on the bed and empties her case. The envelope is still there, along with other envelopes. At twelve hundred dollars a throw, Bronwen earned a lot of money working for Sam. She makes up four thousand dollars in used notes and slips a band around them, replaces the envelopes in her case. When Flanagan emerges, newly brushed, she asks, 'We'll be there tomorrow, won't we?

Flanagan yawns. 'We still got more than six hundred to go, so it'll be Saturday afternoon, I reckon.'

'I'm not going in. You give the matron the money and keep mum about me.'

Flanagan nods and climbs into bed. Within minutes Bronwen is in there with him, her head on his chest, the picture of Chum beneath her pillow.

Chum Kane has checked out of the Four Seasons and caught a limo to Newark airport from where he catches a plane to Miami. As he sits crammed against the window, his mind, as always, is turning over like a well-oiled gear shaft. He is still nervous, has been on edge since he arranged to meet Sam. He is worried by the photograph that is floating around, by the fact that at least two people know his name and face. He can see his priorities shifting in his mind's eye. Whereas before his purpose was to visit Harrison Pen and then visit his mother, these decisions have been reversed by the turn of events. He knows the photograph belonged to his mother, so how has anyone gotten hold of it? Seventeen years ago, he left his mother outside a hospital, the photograph still in her dress pocket. He anonymously arranged for her to be transferred to the Emerald Rest Home and then paid money monthly into the banker's draft account. He hasn't seen the photograph for seventeen years and neither has he seen Iris. Perhaps the time has come for him to see how she is doing?

As the plane begins to descend, causing his ears to pop, Chum decides to change his plans: Harrison Penitentiary can wait (after all, MacDonald and Jefferson aren't going anywhere), but his visit to his mother cannot. A silence descends as the passengers watch the wings wavering and the runway rushing towards them. The heat and humidity hit him as he steps out of the arrivals terminal to collect his hire car, shocking after the sharp, cold late spring in New York. He drives out of Miami and stops at a gas station to buy a burger and a map, then drives west on the US-41, through the Big Cypress Swamp, heading for Naples and his mother.

CHUM KANE

The silent hostility of his fellow students, which the thirteen-year-old Chum felt washing over him in every lecture theatre, made his first weeks at Harvard a misery. He felt small and foolish, under-aged and under-armed, until he realized that he understood concepts other students could not. It was only when the faculty decided to tutor him alone that he began to relish his time there. Each morning when he woke, his mind was hungry for facts, for problems. It would thrash around in his skull until fed titbits of diophantine equations or texts arguing the case for recursive function theory; his mind gorged itself on Goldbach's conjecture and wrestled with Fermat's last theorem. (Years later, in 1993, when he was thirty-four, Chum read the account of Wiles's solution to the problem. At the time he was driving cross-country and he picked up a copy of the *New York Times* as he drove through Sale Creek in Tennessee. The discovery of this fact – that Fermat's challenge had finally been met – depressed Chum unutterably. It reminded him both of the extent of his adolescent ambition and of just how far he had moved away from it.) His days and evenings in Harvard were spoken for, with breakfast in hall, lectures, seminars, tutoring, dinner, reading, problem-solving. He had no time to think of anything except

number theory, until the weekends came. Then he wrote his
letters to Iris and Lydia. He knew Lydia could not read them,
that Iris would have to read them to her and even then they
would mean nothing. But every week he dutifully wrote his
account of what had happened and posted it Sunday
evenings. Saturday nights he'd lie awake in his bed in the
guest room of his tutor's house and listen to the students running in the streets, yelling and calling to each other. It was not
that he wanted to join them but he would have liked to join
someone.

During the vacations he went back home, back to Lydia
and Iris in the house in East Hampton, carrying with him
cratefuls of books and papers. The days he spent with Lydia,
his nights he spent in his room, studying. He felt safest in his
study, in his own place. Each time he returned Lydia had
grown. It was as if the energy that should have fired her intel-
lect had instead been diverted to her bones. She was tall and
rangy for such a young girl. Her skin was flawless, reminding
everyone of Sugar, her aunt; her eyes were the startling Kane
blue, her hair black and thick. In photographs she was a
young beauty; in life she drooled and screamed, lashed out
unexpectedly. But when Chum came home Lydia calmed
down, would sit in his room for hours, watching him work.
Chum would turn away from a legal pad covered in a wild
scrawl of numbers and play Ludo with her, or spend hours
trying to teach her Snap.

Chum was smart enough to realize that he could not,
should not, spend all his life sweating over the conceptual. So
he played tennis, played tag football on the beach, learned to
sail and surf. He went to parties on the beach where he was
surrounded by young girls and grudgingly admired by his

male peers. He was also smart enough to suspect that there was something wrong with his father's relationship with Sugar, but he tried not to think about that. And he always knew that his mother was deeply unhappy and that there was nothing he could do about it.

Chum was liked, loved and universally admired. His studiousness, his commitment, was held up as an example to other, less hard-working, less ambitious students. His patience with and obvious love for Lydia were often remarked upon; he was polite, amusing and imaginative. He had, in short, everything the perfect son would need: diligence, integrity and a sense of civic duty. Theodore would have adored him.

So what, as Sam the Weasel Man asked, had happened to him?

Something happened when he was sixteen which even Chum, in spite of his iron grip on mental processes, could not erase from his memory. It happened during a heat-stunned summer night when it was impossible to eat, to sleep, even to dream. He lay on his sheets, panting, thinking of icebergs and rivers, sweat rolling across his body. It was one in the morning and he dreaded the living of the rest of the night. He had been learning to drive and he thought of the breeze flooding through the open windows of the car. He dressed in shorts and T-shirt and crept down the stairs, took the keys and slipped out of the door. The Eldorado was parked down the drive, a long way from the house, and he climbed in, rolled down all the windows, his skin sticky on the worn leather. The heavy door closed with a satisfying thump and he fired the engine, rolled out on to the road.

The road was dark, the vast, sparse mansions on the

MISTER CANDID   313

seaward side invisible. Chum headed for Montauk Point along the ribbon road, noticed windblown sand glistening on blacktop. The air seemed cooler as it rushed in over his sweating face and when he stopped at the Point and sat on the beach overlooking the Atlantic the sea breeze calmed him. He'd found a pack of Marlboro on the dash and he lit one – his first cigarette – and smoked it as he watched the lighthouses lamps turning. The way he saw it then, tobacco would be his only vice. He sat there in the silence and reviewed his life, pleased by its predictability, its logic. He knew the route he would take, imagined himself as a professional mathematician, an academic, imagined being paid to solve problems.

Chum drove a looping route back, via Amagansett Springs Road, past Three Mile Harbor and on to Sag Harbor, where he passed along the harbour road, watching moored yachts bobbing slightly in the flat, quiet waters. Then he headed south back to East Hampton, driving slowly through the wooded back roads. No lights were on in the houses, just a few security lamps flooding yards, and the only sound was the tyres turning. For the first time – but certainly not the last – Chum felt as if he were guarding the world as it slept. Reaching home, he left the Eldorado as he had found it and crept back into the house. As he passed the open drawing-room door he heard a sound unlike any he had heard before. Chum stopped and looked into the pitch-black room. As his pupils expanded he made out his father's glittering eyes, looking straight back at him. Saw his father locked in an embrace with Sugar on the rug in front of the dead fireplace. He stepped back, stepped back once more, and left the room.

Chum slept late the next morning, forcing himself to dream, so that he need not meet his father over the breakfast table.

Neither did he wish to see his mother, nor indeed any of his family. He slipped out of the house with a towel and a book, and walked down to the shore, an endless beach which stretched east and west until it disappeared. He walked along the water's edge, the towel looped round his neck, trying not to think. But of course that was impossible: it was, after all, what he did best. What had his father been doing with Sugar? How was it that they lived as they did? Why had his father not been shamed? It was as he was thinking this, staring at the horizon, that he stepped on a shard of contaminated glass, washed up from a burst surgical disposal bag.

The fever lasted three days, three days in Chum's life during which he did not think logically. Filmic images of his life, grotesquely detailed and multi-hued, flashed in his mind. His sheets were soaked with sweat, had to be changed by Iris every two hours. Chum ranted, shouted meaningless phrases, laughed aloud, ground his teeth, as Iris sat with him. The dressing on his foot had to be changed hourly, as the wound oozed pus. His foot swelled to bursting point, the skin taut, purple and shiny, veins throbbing as the blood rushed hither and thither, confused by the infection. At the end of the third day he fell asleep and awoke clear-headed. He opened his eyes and saw Iris snoozing on a chair by the bed. Gingerly he searched his memory and found a handful of jumbled, mean- ingless pictures, one of which was of his father watching him in a darkened room as Sugar moved beneath him. So it was that Chum dismissed the memory as fever-induced, the result of his fine-tuned mind losing control.

1997

As the chopper's blades slam through the air, resonating in a light breeze, Keeler thinks that (if he is being honest) situations like these are what had attracted him to the Bureau. He's sitting in a helicopter as it descends, wavering, shifting, into a heliport in downtown Miami. Keeler is wearing shades and a dark, lightweight suit. In his pockets he has the latest miniature sim-chip-driven communication technology. He can contact the world should he wish to. Below him he can see a snaggle of black, unmarked cars waiting for him, men dressed exactly as he is waiting on the tarmac in blinding sunlight, some talking into needle-thin mikes. All his life he has waited for this: for a chopper to jostle to the ground, its door immediately flung open as the roar of the engine rises and he, Keeler, bounds out of the machine to be met by stern-faced men. And then the buttoning of his jacket, a few terse words, followed by a swift departure in an armour-plated car to a stake out. The *power* of the moment.

So why doesn't Keeler feel heroic? Why doesn't he feel that he has finally arrived? Because all of this has been set in motion in order to protect Thomas Jefferson III. Keeler sits in the car as a minion outlines the topography of Harrison Penitentiary using the language favoured by government agencies. Keeler doesn't listen because he is too busy trying to wrestle his conscience to the floor of his mind in a tight arm-lock.

Chum stays on Highway 41 for a couple of hours, passing the turn for Harrison Penitentiary, then finds a diner on the out-skirts of Naples, slides on to a seat and orders coffee. Cars and trucks rumble by, making the glass of the window vibrate. He scrubs at his eyes, realizes how tired he is. How nervous he is. What will he say to his mother? Will she even recognize him? The last time he had looked into her eyes there had been no one there. Or, at least, no one he recognized. He feels he is being stretched by an unseen hand. Standing up, he knocks over the cup and thick coffee dregs spill on the table. As the waitress cleans up, he asks for directions to the Emerald Rest Home.

'Turn round, head south, two miles there's a track for Goodland. Home's a few miles down on the right. Can't miss it. It's not quite in the middle o' nowhere, but you can see it from there.' The waitress smiles at him.

Chum notices his hands are shaking as he grips the wheel; they haven't stopped shaking since the morning he met Sam. The humidity is startling and his shaking hands slip with sweat. In his head white static flickers. What is he going to *say*? Despite the air-conditioning cooling the car, Chum fidg-ets as he drives. The smell of the nearby swamp mingles with the sluggish Gulf breeze, makes him feel he is under-water. He turns left, he drives towards Goodland, the minor road uneven and unkempt beneath him. He keeps looking right and there is a sign for the Emerald Rest Home. He turns into the drive and hits the brakes, the car skidding a little on muddy dust. The windows of the home are boarded up; yards of yellow and black police tape flutter in the wind. The grounds are a jungle. The paintwork is chipped and dirty. Even the palm trees, with their crazy vermilion leaves, look unloved. But, more importantly, there is another car there, in front of the abandoned building, and two people, standing by the imposing double doors of the entrance, are shading their eyes against the sun's glare to look at him.

Chum slams the stick into reverse and slides out of the drive.

Bronwen lowers her hand and turns back to the entrance of the home.

'You'd think there would be a note or something. You know? That they'd leave a number you could ring. What do we do now?' She sounds defeated. Five days she and Flanagan have driven to arrive here, to see Iris, only to find the home is closed. Boarded-up, shut down, finished. Bronwen kicks out at the lintel. 'What's the matter?' She has noticed Flanagan frowning, looking down the drive at the small, swirling cloud of dust left by Chum Kane's car. 'What's the matter, man?'

Flanagan shrugs. 'Don't know. Um . . . what to do? Make a coupla phone calls, I guess.' He jogs back to the car, Bronwen following slowly, utterly depressed.

They drive into Naples, park and cross the road to a diner. Flanagan asks for change and goes to the phone. He calls the number he has for Twyla Thackeray: the phone company comes on the line and tells him the number is obsolete. He asks for a new number. Unsurprisingly, there isn't one.

Flanagan nods silently, thoughtfully, walks over to the table
where Bronwen is tucking into the special, shrimp risotto and
salad. Her forehead glistens.

'Didn't know what you wanted so I ordered for myself.'

Flanagan doesn't answer. He taps the tabletop with the
edge of a quarter, drumming out a rhythm, the same rhythm
that Keeler taps out with his fingernails.

'Are you all right?' Bronwen stops shovelling her food long
enough to ask. 'What happened? What did Matron say?'

'She's not home. The line's dead, disconnected.'

Now Bronwen stops eating altogether: even she can see a
pattern here. 'That's a bit too much of a coincidence, isn't it?
The home closed and Matron's disappeared.'

'You got it.' Flanagan calls the waitress over. 'Excuse me,
ma'am, I was wondering, d'you know the Emerald Rest
Home, down towards Goodland?'

'Sure do.'

'I was wondering, d'you know what happened to it? I
mean, I just been there and it's all boarded up.' The image of
1078 Apaquogue, East Hampton, swims into his mind. Yet
another unloved building which once housed the Kanes.

The waitress slips her order book into a pocket, crosses her
arms. 'Shame, ain't it? Lovely house and all. It was shut down,
let me see, musta been two, three weeks ago? It was all over
the papers. Seems the director just stopped working.
Ever'thing stopped workin'. Place was a mess.' The waitress
shakes her head. 'It was pretty bad. Scandalous, 'f you wanna
know the truth. Ever'one here was real upset – y'know, all
those old folk being treated like that. My husband worked
there for a coupla months – had to leave because he weren'
bein' paid. Works here now as a short-order.'

'Where did all the patients – sorry, customers – where did they all go?'

'Um, ah . . . George?' she hollers, and a ginger-haired man sticks his head through the hatch. 'What happened to the folks in the Emerald? Where'd they all go?'

'They only found two of 'em. Ever'one else had left or died. Now, where was it? Ah, c'mon. I know! Diamond Days, that's it. Diamond Days, just outside Alva, on the Caloosahatchee. Real nice place. I'd like to stay there when I get too old to work.'

'Ways to go yet!' the waitress calls after him. 'Can I get y'anythin'?' she asks Flanagan, fishing out her order book. 'You seen the special. You wanna menu?'

'No, no, thanks. I'll have a Coke. Um . . . how come there were only two of them there? I mean, d'you know who they were?'

'Turned out one was the director – y'know, the woman who was to blame. First they thought she was jus' another patient. There was gonna be some prosecution or something but turned out she died before they could get her to court. Makes you think, don' it? The good Lord took her like it was her punishment.'

Bronwen snorts as Flanagan asks, 'How far's Alva?'

'No distance – maybe forty, fifty mile. If you're heading that way, best to aim for the Parkway and then up the twenty-nine, t'wards La Belle. Seventy-five's closed for some reason and the forty-one ain't movin'. The waitress laughs. 'Seems like ever'one's int'rested in the rest home at the moment – 's good for business, though.'

'What d'you mean?'

'Guy came through this morning, maybe a coupla hours ago? He asked about the Emerald, too.'

Bronwen and Flanagan look at each other. Look back at the waitress.

'What d'he look like?' asks Flanagan.

The waitress frowns. 'You looking for him?'

'Maybe.'

'Well . . .' She looks towards the hatch, unsure about this.

Flanagan flashes his badge. 'Just a description will do fine, ma'am.'

'Well . . . tall, blond. Good-lookin', I guess, 'fyou like that sorta thing.'

Bronwen reaches into her extraordinary cleavage and pulls out the photograph. 'Is this him?'

The waitress puts on the glasses dangling on a chain round her neck and peers at the Polaroid, slips the glasses off. 'Sure, that's him, honey.'

'Need to know, sir. This is strictly need to know.' Keeler is in the prison governor's office and the governor is not happy. He is furious that the Bureau is filling Harrison with undercover agents and armed men.

'Mr Keeler, this is a Grade A secure unit. No one can get in or out of here unless it's on my say-so. I cannot imagine a situation in which it would be necessary to disrupt the smooth running of this operation. Moreover, this facility houses some of the most dangerous and criminally insane men in the state. And from out of state in some cases. To maintain order and control in these situations is a difficult matter. Any disruption, even a minor change, can upset what is a delicate balance, both mental and physical. I would like to speak to your superior.'

Keeler has spotted Jefferson's file, one of a pile on the

governor's desk. 'Your jurisdiction here is superseded if the Bureau is involved—'

The governor explodes, leaps to his feet. 'Just get me your superior on the goddamn line and I'll talk to him. This is not a request.'

Keeler shrugs and picks up a newly installed secure phone. He dials a number, speaks for a moment and then hands over the phone. 'Here you are, sir.'

The governor begins to speak in a quiet, steely voice as Keeler inches Jefferson's file across the desk towards himself. The governor does not notice, turns his back on Keeler to look out of the window at the exercise yard below, criss-crossed by invisible lasers, guarded by four armed men in towers, razor wire stretched along the walls. Keeler flips open the thick manilla cover of the file and finds himself staring at a face it took him nine years to forget. The face he watched for hours in a small, white room as the mouth of that face moved and told him how Katarina Kowalski had died. Oh, how she had screamed. The mouth had told him that Katarina was the first kill and he hadn't known there would be so much blood. Hadn't known a small body could survive for so long.

Keeler flicks silently through the leaves of paper. Scans the psychologists' reports, sees the usual phrases: 'psychotic phase', 'abnormally high intelligence', 'gifted', 'notional psychopathology', 'unpredictable', 'first percentile', 'self-delusional capacity', 'exceptional audio-sensory sequential memory', 'increasing schizothymic factors', 'progress in rehabilitation'. At the back of the file is a pouch of photographs. Keeler flips quietly through them: Jefferson at kindergarten; at high-school graduation; a newspaper clipping of Jefferson in academic gown, winning a prize at UCLA; dressed in a tux and smiling at the camera, handsome and loose, his arm slung round a beautiful woman. Keeler closes the file, closes his eyes. When he opens them he sees the red rubber stamp on the front of the file: *Review date: 03/05/97.*

The governor slams down the phone, glares at Keeler, who doesn't notice. 'Seems I got no choice. All I ask, Agent Keeler, is that you keep your men out of my sight, out of my face.'

'What does this mean?' Keeler points at the bright red square on the Jefferson's file.

'That, Agent Keeler, is frankly none of your business.' The governor picks up the file and slides it back into alphabetical place in a cabinet.

'What does it mean? That he's up for review?'

'I have a meeting scheduled right now. I'd appreciate it if you left my office.'

'Jefferson's case is being *reviewed*?'

'Goodbye, Agent Keeler.' The governor turns his back again.

Chum Kane is sitting in the library in downtown Fort Myers, scanning back copies of the *Cypress Courier*. His head is aching, his hands still shaking, so it takes him a while but eventually he finds it: a report on the scandal of the Emerald Rest Home. He follows the story day by day until he finds what he's looking for: two people remaining, who were moved to Diamond Days, outside Alva on the Caloosahatchee river. It's two in the afternoon when he steps out of the building and his pupils hurt as they contract. He reaches his car, sweat pouring down his back, and drives until he finds a call-box. He is making decisions so fast now that he can hear them falling into place. But making a choice, taking a decision, does not make things so. The line is bad between Fort Myers and Los Angeles but Chum can still hear enough to know that Gideon has disappeared, arrested with thirty thousand dollars in his pocket and taken away, never to be seen again. Gideon is no longer one of his options.

THE KANE FAMILY

The plans for Chum Kane's graduation party, at the age of seventeen, from Harvard University, were described by the Hampton women with whom Iris played bridge as, to say the least, excessive. What these verbal snipers failed to realize was that this graduation was the first rite of passage that Iris had been able to celebrate with her son. Chum had acquired his adult skills at such an early age that Iris had barely had time to recognize one achievement before yet another overshadowed it. High-school graduation had meant nothing to him. His voice had broken and his beard had begun to grow when he was away at college. He had passed his driving test in Boston as well as his degree papers. When he returned to East Hampton in the first week of June 1975, he was already a young man. Iris, it would seem, had missed his adolescence altogether.

To plug this absence she planned a party like the Hamptons hadn't seen before, for the first Sunday in August. Luke Kane shrugged when she explained what she wanted to do, poured himself another drink and said she could do what she liked. After all, they had the money. Then, as he always did, he went to look for Sugar. Iris sat up late that night, sketching plans, drawing up lists. Luke Kane might not have been interested but Chum, seeing his mother content, purposeful for the first time in years, sat with her and helped her to imagine.

Chum stood with his mother in the baking sun, as she explained to the carpenters that she wanted the decking replaced, extended out towards the sea and round two sides of the house, surrounded by a rail. The electricians were told where to bury lights in the garden, where to string up yards and yards of lightbulbs in the trees. José oversaw the planting of hundreds of flowers in the beds, the trimming of trees and bushes. He repainted the picket fencing, replaced rotten shutters and painted them. Iris had the carpenters remove the garage where Lucinda had hung silently for hours, swinging gently. The pool was emptied, its tiles patched and cleaned. A mosaic of a frisky dolphin was embedded in its floor, as the electricians mounted underwater lights. Then the pool was refilled with sterile blue, chemical water. The deck, which now covered thousands of square feet, was clean and raw. Iris had the wood treated and sealed.

Iris lost her unhappiness in the plans for the party, left Chum to look after Lydia. Because of the noise and the milling of so many strangers in the house, Chum took Lydia down to the beach each day, where the other sunbathers watched them with puzzlement. Chum tied up her raven-black hair in a knot, and washed her face and hands before they left the house. Lydia looked quite lovely in her bikini – her skin brown and her limbs long and muscular. Young men would furtively watch her sitting on her towel and move towards her. But when they drew close, they could see the dribble of spit running unremarked down her shapely chin, see the wavering of her cornflower eyes and the fractious movements of her hands in the sand, scattering grains here and there. As the sun rose

higher and Lydia began to sweat, Chum coaxed her down to
the sea, where the two of them paddled, Lydia screaming and
jumping up and down. Often she fell hard but, as ever, said
nothing about the pain and Chum knew she was cushioned by
the water. He sometimes held out his arms and she came to
him and he held her, her head resting against his belly as he
pulled her gently further out, to a depth where she could float.
Her eyes became dreamy and her gurgling stopped as the sea
washed over her, her ears below the surface where she couldn't
hear other people talking.

The month of June passed and while the sun did not rise as
high the temperature inexorably rose. Chum and Lydia were
both salt-tanned and slothful. Luke Kane and Sugar were
rarely in the house: he worried money into wakefulness as
Sugar spent her days in the city, drinking and partying. Iris
noticed none of this. One morning she woke at five o'clock
and went down to the garden, in her robe, with a cup of coffee.
Standing by the fence she looked back at the house and realized it was finished, realized that the shell was pristine but the
interior was shabby. She had enjoyed her new lease of life,
her sense of purpose, so she turned her attention to this next
problem. Once again she consulted Luke Kane and he
shrugged; once again the carpenters were called.

The mirrored wardrobes and twee, skirted dressers were
ripped out of the bedrooms. Old enamelled sinks and toilets
were dumped in the drive as the bathrooms were stripped.
The kitchen was torn apart, the ancient gas cooker leaned
crazily in the drive among the sinks. Iris was a whirlwind, a
tornado, who whipped through the house, destroying it even
as she discussed plans and pored over flooring sanders, curtain materials, linoleum and carpets. Lead piping was torn

out of the walls, electrical circuits were hacked out, renewed and chased, damaged floors were replaced. Luke Kane and Sugar grumbled about the upheaval and took themselves to Luke Kane's apartment in the East Eighties, which he had never relinquished. In his room Chum worried over the mathematical conundrums he had brought back from Harvard and watched over Lydia as best he could. Juanita and José worked around the chaos, frowning and tutting. Iris, meanwhile, was oblivious to all of this, the circled date on the calendar her target – 3 August, when the house would be thrown open to two hundred and fifty guests and Chum would be fêted by them during *the* party of the summer season.

July – and the heat kept rising, through the nineties and into the hundreds. Sugar left the city, made intolerant by the humidity, the pollution, the short tempers of everyone around her. She wanted to be by the sea, wanted to smell fresh air and swim in cold salt water. When she arrived back in East Hampton she found her childhood room stripped of colour and comfort. Chum lay awake and listened to his mother and his aunt shouting in the hot night air. He couldn't hear distinct words but it was clear that Sugar was not happy. But she stayed because the alternative – living in the city – was worse.

Sugar was in her prime when she returned that summer. She was thirty-five years old, sleek and whole, with her figure intact, her beauty more arresting than ever. She was rich, she was single, she was pursued by every man she met. But for nearly twenty years she had had the only man she had ever wanted – her brother – so she toyed with all these suitors and spat them out unused. Luke Kane was the only man she ever slept with, the only man she had ever felt was her equal. From the moment he had appeared on the beach when she was fifteen, and asked her to go for coffee, she had never even considered anyone else. So she lay around on the deck, on the beach, and waited for this madness to be over, for the graduation party to pass, so she could return to her life with her brother.

Gradually the house took on a new shape, a new personality as the last decor that had had Lucinda's hand in it – wallpaper, tiles and paint – disappeared. Iris wondered why she had not done this before; it would have made her life so much easier to have stamped herself on her environment, to take control. Iris was in her element.

Luke Kane, too, seemed content with this change. It was costing tens of thousands of dollars but he was pleased by the sight of his mother's memory being expunged. Still he worked during the week, staying in the city Monday to Thursday, but he came home each weekend to find that 'home' had changed its appearance. Luke Kane was expansive that summer: he didn't hit his wife unless he considered he had good reason; he didn't shout at Lydia unless she annoyed him. He was discreet with Sugar, making sure that Chum did not catch them again. He drank less and tried to talk to Chum occasionally. Indeed, Luke Kane was so content that on the Friday night when he returned for the weekend of the graduation party, he sat out with Chum until late, drinking beer with his son and trying to understand what Chum told him about number theory. Towards midnight, when he was a little drunk, Luke Kane announced that he was giving Chum the 1950 Cadillac Eldorado as a graduation present. Chum whooped and beat the arms of his chair with his fists. 'Yes!' he shouted, and leaped up to hug his father. It was the first time father and son had hugged since Chum had asked him to read during Kennedy's inauguration.

Chum's shout drew Sugar out of the house, dressed in shorts and a vest, her feet bare, her toenails painted a deep, blood red. She sank down by Luke Kane, her back resting against her brother's legs, and smiled at Chum.

'So, nephew, you're a big boy now. Got a car, got a degree, even got a beard coming through. Got a girlfriend to go with all that?' Sugar's eyes were dark in the gloom.

Chum shook his head. 'No.'

'Better get one, then. Got anyone in mind?'

'No.' Chum's blush was invisible. He blushed because there *was* someone, at college. A woman he had seen many times crossing the scrubby square, a woman who had made him thoughtful, almost wistful, each time he saw her. But he didn't want to talk to his aunt about it.

Sugar smiled. 'Won't be long now, I shouldn't think.' She wrapped a hand round Luke Kane's leg and Chum had the same curious sensation as his mother had experienced years before, of imagining the two of them to be twins, Janus-faced. 'Maybe you'll get laid tomorrow, after the party,' she said, shocking Chum.

And his father laughed. 'Reckon it wouldn't be the first time – eh, Chum?'

Chum stood up, said goodnight and left the two of them alone.

The next morning, Saturday, the day before the party, trucks arrived early to remove the debris of the change, as marquees were assembled in the gardens to keep the stunning heat off the guests. All morning neighbours could hear the hollow boom of enamelled sinks shattering in metal skips as the drive was cleared, the shuddering rumbling of gears grinding as the trucks pulled away. Iris had timed it perfectly: the walls were newly papered, woodwork was freshly painted, electricity fizzled along new wiring and water thundered through clean copper piping. Only the hallway needed a few finishing touches: the skirting boards lay, already cut and chamfered, along the floor, waiting to be attached.

Iris turned her full attention to the preparation of the food. All week Juanita had been slaving and sweating in the new kitchen, grudgingly admiring the ease with which she could work in the pristine, ergonomically designed environment, pans, knives and boards all easily accessible, hanging in ordered rows. The meat, fish and seafood had just been delivered and were chilling in the refrigerator. The vegetables were prepared where possible. Crates of wine, beer, spirits and champagne were stacked in the new garages. Iris and Juanita sat together at the kitchen table and ran through the last of the lists, Iris so relaxed by her sense of achievement that she acceded to each of Juanita's suggestions about the responsibilities of the catering staff.

The heat that day, when the Kane house was dusting itself down, settling itself for the party of a lifetime, was crushing. As Iris and Juanita sat beneath the fan spinning above the kitchen table, Sugar lay on her new bed in her newly decorated bedroom, and dreamed of Luke Kane. Lydia was grumpy, unable to understand why she felt so uncomfortable. She and Chum played cards in his room or, rather, Chum laid his cards down just so as Lydia tore hers in half, threw them across the floor. She began to have a tantrum, a spectacular event: a violent monument to the misbegotten and the misunderstood. Chum looked at her in a certain way and Lydia knew what was to follow. Her brother began to tickle her, under the arms, in the ribs, under her chin. Her screams were now interspersed with giggles, as she rolled on the floor, kicking out at Chum.

The distant noise woke Sugar from an imagined delicious union and she shifted on the bed, wiped at the sweat puddling between her breasts. She went to her bathroom, examined her gorgeous but slightly puffed face in the mirror and splashed cold water on her neck. A beer, she thought. I need a beer. The thought of an ice-cold Schlitz drove her from her room. She could hear Lydia screaming and giggling and rolled her eyes as she walked along the static-flashing carpet on the landing towards the sweeping, remodelled stairs (the same stairs that had caused her mother's ankles to hurt all those years before). Lydia's giggles became breathless yips of laughter. Suddenly Chum's door burst open and the two of them tumbled out, Lydia's face distorted by tortured glee. Sugar looked at her niece, surprised as always by her odd beauty, so similar to her own and yet so different.

'Hey, guys,' Sugar called, 'keep it down, OK? It's too damn hot to be yelling.'

Sugar turned and her foot hovered in space as she began her descent. It was at that moment that Lydia broke free from Chum's flying fingers, staggered backwards, laughing her crazy, cracked laugh, and crashed into Sugar's back. Whenever Chum thought of that moment – which was often – he recalled that the expression on Sugar's face was one of mild surprise. She didn't look angry as she was slammed into space by Lydia's muscular, uncontrolled body. Chum clutched at Sugar's T-shirt but only held it for a space of time that couldn't even be called a moment. Sugar landed awkwardly, her hands flailing, snagging on spindles, snapping wrists. She turned and tumbled again, landing this time on her back, flipping over, sliding along the curved wall until she was tipped once more and slammed on to the wooden floor of the hallway. Behind her Chum slithered (for the second time in his life) down the slippery carpeting, scrambling after her, his tanned hands still snatching at air.

It was a spectacular fall, long, winding and breathless. But perhaps Sugar would have survived it – with a few broken bones and a rueful smile – if the skirting boards had not been laid along the floor. If they had already been fixed she might have survived. Instead, as Sugar's sublime face met floor, her forehead was impaled on a two inch oval-head, which stood proud of the shaped wood of the unattached skirting boards.

1997

Even Bronwen breaks into a jog as Flanagan runs towards his car, keys ready. As she thumps into the seat, breathing heavily, the engine fires and the lieutenant looks across at her. 'D'you realize what this means?' he asks.

Bronwen nods, too breathless to speak.

'He's here.' Flanagan looks wildly around, as if he might spot Mr Candid standing nearby, his foot resting on the fender of a 1950 Eldorado. About to smile lazily at the camera. 'He's near. Very close.' Flanagan reverses out of the parking space, shoots off east, heading for Alva. 'Remember that car that came when we were at the home? It pulled in and then pulled out real fast? I reckon that was him. He saw us and panicked. Wasn't expecting anyone there.'

Bronwen swallows hard at the thought of having been that close to the man of her dreams. She had even glanced at the car and not realized.

'It was a white BMW with black trim,' remarks Flanagan.

'How do you know that?'

'Training. Store information, everything you see.'

Bronwen chews her cheek, forgets to smoke. 'So what's the plan? Where are we going?'

'Alva – we'll find him there. An hour, maybe.' Flanagan steps on the gas, takes the old car up to sixty-five, seventy. An hour, he thinks, an hour to compose the question he's been waiting to ask.

THE KANE FAMILY

Luke Kane gingerly negotiated the dump trucks pulling out of the driveway, mindful of the damage flying grit could do to the paintwork of the new cherry-red Ford Mustang he had bought that morning to replace the Eldorado he'd given his son. It was a convertible and all he wanted to do in the world was take the top down and drive the coast road with Sugar by his side. They'd head for Montauk, have a couple of drinks and maybe stop on the beach before coming home. It was as he parked the car, applying the handbrake delicately, that he became aware of ambulance lights flashing, the policemen milling in and out of the house. As Luke Kane ran up the steps a young, wide-eyed cop stopped him, arms akimbo, blocking his path.

There are some events the memory of which does not fade with time. Events which remain frozen, crystalline, clear in the mind until the mind itself dies away. (Even stroke-damaged Iris Chandler, as she lay slowly dying in her soiled bed years later, could conjure clear pictures of some episodes in her life.) That afternoon, when Luke Kane arrived in his new Mustang and ran up to the house, was one of those events for anyone who was there. Indeed, no one who was there would ever forget it: the paramedics, the dumpster drivers, the men assembling the marquees, Juanita and José. The police, the doctor. Chum and Lydia. And, of course, Luke Kane himself.

Luke Kane lost control when he realized that the body under the sheet belonged to Sugar. He was uncontainable. No one there ever managed to erase the sight of Luke Kane – the son of Mr Steel, the man who had everything – crying and mewling like a baby. No one could get near him, just as he made sure no one could get near Sugar. Luke Kane guarded the body, like a lion, like a mother, kneeling over it, howling, desolate, lashing out at anyone who tried to calm him. He pulled the sheet back from Sugar's face, saw the damage inflicted by a single sliver of steel, and his grief redoubled. The sounds he made were inhuman, bestial.

Appalled, unnerved by the rawness of Luke Kane's grief, the people around him melted away. Chum stood, unmoving, at the foot of the stairs. He didn't know what to do; his brain was paralysed. Lydia was fooling and gurgling by the door, fingering the cops' badges. Iris took Lydia's arm, grabbed Chum, waking him from his sleep, and pulled them both outside. She gestured for the cops to get out of the hallway, and they did. The afternoon was strangely silent – no cars passed on the distant road, no gulls called to each other, there were no thin cries floating from the beach. The only sound was the sound of Luke Kane's heart emptying and filling over and over as he bawled. Time passed and the doctor and paramedic tried to approach him again; again he snarled and roared, lashed out. It took more than an hour for the cops and paramedics to grab Luke Kane and drag him away from the body so that he could be sedated. Luke Kane had chewed his lips and his chin was bloodied as if he had gorged himself on his sister's body. Which, in a way, was what he been doing for years.

It was at the moment when the doctor tapped the needle, his hands shaking, that Lydia broke away from her mother and trotted unevenly over to her father, who was sprawled on the (unfinished) hallway floor, his arms and legs pinned. For the second time that day, Chum clutched at thin air too late. Too late to stop Lydia smiling crookedly at her father as she pointed at Sugar's body.

'Lyddie do it,' she said. 'Lyddie push. Sorry.'

As Luke Kane's listened to his daughter's words the needle slid into his arm.

1997

The gardens of the Diamond Days rest home are luscious, trimmed as neatly as a banker's beard, as ordered as a banker's ledgers. The bougainvillaea is espaliered against extensive trelliswork. Hibiscus and poinsettia beds are free of weeds, laid out in pleasing symmetry, in the midst of which an ante-bellum mansion has been expertly restored to former glory, the clapboard painted in shades of peppermint, magnolia and peach pink. As Chum pulls into the parking lot, he sees well-heeled, well-groomed, well-*loved* old folk sitting in the shade of trees on cushioned chairs, nurses hovering nearby. Out back, beyond the landscaped gardens, the Caloosahatchee river runs its burbling way, manatee floating with the current.

Chum sits in the car for a while, looking at his inelegant hands as they grip the wheel. He is preparing himself for disappointment – an activity at which he excels. Seventeen years have passed since he saw his mother and he wonders if she will remember him. Also, it is possible, more than likely, when he calculates the odds (given time/place/number of patients in the Emerald Rest Home), that his mother was not one of the two survivors transferred here. He smooths his hair, checks his stubble in the mirror, opens the car door and crosses the parking lot to the reception area in the building. A young, pretty secretary looks up and smiles when she sees him.

'Good afternoon, sir. Can I help you?' She can't keep her eyes off Chum Kane.

'Hope so. I was in the area and I thought I might drop by and visit with Iris Chandler. I'm a family friend. I believe she was transferred here from the Emerald Rest Home?'

The woman's pretty face clouds and she raises a manicured hand. 'Could you wait there, please, sir?' She lifts the handset of an internal phone system, mutters, nods. Looks up. 'Your name is?'

'Smith. Ivor Smith,' says Chum.

'Could you take a seat, Mr Smith? Mrs Hoffman, the manager, will come to speak with you.'

Chum's highly tuned senses are aching with tension. He is out in the open. He has expressed an interest in Iris. He is a static target. A shadow falls across him and he looks up at the sweeping staircase to see a woman approaching, her face grave.

Keeler is lying, shoeless and tieless, shirt open at the neck, on the bed in his hotel room. He has been working now for nine days straight and he wants time to himself. Not to sleep or eat, not to watch TV as the other agents do. Keeler wants time to think. So he switches off his pager, his cell phone, his laptop, takes the phone off the hook, and he lies down, arms crossed behind his head and he thinks. An observer would not be aware of the speed and intensity with which his mental processes flik-flak back on themselves, because he remains motionless, silent. He does not fidget or cough, or shift about on the mattress. He lies still and unleashes his mental Rottweiler with the instruction to hunt down his convictions. When he is done he picks up the phone and dials Lieutenant Flanagan's number in Miami. He wants to speak to Flanagan, wants to discuss something very important with him.

Harris answers the phone, tells Keeler that Flanagan is still AWOL. No one has heard from him in weeks. Harris is pissed off because his administration load has increased, he is snowed under with paper. 'If you manage to get hold of that asshole, you tell him to get his sorry ass back here. He is in deep, deep shit.'

Keeler drops the phone. Reverts to thinking mode. Reviews the situation. Flanagan now knows who Mr Candid is, probably what he looks like. Flanagan is looking for Mr Candid. As is every federal agency across America. Keeler knows, too, that Mr Candid is heading for Harrison Penitentiary. It is safe to assume that Flanagan knows that as well. Ergo, Flanagan is nearby somewhere. Flanagan will find Chum Kane – Keeler is sure of that – and will have the opportunity to ask him how he lives with himself. Keeler, meanwhile – Keeler, who had watched Katarina Kowalski's pale face bloom out of the sand – is stuck here, detailed to protect Katarina's killer from Mr Candid. The child killer whose case is up for review.

All night Keeler lies on his bed, thinking, stepping cautiously along the mental path that will bring him yet again to the decision he knows he has already made. Keeler lies still and he plans, covers all the angles, takes the logical route. At dawn he sits up and calls his wife, exchanges banalities, tells her he loves her. Asks to speak to his daughters. They tell him about what they've done at school, about the sleep-over the night before. Keeler joshes them, makes them laugh. Then he says goodbye and replaces the phone. He lies back on the bed and sleeps, feeling lighter than he has since he himself was a child. He weeps a little but he thinks that's OK. Permissible.

Mrs Hoffman draws Chum into an office off the reception area, sits him in a plush chair, and perches herself, gracefully, on the edge of the desk. Then she speaks.

'I'm afraid that Iris died a couple of weeks ago. It was a peaceful death, I hope. She died in the night, in her sleep. I suspect she simply slipped away. Iris was not a well woman and I'm sure it was a relief. I am sorry.'

Mrs Hoffman comes to Chum as he cries and wraps a warm, solid arm round his shoulders, comforting him. 'Mr Smith,' she says gently, 'Iris was a damaged woman, as you know. She was a broken woman. Her life – what little we know of it – was a difficult one, a lonely one. Perhaps, and I think you should remember this, it was a relief in the end. Perhaps she wanted to go. The fact that she is mourned, that you're here now, makes me think her life wasn't lived for nothing.' Her honeyed tones transform this platitude into a benediction of sorts and Chum calms himself. He asks, eventually, if he can take Iris's effects.

'There are none, I'm afraid. "Born naked, buried naked – why fuss? All life leads to this first nakedness,"' says Mrs Hoffman, letting her arm slip away from Chum. She walks back to her desk, straightens some papers. 'But perhaps you could give us the details of Iris's family? We were given no information when she was transferred here.'

'I have to go,' says Chum, standing, looking at his watch, striding towards the door. 'I'll mail you what I know.' He passes through the reception area and out into the damp heat and sunlight. A moving target.

Flanagan bought his already used car – a bullet-grey '82 Ford Camero – ten years ago. It's a machine, that's all, and Flanagan loves people (particularly the as-yet-unborn – although he's growing fonder of Bronwen by the minute) more than machines. Which is why he never has it serviced, merely fixed up when it breaks down; occasionally he pours oil and water into it, when he remembers. The car has tried, for years, to be a good servant. But this last journey, from Naples to Alva, during which Flanagan loses his way again and again, is a trip too far. In the space of two weeks the worn, misfiring engine has laboured more than three thousand miles. It's too much; and on a lonely road outside Corkscrew it blows away its head gasket, seizes up and dies.

'Can you fucking believe it?' roars Flanagan, turning the key over and over.

'Bloody hell,' mutters Bronwen, fanning herself with the map. 'Can you fix it, man?'

For an answer Flanagan beats his forehead against the steering wheel.

The two of them sit on the verge, swamp water and sea water seeping into the generous cuts of their clothes as the mosquitoes gather. The hood is propped open, oily, near-smoking air escaping the engine. They sit there for thirty minutes before moving into the shade, Bronwen's nose already pink. No traffic passes by.

THE KANE FAMILY

The weeks following Sugar's death were occupied by post-mortems, interviews, silent evenings, doctors' visits. The restructured, remodelled house, which smelt, unfortunately, of fresh pine, felt like a mausoleum. Luke Kane did not return to work after his sister's death. Instead he took to his bed, where he guzzled pills and bourbon, which rendered him incapable of remembering the moment when he saw the surprisingly tiny, black hole in Sugar's forehead. Iris sat with him, attempting to feed him soup and broth, toast, crackers, anything that would dilute the liquor, but he refused them all. The doctor came every evening and tried to talk to Luke Kane. Since he remained always silent, childlike, the doctor pumped him full of vitamins and left, shrugging when Iris asked any questions. In truth the doctor was shocked by Luke Kane's descent into helplessness. After all, the man had a wife and children; he should shake himself.

Chum steered clear of his father's room, never visited him in his mourning, because he could think of nothing to say that would help him. Nothing he could do would alleviate his father's grief. Iris asked him to ensure that Lydia never went near her father and this Chum did.

August slid away, the evenings pulled in closer and still

the Kane house was silent, shut down, almost. Chum took to sitting out on the deck in the evenings, sitting in the old rocking-chair, just as his grandmother and father had done before him, and as he sat watching the horizon turn scarlet and grey, he pieced together the scattered jigsaw that was the memory of slipping into the house years before and finding Sugar and his father in the drawing room. Had it happened? Chum was never sure but he had his suspicions. No one, he felt, should grieve so long and hard as his father did over the death of a sibling when there were so many other lives to worry about.

Iris, too, had her suspicions but, because the house had become perforce a silent one, she said nothing. The day of Sugar's death had lashed Iris's tongue still in her mouth. That day had become a wall behind which was before and the other side of which was after. For the first time in years she thought of her parents: wondered whether they had thought of the day Iris left in the same way, whether they thought of it as a wall separating before and after. Some nights she would sit at the kitchen table and write letter after letter to them, begging forgiveness, but all the letters were torn up and thrown in the trash can. One morning she came downstairs late to discover that Lydia had woken before her, found the fragments of Iris' pleas and strewn them all over the floor. For the first time Iris lost her temper with her daughter, grabbed her wrist, pulled her to her feet and began to slap the soft, tender skin on the back of her thighs. It was Chum who pulled her gently away, Chum who put his arm round the bawling, uncomprehending Lydia and took her outside.

It was Chum, too, who had been interviewed most frequently by the police. He described again and again what had happened: how Lydia and he had been playing around, how he had been tickling her, how she had laughed. The awful coincidence of Lydia standing and running away just as Sugar began to descend the stairs. Again and again he described the event, because Lydia could not. Whenever she was asked, all Lydia said was what she had said to Luke Kane: 'Lyddie do it. Lyddie push. Sorry.' One policeman, younger than the rest, a rookie new to the area, asked Chum whether perhaps Lydia had not liked Sugar.

'Not liked her?' Chum echoed.

'Yeah. I mean, is it possible Lydia harboured a resentment? Even subliminally? Y'know, a subconscious desire to get rid of her?'

Chum stood up and went to the window, beckoned for the rookie to follow. He pointed to fifteen-year-old Lydia playing in the sandpit, her pouting, rosebud lips covered in grit as she chewed thoughtfully, gurgling and slapping a plastic bucket. Chum turned to the young man. 'I may be biased but I don't think she's capable of harbouring anything, do you?'

The cop looked away, his theories undone by what he had seen.

Eventually a verdict of accidental death was recorded and the Kanes were left alone to their own devices. Chum packed his trunk and cases and went back to Harvard, where he was given rooms and a teaching timetable. Meanwhile, in the Kane house, Iris retreated even further and became like her mother: metronomic and domesticated. Lydia bumbled through her days, watched over by a nanny. Luke Kane lay in his room for weeks, sucking on bourbon bottles, withering away. But even he eventually calmed sufficiently to get up, shower and dress. He went to work, spent his mornings moving money from one place to another, then went for long, alcoholic lunches. In the afternoons he would sit at his desk, looking out over the skyscrapers on the horizon, thinking of Sugar. In the evenings he returned home to ignore Iris and drink some more.

It was a far from perfect life but it was manageable. The Kanes woke each morning and made it through the day to night, when they could all escape into their dreams. With the exception of Chum – who had escaped – they were not happy, but they managed. It might even have stayed that way had Lydia not resembled Sugar quite so closely.

1997

Chum is sitting in the hired car, watching the genteel seniors of the Diamond Days home being herded together beneath a collection of Genoa tents, where they are to be served iced tea and seafood salads, followed by fresh fruit. His mother is dead. For years he has thought of his mother, thought of visiting. And now he has missed her by weeks. He's never even said goodbye. Come to that, he's never said anything, he's never written her, never called. He has even missed her funeral. Chum rests his head on the wheel and cries again.

Keeler, sharp and defined in his white shirt and newly pressed suit, is issuing orders at the penitentiary. He has decided that the spread of agents is incorrect, that they must be repositioned. The governor follows Keeler on his round, smouldering with resentment, as Keeler adjusts the pattern of surveillance. A number of agents comment on the flaws in the new arrangement, pointing out that there are shadows, blind spots, in their cover of the area but Keeler insists and the men move, cradling their guns like babies.

'Mr Keeler,' the governor says, as Keeler instructs an agent to cover an interview room.

'Agent Keeler,' snaps Keeler.

'Is this really necessary?'

'Yes.'

'I thought the threat was an exterior one.'

Keeler turns on his heels and faces the governor. 'When I need advice I'll ask for it.'

'Agent Keeler, I shall need some latitude of movement tomorrow. We're moving an A-grade prisoner and my men need to have access to all exits. I cannot allow the running of this institution to grind to a halt.'

'You're moving a prisoner tomorrow?'

'Yes. The Penal Review Board convenes elsewhere and has requested an interview with the offender.'

'Tomorrow? What time tomorrow?'

'I can't tell you that.'

Keeler smiles a thin smile. 'If you don't tell me, how can I make arrangements to accommodate changes in personnel?'

The governor frowns. 'OK. OK. Eleven hundred hours.'

'Thank you.' And Keeler leaves the man to his anger.

Walking to his car Keeler thinks for a moment that his sight is betraying him. The light in the compound is so flat and so dazzling that all colour has been leached from the landscape; all he can see is black and white. White buildings hatched by black shadows. He drives slowly, carefully, back to his hotel. He wants nothing to happen to him, he must look after himself. He throws himself on the hotel bed and calls his superior.

'Sir? Keeler reporting in.'

'How's it going?'

'Very well, sir. Everything's in place.'

'Good work, Agent Keeler. Just make sure you get him.'

Keeler smiles. 'Yes, sir. I'll get him. I was wondering if you could reconsider and allow me to contact Sam Kowalski. I have a few questions I'd like to ask him.' For instance, what he thought of Mr Candid; if he'd liked him when he met him; if he *trusted* him.

'That won't be possible, I'm afraid.'

'It would be very helpful, sir.'

'I said it wouldn't be possible. Sam Kowalski has been dealt with.'

Keeler puts the phone down quietly. *Dealt with?*

The traffic is still non-existent on the lonely back road and the situation Bronwen and Flanagan find themselves in is getting worse by the moment. Deep in Bronwen's guts a rogue shrimp is releasing its toxins and these combine with the heat to make her nauseous. For a while she sits in the humid shade, swallowing repeatedly, feeling her stomach heave as she sweats and turns pale. Then without warning she throws up spectacularly, all over the sand, grass and soda cans lining the road's verge. Flanagan jumps up as Bronwen groans and hunches over on her hands and knees, expelling the shrimp risotto she had for lunch. He looks round wildly for something to help her but there is nothing. To Bronwen's mortification he kneels next to her and holds back her hair, rubs her back, muttering soothing words as she vomits.

In the driveway of Diamond Days Chum has stopped crying. His eyes are red-rimmed and watery, but he has stopped crying. His mind, which has looked away from this excess of emotion, faintly embarrassed, kicks in again and he begins to calculate. He notices Mrs Hoffman standing in the shade of the portico, frowning, talking to the young receptionist, watching him, and he shifts the car into gear and drives away, into Alva. He stops at the first call-box he sees and parks. He calls Sam the Weasel Man's number and it rings and rings. Chum calls again, unaware of the sweat running down his temples, soaking his collar. The phone rings again and an answer-machine kicks in. A voice. Not Sam's. 'If you'd like to leave a message . . .' A trace. Chum replaces the phone, looks around, imagines children watching him from the blind squares of the school windows. He drives on, not knowing where, keeping to the back roads.

So Sam has gone, as has Gideon. Both disappeared, no doubt, into the bowels of the state, where everything they know about him will be extracted from them and digested. All his mother's papers and effects have been burnt. And his mother is dead. In short, nearly everyone who knows him has disappeared. But . . . but . . . there is the photograph and there was the car parked outside the Emerald Rest Home. What about these facts?

Chum negotiates a lazy bend and sees a woman in distress on the side of the road, a large man practically on top of her. Chum brakes, rolls down the window and calls, 'Hey, lady, you OK?'

Bronwen looks up through bleary eyes, her chin streaked with saliva and vomit, and sees the man of her dreams. Flanagan stops rubbing her back, looks at Mr Candid with amazement. Bronwen throws up again, sickened now by humiliation.

'Can I help?' Chum gets out of the car, but stands by it, leaving the engine running. 'What's going on here?'

'My friend, she's sick. Something she ate.' Flanagan can't take his eyes off Mr Candid, as if he's a ghost or a movie star or something.

'I got some water. Hold on.' Chum finds the bottle and tosses it across the road to Flanagan. Bronwen sips gratefully. Then Flanagan takes out a handkerchief, wets it and wipes her face.

'Thank you,' says Bronwen shyly.

Chum looks at the old Camero, its engine cold now. 'This yours?'

'Yeah. Blew up and seized, I think. We've been waiting for someone to come along. A couple of hours now.'

Chum scans the empty road. Sees nothing. The temperature is in the hundreds, the humidity stultifying. The woman retches loudly once more, helping Chum to come to a decision. The woman is definitely sick: this large, homely couple are in need of assistance. 'You want a ride somewhere? There must be a garage in the next town.'

Flanagan stands up. 'Thanks, that'd be great.'

And so, after months of hunting, Flanagan – who is now himself a fugitive – finds himself sitting in Mr Candid's car, heading back towards Naples. In the back seat Bronwen can't help staring at Chum's profile as she dabs at the vomit on her blouse.

CHUM KANE

Sugar had asked Chum the night before she died whether he had a girlfriend and he had blushed because there was someone who made his heart beat faster. The woman was a student at Harvard, that much he knew, because he'd seen her coming out of lectures, carrying books and laughing with other students. It wasn't that she was beautiful – her face was too long and sharp – but there was something about her that had caught his eye. It was the way she moved, the way she focused on whoever spoke, giving them her whole attention until they finished. The way she waved to her friends and then swung away, already lost to herself. Chum saw her irregularly, randomly walking across the Yard, as he walked back and forth from the faculty to his rooms, or across the campus for meetings and seminars with professors. Sometimes he glimpsed her in coffee shops in Cambridge as he shopped for books on Saturday afternoons. He may not have seen her often but she occupied his thoughts greatly, unbalanced his single-minded commitment to study.

Chum was happier at Harvard than he had been as an undergraduate. His fellowship allowed him the freedom to try to untangle mathematical problems unfettered by fear of examination, and he enjoyed running seminars and attending conferences. Some weekends he would take the Eldorado (the envy of the fraternities) up the coast, to Danbury or Beverley, and sit on the beach reading newspapers or textbooks, smoking his cigarettes, indulging his one vice. He made a few friends among the older undergrads and the younger teachers, all of them young men with a similar diffident disposition to his own. He couldn't visit bars because he was under-age, but they would buy in beers and watch the football, or maybe play frisbee on the Common. Chum played tennis and rowed in the eights: early mornings on the Charles, wrapped in sweats, heart pumping, his oar cruising through water.

He no longer wrote letters at the weekends because nothing he could write would alleviate the atmosphere of the Kane house – that much he knew. His mother sometimes dropped him a note, short and uncluttered by information, and reading between the lines Chum knew how unhappy she still was, how withdrawn Lydia had become, how unbearable his father was. But he knew this anyway, because he still visited East Hampton for Thanksgiving, Christmas and New Year, and maybe for a week each summer, with a few weekends thrown in during the year. These trips were purgatory, full of menace and the unspoken, and each time he left as soon as possible. But he went because he wanted to see Lydia, who, of course, was delighted by him and smiled and played whenever he was there. Chum was not foolish enough to think he could make a difference to this situation; all he could do was behave as a dutiful son.

'Hi,' she said, standing by his table in the Kerouac Koffee Bar.

Chum looked up from his paper on equivalence relation between cardinal numbers, which he was redrafting for presentation that week. It was the woman who moved in a certain way. Chum wasn't surprised by this: he had in some way expected it. 'Hi,' he said, and pushed aside his papers.

'Mind if I sit here?' Her irises, close up, were an odd muddy green, a halo of gold surrounding them.

'Go ahead. Uh, can I buy you a coffee or something?' Chum was already standing, searching his pockets for bills.

'Sure. Thanks. I'll have an espresso.' And then she smiled and Chum knew that everything was going to be all right. For the first time in his life he thought that everything that followed would make sense.

They spent that afternoon in the coffee bar, only leaving when it closed, moving on to an Italian place off Magazine. They sat facing each other, talking, talking, already so comfortable with each other. When they parted, outside her room, Chum took the number of the dorm and promised to call. He memorized the number as he walked back, inverted it, reduced it to binary notation, calculated the possibility of it being another number. It was the most beautiful sequence of integers he had ever seen. In fact, it was such an arresting combination of numbers that he felt compelled to call it the moment he got back to his rooms.

'Hi,' he said, as a sleepy, unknown voice answered. 'Could I speak to Marilyn, please?'

'Moment.' The phone was dropped and Chum waited until her voice came on the line.

'Chum?'

'Yeah. Sorry, I had to call.'

'That's OK, but everyone else here is asleep.'

'Shall I hang up?'

'No. No. Talk to me.'

So they talked through the small hours, Chum lying on his floor, smoking; Marilyn sitting in a dressing-gown, on the stairs by the communal phone. Every now and then they'd break off to fetch a can of soda, or go to the bathroom, then carry on.

After that first encounter they met every day. Marilyn went along to hear Chum's paper on equivalence relation and didn't understand a word of it. He helped her with her work on Math 101. Some weekends they went into Boston and visited the aquarium, went walkabout in Charles Street, ate in Chinatown, spent hours browsing books in Brattle's. They'd wander round Beacon Hill or Back Bay, where Chum's money could have bought them a townhouse. But most of their time was spent in Cambridge, among the students, where they felt most at home.

Late October, and Chum booked a weekend in a hotel in Provincetown. They left early Friday, on a sharp, azure day, wrapped in mufflers, wearing gloves, and Chum drove the length of Cape Cod with the top down. The trees had turned and red-gold, green-veined leaves swirled into the car, Marilyn trying to catch them. They stopped at Buzzard Bay, outside Wareham, and ate fried clams and buttered lobster, looking out over a bullet-grey sea. Then they crossed the canal and took the minor roads to Provincetown, through the small towns of clapboard houses and tall shingled spires dangled above manicured squares. Both of them knew the Nantucket and Martha's Vineyard crowd, from schooldays, from Harvard, and they gossiped about mutual acquaintances.

As they neared Provincetown the conversation faltered and eventually stopped. The heavy car crawled through the town, shuttered now for the winter season, the streets deserted, until they pulled up in front of a grey-shingled hotel with white trim. They checked in and carried their bags to their room, which had a balcony looking out over a shoreline bleached shades of grey, white and pale yellow. Chum and Marilyn stood leaning at the rail, oblivious of the cutting wind. Awkwardly, they turned back into the room and stood with their hands hanging loosely. Eventually Marilyn reached out and tugged at Chum's belt, pulled him on to the bed and lay there with him, and it was that afternoon that she put her mouth inside his head and asked, 'Can I trust you?' The rest of the weekend passed in episode upon episode of skin meeting skin. Chum felt that, after twenty years of waiting, he had come home, found a space into which he fitted.

For three years Chum Kane and Marilyn shared each other's lives. She still lived in Hall, but Chum bought an apartment (paid for by his trust fund, which matured when he was twenty-one) on Magazine and Auburn, and Marilyn spent most nights and weekends there. It was a spacious apartment, with pale, stripped floors and long, triple-glazed windows. Chum had a study, a bathroom with a claw-foot bath, and a vast living room, furnished only with a hi-fi system and a pristine white twill sofa large enough for four. It was certainly large enough for the two of them. In summer the sun threw oblongs of white light on to the floors, turning them peach; in winter the snow on the pavement reflected the streetlight on to the ceiling in strange, unlikely prisms.

Marilyn would arrive Saturday mornings (she never stayed Fridays, insisting on going out with other friends), her arms full of groceries for the weekend. They'd have breakfast, of bagels or pancakes, make love, disappear into the city for the afternoon to see a movie or browse in bookshops. They talked, but most of the time they didn't need to for their communion was silent; they moved naturally in the same direction, towards the same goal. Only once did they argue: when Marilyn, over drinks on the Square, said that she believed in the divine spark. She threw a beer at Chum and walked out. He followed her back to Hall, to see her bend down, looking sad. At that moment he vowed he would never leave her.

1997

Chum drives lazily, his wrist resting on the arc of the wheel, his other hand dangling out of the open window, shifting in the draught. Bronwen watches him surreptitiously from the back seat, the damp patches on her blouse drying out. She is distracted from waves of nausea by the beauty, the symmetry of Chum's profile, which she notices is stubbled with beard. Against her breasts, damp with sweat, the Polaroid picture is sticky. But she is careful with it – it is the silvery back of the photo that rests against her skin. He looks the same yet older in that way that people age. Nothing that Bronwen – who knows his image intimately – can define: his hair, dark blond, is still thick, his eyes still blue. He is still tall, rangy and lean. But there is something about him which makes Bronwen know that nearly two decades have passed since that photo was snapped. An air of dejection almost? As if something has been whipped out of him. But what and by whom?

As Bronwen contemplates this, Flanagan is thinking furiously. What to do? Here he is, sitting next to Mr Candid, and his question is pushing hard against his sternum: *How do you live with yourself?* How to ask it? Flanagan can't imagine any way of casually introducing the issue. How to steer a conversation towards serial killing and child rapists? And, anyway, how would Chum Kane react? Flanagan can't endanger Bronwen, not now. No solution occurs to him so he stares out of the window at the passing tropical scrub.

Chum, meanwhile, is pondering the situation. The image of the car he saw parked in the driveway of the Emerald Rest Home matches the picture of the car broken down on the verge: a silver-grey Ford Camero. Something is askew here. 'What d'you want to do about this? I mean, d'you want to call Triple A or something?'

'Excuse me?' Flanagan looks at Chum.

'I was wondering what plans you have.'

'Plans?' Flanagan feels like an idiot.

'About your car? Doesn't look like it's going anywhere. And we're coming up to a town now – couple of miles. You could maybe call out a tow-truck.' Chum swivels in the seat, looks at Bronwen. 'You OK, ma'am? Feeling better?'

'Yes, thank you,' says Bronwen demurely, dropping her eyes.

'Good.' She's not American – her accent is not American. Chum remembers Sam the Weasel Man sitting on a bench at the Battery, talking about a woman who'd shown him a photograph . . .

Two miles? thinks Flanagan wildly. He notices isolated houses on the outskirts of the town beginning to appear. Two miles? Two minutes. He comes to a decision. Very slowly, he reaches for his holstered gun, unclips it, fishes for his badge. Then turns to Chum, brandishing both. 'Could you please pull over, sir?'

Chum looks at the gun, glances at Flanagan, raises his eyebrows. 'Excuse me?' Keeps driving.

'Could you please pull over, sir?' Flanagan's sweat flows. Chum keeps driving, his wrist resting lazily.

'Flanagan!' Bronwen bleats in the back.

'Look, I don't want to use this.' Flanagan feels desperation rising.

'Don't, then,' says Chum.

'Look, I only want to ask you a question. One question.'

'What? You're not stealing my car or my wallet? You're not a crazy on the make?' Chum smiles.

'No – goddammit. I'm a police officer!'

'You're not arresting me, either?'

'Flanagan!' Bronwen bleats again.

The lieutenant wipes his face, steadies the gun. 'No, I'm not arresting you, Mr Kane. Or Chum, if I may call you that.'

Chum looks at him hard and the car slows, glides to a halt by the kerb. 'What did you call me?'

'Chum Kane. Also known as Charles Kane.' Flanagan falters, collects himself. 'Also known as Mr Candid.' God, but he's a handsome bastard, Flanagan thinks, as Chum stares him out.

Chum adjusts the rearview mirror, checks the wing mirrors. Slowly, very slowly, he scans the horizon: flat and uninteresting, broken by pylons. There is nowhere to hide. Where are they? 'Where's the back-up?'

'There isn't any.'

'You telling me you're here alone? You saying that wasn't a set-up back there – the car, her throwing up?'

Flanagan tries to stare back. 'I promise you. I'm here on my own. Well, actually, I'm on vacation.'

Chum smiles, then laughs. 'On vacation?'

'Yes.' Flanagan drops the gun into his lap, feeling foolish.

Chum rakes his eyes over the lieutenant's face, scans Bronwen's muffin-like features. For some reason – perhaps because the two of them are such an unlikely duo to unmask Mr Candid – Chum believes Flanagan. 'So, what can I do for you?'

'I need to talk to you,' says Flanagan.

'What about?'

'It's too difficult to explain here.' Flanagan holsters the gun, holds out his hand. 'Lieutenant Flanagan.' Chum shakes his hand. 'And this,' he says, twisting in his seat, 'is Bronwen.'

'Bronwen Jones,' says Bronwen, holding out a dainty, if plump, paw.

'Nice to meet you, Bronwen Jones,' says Chum, and she blushes prettily.

'I have a proposition for you, Mr Kane.'

'Chum, if you prefer.'

'OK. I have a proposition for you, Chum. You name a hotel of your choice and we'll pay for the three of us to stay a night, have ourselves a real nice dinner and all that. No catches, no back-up teams, no wires. All we want to do is talk.' Flanagan's lime eyes bore into Chum's. 'If you ask me, you look like a man who could do with a long, hot soak, a couple of drinks and a night's company. If you ask me, you look like a man who could do with not running for a night.'

Chum feels a rush of tears as this huge, hairy man – whom he does not know, whom he has never met before – expresses more concern for him than anyone has for a long, long time. For seventeen years. He stares at the swampy land around them. 'I read about a place once, outside Boca Grande. Antebellum house on the beach with water villas. Each villa has a

pier and a dinghy tied up. The bathrooms have no ceilings –
you can lie in the tub and look at the stars.'

'How far is it?'

'From here? Not far. Not sure. An hour, maybe.'

'Well, Chum, Bronwen and I would love to buy you a night
there in exchange for the pleasure of your company.'

'It costs more than five thousand bucks a night.' Chum
could buy the complex for cash but he realizes that others
might have a difficulty with this.

'No problem,' says Bronwen, thinking of the crumpled
envelopes in her suitcase. Flanagan looks at her, dumbstruck.
'Let's get going, man,' she says, and Chum shifts into reverse,
turns the car round and drives north towards Fort Myers,
heading for Gasparilla Island.

As the sun slips away, heading for Mexico and all points
west, Keeler brushes his teeth and slides into bed in his air-
conditioned hotel room. He lies in the cool, darkening room,
thinking of his family, how he wants to be with them.
Turning on his side, tucking his hands beneath his chin, he
thinks of Gideon and ponders the problem of what will
happen to the young black man. Keeler hopes he will be par-
doned, that he will make it to college somehow, for Keeler
realizes that Gideon – given his background, given what he
was born into – can hardly be held responsible for what he
has become. He thinks of Sam Kowalski and wonders what
has happened to him, how he has been 'dealt with'. Surely
the man, whose only daughter was found in a shallow grave
on a beach, has a right to live out his days – playing domi-
noes, walking round the neighbourhood, eating lunch in his
favoured deli, whatever – as he wants to? Keeler fervently

hopes that Sam Kowalski, the Weasel Man, will be allowed that dignity.

Panic suddenly hits Keeler and he jumps from the bed, crosses the room, picks up the Magnum he cleaned the night before, slides back the chamber and hears the comforting click and whisper of a well-oiled piece. He climbs back into bed. Gets up again, visits the bathroom. Drinks a glass of water. Gets back into bed. He has to sleep. He needs to be in good shape for the morning. He tucks himself in again, knees up, hands folded. And thinks of Katarina Kowalski, how she had looked. Lonely was how she had looked on that dark beach. Sad and lonely and more dead than anything he had ever seen, with her ragged wrists crusted with sand. Keeler begins to weep and wishes Flanagan was there with him.

Flanagan, meanwhile, is sitting on the pier of the water villa he, Bronwen and Chum are sharing, sipping a vodka martini and watching the sky blacken. The water is phosphorescent, a green glow snapping across the horizon as the last fragment of sun disappears. He has showered and clipped his beard, dressed in clean, pressed shorts and shirt, and now he awaits the arrival of Bronwen and Chum, who are completing their own ablutions. A veritable banquet has been ordered – lobsters, shrimp gumbo, clams and steak. He is, he realizes, completely content, his quest nearing its end. Then Bronwen sits next to him, wrapped in a robe, her hair still wet. The two of them say nothing; they sit and watch the phosphorescence dance, occasionally hear the splash of a fish leaping. A while later Chum joins them, clean-shaven and scrubbed, wearing T-shirt and shorts. He takes a beer from the ice-box and comes to sit with them, his feet up on a rail, his head thrown back,

watching the stars appear. The three of them sit there in com-
panionable silence, as if they have known each other for years.
Chum and Bronwen smoke as Flanagan keeps the glasses full.

'When I was in the tub, I realized I was looking at
Andromeda and Pegasus. Markab was so bright you could
read by it.' Chum's voice makes the others jump a little. 'I
haven't stopped to look at the stars for years. You can forget
they're there.'

A handbell sounds and a troupe of waiters wheel trolleys
down to the pier. A table is erected and laid and the three of
them are called to sit for dinner. Cold, sharp Entre Deux Mers
is poured as they settle and the lobster is served. For an hour
they eat, Chum marvelling at Bronwen's capacity for food,
given she only hours ago was sick. Course follows course,
the meal punctuated by murmurs of appreciation, comments
about the luxury of their rooms, the pleasing air temperature.
Finally the plates are pushed aside and the waiters sweep
them away, clean the tablecloth with tiny brushes and dust-
pans, serve coffee and leave.

Flanagan is about to belch his appreciation when he
remembers that he and Bronwen have company. Instead he
pads into the water villa, passing Chum's bedroom, where he
sees new shirts laid out. The man has brought nothing with
him – travelled so light he could blow away in a wind. When
they had arrived at the hotel he had asked for fresh clothes to
be delivered to the water villa for all of them, insisting on
paying for them. Flanagan selects a thick Cuban cigar from a
compact humidor and finds Chum and Bronwen sitting back
down on the pier, lit now by a swinging chain of tiny, mellow
candle-lights. They are sipping Armagnac, as Chum points
out the constellations, naming them and explaining their

significance. Flanagan experiences a rush of jealousy as he recalls the photo of Chum that Bronwen wears next to her heart. He throws himself into a cane chair, which creaks and protests at his newly laden weight. It is this jealousy that makes him speak harshly.

'Right, I guess we'd better get on with the business of the night.' Even in the dim light he sees Chum's expression of hurt – Chum has forgotten this was a business arrangement. For a while there, he thought he was among friends. Flanagan's huge Irish heart contracts. 'All I mean is, well, you know. It'll get late and all.' Flanagan busies himself with his cigar, clipping and teasing it, to distract himself.

Chum settles, pulls the bottle towards himself, having refilled Bronwen's glass. 'How can I help you, Lieutenant?'

'Oh, call me Flanagan. Everyone does.'

'Don't you have another name?'

'Well, I suppose I do.' Flanagan frowns, trying to remember it.

'I mean, what did your mother call you?'

'Padraig – Patrick. But everyone called me Paddy and I hated it. So now it's Flanagan. Has been for years.'

'I didn't know that,' says Bronwen, smiling at him, flanked by her two favourite men in the whole world. 'I don't think I could call you anything but Flanagan now.'

'Good,' says Flanagan, and laughs.

'My mother called me Charlie, and everyone else called me Chum. But I'm not telling you anything you don't know already, am I?' Chum rocks a little in his chair. 'How about I ask you how you know that, in order to kick off our little discussion? I mean, as far as I'm aware, everyone who knows that is either dead or disappeared.'

Flanagan exhales Caribbean smoke. The moment is here and he cannot lie; has never been able to. 'Bronwen told me.'

Chum turns to her, his expression unreadable. 'And how, Bronwen, did *you* know that?'

Bronwen lowers her heads, runs a pale finger around the rim of her glass. 'Your mother told me.'

It is too dark for Bronwen to see the water that gathers immediately in Chum's eyes, and he looks to the horizon, blinks it away. 'I found out today she's dead.'

Unthinking, Bronwen reaches out her hand and lays her palm on Chum's smooth cheek. 'Oh, I'm so sorry.'

As Chum stares into the distance, Flanagan wonders where to go from here. This is not working out as he planned. But he has not allowed for Chum's powers of self-control: within minutes he is composed once more. 'When did she tell you?'

'A few months ago. I was her nurse.' And, holding Chum's hand, Bronwen tells him about the Emerald Rest Home, about the matron, about Iris always talking about Chum, about how she, Bronwen, left. But she is less than candid about *why* she left: to find Chum Kane.

'So, she was happy?' Chum asks.

' I think so, Chum. I really think so. She had a lovely room.'

'But how did you know who I was? How d'you recognize me?' Chum already knows the answer.

Bronwen releases Chum's hand and reaches into the pocket of her gown, pulls out a Polaroid photo. 'She gave me this' (and she apologizes silently for the lie).

Chum takes the Polaroid from Bronwen, stares at it in the pale light: himself, seventeen years ago, young, handsome, his foot on the fender of an Eldorado, about to laugh. He turns it over in his hands. 'Thanksgiving 1980'. A familiar hand. Written a lifetime ago.

'Chum?' Flanagan's voice seems loud in the dark night. 'Chum? You been asking a lot of questions. I think it's my turn now.'

'Go ahead,' Chum says, his eyes locked on the photograph.

'What happened to you?'

'Sorry?'

Flanagan turns the cigar in his unsure fingers and it snaps. He has waited so long to ask this. Travelled so far to arrive here. 'I know your background. I know where you came from. What happened to you?' Flanagan looks up at the stars, notices Markab winking. 'What was it that turned you into a killer and – let's be fair – such a successful one?'

CHUM KANE

Chum woke up early that Thanksgiving morning, disturbed from sleep by a hangover – a rare occurrence for him. Marilyn and he had been to a party in West Roxbury the night before and he had drunk too much beer, talked for too long, too late. He lay in bed, gingerly probing his mind, testing it for efficiency. He eased himself from the bed and slopped his way to the kitchen, where he made tea, standing scratching himself as the water boiled. He took the tea to the bathroom, drenched his head with cold water from the shower and then lay in the bath soaking himself in steaming water, watching snow fall on the skylight. As he combed his hair in the mirror, his eyes stared back bloodshot, and he sighed, disgusted that he felt so shabby on a day when he had to drive to Long Island and face the remains of his family. As he pulled on jeans, a key turned in the lock and Marilyn appeared carrying a bag, which she dropped in the hall.

'Hope you feel as bad as I do,' she said, throwing herself on the bed, rubbing her forehead.

'Reckon I do,' Chum said, leaning over her and kissing her hair. 'Want breakfast before we leave?'

'God, I dunno.'

Chum made a pot of coffee and pancakes and the two of

them sat in the kitchen eating, reading papers. As the clock inched round to ten o'clock, Chum made a move. 'C'mon, we'd better go. I'll get the car.'

He clattered down the stairs of the apartment block, slipped on his overshoes and walked out into the freezing air, which cleared his head immediately. A different ache replaced the hangover – it was so cold his jaw ached (genetic memory?). He crunched down the drifts of a snowstorm which had passed through the city three days before, and walked to the garage. The padlock was frozen and he had to warm it surreptitiously with his urine. He ran the Eldorado for five minutes before reversing out, glad the snow chains were already fixed. The heater blew noisily but it was effective, clearing the windows in moments. He drove back to Magazine and there she was – the only woman he'd ever wanted – waiting on the kerb.

Marilyn got in, her nose red at the tip, slapping her hands and shivering. 'Christ, it's cold. Y'know, you live here all your life and you never get used to it. Every summer I forget what winters are like. Every frigging winter I swear I'm moving out west. California or somewhere – somewhere warm.' She spotted Fergus across the street and called a greeting to him, waving as the Eldorado pulled away.

The traffic was heavy as people headed home for the weekend and Chum turned off the I-93 south out of Boston, taking the 3A coast road down towards Plymouth instead. The snow was thicker on the two-lane road but the weight of the car and the chains on the tyres ground them onwards, through slush and ice. Men in tartan wool jackets, heavy boots and caps, hands heavily gloved, cleared driveways, each of them stopping for a moment to gaze longingly at the car as it glided past, resting on the handle of their shovels. The sky was pregnant with snow, low and grey, and the porch lights of the houses looked warm and yellow; even the streetlights glistened. Chum and Marilyn held hands and talked, warm and toasty inside the shell of the car.

On the outskirts of Plymouth, Chum turned off the road down a track, driving at walking pace, slithering on frozen, packed ice. He stopped in a deserted spot by the ocean, where he had Marilyn had often canoodled during their early days, when they could not keep their hands to themselves, when they had few places to canoodle.

'What're you doing?' Marilyn asked, surprised by this detour.

'Um.' Chum rested his hands on the wheel, watched the lighthouse beam swing round on Gurnet Point. 'Um. I've got something to ask you.'

Marilyn sat suddenly still, stopped fidgeting, and turned her muddy eyes on her lover.

'Will you marry me?' Chum asked.

'Yes,' Marilyn said, 'I will. I'd love to.'

And Chum smiled.

Once again, they couldn't keep their hands to themselves and – with the engine running, making the car throb, keeping the heater blowing – they crawled over on to the huge back seat, giggling, pulling at each other's clothes and made sweaty love. The Eldorado had always been their second bedroom and they were expert in turning each other in its confines, avoiding handles and sharp metal corners. When they were done they sat naked on the red leather seat and watched the sky tear, clouds pulling apart, releasing more snow.

'When shall we do it?' Chum asked.

'Soon – as soon as possible. No point waiting.' Marilyn fished for her clothes in the footwell, began to dress.

'I'd just want a quiet wedding, a small civil ceremony, y'know? I don't want families involved.'

'Sure, that's fine.'

'I love you.' Chum took her hand and held it, kissed it.

'Hey,' Marilyn said suddenly, 'I got an idea.' She fished in her tote bag and brought out a Polaroid camera. 'Let's capture the moment.'

'What, now?' asked the naked Chum, appalled.

'No, course not. Get dressed.'

They each took a picture of the other, standing by the car, Plymouth Bay behind, and wrote on the back of their prints so they would never forget the moment when they agreed to marry.

Chum dropped Marilyn at her parents' home in town, not going into the house, wanting to move on, worried by the weather. Marilyn hugged him before she got out. 'Drive carefully. It's getting worse. Where are you going to get the ferry from?'

'New London if it's running. If not, I'll have to take it from Bridgeport.' He checked his watch. 'Should be there by five.'

'Call me when you arrive? Otherwise I'll worry.'

'Sure I will. I'll pick you up late Monday.' And Chum kissed her, kissed her again and let her go. How was he to know, as he drove off, waving through the window, that he'd never see her again, Marilyn, the woman he believed he'd never leave?

The ferry at New London was at dock, crippled by a broken oil pump, so Chum drove on to Bridgeport, cursing as the snow thickened, blown across the highway in shifting clouds.

He had to wait an hour for the ferry to Port Jefferson, and he stood in the waiting room sipping bitter coffee, wishing he was back in his apartment in Cambridge with Marilyn. The crossing to the Island was choppy, wind whipping round the ferry's deck, and he distracted himself by imagining married life with Marilyn. Two kids or one? And what would they call them? He fished for the Polaroid and cursed when he realized he'd taken the wrong one – he'd pocketed the photograph of himself. Then he dozed, his head lolling against the window, and was woken by the jolt of the ferry docking. By the time he began to drive east towards the Kane house it was dark – he was running hours late. He was cold and hungry, so uncomfortable that he was, for once, actually looking forward to arriving at his family home.

Chum pulled into the driveway, the gravel covered with deep snow, and parked by his father's Ford Mustang, Juanita's jalopy behind. The house was in near darkness, bar the lights in the living room. He grabbed his bag from the trunk and jogged over to the back door. Juanita was tidying the kitchen, wiping bowls and surfaces, and she smiled when she saw him burst in, stamping his feet and brushing snow from his shoulders.

'Mr Charlie! You late!' She hugged him. 'You want coffee? I made some for you.'

'Love some.' Chum shook off his jacket, emptied its pockets on to the table, then struggled out of his damp boots and socks. 'How you doing?'

'I fine, José too.' Juanita looked old and tired.

Chum felt sorry for her.

'What's cooking? Smells good.'

'What you think? Turkey, pumpkin pie, what else?' Juanita smiled.

'Where is everyone?' asked Chum as he poured a coffee.

'Mama in living room.'

'And how's my father?' Chum watched Juanita closely; she, after all, spent longer with his family than he ever did.

Juanita shrugged on a long, padded coat and waggled her hand, her mouth turned down. 'Papa? Up, down, up, down. I go now.' Juanita nodded to the clock. 'I late and José he worry. I just wait to see you. I maybe see you Tuesday?'

'Have a good weekend.' Chum kissed her cheek and Juanita left, the kitchen door slamming behind her. Chum stood for a moment in the kitchen, gathering his strength to encounter his kith and kin, then crossed the hall to the living room. His mother was asleep on the sofa, a photograph album open beside her. He looked at the page: the photographs she had taken when the house was renovated. Chum leaned down and kissed his mother's forehead to wake her.

'Hey, Ma.'

Iris woke with a start, saw Chum and smiled. 'Hello, stranger.'

'Sorry I'm late – the weather's turned bad.'

'What time is it?'

'Seven.'

Iris sat up, pushing her rumpled hair back. 'Shoot, I must have fallen asleep. Juanita still here?'

'No, she just left.' Chum wandered around the room, touching the ornaments on the shelves, reminding himself of his childhood. He paused in front of the rows of framed certificates, prizes and photographs that had punctuated his academic career – they'd always embarrassed him.

Iris held up a picture of the house when it was finished,

when the paint had just dried. 'I found a silver frame this morning that'd fit this. It would look real pretty. What d'you think?'

Chum shrugged, not wanting to think of the time the house was last decorated. 'Why not?'

'Well, I guess I'd better see to dinner,' said Iris, hauling herself to her feet, smoothing her skirt, slipping the photo into a pocket. Chum followed her back into the kitchen and he saw her pick up the Polaroid of him standing beside the Eldorado. 'Hey, this is even better.' Iris smiled, turned to him. 'Can I keep it? Frame this instead?' Chum paused. He wanted to please his mother and he wanted to keep the photograph equally. Iris mistook his silence for acquiescence and slipped it in with the other picture. Chum stood there, wanting to tell his mother that he was to be married, wanting to tell her he loved someone, but was tongue-tied by sudden embarrassment. 'Where's Lyddie?' he asked instead.

'Upstairs in her room. I told her you were coming but . . .' Iris shrugged.

'And Dad? He around?'

'Yes. He's having a bath, I think.'

Chum leaned against a counter and crossed his arms. 'Juanita said he's up and down.'

'That's about it.' Iris opened the oven, lifted the tin foil covering the roasting bird and stabbed its skin, the flesh running with thin blood. 'Hour should do it.'

'Is he still drinking?'

Iris straightened and looked at her son. 'Charlie, he's never going to stop drinking. But it's better. A bit better. I don't know.'

Chum stared at the slate floor – Iris had had it laid when the house was refurbished. This made him think of Sugar, the picture of her falling down the stairs blossoming in his mind. 'Why don't you leave him, Ma?'

Iris put down the knife she was holding. 'Charlie, I married him. I can't just go. It doesn't work that way. Anyway, Lyddie's happy here. This house is all she knows.'

'How is she?'

'Why don't you go find out? She'll be happy now you're here. Then I want the two of you to set the table – Juanita cleaned the silver yesterday, so use the best.'

'Will do.'

Chum ran up the stairs, two, three at a time, not wanting to linger, trying not to think of Sugar's forehead meeting a nail. He crossed the landing, began to head down the hallway to Lydia's room. Then stopped. Stood still. He'd heard an unexpected sound. Not an unfamiliar sound but an unexpected one. He had heard it once before, years ago, but had assumed it was a product of his fevered mind as his body fought the infection in his foot.

He turned back and headed for the door to a spare guest suite, opened it slowly. The room was in near-darkness, lit only by a slice of light from the bathroom. And there, on the bed, were Lydia – who in the gloom looked so like Sugar Chum's breath stopped for a moment – and his father. Luke Kane looked up at his son with an unwavering stare. Lydia began to gurgle, struggled to hold out both her arms.

'Chum! Chummie here!'

Charlie 'Chum' Kane could have stopped then. He could have asked his father just what the fuck he thought he was doing. He could have walked out, fetched his mother, called the police and brought the crushing weight of the state's

judgement down on Luke Kane. But he didn't. Instead he
strode over to the bed and – mirroring Theodore's actions of
forty years before, when he had pulled his son off his mother
in the same house, in the same room – Chum dragged his
father off his own daughter.

Luke Kane was drunk, stumbling, dangerous, knew he had
miscalculated his son's rage should he ever find out what was
happening to his sister. Because of the bourbon, when he hit
the floor after Chum's first blow he fell like a sack, a clown,
landed undamaged. Chum kicked him as he lay, kicked him
hard in the softest, bloodiest part of his stomach and the wind
left Luke Kane's lungs.

'Chummie here!' cried Lyddie again, kneeling, now, at the
end of the bed, her arms still extended towards him. Chum
turned to reassure her and noticed the smudge of blood at the
side of her beautiful full lips, as Luke Kane smashed a chair
across his shoulders, pitching him into Lydia, who caught her
brother, wrapped her arms round him and laughed. Chum
could hear Luke Kane blundering out of the bedroom, breathing heavily, his footsteps uneven. Lydia was strong, had
always been a well-toned, muscled young woman, and she
clung to Chum as he tried to break free. To his eternal disgust
she began to grind her hips against his, tried to kiss his neck,
her hand slipping to his belt. He yelped and caught her hands,
pulled them away.

'Bad Chum,' said Lydia, rubbing her wrists, pouting.

This was what their father had been teaching her in his
absence? *This* was what he, Chum, had abandoned her to?
Chum sprinted out of the room, along the landing and skit-
tered down the stairs, his heels flying on carpet. He slammed
into the kitchen, the swing doors bouncing, flapping again

and again, in time to see Luke Kane push Iris aside and swig from a bottle of bourbon on the counter.

'What's . . .' Iris, shaking her hands which were covered in flour from rolling out pastry, looked from her husband to her son and her eyes widened because she saw in Luke Kane's eyes the casual violence spark there, with which she was so familiar. 'What's going on?'

But her question was lost in the sound of the bar stools around the kitchen island being knocked to the floor as Chum came roaring through, slipping slightly on the slate floor, homing in on his father. Luke Kane judged the moment with the eye of a practised drunk and tossed the bourbon bottle, which smashed at Chum's bare feet. But Chum didn't falter, didn't feel the pain, just kept barrelling through, catching his father round the neck, pummelling the side of his head with his fist.

Lydia appeared at the swing doors, naked but for the bruises on her thighs and a garish diamanté necklace she'd taken from her mother's jewellery box. She stood, one leg slightly bent, an arm across her breasts, in classic courtesan pose, and said, not for the first time, 'Lyddie do. Lyddie sorry.'

Luke Kane, who had been made heavy and stolid by beer, bourbon and high living, bent over, swung his arm back and caught his son in the groin. Chum gasped and crumpled, breaking his fall with his hands, slashing them on glass as Iris asked – who? Just *who* was she asking? – 'What's going on? What's happening?' Her husband stood, panting heavily, rubbing his temples and casually kicked his son in the ribs. Chum lay on the slate, curled over his damage, hands and feet bleeding, dribbling with pain.

Luke Kane went to the pantry, snapped open a fresh bottle

of Jack Daniel's and toasted his wife. 'Happy Thanksgiving!' Lydia giggled. Iris went to Chum, bent over him.

'Leave him the fuck alone!' Luke Kane shouted, moving towards them, but Iris stayed put. Lydia left her post by the door and moved vaguely around the kitchen, running her hands along clean counters, smiling faintly. Her father watched her appreciatively.

Iris looked up at Luke Kane. 'What's happened?' Her voice was hard, sounded different, sounded as if it belonged to a larger woman. 'What's Lyddie done?'

'Lyddie naughty girl,' said Lydia conversationally, stopping by the sink to play with the drips from the tap.

Chum suddenly rose up in a single movement, catching his father unaware. He slammed Luke Kane against the walk-in refrigerator, making it rock and spill the tins and jars resting on its top. Red, glistening footprints followed Chum's every move. The two of them wrestled, spilling plates and glasses, rocking the oven, causing the turkey to hiss under its foil. Iris looked round wildly as Lydia gazed at her reflection in the darkened window, smiling, adopting the pose her father preferred. Iris knew she was helpless to stop this and she ran to the telephone to call for help, pulling the cord out into the hall, away from the noise, away from the sight of her husband and her son trying to kill each other as her daughter smiled.

Luke Kane thought he was dying as Chum pinned him against a wall, pressing his thumbs hard into his neck, closing his windpipe. Luke Kane looked blearily at his daughter and motioned for the fish axe, which hung above the drainer. Lydia pointed at it, puzzled, and Luke Kane nodded as much as he was able; so Lydia dutifully placed the weapon in her father's hand. He chopped at Chum and felt the immediate relief of air rushing to his lungs as Chum fell back. Rubbing his neck, Luke Kane chopped the cord of the telephone as it stretched out of the kitchen. Then he beckoned to Lydia, who came to him, frowning. 'Bad Daddy,' she said. The two of them, father and daughter, stood silently, Luke Kane's arm around Lydia's neck, as Chum pressed a hand to his wound and Iris reappeared in the kitchen, still holding the phone, the cord trailing behind her.

Iris took in the situation, looked at her family in their Thanksgiving pose. Turned to Luke Kane. 'You were fucking her, weren't you? When Chum went upstairs he found you fucking her, didn't he?'

Her husband shrugged.

'Just like you fucked Sugar. Poor, dead Sugar.'

Luke Kane's face crumpled at the sound of that name. He had forbidden it ever to be said, had not heard it for years. With a vicious shove he sent Lydia spinning from him and he watched as she stumbled and stopped beneath a discreet downlighter set in the false ceiling. He looked at her in the harsh, unforgiving halogen light and saw she was nothing but a travesty of the sister he had loved, looked equally like her and not like her. In two paces he was on Lydia, with one sweeping movement of his arm he cut her throat. Lydia fell without a sound, her voice box slashed.

Iris – who was small enough to break her parents' heart, small enough to buy children's clothes, small enough to be forgotten – screamed and lunged at her husband. He pushed her aside as easily as an unpleasant thought, brought the axe down again and severed his wife's arm above the elbow. Iris made an odd noise, like a puppy dreaming, and fell as her hand, still holding the phone, slid across the slate floor away from her.

Luke Kane knew – as in a way he had known from the moment Chum had pushed open the bedroom door – that it was all over, whatever it was, it was over. Even Luke Kane, son of Mr Steel, would have trouble getting out of this one. A part of him was grateful. Since Sugar had died nothing had been the same. It was a shame, because he liked living, he enjoyed drinking and laughing and fucking and working and lying in the sun. But, when he came to think about it, none of those things had been the same since he'd seen Sugar lying broken at the bottom of the stairs.

He sighed, looked up and saw what he'd hoped to see: his son looking murderous, as blood flowed from the cuts on his hands, feet and ribs. Luke Kane thought for the first time in a long time about Theodore and Lucinda, his mother and father. He thought about the priest at Mono Lake, the boy at prep school, the black woman in the hotel in Harlem. Perhaps it could all have been different; perhaps he could have made everything happen differently – but with his looks, his money, his privileges, his disposition? Well, maybe sometimes there was nothing that could be done.

Luke Kane held the axe out to his son, took a last swig of bourbon, and waited.

1997

Flanagan and Bronwen are staring at Chum, whose face is shadowed by candles and moonlight. They have not spoken for a long time.

'What happened then?' asks Bronwen, eventually, in a whisper. 'Chum, what happened then?'

Chum pours another brandy, sits back in his chair. 'I took the axe and I killed him. I killed my father.'

For minutes the three of them sit in silence, Flanagan and Bronwen pondering what this urbane, articulate, charming man has said. 'That's why you disappeared,' says the lieutenant eventually.

'Yes.' And Chum tells them how he carried Luke Kane's and Lydia's bodies to the car, put them in the trunk, along with the axe. How he tourniqueted his mother's wound, wrapped it in ice, picked up her forearm and wrapped that, too, in ice. Carried her to the car, laid her on the back seat and drove like a madman out of Long Island, across Staten Island into New Jersey. He stopped to call the emergency ward of a hospital, warning them of her arrival, directing them to a deep snowdrift back of the laundry block, where he left her, left his mother, her arm in her lap. He drove on, found a track off a minor road outside Readington, drove deep into the woods and buried Luke Kane and Lydia there, his hands and feet in agony and his ribs aching, still oozing blood. Then he moved on, moved west, across one state after another, napping in the car, dressing his own wounds, living on soda and burgers, until he was in Missouri, far enough from East Hampton to abandon the car and hitch to Las Vegas.

'But why?' asks Bronwen. 'Why didn't you call the police? It wasn't your fault.'

'I'd killed my father.'

'But you were *provoked* – it was self-defence.' Flanagan is stunned.

Chum looks at him. 'I had no defence. I might have killed them all. That's what they would have argued.'

'But your mother could have told them – she would have explained.'

'My mother didn't work any more. I don't know if she lost too much blood, if she got too cold. I tried to talk to her in the car.' Chum stops, looks away, looks out over the water, remembering that ride: Iris laid out on the back seat, moaning occasionally as Chum yelled, yelled that she'd be OK, that he was taking her somewhere, just yelling, trying to keep his mother in this world, as he cried and hurtled past the small coastal towns and then through the suburbs at over one hundred and twenty miles an hour, ignoring stop lights and crossings. The roads were empty, because, of course, all America was sitting at groaning tables giving thanks for its good fortune, as Chum in his makeshift hearse tried to save his mother and himself in the best way he knew how. 'I tried to talk to her. When I lifted her out, there was no one there, in her eyes, there was no one there. She didn't know who I was. She just burbled like a fool. You'd know about it, Bronwen, you knew her.'

'I met her, too,' says Flanagan. 'I met her in the home. She seemed OK to me. Well . . .'

'No, she wasn't, she was nuts,' says Bronwen bluntly. 'Matron said they thought she'd suffered a trauma. She never made any sense, not really. But she talked about you a lot, Chum. Actually you were *all* she ever talked about. You must remember that − you were all she ever talked about.'

Chum swallows, unable to think about this. 'So now you know what happened. Has that answered your question, Lieutenant?' He looks at Flanagan.

'You haven't explained *how* you changed. Why you do what you do. Why you've killed so many people.'

Chum smiles faintly. 'Because they deserve it.'

'You're sure of that?' asks Flanagan sharply.

'Yes. And I'm pretty sure you are, too.'

Flanagan rubs the top of his head, frowns. 'I'm not.'

'I wasn't there for Lyddie. I didn't save her. I couldn't make it right.'

'So you do it for the as-yet-unborn.'

Chum looks at the lieutenant again. 'That's exactly how I think of it.'

Flanagan draws a deep breath. 'But how do you live with yourself? How do you forgive yourself?'

'It's not my forgiveness I'm looking for, it's Lyddie's.' Chum sighs, lights a cigarette, turns the lighter in his hand. 'But I'm nearly done now.'

It is Bronwen's turn to frown. 'What d'you mean, man?'

'I'm tired. You want to know the truth, I'm just about wiped out. And I know now I'll never be forgiven. Lyddie's gone and nothing I ever do brings her back.'

'You say you're nearly done?' Flanagan stands up, stretches his back. 'You got plans?'

'What's the problem, Officer? You going to arrest me? You going to stop me? I came here to see my mother and I find she's dead. I promised a man I'd do him a favour and he's disappeared. Everything is closing down. But I owe that man, I gave him my word.'

And Flanagan wonders what kind of world he's living in when the word of a serial killer is the only constant he can believe in.

'What are you going to do?' asks Bronwen, who can't believe anything she's hearing.

'I'm going to visit a man called Thomas Jefferson the Third.'

Flanagan wheels round. '*Who* did you say?'

'A guy called Thomas Jefferson. Nice guy. You'd like him. He killed nine kids and cut—'

'I know exactly what he did,' says Flanagan, his voice harsh. 'I found the first victim. Katarina Kowalski.'

'Well,' says Chum, 'it was her father who asked me to do the job. And I have to be honest, it'll be a pleasure.'

Flanagan is thinking furiously. A memory: a man with dazzling teeth who had sat in a limo in the Upper Eighties and warned him not to mess with Bronwen. 'Sam Kowalski, *that's* who it was. It was Katarina's father.'

Bronwen knows Sam too, of course, but she doesn't make the connection, doesn't recognize the name.

Flanagan comes to a decision – a decision which is at odds with every principle he has ever held true. 'How can I help?' he asks Chum.

Keeler is dreaming of explosions – bridges falling, cars

tumbling, roads cracking. Whole walls collapsing. He keeps waking up in the cold hotel room, looking at the clock and turning back to sleep with a groan. He wants it to be morning. Each time he falls asleep he dreams again of explosions and shouts, flashes of orange.

Chum searches his pockets until he finds the name and number of Junior Troy, the contact at Block C, Harrison Penitentiary. He dials and a sleepy voice answers.

Minutes later Chum walks through the water villa to the room where Bronwen and Flanagan are sleeping. The door is unlocked and he creeps in, smiles faintly when he sees the two of them, chastely dressed in pyjamas, holding each other close. He notices the Polaroid of his younger self on the bed-side table (and perhaps this would have saddened him, had he known that before she met him Bronwen had slept with the photograph under her pillow). He shakes Flanagan's shoulder gently and the lieutenant wakes with a start. 'What?'

'I just called someone,' Chum whispers. 'Thomas Jefferson is being moved tomorrow at eleven a.m.'

'Shit.' Flanagan sits up and Bronwen grunts and rolls over.

'We have to leave early. Six o'clock.'

'I'll ask for a call.'

'No, it's OK. I don't sleep so good. I'll wake you. G'night.'

Flanagan grabs Chum's T-shirt. 'Hey, I been thinking. I got a problem.'

'What?'

'I got a warrant out for me.'

'Huh?'

Flanagan sighs. 'I just walked out on work and I been using my badge when I shouldn't. Plus the FBI might be interested.'

'Shit.' Chum crouches down by the bed. 'You known round these parts?'

'Depends who's around.' Flanagan rubs his beard. 'Might be OK.'

Chum bounces on his heels, thinking. 'What d'you wear? When you're at work, I mean.'

'Brown suit.'

'Always the same?'

Flanagan laughs and Bronwen shifts again, rocking the bed. 'How d'you know that?'

'Figures. Right. This is what you're going to do: shave your beard, change your hair and call the desk. Ask them to get you a black lightweight suit, white shirt, dark tie, some shades – you have a meeting in the morning and the airline lost your case. Charge it to my tab.' Chum stands. 'So you might as well make it Armani.'

CHUM KANE

His first week in Las Vegas Chum Kane lay in a motel room, the TV constantly murmuring to blot out the sound of his grief. He lay on his back on the bed and tears poured out of him. His mind, which before had always consoled him, instead tortured him with the image of Lydia falling in the kitchen, crumpling as gouts of blood fanned out around her. She hadn't cried out, hadn't registered any emotion, and Chum clutched at the idea that, as always, she had been unaware of pain. If he turned away from that image it was to see his mother's arm lying on the slate floor, holding the phone. Or the picture of his father offering him the axe and even *that* memory – of taking it and chopping – couldn't stop the tears coming. Sometimes he would pick up the telephone, intending to call the police, to give himself up. But as his finger stabbed at the numbers he couldn't work out what he'd done wrong. So he'd put the phone down and stare at it for hours.

One morning the tears dried and Chum slept deeply. When he woke he realized that for that week he had lost his mind. Mislaid it, forgotten how to use it. So he lay a little longer in the bed, thinking. Going to the bathroom, his feet still painful, he looked at his face in the mirror, decided not to shave, to grow a beard. He showered and dressed, then went out on the

JULES HARDY

streets of Las Vegas. Scanning the papers, national, local, east coast, west coast, he could see nothing to worry him. The Kanes had simply disappeared and no one had any idea of where they might have gone.

But what, then, of Marilyn? He had been due to collect her from Plymouth on Monday past and he had never shown up. Surely she'd have tried to call him? Raise the alarm? What would she be thinking? He ached to phone her, to hear her voice, to cry over her and explain what had happened. But then she would no longer love him. It was then that he remembered his mother slipping the photographs into her skirt pocket. She would have them with her, a picture of him smiling with his foot on the fender of the Eldorado, and an image of the Kane house.

Chum put his head down and walked the streets, blanketed by the anonymity of an unfamiliar city, getting used to a new way of life, the life he lived for the next seventeen years.

1997

Keeler sits at the table in his hotel room and reassembles his gun, sliding home the clean, lightly oiled sections, all perfectly engineered. Hair still damp from the shower, he slips on his linen suit jacket and collects together his keys, cell phone, palm-set. Leaving the room he locks the door, straightens his tie, then walks in a certain way he has, a way he hasn't walked for years: like an Ice Man. He takes the elevator to the desk, strides over to his car and drives away. Anyone looking at him would be puzzled by the set of his face, by its immobility. He arrives at Harrison Penitentiary at 08.00, shows his pass to the guard at the gate and drives into the compound.

The next hour is spent overseeing the change of personnel surrounding the periphery and fielding questions from the governor. Then there is the paperwork, the signing of expense forms, the clearing of the distribution of ammunition, the accounting for the way men spend their hours. As he signs the last docket Keeler glances at the clock: 09.29. One hour thirty one minutes. The phone rings; it is his superior.

'Keeler?' The voice is as thin and cold as ever, like the stem of a bullrush pulled through small fingers.

'Yes, sir?'

'Everything OK down there?'

'Yes, sir.'

'Seems to me if Mr Candid – or . . . what's his name?' – the sound of pages being flicked, which does not fool Keeler – 'Chum Kane is going to make a move he'll do it this a.m. I've been informed of the movement down there. I want you to keep on that job.'

'No problem, sir.'

'Good luck, Keeler.'

'Thank you, sir.'

'Get him.'

The conversation ends and Keeler stares at the buzzing handset. It is 09.31. Less than an hour and a half.

As Keeler is reassembling his gun, Chum, Bronwen and Flanagan are already on the road. Chum hired a second car at the hotel, thinking Bronwen could tail him and Flanagan, but he did not allow for the fact that Bronwen couldn't drive.

'You can't *drive*?' he asked with incredulity at dawn, as the two of them stood shivering in the strange cold of a tropical morning.

'No, I can't drive. Where I come from a car is a luxury, man.' Bronwen was disgruntled.

'Shit,' said Chum. 'Everyone knows how to drive.'

Flanagan joined them, unrecognizable, clean-shaven, well groomed, sharp-suited.

'Look,' said Flanagan, the peace-maker, once the situation had been explained. 'Why don't I drive the other car and Bronwen travel with you? When we get there, she can wait for us in this car.'

'OK. OK. It's just not what I was planning.' Chum sighed.

'Hey,' said Bronwen. 'Look you, I don't come from where you're talking about. I'm not like you.'

'What do you mean?'

'I'm not rich, I'm not educated. I never had many things. But, then, I don't come from the same place as you. All right?' Bronwen has been stung by his attitude.

'All right Bronwen. I'm sorry.' Chum walked over and hugged her – everything she ever dreamed of. 'I'm really sorry.'

Flanagan frowned. 'Let's get going.'

So it is that Bronwen and Chum are trail-blazing across the flat, swampy heartland of Florida, via deserted country roads, with Flanagan following on his own.

'Where are we going?' asks Bronwen, as Chum turns off one road on to a smaller, unmetalled track.

'Harrison Penitentiary,' says Chum, glancing at the digital clock.

She unwraps a Snickers bar and bites hard on it. 'Why?'

'Ah, well, Bronwen, there's a question. Where are you from, anyway? It's a cute accent you have there. Are you English?'

'I'm Welsh, man, and proud of it.'

'Right.'

'D'you know where Anglesey is?'

Chum turns one of his lazy turns, wrist on the arc of the wheel, and smiles, which would be enough to break most hearts. 'Can't say I do.'

'You want some of this?' Bronwen holds the rest of the candy bar in front of his mouth and Chum bites. As he chews, Bronwen asks a question. 'How long have you been doing this? Killing people.'

'I don't kill people, Bronwen. I kill child rapists.'

'OK, fair enough. How long have you been doing it?'

'Too long. Seventeen years. Nearly eighteen.'

'What do you do when you're not doing that?'

'Nothing. Drive, move around. Try to find out where they are.'

'Don't you have a girlfriend?'

Chum smiles. 'No, I don't. As a profession this is a little unpredictable. Difficult to work around, y'know, to plan vacations and that kinda thing.'

'Don't you ever get lonely?'

'Yes. I'm lonely all the time. Now you ask, I can't remember not being lonely. Y'know,' and Chum laughs, 'I used to have a name for it. Mrs Blue Cube – or was it Mrs Ice Blue Cube? Can't remember. Thought if I gave the loneliness a name it might become a friend. You and Flanagan are the first people I've talked to, y'know, sat around and talked to, for as long as I can remember.'

Bronwen is shocked by this confession, far more shocked than she had been the night before when Chum described the carnage of the Kanes. 'You don't have *anyone*? Wasn't there anyone ever?'

'Yeah, there was someone.' Chum looks away, swallows. 'I was going to get married once. I asked someone to marry me.'

Bronwen remembers something Flanagan had said and she takes out the Polaroid. 'Did she take this?'

Chum glances at the familiar image. 'Yeah. On the day I asked her to marry me. It was a memento of the moment. I'd kind of like it back, if that's OK.'

Bronwen leans over and pushes the photograph into Chum's shirt pocket. 'Tell me, what was she like?'

And so Chum tells Bronwen about Marilyn as he drives,

about the way she laughed, the way she spent an age spreading butter to every corner of her toast, how she slept on her
front with one leg cocked awkwardly, about the crooked
canine that made her face interesting. That her voice was so
mellow it made him think of burned umber, that she took
three sugars in her coffee and couldn't stand the smell of
celery. As the car heats up in the blinding sun and the swamp
around them bubbles, Chum tells Bronwen everything he can
recall about Marilyn, which is a great deal.

'She sounds wonderful,' says Bronwen generously.

'She is.'

'So, do you know where she is? Don't you want to see her
again?'

'Thing is , would she want to see me? Eh, Bronwen? Would
she want to see me?'

A sign looms, pointing the way to Harrison Penitentiary –
five miles north – warning the unsuspecting motorist to turn
back. Chum pulls over and waits for Flanagan to arrive.

CHUM KANE

When he walked away from the shack in Las Vegas, that he had described to Sam, leaving a smouldering videotape in the kitchen sink and four dead child rapists in the living room, Chum knew he'd found something he could do. Something he could do well; something that eased the constant guilt he felt for failing Lydia. As he walked back to his car he decided that this was what he would do. It wasn't quite the career he had anticipated but it was something he could give back to the community: the absence of people who really, really shouldn't be there.

He needed money for travel, for accommodation, for false papers, for hire cars, food, cigarettes. So he began to visit the tables, his memory and his ability to calculate probabilities lining his pockets, filling the bank vaults. He had always excelled at research and he discovered new tools to unearth facts: reading local and national papers, court reports, school reports, tuning into police-band radio, talking to scum and extracting information from them. The advent of the personal computer released him from the drudgery of visiting libraries and courts and he became an expert hacker, accessing data bases which told him all he needed to know. Still he culti-vated contacts in major cities, all of them useful – although when he discovered Gideon he struck gold. Having flushed out his prey, he never made a mistake, he never shot an innocent.

Over the years he got used to the life of the itinerant. His car or ute or RV, whatever he was driving, was his home for days or weeks. He travelled on Greyhounds, on Amtrak, on ferries; he hitched, he delivered new cars across the country. He never stayed anywhere, never bought a chair, a TV, an oven. Why would he? All Chum Kane ever did was keep running from the thought of just how long his father had been raping his infant-like sister, scything down the rapists as he ran.

It was, he thought when he looked back, inevitable that he would begin to drink bourbon and snort cocaine. (Genetic memory?) The loneliness was a chronic disease, debilitating and corrosive, eating away at him, as the acute memory of Lydia falling in the kitchen stabbed his conscience over and over and over. He felt Prometheus-like despair, knowing it would never fade. The cocaine and the booze soured his mind and he became an automaton, ceasing to reflect on what he was doing and why. Strangely, he never considered the paradox of his buying up and destroying the drugs on the streets, then snorting the white lines himself as reward. He even stopped keeping tabs on the body count. But no matter how damaged he became – and he did become very damaged – he knew he would never be caught.

Then one day, as he walked the streets of New York City, he remembered Marilyn and who he had been. It was one of those rare, beautiful spring mornings, and he walked into Central Park and lay on the grass until evening, considering his options. It was then that he made his vows: to give up bourbon, stop the coke, stop the killing and to contact Marilyn. He might not have managed to do all these but he did save himself when he made those vows, clawed back pieces of himself that he was in danger of losing. Later still, he vowed yet again to forget it all, to disappear, shake off Mr Candid; only to discover that Mr Candid always went with him, even behind the fence into Alaska.

But this time, right now, as he sits in the car with Bronwen five minutes from Harrison, he means it. These deaths are the last. He wants to be there when Thomas Jefferson III walks, blinking, into the light, chained hand and foot. He wants to look into Jefferson's eyes. He wants revenge for Katarina Kowalski and eight other children whose names he doesn't even know. Revenge which the state, in its wisdom, has withheld. Revenge which Governor Jefferson, with his money and power, averted. Ray MacDonald has become an optional extra.

1997

Flanagan is mopping sweat from his forehead as he raps on the car window. Chum lowers the glass.

'Let's go,' says Flanagan.

'OK.' Chum gets out, leaves the keys with Bronwen.

Flanagan squats down and looks at her. 'Bronwen, we'll be back in around an hour. OK?'

Bronwen looks suddenly frightened. 'You *will* come back?'

Chum's face appears next to Flanagan's. 'Don't worry – an hour max.'

Bronwen chews her lip. 'You're going to kill someone?' It is only now the moment is here that the enormity of what is happening, of exactly where the girl from Ynys Môn has ended up, hits her.

Flanagan reaches in and puts his hand on her arm. 'Bronwen, you know me better than most. Would I do this if I didn't think it was right?'

Bronwen shakes her head.

'Bronwen? I think . . .' Flanagan pauses, looks at the sky. 'I think it's the right thing to do.'

'Just come back, please, just come back and get me.'

'Lieutenant, we have to go. Time is passing.' Chum walks away.

Chum and Flanagan slip on jackets, drive away, and
Bronwen watches the dust rise as they turn on to another
track. The car ticks in the sudden silence as metal contracts
and the engine cools. She turns on the radio and tunes it to a
Nashville station, remembering that Sam the Weasel Man
liked C&W, and she wonders what has happened to him.

When they reach the guardhouse, Chum flashes the FBI IDs
that he chose for them both early this morning from a large
selection in his tote-bag. The guard looks closely at the IDs,
aware that the pen is on high-security status this morning,
but eventually waves them through. Three more times their ID
is examined but the two of them, in their dark suits and
shades, with their bored, arrogant manner, are so casual, so
convincing, that no one thinks to question them too closely.
The last guard, a man called Junior Troy, accompanies them to
a parking lot and watches as they park, button their jackets,
and then he walks with them into the compound. It is 10.55
a.m.

Mr Candid scans the area, his eyes and brain working fast,
counting bodies, counting rifles and semi-automatics, calculating possibilities and probabilities. He walks with purpose
around the concrete square, watching for movement in the
towers, on the walls. But what Mr Candid is really searching
for is the deepest, darkest shadow.

Flanagan – who hasn't thought this through, who has acted
on impulse – is beginning to panic. He has recognized a
couple of cops. And why wouldn't he? He is, after all, in
Florida. More to the point, have they recognized him? And,
anyway, how are they going to get out of here? The compound
is strangely silent, anticipatory. No one moves. But before

Flanagan can think further, a siren sounds and everyone turns to the armoured doors opening in the wall. A security truck rumbles in and stops, reverses and then its rear doors are opened by remote control. Guards snap to attention and shoulder rifles. The bullet-proof, reinforced doors leading into Block C open and Thomas Jefferson III, dressed in a lurid orange jumpsuit, chained at the ankles, cuffed at the wrists, stands there, smiling and squinting at the sun, scanning the sky. Flanagan has never seen him before, yet sudden rage swamps his panic. He looks around for Mr Candid but can't see him. Mr Candid has disappeared. Thomas Jefferson III, a beacon of colour in the midst of black suits and grey concrete, shuffles awkwardly towards the truck, the crunch of his boots grinding gravel the only sound. 'Come on, come on,' mutters Flanagan, furtively searching for his accomplice.

A movement catches Flanagan's eye and he whips back to Thomas Jefferson. A man is walking swiftly behind the child murderer, a man Flanagan knows. Edison Keeler. Edison Keeler, striding out, a gun held easily in his right hand. Keeler reaches Thomas Jefferson, wraps an arm, rather gently, round Jefferson's neck, pulling his head back as he empties the cartridge into the multiple-child-murderer's spine, lungs and heart.

Flanagan is surprised by the moment of complete stillness that follows this violence. He looks up and sees the birds, which have been disturbed by the gunshots, wheeling around the visible sky. Then mayhem erupts. Keeler is gunned down, falls in a graceless tangle of limbs on top of the rapidly dying body of Jefferson. FBI agents burst from corners, clatter down metal stairs, guards yell into radios as the siren sounds again. A blond, lean, dark-suited man floats to the edge of the chaos, skirts the frenzy and slips away. Muted howls can be heard from the cells adjoining the walls.

Flanagan breaks into a run, heads for Keeler. Guards attempt to bar his way but Flanagan is unstoppable. He kneels by his ex-colleague, who is still bleeding, still breathing. Flanagan hauls him up, lifts the dead weight on to his chest, looks down and sees Keeler's eyelids move. And he holds Keeler against his broad, bountiful, heart-thumping chest, just as he's always known he would do: until one of them died.

EPILOGUE

Ray MacDonald lived for a further six weeks after the turmoil of the killings at Harrison Penitentiary, unaware that he had been reprieved by that turmoil, unaware of the chain of events his crimes had forged. Unaware, really, of very much at all. As Chum suspected, MacDonald did indeed strut around the exercise yard like a hard man, basking in the fading glory of having killed Addis Barbar, his brain always addled by the constant supply of drugs to the security blocks. It was an argument over the theft of a DC comic that occasioned his death – he was found in the kitchen gardens of the pen, lying among green, waving stalks of scallions, with a shard of sharpened metal buried in his chest.

The parents of Addis Barbar, lured ever deeper into the labyrinthine bowels of criminal law by the fabulous sums of money promised by their lawyers, eventually managed successfully to sue the state for tortious negligibility. The Barbars argued that the state of Florida had failed to discharge an objectively tested duty of care towards their beloved son and found, rather surprisingly, that the jury agreed with them. The $17,000,000 they received exceeded even their wildest dreams and represented generous recompense for a son whom they had not seen for more than twenty years and had not much liked then. But, as Mrs Barbar was heard to say in numerous interviews, 'Ain't nothin' that can replace a chile or put right a mother's pain.' It seemed to some that she had conveniently forgotten the nature of her son's crimes.

Gideon never did get to college; instead he went to prison, being found guilty of three drive-by shootings and sentenced to life. But once he settled into the routines of boredom and threat that he found there and recognized the same patterns of life that he had known outside, he did begin to study. He learned to read and write, then enrolled on a college correspondence course and discovered he had an aptitude for understanding and making sense of history. He immersed himself in the history of the slave trade, read tales about the movement of molasses, salt and black bodies around the West Indies. Racial oppression, civil rights, indentured labour – Gideon became an expert in all of these. Eventually he wrote a book arguing that tourism in the Caribbean was nothing other than neo-colonialism, a text which was published by a small Southern university press. It received favourable reviews in the literary supplements. Often, as the years passed, he thought of the strange blond man who had given him thirty thousand dollars in a café in Venice Beach and wondered what had happened to him.

Sam Kowalski was sitting by the swimming pool at his highly desirable Santa Barbara villa when he read in the papers the official accounts of Thomas Jefferson III's death: how Jefferson had tried to escape and been shot within the limits of Harrison Penitentiary. Sam smiled when he read this, smiled for two

reasons: first, because Thomas Jefferson III, who had murdered Katarina, was dead, and, second, because he knew that
it had not happened that way. It was over. Sam Kowalski felt
old and tired, but happy. It had taken him a long, long time
but he had finally avenged Katarina. As for Governor
Jefferson – who must have abased himself to save his son from
the chair – well, he could live and suffer. Without his wife,
without his child. Just as Sam Kowalski did.

Edison Keeler's superior managed somehow to convince the
authorities to issue amended stories, stifle the truth about the
nature of Keeler's death. The chief did this because whenever
he thought of Keeler he remembered him asking one day, 'If
you thought you could get away with it, would you give Mr
Candid Scott Graves's name?' And the answer, although he
never told Keeler, was 'Yes.' The chief ensured that Keeler was
buried with full honours; Keeler's wife was given a folded
flag as she listened to the gun salute, and was told her husband had been shot in the mêlée, trying to restrain Jefferson.
Keeler was, they said, an American hero. Which, of course, he
was. But his wife never knew the extent, the manner, of his
heroism; never knew for how long he had cried as he reached
the decision to take justice into his own hands; how he had
feared for his daughters' futures. How he died wishing he
could have shaken Chum Kane's hand.

Padraig Flanagan and Bronwen Jones married and moved to
Iowa. Bronwen realized she loved Flanagan when she was sitting on the pier with him by the water villa on Gasparilla
Island, watching the stars. As she had often said, she might
not be educated but she was bright enough to know what she

wanted. Also bright enough to realize that Chum Kane – the man she had pursued up and down the eastern seaboard, the man who was about to smile in a seventeen-year-old Polaroid photograph – did not exist. But Flanagan did. The two of them never saw Chum Kane again, rarely mentioned him. (But both of them would sometimes think of him and, had they known it, always in the same way: sitting on the pier, a drink in his hand, smiling about the luminance of Markab; just sitting there, sitting among friends for an evening.) The lieutenant left the force and became a private investigator, chasing errant husbands and debt defaulters. He was madly proud of his wife and four children. It was an easy life of wide horizons and plentiful, home-made food. Some summer nights, when the kids were asleep and the breeze was up, Bronwen would dance her exotic dance for an appreciative audience of one, against the endless, corn-waving Iowan backdrop.

And Chum Kane? He spent six months searching for Marilyn before he found her, in Weston, Connecticut. She was married, as he had thought she might be, and had three children. Her husband was a psychologist and the family lived in a three-storey clapboard house, in acres of grounds, with a tennis court, swimming-pool and an orchard. Marilyn was a freelance writer and her life consisted of work, school runs, junior league, beach parties and tennis in summer, skiing and the Virgin Islands in winter. Chum knew these things because he stopped running, stopped moving when he got to Weston and rented a house there.

The first time he saw her he had not anticipated the meeting. He was in King's supermarket, standing at the deli waiting for pastrami to be wrapped, when he heard a familiar, cracked voice say, 'You know that's not what I meant. Don't try to pull a fast one on me, young lady.' And Chum stopped breathing. Imperceptibly he turned his head and in the corner of his eye he saw her, standing with a sullen teenage girl, her daughter. He waited until they had been served, then watched them leave. Nothing about her had changed. Nothing. The way she walked with a tiny hitch in her left leg, the way she moved her hair around with her left hand. She still wore the same style of suede jacket, long shirt and jeans of her student days.

Chum's rented house was a mile from hers and for a few months he watched her – not from his car across the road or anything, he just made sure their paths often crossed. He learned where she played tennis, where she shopped, where the kids' schools were, and he tried to see her every day. He'd spent years perfecting invisibility and Marilyn never noticed him. Many times he wanted to walk up to her and ask if she remembered the drive through the snow that Thanksgiving and what had been said. Ask if she had forgiven him for not coming back for her, if she would forgive him for all he had done since. But as the months passed, the snows melting, giving way to a late spring, and Chum saw her out with her husband, or bending down to wipe her son's grazed knee, or laughing over a beer with friends at the tennis club, he knew he'd never ask. Because Marilyn was happy.

So Chum wrapped up the rental of the house, threw away the possessions he'd accumulated over the time he'd been there, sold his car and bought a plane ticket out to the West Coast. He knew now he'd never see Paris with her, or walk across the Crete in Tuscany, or swim in the Aegean, and it saddened him more than he thought possible.

The day he was due to leave, before the limo came to take
him to La Guardia, he walked the road down to her house. He
could see her sitting out on the porch-swing, dressed in sweats
and a jumper against the still-chill spring breeze. Her husband was in the city, working, and her kids were at school, so
she was alone. Chum sat at a distance, on the grassy bank of a
neighbouring house, pulling at blades of grass with his fingernails, watching her for the last time. He imagined crossing
the road, sitting next to her and taking her hand. He'd noticed
that she sometimes looked as sad as the time, years before,
when she had dropped some books and bent down to pick
them up, in the Halls of Harvard, and there was nothing he
could do about that sadness. It would seem, after all, that neither of them was destined to retrieve the divine spark. He
stood and brushed the grass from his jeans, looked at her once
more and walked away. Hours later, as he walked towards
Departures at the airport, he stopped and dropped a bound
bundle of letters in a trash can.

Chum Kane never managed to shake Mr Candid loose. He
continued his strange, looping odyssey around the States,
righting wrongs the best way he knew how. Renegade?
Recidivist? Apostate? Saviour? He was never sure. But, as he'd
written, it was just that there were always so many
Tinkerbells.